A DAUGHTER'S LOVE

Nell Goodman is a good daughter. Her job in the local brewery is the only thing keeping her and her mother afloat. But with her mother becoming increasingly eccentric, Nell is starting to feel the burden of her responsibilities. When Nell goes to George Wilmot, the brewery's owner, for help he offers her a job as a live-in servant. She begins to grow closer to Devlin, George's son, and it looks like Nell's luck is finally changing. An unwelcome discovery and tragedy mean that things suddenly change. Devlin pulls away from Nell, her mother's behaviour is becoming worse and there are secrets around every corner.

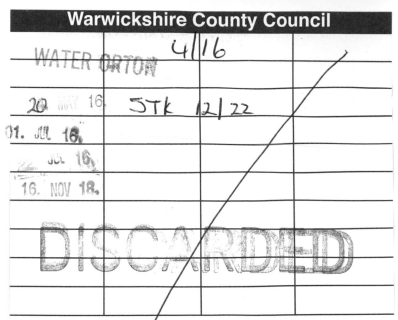

A DAUGHTER'S LOVE

A DAUGHTER'S LOVE

by

Catherine King

Magna Large Print Books
Long Preston, North Yorkshire,
BD23 4ND, England.

British Library Cataloguing in Publication Data.

King, Catherine
        A daughter's love.

        A catalogue record of this book is
        available from the British Library

        ISBN   978-0-7505-4252-4

First published in Great Britain in 2015 by Sphere

Copyright © Catherine King 2015

Cover illustration © Gordon Crabb by arrangement with
Alison Eldred

The moral right of the author has been asserted

Published in Large Print 2016 by arrangement with
Little, Brown Book Group

Magna Large Print is an imprint of Library Magna Books Ltd.

Printed and bound in Great Britain by
T.J. (International) Ltd., Cornwall, PL28 8RW

PART 1

South Riding, Yorkshire, 1887

Chapter 1

Mabel stood in the middle of the Master's office. A welcome fire glowed in the grate and she felt the warmth through her coarse scratchy gown. The square of carpet under her stiff boots was soft and silent.

The workhouse Master sat behind a large wooden desk and reread her schoolteacher's report. It wasn't good. The teacher had never liked Mabel very much because she wasn't clever and had a tendency to be outspoken. Now, the guardian peered over the spectacles on his nose and grunted. His wide forehead creased. 'Factory or domestic?'

'Factory,' she replied. She had had enough scrubbing in the workhouse to last her a lifetime.

'Speak when you're spoken to,' the Master snapped. His forehead creased even further as he added, 'Matron?'

Matron stood beside Mabel on the carpet. 'Domestic,' she said. 'This one can sew as well as clean.'

The Master nodded and picked up another sheet of paper. 'The Navigator wants a general help to live in.'

The Matron sniffed. 'It's that woman who runs the Navvy!'

'She's a ratepayer.'

'She's a trollop.'

'Aye, well, that's what happens when women have their own money. Our relieving officer speaks highly of her.'

It was the relieving officer's task to decide if folk could be admitted when they arrived at the workhouse. He was responsible for spending the Parish Relief wisely.

Matron grunted. 'Mabel's only fourteen. I don't think the Navigator is– '

'You're not paid to think or to tell me how old my inmates are. Besides, she's nearly fifteen and I've only kept her on because you wanted her as a cleaner.'

Mabel pursed her lips and flared her nostrils. She had wanted to leave as soon as she was old enough, but Matron had told her that she had to stay because nobody in town had a position for her.

The Master picked up his pen and dipped it in the inkwell. 'Domestic, Navigator Inn, Mexton Lock,' he said. The nib scraped along the paper as he wrote. 'Next,' he called, without looking up.

Matron ushered Mabel out of the room. 'Do you know where the Navvy is?' she asked.

Mabel shook her head.

'You go down to the canal and follow it towards Doncaster until you get to Mexton Lock. You can't miss it.'

'What's a trollop?' Mabel asked.

In answer, Matron clipped her round the ear and told her not to be cheeky.

Mabel rubbed the side of her head and pro-tested, 'I'm a girl! You're not supposed to hit me!'

'You'll get worse than that at the Navvy if you

12

don't keep your tongue between your teeth.'

Mabel sat in the receiving ward while she waited for a piece of paper to take with her to the Navigator. Her corset dug into her skin. Matron insisted she wore it now she was leaving but she couldn't imagine scrubbing floors in it. It was second hand, just as her stiff brown gown was second hand, but they were all she had in the way of clothes apart from her calico shifts and drawers.

The letter when it arrived was sealed in an envelope with 'Union Workhouse' stamped in the corner. She stowed it in her skirt pocket, hooked her bundle over one arm and wrapped her coarse woollen cloak around her. Then she set off for her new home without so much as a backward glance at the cold and draughty prison she had lived in for as long as she could remember.

She went through town towards the canal, past the church that she'd walked to every Sunday with other workhouse inmates, and down the high street. No one moved her on when she stopped to gaze in shop windows or stare at fine ladies in their carriages.

She didn't see many fine ladies, though. This was an industrial town driven by steelworks, glassworks and factories. There were more rough-hewn carts than carriages lining the pavements outside the shops. She passed the doorway of a cooked meat shop and a working man came out with a bread-cake oozing roast pork. The smell made her realise how hungry she was. But she had no money so she dared not linger and quickened her step towards the canal.

The air was damp and chilly by the water.

Some of the older buildings along the canal were derelict; others had been fitted out as workshops or factories, turning their backs on the waterway. A railway line ran alongside the canal now and it had taken most of the barge trade. The line followed the same route along the valley and steam engines pulling carriages chugged straight past the decaying wharves and horse marines that had kept the barges going in days gone by.

Mabel began to have misgivings about being all alone and away from the town throng. Suddenly she wanted to be back in the workhouse with the other children and Matron barking orders at her. But she was on her own now and fretted about coming face to face with thugs on the towpath.

A man pushing a handcart loaded with coal came towards her. The handle of his shovel stuck out of the top. As he got closer she noticed his clothes were grubby and dishevelled, and his face was grimy with coal dust. She slowed her step and looked around: there was the dingy water of the canal on one side of her and a prickly hedge on the other. Thinking of the lurid stories she had heard in the workhouse dormitory, from girls younger than she, about what men had done to them, she backed away against the hedge.

He was a tall man, but fresh-faced and young with dark hair and eyes, and he smiled at Mabel as he approached with his laden barrow. As he drew level with her, he stopped, touched the brim of his greasy cap and said, 'Thank you, miss.'

He's just a lad, she said to herself, not much older than the workhouse boys, although he was broader and ... and obviously stronger. She froze

14

to the spot. No one had called her 'miss' before. Why was he being nice to her? What did he want?

'I haven't got any money,' she said in a rush.

His smile broadened. 'Hey, steady on! I'm not going to rob you, miss. Where are you heading?'

'Why do you want to know?'

His expression became serious and he put his head on one side. 'Well,' he said, 'you're a pretty young lass out on your own and there's not much back that way apart from Mexton pit.'

'Oh!' Had she missed the inn? Perhaps it was on the other bank? 'Not the Navigator Inn?' she queried. 'Isn't that this way?'

'Oh yes, it's not far. You come to the black-smith's forge first and the Navvy is next door. I've just come from there.'

'Have you? What's it like?'

'Cheap enough, if you're looking for a bed for the night.'

'I'm going to work there.'

'Are you? Well, the landlady could certainly do with more help. I'll look out for you when I next call in.'

Mabel liked that idea and relaxed enough to manage a small smile.

'I'm Harold, by the way,' the young man said.

'Mabel.'

He took hold of his handcart again. 'Ta-ra, then, Mabel.'

'Ta-ra,' she said and watched him push on with his coal. After he had gone a few yards he looked back over his shoulder and, caught out staring at him, Mabel flushed with embarrassment. She hoped he was too far away to notice.

15

Pretty girl, Harold thought as he glanced back at her. He liked girls with fair hair and blue eyes; and if she'd be working at the Navigator he would see her again. This had been a good day for him with a new order to think about. He wasn't keen on the landlady at the Navvy, especially the way she had given him the glad eye. She must be ten years older than him at least! Still, she wanted a carter and she could pay. But if he was going to carry sacks of grain and barrels of ale for her on a regular basis, he would need a horse and cart, which he couldn't afford yet.

Harold had a fair business going now, carting coal by hand all the way from Mexton pit head to the rows of terraces in town. The profit was good, especially if he shovelled the coal into the cellar for his customers. He had been thinking of going into coal haulage proper until he'd seen the brewhouse in the back yard of the Navigator and the line-up of small barrels waiting to be collected by farmers and shopkeepers and the like. If he delivered the barrels for her she'd have more orders. But would she pay enough for him to afford to keep a horse?

Harold made his coal delivery then moved on to the flour mill to pick up a few sacks of flour that he paid for with his coal money. The flour was ordered and the miller gave him some old sailcloth to put down in his cart over the coal dust. Harold dropped off the sacks and collected payment for them on his way home. One of his regulars for flour baked bread and cake to sell from her front room. She always kept back one of her loaves for him and he was grateful.

His mother had baked her own bread until Father died. After that, she took poorly herself and never completely recovered. It was her heart, the club doctor said. He'd said that about his father, too, and Father had gone suddenly, whereas Mother was lingering, growing weaker and weaker by the month. Thank goodness he was fit and strong enough to work, Harold thought as he headed for home. It was a good couple of miles out of town but with an empty handcart he fair raced along.

Home was a farm labourer's cottage. The farmer, Mr Hawkridge, was a kindly gentleman and hadn't turned them out when Father died. His wife had a similar nature and looked in on Mother every day while Harold was out making a living. She was at the front door when Harold arrived so he knew something was up.

'She's had another turn – a bad one,' the farmer's wife said. 'I had to send for the doctor.'

Harold was shocked. The doctor had told him Mother would be fine provided that she didn't do too much. 'Where is she?' he queried.

'Upstairs. The doctor is with her now.'

Harold took the stairs two at a time, fearing the worst. The front bedroom door stood open. 'How is she, sir?' he asked, but one glance at his mother's grey face told him. He knelt down beside the bed. 'Mother,' he said, 'it's me.' She didn't move – not even a twitch. Harold's eyes were scared when he looked up at the doctor. 'Is she asleep, sir?'

'You must prepare yourself, son,' the doctor replied quietly.

'You don't mean she's going to die?'

'Her heart is very weak now.'

Harold picked up his mother's hand. The fingers were cold to his touch but he saw she was still breathing: in short shallow snatches, barely enough to notice.

'It won't be long now, I'm afraid,' the doctor added.

She didn't last through the night. The doctor stayed with her to the end and the farmer's wife came back before breakfast. Harold's head was heavy. His neck didn't feel strong enough to hold it up. He had never been a lad to cry easily but a few tears squeezed through his tightly shut eyelids.

The hours ticked by slowly and the day passed in a blur of visitors: the vicar and a stream of church wives bringing him sustenance and sympathy. The funeral arranger called and later came to take Mother away to his chapel of rest. At the end of the long day, the farmer arrived with a flagon of ale, some cheese and a jar of his wife's pickled onions. They sat down at the kitchen table, sawed hunks of bread from yesterday's loaf and talked together, man to man.

'Your father was one of my best labourers,' Mr Hawkridge said. 'I hoped you would follow in his footsteps.'

'I like what I'm doing, sir,' Harold replied.

'I can see that, son, and you're good at it. You've got more about you than he had, God rest his soul. Have you plans?'

Harold hesitated. His mother had just passed away and all thoughts for his future had flown right out of his head.

'I'm not rushing you,' the farmer added. 'You can stay here as long as you like. You've always paid your rent and the doctor's club on time. The vicar would've liked to see more of you on a Sunday, but his church ladies all took to you, right enough.'

Harold agreed and gestured towards the dresser, loaded with jars and covered dishes. 'Can you take some of this for the old folks' dinners?'

'Nay. I can't do that, son. It's for you and it's more than my life's worth to upset the womenfolk. It'll keep in the pantry.'

Mr Hawkridge crunched on one of wife's pickles. 'You see, son, what I need is another farm labourer as good as your father was...' He paused, then went on, 'And somewhere for him to live.'

Harold closed his eyes and nodded. That's what this was about. His home was a tied cottage. Since his father passed on two years ago, Harold and his mother had been able to stay by paying rent. He had worked on the farm out of school hours since he was ten so the farmer knew and trusted him. Harold had saved his meagre pay until he'd had enough to buy wood and wheel axles to make his handcart.

As soon as he left school, he was ready to trade and bought up produce from local allotments that he took to market and sold for a profit. When his cart was empty he carried anything anywhere for pay in the town until it was time to go home. Forges and factories were thriving and expanding; folk had work; they were busy and they had wages to spend, so he was busy, too. He was eighteen now, saving for a horse and cart and doing all right for himself and his mother. But now Mother had passed on as well as Father, he was at a loss to think straight.

'I'd be more than happy to take you on, Harold,' Mr Hawkridge added.

'I understand, sir,' he replied. But if he didn't want to be a farm labourer – and he didn't – Mr Hawkridge wanted his cottage back. He felt sad and said, 'When do you want me out?'

'Nay, son, I'll not turn you out. There's no rush, but I do want you to think on it.'

'I will,' Harold said with more conviction. 'I'll give you a decision after the funeral.'

Harold couldn't remember ever being alone in the cottage at night before. He wished he had brothers and sisters to talk to. Mother had been getting on in years when she had him and father was even older so no more children appeared after him. But he had never felt proper loneliness until now. Now, he was quite alone in the world and during that night he felt it keenly. He couldn't sleep and ended up resurrecting the kitchen fire in the small hours and sitting by its red glow, staring out of the window into the darkness. Eventually he felt so sorry for himself that he allowed himself to cry until he pulled himself together and took the farmer's advice to 'think on it'.

He supposed he'd been marking time since Father died, gathering more customers and bringing home treats for Mother. This cottage was his home and he loved it. But he was a long way out of town and where his customers lived.

His new order for the Navigator was the other side of town. If he had enough saved for a horse and cart it wouldn't matter, but he hadn't.

Then he remembered, as a nipper, seeing an old fellow take his potatoes to market in a donkey cart, because that had given him his original idea for a handcart. He perked up. He could afford a donkey with a bigger cart and that would be enough for the Navigator order to start with!

The dawn broke and Harold turned down the lamp. Did he want to stay here on his own, anyway, with only a donkey to talk to? That landlady at the Navvy was a handful by all accounts but she put on good dinners and had cheap rooms to let. She did have a reputation for the fellas, but that was none of his business. She had stabling at the back where he could keep a horse and cart. In spite of his overwhelming sadness, his spirits lifted for a moment. The Navigator also had Mabel. Mabel, sweet little Mabel. Her pretty face came to mind and he smiled. Just the thought of Mabel took away some of his loneliness.

Chapter 2

Mabel's initial nervousness when she arrived at the Navigator disappeared quickly as she was thrown into work. A shrivelled old couple seemed to run the place – she cooked food and he brewed beer – while the landlady stayed in her bed or went into town all dolled up to collect her rents.

Nobody appeared to have done any cleaning before Mabel arrived.

The old couple slept in one of the attics. It had the kitchen chimney breast going through it so it was always warm. Mabel's attic was not only cold but damp as well because water dripped from the rafters when it rained. But it did have a small fireplace and a spotty mirror that she leant against the wall. She didn't meet the Missus, as the landlady was known, until the following day when she took her breakfast in bed and was amazed by the red velvet and gold-trimmed furnishings in the landlady's bedroom. It contrasted sharply with the dingy curtaining downstairs. She deposited the tray of tea, bacon and egg and fried bread across the Missus's lap as she sat up in bed.

'So you're Mabel,' the Missus said. 'Well, you look strong enough. The old duck'll tell you what to do and I don't want you under my feet, d'you hear?'

'Yes.' Mabel stared at the smeared red on the other woman's lips, the creased ribbon in her tangled dark hair and the way her bosom swelled out under her nightgown.

'Yes, *Missus*,' the landlady corrected.

'Yes, Missus,' Mabel repeated.

'I'll have another cup of tea in quarter of an hour and hot water for the washstand.'

'Yes, Missus.'

'Knock and wait for me to say before you come in. I might be on the po.'

'Yes, Missus.'

'Stop staring then, and clear off.'

'Can I have coals for my attic?' she asked.

'Help yourself from the coal hole,' the Missus answered and waved her out of the room.

Mabel decided she would be very pleased to stay out of this woman's way. In fact, the Missus took most of the morning to get up and dress herself like an actress on a music hall poster. She sometimes had a word with the old couple and inspected the brewhouse before she went off for the day in a hired trap with a driver who came out from town to collect her.

The 'old duck' in the kitchen was called Elsie and seemed grudgingly glad of Mabel's help. Her husband, Sid, brewed good beer and folk came from miles around to take home a keg to set up in their outhouse or scullery. Beer was safer to drink than water these days and the Navvy did a steady trade. When Mabel pegged out washing in the yard, the yeasty smells from the brewhouse were quite heady.

Mabel worked hard. The taproom at the back of the inn was the worst to clean because coal miners drank in there on their way home from the pit, and coal dust stuck everywhere. Sometimes she was still there scrubbing when they came in after the early-morning shift and the younger ones often slapped her bottom or made suggestive comments, surrounding her until an older fellow came in and told them off.

But no one ever told *her* off, except once, one morning, when the Missus was so angry with her that she expected to be sent back to the workhouse. It happened after a particularly noisy night in the saloon. Mabel wasn't allowed in the taproom or the saloon at night. She was sent to bed early with instructions to do the clearing up in the morning. But the carousing kept her awake until late. Even later she was roused by creaking stairs and whining door hinges. That was normal as the Navigator often had one or two lodgers – working men who liked a drink or two.

Mabel got up as usual the next morning to find that Elsie hadn't laid up the Missus's breakfast tray. The range was going and the frying pans were out. A pot of tea stood on the side but there was no sign of Elsie. Thinking the old lady might be out of sorts after all the noise last night, Mabel set to cooking the Missus's breakfast herself. She found the bacon and eggs in the pantry, laid up the tray and took it to the Missus as usual.

She paused for a second outside the Missus's bedroom and raised her hand to knock. But she heard cries of pain coming from inside. Dear me, she thought, the Missus was ill! Instead of knocking she balanced the tray on one hand, grasped the door handle and rushed in, splashing the cup of tea into its saucer.

The Missus wasn't alone. The bedding was on the floor along with a jumble of discarded boots and clothes. The Missus's nightgown was draped over the iron bedstead. She was stark naked and kneeling astride a man, also starkers, who was wild-eyed and grinning. Her head was thrown back so that her tangled black hair straggled down her white back. A tortured cry came out of her open mouth with each descent of her body as she moved up and down on top of the man as though she were riding a horse. Mabel was rooted to the spot by the vivid vision of the man's sweating hairy chest and the Missus's wobbly white bosoms bouncing up and down.

The man caught sight of her. His grin vanished and he croaked, 'We got comp'ny.'

The Missus didn't appear to hear him but her movements slowed. 'What's wrong with you?' she panted. 'I haven't finished yet.'

'I can't do it in comp'ny, Missus, not even wi' you.' His voice was strained.

The Missus looked over her shoulder with fury in her smudgy dark eyes. 'What are you doing in here, you evil little witch?'

'I ... I've brought your b-breakfast.'

'I can see that,' the Missus seethed. 'Now get out of here.'

'I thought you were poorly,' Mabel squeaked.

The man didn't look very happy either. 'Have you seen enough now, love?' he asked sourly.

Mabel put the tray on the floor and fled. Elsie was going down the stairs and Mabel caught up with her. She had taken a mug of tea up to her husband in bed.

'No sense in you being up,' Elsie said. 'There'll be nob'dy about for a while yet. Mind you, I can smell bacon. Who's in my kitchen?'

'It was me,' Mabel admitted. 'You weren't around so I took the Missus her breakfast.'

'At this hour? After last night? Gawd 'elp you, then. Gawd 'elp me an' all. She'll be in a right paddy now.'

'She was,' Mabel agreed miserably.

'Well, she's gorra fella in there, 'a'n't she?'

Mabel pressed her lips together, blushed and nodded.

25

'You've gone red. Were they at it?'

Mabel's blush deepened.

'You'll be lucky if she don't gi' yer the boot.'

'But she can't! I've nowhere else to go!' Except back to the workhouse with a black mark against her name, she realised with a sinking heart.

Elsie tutted, shook her head and muttered, 'You should've known she'd 'ave a fella wi' her after a booze-up like last night.'

'I'm sorry.'

'Aye, yer should be. Come on, we'll have our breakfast afore the men get up.'

Until then, Mabel had eaten breakfast alone because Elsie normally ate hers early with her husband. She could have what she wanted if she cooked it herself. After a lifetime of porridge in the workhouse, she fried bacon rashers and ate them between two slices of bread with a big mug of tea every morning. But today she sat down with Elsie to butcher's sausages and fried bread.

'I can put in a good word fer you wi' the Missus,' Elsie said over their second mug of tea.

'Will you? I don't want to go back to the work-house.'

'You and me can be friends then, can't we?'

Mabel knew she couldn't afford to have this woman as an enemy and mumbled, 'I suppose so.'

Elsie didn't smile very much because she had no teeth, but she did now. 'Good lass,' she said. 'Now then, tell me what he was like, this fella?'

Puzzled, Mabel raised her eyebrows.

'The one wi' the Missus,' Elsie prompted.

Mabel had no idea what he was like so she hunched her shoulders silently.

'What did he look like? Dark or fair?' Elsie's tone had hardened. She wanted to know.

Mabel blew out her cheeks. He was dark, she thought. She suddenly remembered his legs stretched out on the white sheet and the Missus's round white bottom contrasting with his dark skin. 'He had black hair, all over him,' she said.

Elsie chewed the inside of her mouth. 'Oh, that one this time. What were they doing?'

Mabel didn't know quite how to answer her. 'What do you mean?'

'Tell me what they were doing. Yer saw 'em, di'n't yer?'

She sounded like the wardresses in the workhouse and Mabel felt cornered. In there they did something horrid to you – like putting you on cleaning the privies – if you didn't tell them what they wanted to know. 'Well, yes. They were ... you know, like you said, they were ... they were at it.' She finished in a rush and looked down at her empty plate.

'I know that, but tell me how they were doing it?'

Mabel was shocked that she should ask. She didn't want to say. It embarrassed her and made her blush even more. It was private anyway, she thought. 'I can't really say, Elsie,' she muttered.

'I thought you wanted to be my friend,' Elsie reminded her.

'Yes, but...'

Elsie sat back in her chair and grinned her toothless grin. 'Get on wi' it, then. Did they have owt on?'

Mabel shook her head slightly. 'He ... he was on

27

his back and the Missus was … well, she was sitting on top of him.'

Elsie folded her arms and started to laugh, but more by shaking her shoulders than with her face. 'Oh aye? Whereabouts on top of him?'

'On top of him!' Mabel exclaimed. 'And I'm not telling you any more!' She pushed back her chair and rushed out of the kitchen into the scullery to find her bucket and brushes.

'Come back here you!' Elsie called after her but Mabel ignored her.

The taproom was a pigsty after last night and it kept her out of Elsie's way for a while. But later, as she was trimming the wicks on the oil lamps, she began to see the funny side of the Missus 'eing caught 'at it', and chuckled to herself. No wonder she was cross!

After a couple of hours, Elsie came to find her, when she was on her hands and knees, washing the sticky floorboards in the saloon.

'The Missus wants yer,' Elsie said, with a hint of triumph in her voice.

The Missus was in a small room at the back of the stone-flagged entrance hall. The way she was sitting behind her desk reminded Mabel of the workhouse guardian. But that was all the Missus had in common with him. Her lips were painted red and her hair was done up in coils and jet combs, with ringlets at the back of her head. She wore a low-necked gown fit for a ball in dark red satin with black lace trimmings.

She waved a piece of paper in the air and yelled, 'Do you know what this is? It says that I am your guardian for the next seven years. Unless I decide to send you back to the workhouse – and I can, you know. You are *my* property until you're twenty-one. That means you do as I say.'

'Yes, Missus. I'm sorry, Missus.' Mabel had had years of learning how to be contrite and humble before her betters.

It wasn't wasted on the Missus. She lowered her voice and scowled. 'Remember that in future.'

In future? Mabel's heart leaped. 'Does that mean I can stay, Missus?' she asked.

'As long as you do as you're told. If I have to send you back, your next guardian won't be so forgiving.'

'It won't happen again, Missus.'

'No, it won't. You're on the rough work outside until I see fit to have you indoors again. See Sid in the brewhouse. He's got plenty for you to do.'

'Yes, Missus. Thank you, Missus.'

The landlady waved her away impatiently and Mabel escaped into the hallway. Well, she thought, I'm still not sure what a trollop is, but I'm finding out.

Elsie was hovering in the shadows. 'She's kept you on, then?'

Mabel nodded. 'She's put me outside, though.'

'Bugger! I'll have to carry her tray up them damn stairs again.'

'I can come in and do it for you,' Mabel volunteered.

'If the Missus says you're outside, you're outside! Any road, I've got an 'usband who'll do it fer me, ta. He can do a lot more fer me, an' all, wi' you doing his job.'

'But I don't know how to brew beer!'

'No, but you can muck out stables, keep the yard clean and do the privies.' Elsie grinned maliciously and added, 'The gen'lemen's privy, an all.'

Mabel grimaced.

Elsie chuckled. 'Serves you right. You should ha' been nicer to me, shouldn't you? I'll keep all the washing-up fer you to do an' all, after yer come in fer yer tea.'

Mabel thought that she might as well be back in the workhouse, until she remembered her attic room. She had never had a space all to herself before and if she put a bucket under the leak in the roof she could arrange the furniture quite nicely. It was old and dusty but it had cleaned up well. And the Missus hadn't stopped her taking coal for the fire. But she fretted that Sid might be as nosy as Elsie about the Missus.

Mabel soon discovered that Sid wasn't interested in anything except brewing his beer and he had never cleaned out the stables or the privies. The muck and the smell from both were disgusting and it made her stomach heave just to go into either. It was back-breaking work, too. Luckily for Mabel, the stables weren't used every day because the Missus didn't keep her own pony and trap and few if any of the lodgers at the inn arrived with their own horses.

But she couldn't get rid of the appalling smell in the privies. Even the workhouse privies had smelled of carbolic instead of what they were used for. She did her best with them each morning but they would be just as bad again by dinner time.

She couldn't go into the wash house to get away from the pong because the washerwoman, who came in once a week, kept it locked so that she could store her gin in there. So instead she would escape into the brewhouse when she could, just to inhale the yeasty fumes!

On one frosty morning, she stepped outside the warmth of the brewhouse into the yard to find a young man standing beside a handcart in the middle of the cobbles. He was looking about for something – or someone – until he spotted her.

'Mabel?'

Chapter 3

She had forgotten all about meeting Harold on the towpath but he had said he'd look out for her.

'Harold?'

'You remembered me. How are you settling in?'

'All right,' she answered, walking towards him. She noticed a black band around his arm and added, 'You've had a loss.'

His face looked sad. 'My mother; I buried her a few weeks ago.'

'I'm sorry.' Death had been a regular part of life in the workhouse. Old folk, young folk, babies even; death was no respecter of age.

'She'd been poorly for a while, since my father passed on.'

'Oh.' He was an orphan, the same as she was. But he was a few year older than her, and a

31

handsome young man with his own trade. She peered into his barrow. The contents were covered with a piece of string netting.

'Sacks of grain for the brewhouse,' he explained. 'The old boy here is fussy. He only uses barley from one miller. Where is he?'

'Sid? He's indoors with the Missus, I think, talking about new barrels.'

'I'm not in any rush. What's it like for you living here?'

It could be worse, Mabel thought. At least she was warmer and better fed than in the workhouse. She said, 'The Missus doesn't stint on coal or food, but it gets rowdy at night. The men who come here drink a lot.'

'Aye, that doesn't surprise me. There's a pit village up the road and she does serve the best ale for miles.'

'Does she?'

'Oh aye. Well known in these parts. She sells barrels of the stuff to local farmers and bigwigs. And she'd sell more if Sid could brew more.' He paused for a second before adding, 'I'm thinking of taking a room here.'

Mabel's eyes widened. 'What, like, move here to live?'

'I've got to get out of my mother's cottage and this is handy for some of my regular work.' He suddenly smiled – a broad friendly smile that lit up his sad face. 'And there's a really pretty lass called Mabel who works here.'

Mabel blushed and looked down at her feet, at her sacking apron and scuffed boots. She couldn't think of anything to say so she just pushed a stray lock of fair hair under her plain calico cap.

'I didn't mean to embarrass you,' he said and went on quickly, 'I'm buying a bigger cart, you see, and a donkey to pull it, so I need to have stabling as well.'

'Oh, I see.' He was just being kind to her and she wasn't used to it. She said, 'The Missus has stables. It's my job to keep 'em clean.'

'Isn't that a lad's work?'

'It's Sid's work, I think, but he's too busy brewing his beer.'

'Can you show me the stables?'

'I can. The Missus has six stalls and space for two carriages. None of it gets much use at all.'

They went inside. Mabel had finished clearing out all the muck and had sluiced the floor days ago so it was clean and dry. She had piled the old straw in a heap against a wall.

'I'll only want one of the stalls to start with,' Harold said, as he looked around.

'To start with?'

'I'll be getting a heavy horse and bigger cart eventually.'

'Oh, I don't look after animals. At least, I never have done.'

'I'll take care of him myself. I was brought up on a farm. What's upstairs?'

Mabel raised her eyes to the ceiling. Doing out upstairs was next on her list. 'I've not been up there yet.'

'A hayloft, I expect, and somewhere for the servants to sleep.'

'I don't think the Missus ever had folk staying with servants.' Mabel's tone was disparaging and

Harold noticed.

He glanced at her and said, 'Don't you like the Missus?'

'She's all right.'

Harold raised his eyebrows. 'But...?'

Mabel felt uncomfortable. She liked Harold and didn't want to put him off moving here.

He went on, 'I have heard she's got a liking for the fellas.'

Mabel was quite relieved he knew and said, 'I heard she was trollop.' His eyes widened and Mabel realised he was shocked to hear her say it. She had an idea of what a trollop was but still wasn't sure. 'That's not a ... not a ... not a whore, is it?' she asked.

Harold's eyes widened further but he found this amusing and laughed, 'No, a trollop doesn't charge for it. The constable can't shut her down for being a trollop.'

Mabel blushed but she was pleased he was good-humoured about it. To cover her embarrassment she said quickly, 'I've seen the constable here a few times.' He was a friendly young man, new to his responsibilities and always had a word with her if he saw her.

'Well, that's a good sign. He'll keep a bit of order about the place.'

'Have you gorra lad in there wi' you, Mabel?' A gravelly voice floated in from the yard.

'That's Sid,' she moaned. 'I'll have to go.'

'No, you stay here. He's waiting for those sacks of barley out there so I'll talk to him.'

'Ta,' she said gratefully. He gave her a brief smile and turned away. On impulse, she added,

'Will you really come and live here?'

He stopped and looked back over his shoulder in exactly the same way he had done on the towpath when she first met him. 'You can count on that,' he answered.

Mabel folded her arms and hugged them to her body, thinking how much she liked him. She heard him talking to Sid in the yard and then the wheels of his cart rumbling on the cobbles as he took the grain into the brewhouse. Then she heaved a sigh and went out to fill her bucket from the outside pump. She still had the privies to do but she hardly noticed the smell. Her mind was full of Harold's smile and a dream that he was coming to live at the Navvy.

The day that Harold moved into the Navigator marked a turning point in Mabel's life. He became her friend and confidant, her secret ally. He would praise her to the Missus when he could, which resulted in Mabel being reinstated to indoor work. Harold also suggested to the Missus that he kept the stables clean in return for a reduced rent as he was in there every day to see to his donkey. But he worked long hours and frequently Elsie had to leave his tea to keep warm in the oven because he didn't get back for dining-room hours.

The evenings were the best time of the day for Mabel because she had finished most of her work and if the drinkers were gathering the Missus would tell her to leave any washing-up until morning and 'make herself scarce'. Sid served beer in the taproom and saloon in the evenings, helped by the Missus, who would appear, tightly corseted into a low-cut gown that her bosoms were bursting out of. But once the Missus was distracted by her customers, instead of going up to the attic, Mabel would creep out to the stables where, quite often, Harold was still tidying up.

She would pet the donkey or sit on straw heaps and watch Harold, enjoying the way that his shoulder muscles flexed underneath his shirt. She had seen the Missus look at him in the same way once or twice and was glad that he never joined the drinkers in the saloon. It wasn't always a different fella with the Missus because she had her favourites whom Elsie called her 'young stallions'. But when a new face came along the Missus would often take a special interest in him.

One evening Harold had been upstairs in the cleaned-out hayloft when Mabel crept into the stables, so she talked to his donkey until he had finished. Eventually, he clattered down the narrow wooden stairs full of his new idea.

'I can get Sid's barley cheaper for the Missus if I buy more sacks at a time. The Missus said Sid had nowhere to keep it but if she has a pulley put in that hayloft door we could keep it up there.'

'You'll be running the place soon,' Mabel laughed.

'Well, Sid'd have more space for brewing if he kept all his grain and barrels in here.'

'P'raps he doesn't want to?'

'He does. He likes making beer. I'm going to talk to the Missus about expanding.'

Mabel tried not to show her feelings on this. But she knew the Missus had taken a fancy to Harold and it annoyed her because the Missus had plenty of other young men to make eyes at. The image of the Missus, with her rouged smile, nearly falling out of her bodice as she handed Harold a glass of foaming beer unsettled Mabel and she said sharply, 'You're not going in there tonight, are you?'

'No fear,' he said. 'I come out here at night to get away from her. She's a right man-eater, she is.'

Mabel laughed, because she agreed with him and 'man-eater' was somehow more repeatable than 'trollop'. She stroked the donkey's coarse hair and fondled his ears. She knew that Harold was watching her and gave him a shy smile. 'I do like you, Harold,' she said.

'We get on all right, you and me, don't we?'

Mabel nodded silently.

He continued to watch her and eventually he said, 'I was going to get rid of the donkey when I get my horse and cart.'

'Oh, that's a shame. He won't go for dog meat, will he?'

'No, he's got plenty of work left in him yet but I shan't need him.' He paused. 'You might, though.'

'Me?'

'He won't cost you anything because I'll still look after him. You'll be able to go into town with the cart when you have time off.'

'Oh, could I?' Mabel warmed to the idea of getting away from Elsie and the Missus once in a while. 'D'you think the Missus'll let me?' Mabel hesitated then added, 'I ... I don't know how to drive a donkey and cart.'

'I'll show you. It's not difficult. I'll explain to the Missus how useful you'll be to her if you can run a few errands when she needs it.'

'Oh, you are clever, Harold. Will she listen to you?'

'You just have to catch her in the right mood if you want to ask for anything.'

'Well, be careful she doesn't eat you,' Mabel warned and they both laughed.

Mabel hadn't laughed much in the workhouse, and she had laughed even less when she first came to the Navigator. But since Harold had arrived, she laughed more often and it made life with Elsie and the Missus easier to bear. She skipped up the stairs to her attic that night thinking that Harold was the nicest lad she had ever met. But he wasn't a lad. He was a man, a strong, fine-looking young man that she wanted to hug and claim as her own. Instead, she hugged her pillow and dreamed of a life with him, as his wife, with a little baby, their baby, living in a proper house in the town...

With Mabel keeping the inside of the Navigator clean, the Missus had more lodgers coming and going, as well as Harold and another older man who lived there all the time. The Missus called them guests and Mabel was put on fettling their rooms and helping Elsie with their meals. She served breakfast to them in the dingy dining room next to the saloon. She always gave Harold extra attention and, later, lingered over the dusting in his bedroom because she felt close to him, even though he wasn't there.

Three months after Mabel left the workhouse, the relieving officer visited to check up on her

38

welfare and report back to the Board of Guardians. Mabel was summoned to stand before him and the Missus in the tiny office at the back of the hall. The door had a glass panel in it so she saw the tankards of foaming beer on the desk before she went in. They drank as they talked about her, though the relieving officer spent most of his time looking sideways at the Missus.

'Is she in good health?' he asked.

'Oh aye. She eats plenty and she's filling out. She's turned fifteen now so I have to keep an eye on her with the lads.'

'Has she done 'owt she shouldn't?' He appeared to be talking to the Missus's white bosom, bulging out of her red low-cut gown, the one trimmed with black lace.

'Nay. She's still an innocent. You can tell that just by looking at her.'

'That new constable says you're not sending her to church.'

The Missus grinned at him and said, 'Are you going to give me a spanking then?'

Mabel pressed her lips together to stifle a giggle. She had seen the Missus's round white bottom and she could imagine the mean relieving officer giving it a good spanking.

He wagged his finger at the Missus and answered, 'One or two of the guardians don't trust you with her welfare and you don't want 'em to be right. You'll have to send her.'

The Missus looked cross. 'Oh Percy,' she protested, 'I need her here to help with the Sunday dinner.'

'It'll be worth it for you in the long run to send

her. If she turns out all right, the Board of Guardians will ask you to take one of our lads.'

'I don't need a lad.'

'Sid does, though, in the brewhouse. He'd have proper apprenticeship papers, and you'd get a premium.'

'A premium, eh? I'll think about it.'

'Only think about it! This one's not giving you trouble, is she?'

The Missus shook her head and her dark ringlets jiggled. 'No, but you'll have to persuade me to take on another 'un,' she murmured. She arched her eyebrows at Percy, opened her rouged mouth and ran her tongue over her teeth.

The relieving officer gave Mabel the briefest of glances and said, 'You can go now.'

'Pull the blind down as you leave,' the Missus instructed.

She obeyed and as she closed the door she heard the Missus giggle, 'Now then, Percy, take off your jacket first.'

Trollop, Mabel thought and, instead of being shocked as she used to be, she shook her head slightly and laughed to herself. Then she fretted that the Missus might not keep her if she took on a lad and she'd have to go back to the workhouse. She didn't want to leave the Navigator because she didn't want to be parted from Harold!

Later that day, the Missus came to find her in the scullery. She was washing up the dinner pots. 'Right, lass,' the Missus said, 'dry your hands for a minute.'

Mabel's heart stopped. 'Have I got to go back to the workhouse?' she asked.

'Not as long as you stay away from my drinkers at night.'

Mabel inhaled deeply and blew out her cheeks. She wasn't the least bit interested in the Missus's beery boozers who made lewd comments about her until somebody with some common decency shut them up.

The Missus continued, 'You should have been going to church every Sunday so make sure you're seen there from now on. Right?'

Mabel nodded. 'Yes, Missus.'

'You'll need a respectable gown. I'll put one of my old 'uns over the banister for you. You'll have to alter it.'

Mabel wondered how she would make anything from the Missus appear respectable but she didn't argue. She was a good needlewoman, although she'd only ever made calico aprons and caps in the workhouse.

The Missus pushed a small leather pouch into her damp hands. 'Here's your wages. You'll get that every quarter, provided you earn it and you behave yourself.'

Mabel clutched the purse of coins tightly and breathed, 'Oh, I will, Missus, I will.' Her own money! Her very first own money!

'Keep back a ha'penny for the church collection every week, mind.'

'Yes, Missus. Thank you, Missus.'

The Missus's silky red skirt rustled as she turned away.

'Missus?'

'What is it now?'

'Can I ask Harold to take me to church in his

41

donkey cart?'

'Harold? Harold? He's Mr Goodman to you and he's a guest so no, you can't.'

'I'd save time and Elsie won't be on her own too long with the dinner,' Mabel added.

After a pause, the Missus said, 'Well, I suppose Harold does work for me as well. But *I* shall put it to him, and listen here, you, you make sure there's no hanky-panky when you're with him.'

Like you with your fellas, Mabel thought, but she remained silent. The Missus went on, 'I mean it! That new constable will have his eye on you.' Then she swept out, leaving a heavy, sickly scent in the air.

'Thanks, Missus,' Mabel called after her. She lifted up her scratchy brown workhouse skirt and stowed the pouch in the pocket of her drawers.

The gown when it appeared was plain compared to the Missus's red satin and black lace. It was made of a faded blue woollen material with long sleeves, a high neckline and a white tatting collar. It had similar cotton trims down the bodice and around the bottom edge of the skirt. The Missus had probably discarded it years ago in favour of the low necklines that showed off her ample bosom. Anyway, Mabel reckoned, even with her tightest corset the Missus would never fit into this gown now; she was too fat.

Old and worn or not, the Missus had kept away the moths and Mabel thought that it was the prettiest gown she had ever seen, and it was hers. It had underskirts, a matching sash for her waist and a straw bonnet trimmed and tied with the same fabric. Her eyes shone and as soon as she saw it, draped over the banister, she gathered it up and took it to her attic, where she laid it carefully on her bed. It was too big for her but she was still growing, outwards if not upwards and while her bosoms would never be as big as the Missus's, they were quite rounded now.

She had time to shorten the skirt before Sunday but that was all. So she laced her corset tighter to push up her bosoms and fill out the bodice, then tied the sash firmly around her waist to take in the extra inches. Her fair hair fitted under the bonnet when it was coiled round her head and she fashioned a bow on the side of her face with the ties. Her mouth dropped open with surprise as she looked at her image in the spotty mirror. She was a young woman, and a respectable young woman, too! No one would mistake *her* for a trollop, even though she did live at the Navigator.

She put her ha'penny in the gown pocket and went downstairs and straight out into the yard where Harold was waiting with his donkey cart.

Chapter 4

It gave Mabel such a thrill to see Harold's reaction. His mouth dropped open and his eyes widened.

'Do you like it?' she asked, holding out her skirts.

He recovered enough to say, 'You look ... you look lovely.' He seemed lost for words but he added, 'You're beautiful, really beautiful, and your carriage awaits, miss.' He held out his hand.

She giggled at his formality and took his hand, allowing him to help her up onto the plain wooden board that served as a driving seat. She felt very proud to be riding beside him and, when they reached the parish church in town, even prouder to be recognised in her new gown by the workhouse matron and the young constable. Matron acknowledged her with a nod and the constable smiled. After the service she chatted about her life outside the workhouse to one or two of the inmates.

On the way home Harold walked the donkey, leading him by his bridle, while she sat in the driver's seat and held the reins to get used to the feel of them in her hands. It was not much quicker than walking, but far less tiring for Mabel and she skipped up to her attic to take off her bonnet and change her gown before rolling up her sleeves in the kitchen.

After a month of similar Sundays, Mabel took the reins on the way to church and tethered the donkey while Harold watched discreetly. She wanted to take his arm as she walked into church with him and she was hurt when he wouldn't let her. He said they must walk side by side and be careful not to touch each other.

But Mabel's feelings of wanting to hug him and claim him as her own grew stronger as the weeks passed and she vowed to tackle him about it in the stables one evening. She thought he felt the same way about her, but how could she be sure if he wouldn't even hold her hand in church?

Mabel chose her time carefully. She waited until the saloon was busy and the Missus was fully occupied keeping her drinkers happy. Sid was looking after some thirsty young miners in the taproom and Elsie was sozzled, as usual, in the kitchen. Mabel picked up a lantern and went outside.

She found Harold cleaning out and repairing the biggest stall for his heavy horse. He had arranged to collect it from a farm as soon as he had enough money to pay for it and the substantial cart that came with it. Mabel knew how to feed and bed down the donkey by now and they worked in an easy companionable silence until Mabel had finished.

Harold was whitewashing the back wall before he refitted the manger. Mabel stood and watched him for a few minutes, admiring him as she always did, then she said, 'You do like me, don't you, Harold?'

He put down his whitewash brush and turned round.

'I like you very much. I thought you knew that.'

'Well, why won't you hold my hand in church?'

'Because the constable is watching me.'

'You haven't done anything wrong, have you?'

'No, but if he's not there, the workhouse matron has her beady eyes on you.'

'Oh, I see. Well, they are supposed to keep checking up on me until I'm sixteen. What do they think you're going to do to me in church?'

'Ravish you in the aisle!' He laughed and she laughed with him. 'It's not that I don't want to,' he added.

Mabel stopped laughing and said, 'We're not in church now.'

'I know.' He took a step towards her. 'I want to do more than hold hands, Mabel. I want to kiss you.'

She sighed at the sound of such sweet words and ran towards him, bumping against his chest.

'Be caref–' he began before she reached up, pulled his head down towards her and planted a kiss on his lips.

He needed no more encouragement. He gathered her in his arms and kissed her deeply and – and – oh Lord, he wanted her, he wanted her passionately; and she wanted him ... she didn't want the kiss to end ... she wanted to tear off her clothes ... and his too ... and...

She had to drag her mouth away from his eventually in order to breathe.

He was panting slightly and his face was flushed. They both looked towards the heap of straw against the wall. A bed of straw, Mabel thought, our bed. He must be thinking the same, she thought, he must be. Her body was alive with desire for him and she pleaded with her eyes for him to make the move.

'I want to, Mabel...' he croaked.

'Me too,' she said quietly.

'...ever since I first met you on the towpath, so it's not that I don't want you.'

Mabel's heart stopped for a moment. He was saying no. She heard the sorrow in his voice as he went on, 'We can't do it, Mabel. We mustn't. If the workhouse find out, they'll make you go back and the Missus'll get rid of me, too.'

'Oh, but it's all right for her to carry on...' Mabel protested.

'It's *her* they are watching. She has her friends on the town council but she has enemies as well, just waiting for her to put a foot wrong.'

'Well, I know the workhouse matron doesn't approve of her.'

'Any sign that you're in moral danger and they'll say that they were right about her. They're jealous of her, you see. She's over thirty and not wed and she's got money to burn, so they think she's a ... she's a...' He shrugged. 'You know what I mean.'

A whore. Mabel had thought the same when she arrived. But the Missus wasn't a whore. She just liked the young fellas that drank at her inn. She actually encouraged the constable's regular visits to see off any roaming 'ladies of the night'.

Harold heaved a sigh and added, 'Besides, you're too young to get married.'

'No I'm not!'

'You are. Oh, Mabel, I do love you and in a few years I'll have enough put by to rent a house and give you a proper home. Then I can marry you and take you away from here.'

Mabel's heart swelled. Her dream has suddenly become a possibility. 'Oh, I'd like that, Harold, I really would. I love you too.'

He stepped back, allowing the cold air to rush in between them. 'That's all right then, isn't it?' he said. His voice took on a serious tone. 'But we do have to wait until I can afford to marry you. And you mustn't tempt me because I really do want you, and it's hard for me.'

Mabel looked down at the bulge in his trousers

and suppressed a guffaw, putting a hand over her tightly closed mouth. But her eyes danced. He saw the humour, looked down at himself and laughed as well. 'It's not funny,' he protested. 'Now go away before I jump on you.'

She picked up the lantern. She reckoned she could easily get him to jump on her and she wanted that because she loved him. But she loved him too much to *not* do as he asked. He was right. They had to wait. In two years she'd be seventeen and plenty old enough to be married. Two years, though! She blew out her cheeks. It seemed like a lifetime to Mabel.

Before she left, Harold said, 'We'll have to keep it quiet about you and me. The Missus being how she is, she'll never believe we haven't been at it like her.'

Mabel was disappointed because she wanted to tell everyone that she had a sweetheart. Nevertheless, she saw the sense in what he said. Harold thought about these things and he knew more about how folk in town behaved than she did. She crept into the Navvy by the back scullery and was reflecting on this, when a voice called out, 'What are you doing out here, young lady?'

She whirled round and lifted the lantern. It was the constable. He often walked about outside looking for women from town attempting to ply their trade at the Navvy. Most didn't bother trying because he always caught them, threatened to arrest them and lock them up for the night. Mabel was ready for him or anyone else she might meet on her way to and from the stables. 'Just been to the privy,' she said cheerily. 'Goodnight, sir.'

'You've got whitewash on your sleeve,' he commented. She didn't care. She was in love with Harold and he wanted to marry her. It was all she wished for and the constable and the matron and the relieving officer wouldn't give a tinker's cuss about her once she was past sixteen. She could wait for Harold until then and her behaviour would be exemplary while she did. The workhouse had trained her well to 'shut up and put up'.

Harold's deliveries for the Missus increased and he became more involved in the brewing side of the Navigator Inn. With the stables and outhouses cleared for storage and barrels, Sid had room in the brewhouse for two new vats, and regular orders soon started to come in from taverns across the Riding. Harold produced a recipe of his grandmother's for barley wine – a strong ale that needed longer to mature than Sid's beer. Harold said it should be bottled as Navigator Barley Wine and delivered in crates to the taverns, which Sid didn't want to do but the Missus did because it would be popular with women-folk and therefore profitable.

The Missus had her own way, of course, and promised Sid a proper apprentice to help. But Sid, always a surly sort of fellow, thought Harold had 'interfered' and the atmosphere was strained for a week or so. Mabel, on Harold's advice, kept out of it. She had to work with Elsie, who could make life difficult for her if she chose. But the Missus's word was law at the Navigator and Harold's recipe was used.

Eventually, too, the Missus allowed Mabel to

take the donkey cart into town on her own and she began to go in on market day to make a few purchases. Her scratchy brown workhouse gown was too tight and it had no more in the seams to let out. She needed a serviceable skirt and bodice for everyday and a pair of smart boots for Sundays from the second-hand stall.

Now that Harold had a horse and cart he made deliveries over a longer distance and even stayed away overnight on occasions. Mabel missed him hugely when he was away and waited in the stables for him to return the following night. She would help him bed down his horse and then they would sit and talk about his journey and kiss each other passionately – far too passionately – before he sent her away. She could tell he didn't want to. He was strong-willed, though, and it needed one of them to be able to say no because Mabel would never refuse him. He didn't shave when he was away and her face was often red and sore afterwards but it was worth it. She bought a soothing salve from a market stall and it worked a treat on her skin.

She made small purchases in the market for Harold as well. He would give her a list and some coins when he wanted saddle soap for his tack, or dubbin for his boots. She was proud that he trusted her with his money and felt like his wife already. However, as the days grew longer and the evenings were lighter it became difficult not to be seen when she went indoors after her visits to the stables. Inevitably, the Missus found out.

Until then, Mabel hadn't been aware that the Missus didn't know and had assumed that she

50

didn't mind. Harold was a carter in his own right; he was respectable and trustworthy. Mabel behaved herself indoors and ignored the miners' suggestive comments about her. So she was surprised when the Missus stormed into the taproom one morning as she was on her hands and knees scrubbing the floor, and grasped the back of her bodice.

'Get on your feet and explain yourself,' the Missus demanded. 'I've told you before to stay away from my guests!'

Mabel scrambled up, shook the soapy water off her fingers and wiped them down her apron, unsure of what she had done wrong. 'I ... I have to clean their rooms,' she said. 'Sometimes they come back early. I leave straightaway if they do.'

'I'm not talking about that. I mean after hours; you and ... and men in the stables!'

'Me and men? What men?'

'Don't play the innocent with me! The constable says he's seen you coming out there of a night-time when you should be upstairs, and Elsie says you're always in the stables after tea.'

'I have to see to the donkey.'

'You do that before tea and you do the washing-up after.' The Missus glared at her.

Mabel guessed this was no time for half truths and admitted, 'I go back to the stables when Harold gets home and help him with his horse.'

The Missus clipped her across her head and shouted, 'Haven't I said he's Mr Goodman to you! Sid saw you coming out of there with coins in your hand! Is that how you got the money for them new boots?'

'No!' Mabel protested. 'My boots were second hand off the market. I had enough for them from my wages.' She rubbed the side of her head. 'And you're not supposed to hit me 'cos I'm a girl.'

'You don't have to tell me that. I can see how you've filled out while you've been here. Who else have you had in the stables?'

'I haven't had anybody in the stables!'

'Don't lie to me! Is Harold finding fellas for you? He's certainly not short of a bob or two himself these days.'

'He works hard! And he gives me money to buy things!'

This made the Missus more furious and she shouted even louder, 'I knew it! He's got you on the game! How many fellas have you had in there?'

'The money is to buy things for him, things he needs off the market!' Mabel protested.

'Oh, he's a right clever one, that one is. Has he told you to say that?'

'It's the truth! When he's away all day, he can't get to the market.'

But the Missus wasn't listening to her; and she didn't lower her voice either. 'If that young constable finds out he's running a brothel in my stables, he'll close me down! And you, you little witch...' The Missus raised her hand to clip her again, but Mabel dodged out of the way.

'I haven't done anything,' Mabel protested, 'and neither has Harold. He's decent. He's not like your fellas...' She wished Harold were here to explain to the Missus. He was cleverer than she was and the Missus would believe him.

'Now then, ladies, what's going on? I can hear

52

you from the dining room.'

The Missus whirled round. 'Mr Wilmot!' Her demeanour changed immediately, as though she had forgotten Mabel was there. She patted her hair and smoothed down her skirt. 'Mr Wilmot, I am sorry I have disturbed you. I have to chastise my servants from time to time. What can I do for you?'

Chapter 5

Mr Wilmot had arrived the night before looking for a lodging and Mabel had served him breakfast that morning. He had taken his breakfast later than the other guests, including Harold, who had already left for work. Seeing him enter the shabby dining room, Mabel had wondered if he wouldn't have been better off in the hotel in town. He was smartly dressed in long jacket, matching trousers and polished boots. He'd carried a bowler hat and a tweed overcoat with a rain cloak attached to the shoulders and he'd asked Mabel to hang them on the coat stand in the entrance hall.

Now, he gave Mabel a kindly smile and spoke to the Missus. 'My hat and coat need brushing. Railway trains are so smutty. Will your maid do it for me?'

'I'll see to it myself, Mr Wilmot.'

'I'm sure the girl can manage. I was rather hoping to have a talk with you about property in the town. I'm told you know the area well.'

53

The Missus was flattered. 'Indeed I do. I have many interests in town myself.'

'Perhaps you will advise me? Can you recommend a legal man as well?'

Mr Wilmot gently plied the Missus with questions and Mabel was ignored. As they moved out of the taproom towards the entrance hall, the Missus suddenly remembered her, turned and said quite calmly, 'Do the hat and coat now.' Her anger, it seemed, had evaporated with the appearance of Mr Wilmot.

Mabel followed them and listened in on the conversation, amused by the way the Missus preened herself in response to Mr Wilmot's attention. He was more the Missus's own age than the 'young stallions' she favoured from her saloon bar. Besides, men his age usually saw the Missus for what she was – a trollop – and they had wives waiting for them at home so they stuck to their drinking.

She heard Mr Wilmot say, 'Oh, I cannot be beholden to you, my good lady. If you insist on taking me in your trap then you must allow me to buy you dinner.'

'Come into my office, Mr Wilmot,' the Missus murmured. 'I have a newspaper with lists of properties for auction.' She glanced back at Mabel and called to her, 'Tell Elsie to bring coffee.'

Mabel grabbed the hat and coat and rushed into the kitchen, knowing Elsie would be her friend for a week if she shared this piece of gossip. She had never known the Missus invite a lodger into her office before.

'Who is he?' Mabel asked.

'Dunno,' Elsie replied, 'but he's a Yorkshireman by the way he talks. I made him a bit o' supper when he arrived last night and Sid showed him upstairs. He's a charmer, right enough. He's got money an' all, by the look of it. Your Harold might know of him from his rounds.'

'*My* Harold?'

'Yes, *your* Harold. Sid reckons you're having it off wi' 'im in the stables.'

'Well I'm not, and I'll thank you to stop spreading lies about me. I've had a right telling-off from the Missus this morning.'

'Aye, I were listening. Sid never said Harold were pimping yer, though. But y'are sweet on him, aren't yer?'

'What if I am? We're going to be wed when I'm seventeen.'

'Seventeen?' Elsie squeaked. 'He'll never wait that long. His blood's up as far as you're concerned, my lass.'

'Well, he won't get the chance because the Missus will send me back to the workhouse after what Sid told her!' The thought of leaving Harold made her miserable. If they decided she was 'in moral danger' at the Navvy, they'd place her at the opposite end of the Riding and she might never see Harold again. She had to talk to him, whatever the risk, before the Missus sent her away.

But Mr Wilmot's arrival at the Navvy had an unusual – and for Mabel a welcome – effect on the Missus. George Wilmot was a flatterer and the Missus was smitten by him. He was an easy fellow to like because he was charming to all the women, even Elsie and Mabel, although this made the men who frequented the Navvy suspicious of him. However, the Missus thought he could do no wrong. She appeared to forget all about Mabel's evenings spent with Harold in the stables as her time and attention became devoted to Mr Wilmot.

He brought the Missus small gifts from the best shops on the high street and took her to Doncaster races where she could show off her ostrich feather hats. When they returned, merry and tired, she retired to her bedroom while he served the pints in the saloon bar for the Missus and handled any rowdiness to the approval of the constable. If it was a quiet night, he took himself off upstairs with a glass of stout for the Missus and a brandy for himself.

It was noticeable that the Missus lost interest in her 'young stallions' and Mabel knew why. Mr Wilmot frequently entertained the Missus in her bedroom and stayed with her all night. However, he didn't go off to work the morning after. He took her breakfast upstairs, and Mabel had to go out and find flowers to put on the tray.

But, as Harold said to Mabel on their journey home from church one Sunday, 'He's not that well off. She still hires a horse and trap for them to travel around in, although he does the driving nowadays.'

Mabel was confident holding the reins all the time now, even if she only had a donkey, and conversed easily. 'He told her when he arrived that he was looking for property in town,' she commented.

'He was spinning her a line,' Harold grinned, 'to get his feet under her table.'

'Well, it's worked. He goes with her to collect the rents. Do you think he knocks on the doors for her?'

'She's never done that for herself. All the Missus does is see her solicitor and her bank manager. Then she hobnobs with the councillors and municipal officers in the Red Lion.' He chuckled. 'Shall I tell you what the women say about her?'

'What?' Mabel giggled. Nothing about the Missus surprised her any more.

'The workhouse guardians have been trying to get their wives to take her onto one of their charity committees. They won't have her, of course.'

'Why not? She's got plenty of money.'

Harold put on a high-pitched voice. 'Far too rough and ready for us, my dear, and what can you expect with someone from *that* family?'

'I didn't think she had any family.'

'Well, she hasn't now. But they were well known for the men being thugs and the women being coarse. She lost 'em all to the cholera.'

'I remember that. The doctor made us boil all the water in the workhouse.'

'We were all right on the farm because we had our own spring, but it was bad in town.'

'A lot of folk died.' Mabel shivered at the memory. 'You never knew who was going to be next.'

'The Missus's father and brothers owned all the property around Mexton Lock, even the engineer's house on the other side of the canal. They all went down with the cholera, including the wife and kids.'

'But she didn't?'

'Her mother had sent her away to school so she

57

could better herself and she was in Scarborough with a la-di-da friend. Apparently, the solicitor wrote and told her to stay where she was.'

'Poor girl, though.' Mabel grimaced. She knew what it was like to have nobody. So did Harold and a lot of other folk in these parts. She reached across for his hand and added, 'I'm glad we've got each other.'

He squeezed her fingers gently. 'Me too. Mind you, all the property came to her.'

'I wouldn't want to be well off in that way.'

'Neither would I, but don't you worry about us, Mabel my love, I'm making good money with my horse and cart and I've a fair amount put by already.' He shuffled closer to her and put his arm round her shoulders. 'We might not have to wait until I'm twenty-one after all.'

Mabel wanted nothing more than to marry Harold whether he was well off or not and her eyes shone. 'I do love you, Harold.'

'I know. I love you too.' He paused for a moment, then went on, 'I've had a word with the Missus about us.'

Mabel tensed. She didn't want to be sent away. 'I shouldn't have told you what she said.' Her years in the workhouse had taught her to accept her lot and keep quiet.

'Yes you should. She was wrong about us and I explained. She's been all right with you since, hasn't she?'

'Well, she's got Mr Wilmot to keep her happy now.'

'And I suppose she knows what it's like to be in love.'

'Do you think so?'

'Oh yes. She's fallen for him proper.'

'D'you think he loves her?'

Harold shook his head. 'He loves her money. But we've been talking and he agrees with me about expanding the brewhouse even more. Everybody wants Navigator Ale so I told him about the horse marine next door.'

'It's derelict.'

'Yes, but it belongs to the Missus. So does the blacksmith's. They made her folks rich in the heydays of the canals.'

The Navigator was in sight, and smoke from the chimney indicated that the range was going strong for Elsie's roast mutton. 'Are you sure the Missus is all right about us?' Mabel queried.

'She's easy to flatter and, as she is your guardian, I asked her permission to court you.'

'What did she say to that?'

'Well, she was impressed that I'd asked her, but she ummed and ahhed and then told me to wait until the workhouse had stopped checking up on you.' He glanced sideways at Mabel and grimaced.

Mabel wondered why he was frowning. 'We were doing that anyway, so what else did she say?'

'Well, I agreed with her. I was happy that it was out in the open, so I mentioned that both of us were really keen to be wed as soon as possible and then she got really twitchy. She marched about saying she was responsible for you and–'

'And what?'

'And she didn't want any gossip and what if I changed my mind about you? She'd send you

59

back to the workhouse rather than have any little...' He glanced at her before going on, '... any little bastard at the Navvy.'

'But you'd marry me!'

'Of course I would! We both know that. She doesn't, though, and she thinks every woman is like her. Anyway, she made me promise not to touch you in that way before we wed.'

'Oh.' Mabel was disappointed. She didn't see anything wrong with loving each other like man and wife once she was sixteen and they knew they were getting married. But the Church said you shouldn't and she didn't really want to walk up the aisle with a swollen belly under her gown and everybody saying 'I told you so'. Mabel raised her eyebrows at Harold. 'You're all right with that, aren't you?'

'Not really. Are you?'

'No,' she admitted.

'At least she didn't say no to us outright, and she didn't mean I couldn't kiss you.' He snuggled even closer and slid his hand from her shoulder and around her waist.

When he kissed her ear, her whole body came alive with desire and she turned her head to kiss his lips. The reins fell from her hands and she was locked in an embrace so passionate that the cart rocked and she almost fell off. The normally passive donkey veered off track and nearly went in the canal. Harold broke away from her and jumped down to take the bridle just in time to prevent a disaster.

They didn't speak. They just smiled at each other wistfully. Mabel tried to lift their mood and said brightly, 'Well, when you do start to court me proper, you can drive me around, just like Mr Wilmot does for the Missus.'

Harold laughed but he took the reins for the rest of the way. When they reached the Navvy and he helped her down, he said quietly, '*She* never falls for a baby, though, does she?'

Mabel shook her head. Elsie had made the same comment because 'she knew for a fact them young stallions never wore owt when they did it'. Elsie had concluded that the Missus must be barren, but Mabel knew different. She had seen the tin box in the Missus's bedroom when she was fettling it. But she didn't have time to dwell on that now. She ran upstairs to change before joining Elsie in the kitchen.

The Navvy wasn't allowed to sell drink on a Sunday but lodgers and other diners could have ale with their dinner. There was often an extra table or two for folk who walked down from Mexton to eat. They were local men who were bachelors or widowers and had good wages from their work as pit suppliers, like the blacksmith next door and the mine's engineer.

The Missus never went to church or chapel. She took all morning to doll up and serve the dinners while Elsie dished up and Mabel washed up. But today the Missus asked Mabel to serve at table because she was sitting down to eat 'with her guests'.

The Missus liked her food as well as her ale and had a good appetite. She was sitting with Mr Wilmot and a gentleman who had arrived wearing a top hat and driving his own trap.

'Who is he?' Mabel asked Elsie.

'He's her fancy lawyer from town. He's been 'ere before. See if you can listen in to what they talk about. I can manage t'kitchen on me own.'

Mabel usually hovered near Harold's table but today he was sitting with the blacksmith and the engineer and they were deep in conversation. Sid came in with jugs of ale for the tables and it was Mabel's job to keep them filled. Sunday dinner always started with Yorkshire puddings and Elsie's were well known as some of the best. She made plenty of thick gravy to pour over them so Mabel had time to linger as they ate.

'I am ready to expand the brewhouse further, Mr Belfor,' the Missus said, 'and Mr Wilmot has some experience in brewing.'

'Your new barley wine is proving popular, especially with the ladies in town,' the lawyer responded.

Mr Wilmot said, 'We need a bigger set-up for bottling, though, and another building.'

'Reliable delivery is important, too,' Mr Belfor added.

The Missus gestured towards Harold. 'I have my own carter.'

The lawyer nodded. 'Young Goodman; well named, that fellow is. He's reliable and doing all right for himself. Will he invest? It will keep him with you.'

'He's saving to get married,' the Missus said.

'But he's ambitious,' Mr Wilmot added. 'The barley wine was his recipe. He gets a royalty on each vat.'

'Does he now?' Mr Belfor commented. 'He's

clever, as well, then. You'd better watch him.'

'He's honest,' the Missus said, 'and the horse marine was his idea.'

'I'll take a look before I leave.' Mr Belfor turned to the Missus. Mabel had noticed that *he* never looked at her bosoms, nor did he smile, and she might as well have been invisible for the want of any sort of acknowledgement of her. 'No need for you to come with us, dear,' he said to the Missus. 'Wilmot will show me round.'

The Missus reached across the table to place her hand on Mr Wilmot's. 'Well, George is part of my life now.' She smiled.

Mr Wilmot returned her smile then indicated to Mabel to clear the plates.

Mr Belfor added, 'Ask young Goodman to join us.'

Mabel felt excited about this. Mr Belfor was well connected in the town and he had noticed her Harold. Harold was already going up in the world!

Mabel brought in dishes of roast potatoes, carrots, greens and mashed turnips while Sid carried in a leg of mutton and tackled the carving. Elsie put out more jugs of gravy then she disappeared with Sid for their own dinner. There was another smaller joint for them in the kitchen and Mabel's would be waiting for her as soon as all the guests were eating. Walter, Sid's new apprentice, who slept in the brewhouse, had his dinner with them, too. He was a quiet lad, not yet fourteen and, like most workhouse kids, he did as he was told without question.

The Missus came into the kitchen to say they were ready for pudding. 'Mr Belfor is in a hurry,' she said to Mabel. 'Bring us the apple pie now; I'll dish up. Mr Belfor wants coffee so you'll have to take it out to them, make enough for three.'

'Where will they be?' she asked.

'In the old horse marine.'

Mabel grimaced, and so did the Missus. 'I know it's filthy dirty. Leave the tray on the mounting stone outside and they can help themselves.'

Mabel and Elsie left their plates to carry in the warm pie and custard waiting on the range. They brought out the used pots, piled them in the scullery sink and started the coffee. Mabel saw Mr Belfor crossing the back yard with Mr Wilmot and Harold on their way to the horse marine as she put the finishing touches to her tray. She wrinkled her nose. She didn't like coffee, not even the smell of it, but Harold took it sometimes.

The horse marine was bigger than the brewhouse and stables put together. It was cold, dank, full of spiders' webs and still smelled of the farmyard from the days when heavy horses pulled canal barges. The doors were wide open and Mabel stood in the light with her tray. 'Your coffee, sir,' she said.

Mr Belfor continued his conversation. He was talking about stonemasons and carpenters and delivery drays pulled by two horses. Mabel could see that Harold was interested. 'I'll leave it out here,' she added.

Mr Belfor stopped talking and said irritably, 'Bring it inside, stupid girl, and pour it before it goes cold.'

She ignored his rudeness, looked around for a flat surface, which she found in a dark corner, and took him his cup first. Mr Wilmot and Harold both gave her a brief smile when she handed over theirs, then Mr Belfor took out his gold pocket watch and said to Harold, 'Goodman, fetch my trap around now.'

Harold put his cup and saucer on a ledge and avoided looking at Mabel as he left, which is just as well because she might have said something about Mr Belfor's manners. Harold wasn't his personal servant. She stayed in the shadows by her tray in case they wanted a refill.

'She's taken to you, Wilmot,' Mr Belfor said. 'I thought she would.'

'Aye, she has. I think she'll wed me an' all.'

'Excellent, but she has to make you a partner. Wives keep their own property these days, more's the pity.'

'She does like being in charge.'

'What you'll have to do is give her a few bairns to keep her busy. I know a young fellow who's already tried that with her. He had no luck but if she really can't have them, you'll have to adopt. You can be sure you get boys then. You don't think she's barren, do you?'

'No,' Mr Wilmot replied. 'She uses stuff she gets from the chemist.'

'Good God, Wilmot, is that how she does it! What is the country coming to? I hope you put a stop to that right away. It doesn't do for women to have all that money and freedom. Their job is to marry and have children.'

'I think I've persuaded her to give me a go,' Mr Wilmot said. He shuffled his feet and went on, 'She is a handful, Belfor. I ... I ought to buy her a ring, you know, for a proper betrothal.'

Mr Belfor sniffed. 'And I suppose you want me to fund it? You know I can't. I've only got clients' money until I'm wed myself.'

'Call it an investment,' Mr Wilmot suggested.

Mr Belfor sniffed again. 'Come into my office next week.' He stepped back, viewed the whole of the building and gave a satisfied nod. 'This'll be a gold mine. But I won't be greedy, Wilmot, just as long as I get my percentage. You concentrate on out here. Keep everybody happy, especially that young Goodman.'

Chapter 6

Building work was under way on the horse marine within a month. The Navigator was busier than ever, with labourers from the site and those simply curious, who walked down the towpath from town for a drink. Elsie made dinner-time pies for the men and the Missus gave each one a free pint. She also arranged for another girl to come from the workhouse. Vera was younger than Mabel and shared her attic. Mabel remembered her from school and felt very grown-up as she showed her what to do. An extra pair of hands for Elsie meant that Mabel could concentrate on serving in the dining room and cleaning for the lodgers.

There had been a scandal at the workhouse where complaints about the matron had un-covered an affair with Percy, the relieving officer, who was a married man. Matron had been asked to leave and Vera was happy to tell Elsie all the inside gossip, so Elsie was happy too.

But Mabel wasn't happy because she saw less and less of Harold. Vera came to church with them and, as she was so small, she sat between them so as not to fall off. Harold smiled wistfully at Mabel over her head. She was becoming used to it because they were hardly ever alone these days. When Harold was home from his deliveries he was in conversation with Mr Wilmot and Sid, or Mr Wilmot and the Missus, or Mr Wilmot and the builder, or even Mr Wilmot and the blacksmith from next door.

Harold began to refer to Mr Wilmot as George when they spoke about him and, eventually, Mabel did too. George encouraged this and frequently referred to the Navvy as 'his big happy family'. He charmed everybody with his winning ways and once flattered Mabel that 'he'd marry her himself if Harold hadn't already claimed her'. Fortunately, the Missus didn't hear him.

George became part of everyone's life at the inn. He sat in the crowded office with them instead of the Missus when Percy from the workhouse visited. Percy was more interested in Sid's apprentice than he was in either the new girl or Mabel. This suited Mabel. She'd be sixteen by the time the horse marine was finished and fitted out.

The Missus told Elsie to bake a Dundee cake for her birthday, and George's 'big happy family' sat down to an afternoon tea – the sort the gentry had – in the dining room. There were eight of them and it did feel like a family to Mabel, not that she had ever had one of her own to compare it to. She was asked to cut the cake and the Missus gave her a present – a lovely length of cloth to make a gown. Mabel's eyes shone. She'd have a new gown, a proper new gown, not worn by anybody else!

Harold gave her a soft woollen shoulder cape lined with silk that had been in the draper's window in the high street. She had coveted it for weeks and remembered being so disappointed when it disappeared from the window.

George made a little speech about how well she had turned out and how the workhouse was proud of the Missus's efforts. But tea was over quickly. There was a dinner to cook, a vat of foaming ale to check, a delivery to make to a new hotel on the Bawtry Road, and Mabel had to make sure the washerwoman finished the bed sheets before she finished her gin.

While the day-to-day work of the Navvy went on, the Missus and George occupied themselves planning a grand opening for the new brewhouse: local bigwigs, the colliery brass band, pork pies and cheeses with unlimited ale. Elsie had the new girl to help her but Mabel was left to cope with the lodgers and cleaning the rooms by herself. This had its compensations, but only if Harold wasn't out on deliveries. He was often late back and Elsie would put his tea in the bottom oven of the range to keep warm. Mabel would wait patiently for him to return, and make sure he had anything he wanted from the pantry.

On one particular evening she stood quietly by the sideboard while he ate – ravenous as usual –

then went to collect his plate. He caught hold of her hand as she walked by. 'Sit down, Mabel love. I have to ask you something.'

'What is it?' Mabel drew out a chair. They normally chatted about his day while he finished his beer.

'We never get a chance to talk these days.'

'You work hard. I understand that.'

'We're never alone any more either. This place is like Sheffield station these days!'

Mabel agreed. 'It won't be for ever,' she said.

'I know but I really can't go on like this. I want to marry you – soon.'

'I know, my love. I want to marry you, too. I think the Missus might let me an' all. Can you afford it?'

He nodded and her heart leaped. Then she saw his serious face and calmed.

'The thing is,' Harold said, 'George wants me to invest in the brewery.'

'The brewery?'

'That's what this place will be when the new building opens. The Missus will still sell ale, of course, but she'll stop taking lodgers. Elsie and Sid are getting on in years and–'

'What have they got to do with us?' she interrupted.

'Nothing, it's just that George wants me to invest my savings. I'd be a partner. It'd be worth it in the long run, but...' He grimaced. 'Well, we'd have to put off getting married.'

This was a blow for Mabel. Harold had a lot put by for them so they could have a nice house in a better part of town and it wouldn't matter if she had babies straightaway. 'For how long?' she asked.

'I can't say. I've talked to George and he knows how we feel about each other. He thinks we should wait until you're seventeen anyway. He said we could have one of the Missus's houses in town then and I wouldn't need a guarantor for the lease.'

'Another year, though,' Mabel groaned.

'He ... er ... he reckons the Missus wouldn't mind if we had a bit of time alone together now and then.'

Mabel shrugged. 'Well, we do when we can find the time.'

'In my room,' he added quietly.

She looked at him sharply. 'You mean she wouldn't say anything?'

'He can handle her.'

Mabel had to agree. Elsie had said that George had the Missus 'eating out of his hand' these days.

Harold went on, 'You needn't go up to the attic of an evening. You could come to my room.'

Oh, what joy! She'd be able to kiss him without fear of interruption, without fear of anything. He would hold her in his arms and love her properly; as she wanted him to. She loved him. He loved her. Mabel began to melt inside at the thought.

His eyes had darkened too. 'I want you so much, it hurts,' he groaned. 'But ... but we won't do it if you don't want to.'

'Oh, I do, I do. You know I do. It's just that if we can't wed straightway, I'd worry about...'

'Having a baby? Me too. I'll wear something.'

'I thought fellas didn't like them things.'

'I could try.' He shrugged.

'Don't bother. In the workhouse the women used to say that their men said they'd use something and then wouldn't. So the women had their own things.'

Harold stared at her. 'What things?'

'The Missus has them. She keeps them in a tin in her drawer with a piece of paper showing you what to do.'

'What things, Mabel?' Harold persisted.

'They look like little sponges and you soak them in ... in this stuff and ... and...' She chewed on her lip and looked down. 'You ... you put them inside you before you ... you do it.'

'Inside? I don't like the sound of that. What does it do to you?'

'It stops the babies coming. It smells like vinegar. It must be all right because the Missus uses it all the time.' Mabel thought for a minute. 'Mind you, I haven't seen it lately.' After a further pause, she added, 'You buy it from the chemist but he only sells it to married women.'

'It's no good for us then,' Harold moaned. 'Maybe we should just stay away from each other.' He looked miserable and Mabel felt the same.

After a few minutes she said, 'I could say it was for the Missus. I buy things for her all the time from the chemist; you know, women's things. I'll take the tin to show him.' The Missus cut out advertisements from the newspapers that Mabel took into the chemist. He had ordered her a rubber douche contraption especially, and some patented pills for 'women's problems'.

71

She saw Harold's eyes light up. 'You wouldn't mind?'

She shook her head and smiled. Simply thinking about loving Harold made Mabel want him even more. The pit of her stomach had this empty space that yearned for him and she didn't know what to do to make it go away. She was hungry for him and when they talked of love she became ravenous.

They chose the day of the 'grand opening'. It was a fine sunny day, breezy with a nip in the air. A crowd had gathered, dressed in their Sunday best, to see a local dowager countess something-or-other in a very fancy hat cut the ribbon. She brought her spinster niece with her, who Mabel thought was very plain in spite of her silk gown. George and Mr Belfor fawned all over them, much to the Missus's annoyance. Then the band started playing and the ale and pies were on offer so Harold and Mabel crept away.

Mabel prepared herself for him in her attic and hurried downstairs to his room. She was nervous and she guessed Harold was too. They carefully removed each other's clothes, folding them neatly until they stood naked in front of each other, relishing their shared pain of waiting, of suppressed passion and frustrated desire.

He's beautiful, she thought, so tall and strong and he wanted her – oh, how much he wanted her! It is so obvious in a man, she thought. But she, only she, knew how much her insides were melting for him. He carried her to his bed and gazed at her with love in his eyes. She was trembling with excitement. The sounds of the outside celebrations faded in her ears. She wasn't sure what to do but he was. He kissed and fondled her until she begged him to help her. And when he did she felt complete. He possessed her with an assurance that gave her the confidence to respond. And respond she did, with instinct and craving and, above all, with love.

He was hers, she was his; they were as one, carried away on a turbulent sea of joy and fulfilment. Eventually, she resurfaced into reality, spent and sweaty. The music had stopped. They rolled off the bed and peered through the net curtain. The gentry and the town mayor were leaving but many ordinary folk lingered to enjoy their free feast. Mabel noticed the Missus sitting in the shade. George was beside her, holding her hand.

'The Missus has had too much of her own ale,' Harold commented. 'That's not like her.'

'We'd best go down and give a hand,' Mabel said.

Harold squeezed her naked bottom. 'Just once more,' he urged.

She grinned at him, loving his large warm hand on her flesh. 'Oh, all right then,' she said.

The Missus wasn't well. Mabel had not known her to have a day's illness during the time she had been at the Navvy. George fussed around her but it was Elsie who worked out what was wrong with her.

'She's got a bun in the oven, you mark my words.' Then she added, 'Fancy that, having a bairn at her age!'

It turned out that Elsie was right, although no

one actually said so. Mabel should have guessed when the Missus stopped using her sponges. Mabel wished she could do the same. She was envious of the Missus because she wanted a baby, too. She wanted Harold's baby. But they had agreed. She was too young and they had to wait until they were wed and had a proper house to live in. Meanwhile, they had their secret, thrilling trysts whenever a chance presented itself. Waiting for an opportunity made it all the more exciting, for they were bursting for each other by then.

Walter had been ordered to church by Percy as Mabel had before him and so the four of them went each Sunday in the donkey cart. The youngsters sat on grain sacking in the back. Vera decided she'd rather sit with the lad than up front with 'them two lovebirds'.

Several weeks after the brewery opening they were installed in their pew in church when Mabel suddenly sat up straight, her eyes wide, as the vicar read the banns for forthcoming marriages: *Miss Gertrude Dorinda Jackson of the Navigator Inn, spinster of this parish.*

She didn't hear any more. Harold glanced at her and smirked. Gertrude Dorinda! Mabel swallowed a giggle. No wonder she preferred 'Missus'! She was marrying George, of course, but neither had seen fit to attend church that day or indeed any other.

However, Mr Belfor was present with his ageing mother and father. He acknowledged Harold on his way out and gave the briefest of nods in Mabel's direction. He knew their business because he had drawn up the papers for Harold's investment in the brewery, and stood as his trustee until he was twenty-one. Outside the church, he helped his parents into his trap then walked over to them.

'Goodman, a word.'

'Sir,' Harold responded politely.

'One of Miss Jackson's larger properties will be vacant in a year or so. Wilmot has suggested it might be suitable for you.' He gave the address, on a road where better-off folk lived, and added, 'You might care to drive by and take a look.'

'Thank you, sir,' Harold replied. He turned to Mabel and raised his eyebrows. 'Shall we?'

Mabel blew out her cheeks. 'You won't be able to afford the rent for us to live there!'

'It'll be rent-free now I'm a partner and I've got the barley wine money. My investment's not paying much yet but George says if I give up all my other deliveries in favour of the brewery I'll be an equal with him.'

'You mean you'd stop being a carter in your own right?'

'I'd have a proper brewer's dray and two shires. I've always wanted a shire horse.' Harold was excited by this prospect and went on, 'I'll be in charge of haulage and have a stableman to help. The Navvy's a real moneyspinner now. You'll have your own pony and trap one day.'

Mabel's heart swelled with pride for the man she loved. He was so hardworking and clever. She worried about him sometimes, at the end of a long day when his face was grey and he fell asleep over his dinner. But today she was as excited as he was. 'Shall we look at that house then?' she said.

The house was Mabel's dream, built of mellow

stone with a bay window at each side of the front door and railings to separate them from the pavement. They walked up and down the road several times, admiring the brass door knocker and lace curtains at the windows.

'When can we be wed, Harold?' Mabel asked.

'Soon, my love, soon.'

The youngsters complained loudly from the donkey cart that they were hungry.

'Better get a move on,' Harold suggested. 'Elsie will be cross.'

'She won't mind today. I've got some gossip for her.'

'Well, it's good news for us, too. I don't suppose the Missus will want us cluttering up the inn when she's married with a baby.'

'Knowing her, she'll have a proper nursery with a nursemaid who won't want to sleep in the attic like the rest of us.'

George married the Missus within a month. The Missus went to Sheffield for a pink satin gown with white bows and a veil. She did look pretty, in an overblown way, and her belly showed quite a lot. The Missus didn't seem to mind, though. After the ceremony they had a celebration with French wine and plates of cold chicken and ham in an upstairs room at the Red Lion. George took her to Scarborough on the railway train for their honeymoon and they stayed in an hotel on the seafront, leaving Sid and Harold in charge of the brewery.

When they came home the Missus was still feeling poorly. The doctor advised her to rest and drink a glass of stout every day. So she took to staying in bed for most of the time. Now there weren't any lodgers at the Navvy, the Missus had decided that Mabel could look after her; and the baby, too, when it arrived.

'She won't want me to leave, now,' Mabel moaned to Harold.

'She'll have to let you go when we marry. George said we could when you're seventeen.'

'Is he my guardian now they're wed?'

'I don't know but she does what he says anyway.'

They were lying on his bed, side by side and naked. Harold adored her body, gazing at her as though he worshipped her. She hoped so because she worshipped him. He gave her so much pleasure in these stolen moments and she was so very, very proud to be his sweetheart. His love had matured her into a confident young woman and sometimes she imagined her heart was bursting with love for him.

'Don't you have a guardian as well?' she asked.

Harold shrugged. 'I've never needed one. I've always paid my way. When my father died the farmer who was my landlord said he would vouch for me. But George does that now.' He paused a moment as though not sure whether to go on.

'What is it, Harold?'

'George has set me up a bank account.'

Mabel's eyes rounded. A bank account! Only rich people had those. The brewery must be doing well. She wouldn't have to wait before she had babies and she could have lots of them, just like the Queen.

He went on, 'Shall we decide exactly when we'll

get wed?'

Her heart was full. She rolled over, half on top of him. Her soft breasts fell against the hard wall of his chest. 'Oh, yes please,' she murmured, 'on my seventeenth birthday.'

She felt his need for her stir against her thigh, and snuggled her soft and pliant flesh closer to his. He groaned with desire, and she knew she wanted him just as much as he wanted her.

Chapter 7

The Missus's baby took a long time to be born and the Missus screamed a lot during the birth. When the infant arrived, she took over the screaming and continued to scream with a permanently cross expression on her little red face. The Missus was exhausted and shouted loudly that she was never going through that again. The doctor said she'd lost a lot of blood and had to rebuild her strength but any subsequent births ought to be easier for her.

The Missus employed a monthly nurse to look after her and the baby, much to Mabel's relief because she still had the inn to look after. George had masons and carpenters in to change it into a family home and she was always cleaning up after them. He bought a proper carriage with a sleek horse to pull it. The Missus had grand ideas, too. She had a bedroom turned into a dressing room for her and George, and an indoor privy that flushed itself clean from a water tank over your head. The nursery too had an adjoining room for the nursemaid to sleep in.

Meanwhile, Harold worked harder than ever. He delivered Navigator Ales far and wide and, although he was young and strong, sometimes in the evening his face was grey and Mabel thought he looked older than his years. George took on more men to work in the brewery. If the way he spent money on the inn was anything to go by, the profits must be pouring in.

Baby Wilmot was christened Phoebe – 'A gentry's name if ever there was one,' Elsie commented – and she was a difficult child. She cried when she was left on her own and continued crying until someone rocked her or sang to her. George was always happy to oblige, which caused a disagreement with the nursemaid. When the Missus fed Phoebe, the child would spit out her milk and cry some more. It was enough to put Mabel off the idea of having a baby.

But Harold changed her mind. He bought her a betrothal ring, a delicate gold band with a real garnet surrounded by tiny pearls, and their marriage banns were read out in church. She suggested that she give up using the sponges and Harold agreed. Even if she did fall for a baby straightaway, she'd hardly be showing on her wedding day.

Her heart was set on the stone-built house with railings at the front. The tenants let them look round for her to be sure, as their move had been delayed. The man of the house owned a forge and he was having a house built on the Moorgate Road. Furniture was included in the lease and all of it was so much nicer than anything Mabel had known before that she loved it even more. And it had gaslights on the walls! It didn't have a stable for a pony and trap, though, but it was close to town so she could walk to market. Mabel didn't want to change anything but Harold pointed out that they would need a nursery. He placed a hand on her stomach and asked if there were any signs yet.

Mabel was disappointed every month when she had a bleed. She began to think the sponges had done something nasty to her, although the Missus had had a baby soon enough with George. But as her birthday drew closer she became so excited about the approaching ceremony that she forgot to count the days. She made a new gown in pale blue satin with a draped bustle and the Missus lent her her own wedding veil and white satin pumps. George took her to the church in his new carriage.

Mabel had not expected to see so many people. There were people from the workhouse and the Navvy, Harold's former customers, even Mr Belfor and his young wife. The constable was there and Mr Hawkridge, who stood for Harold and had the ring. The Missus had asked them all back to the Navvy for a wedding breakfast and they had sherry wine followed by a sit-down tea of ham with lettuce hearts and bread and butter. Elsie had made a celebration fruit cake, which Harold and Mabel cut together accompanied by everybody clapping.

Mabel was overwhelmed by so many well-wishers. She had not experienced being the centre of attention in this way before. But Harold was there, squeezing her hand gently and talking easily to everyone from the stiff and starchy Mrs Belfor to the farm labourer who now lived in his mother's old cottage. It was exciting for her, though she was pleased when everyone had left. She and Harold escaped to his bedroom, now hers too until their house became vacant. It had been a long day and she was too tired to enjoy their wedding night as she should. But so was Harold and they both fell asleep without indulging their passions. Mabel didn't mind. She had a lifetime with Harold to look forward to and they compensated for it in the morning.

Being Mrs Goodman made a difference to the way folk treated Mabel. She was a married woman now and Harold was a partner in the Navigator Brewery. Suddenly tradesmen and shopkeepers were admiring and respectful towards her. Her husband – oh, how she adored to describe him so – was a man of means and not yet one and twenty. He was a man to be reckoned with; as his wife, Mabel's origins in the workhouse counted for nothing. Even Elsie recognised her new status and shared her kitchen secrets willingly.

But the Missus was ill again and everyone knew the reason straightaway. George fetched the doctor and he prescribed a glass of stout and rest as before. He said George need not worry as his wife had servants to look after her. But the Missus still felt poorly most of the time and Mabel hoped *she* wasn't going to suffer in the same way when she was with child!

Mabel continued to take her donkey cart to market once a week. Having her own money to spend was still a novelty for her and she liked to make it go as far as possible. She usually had a list from the Missus and Harold as well and shopping was one of her pleasures. So she was in a particularly cheerful mood when she returned to see the doctor's trap outside the Navvy, and a morose George with his head in his hands sitting at the kitchen table.

'What's happened?' she asked Elsie, who was mixing a powder in a medicine glass.

'It's the Missus,' Elsie said quietly. 'She's lost the baby.'

'Oh, I'm so sorry.' Mabel pulled a chair near to George and put her arm around his shoulders. 'She's strong, George, she'll have others.'

'She won't,' he moaned. He sat back and wiped a tear from his eye. 'She's mad at me. She says she's not having any more.'

'She doesn't mean it, I'm sure. Give her time.'

'Aye.' He picked up her hand. 'You're such a good little lass. Harold's a lucky fellow. Will you go and talk to her?'

'If you like.'

'Doctor's still with her but you can take her this powder,' Elsie said. 'Shall I get you a drop o' brandy, George?'

Mabel – and Harold – used to chuckle at the Missus's antics and language. But there was no humour in this. She saw the doctor to his trap and asked if, perhaps, a brewery wasn't a healthy place to have a baby.

'Nonsense, Mrs Goodman, Miss Phoebe is

thriving.' He must have guessed her reason for asking for he added, 'And your little ones will too.'

'But I haven't got any yet,' she said.

'You will and soon, if I am not mistaken.' He took the reins, climbed into his trap and added, 'Come and see me at my surgery.'

Mabel sat down and thought and counted and realised the doctor was correct. Harold was absolutely delighted by the news, but as her belly swelled, they both grew restless to move to the house in town for the birth. Mabel was a married woman, after all, and she wanted her own home.

But as it turned out, Mabel was glad she had been at the Navvy because both the Missus and Elsie knew what to do when the time came and the three of them just got on with it. Mabel's labour was long and she cried out every now and then because it was painful. But she was nowhere near as distressed as the Missus had been and insisted that she didn't need a doctor. However, urged on by George, Harold eventually sent for him.

The baby – a beautiful little girl they named Nell – was out and yelling by the time the doctor arrived. After fussing that he ought to have been called earlier, the doctor pronounced that mother and daughter were both 'doing well'. Mabel was exhausted but she forgot the pain because she was unbelievably happy. Since getting wed to Harold she didn't think she could become any happier but she had. She was happy, proud, thankful to God, and so much in love that it hurt.

Two months later Mabel and Harold moved into their new home with their infant Nell and Mabel's life was perfect. They had a whole house to live in – a proper house with two front rooms and a nursery for Nell.

As soon as she felt able, Mabel walked proudly to market with Nell in her arms. The constable went out of his way to take a peek at her baby and said how pleased he was for her and Harold. The stall holders and shopkeepers addressed her as 'Mrs Goodman' or 'madam' and even Mrs Belfor nodded an acknowledgement in the high street draper's shop. Mabel was able to give a lad a coin to carry her basket home and have a fire in the nursery all day. Once a week she hired a trap and driver to take Nell to see the Missus and Elsie at the Navvy.

Miss Phoebe was toddling around and despite having her own nursemaid she was a fractious and demanding child. Oh dear, Mabel observed, she was rather like the Missus in that respect and she vowed that her Nell would grow up with better manners. But the Missus was expecting again and needed to be flattered, so Mabel complimented her on her pretty and accomplished child. Elsie, she noticed, hardly ever said anything about her.

The Missus had a daybed in her fancy downstairs drawing room. As her pregnancy progressed, her legs became so puffy she could barely walk and she was permanently exhausted, so much so that she was quiet and submissive for most of the time when Mabel called on her. Mabel found this more worrying than her tantrums. She would go home quite unsettled by her former guardian's pregnant state. And then one evening, Harold came home with the devastating news that the Missus had given birth early, and her baby – a son – had died. She was very weak but the doctor was with her and Mabel could visit the following day.

Early the next morning, before Harold had left for the brewery, Mr Belfor was at the front door with more shocking information. He wouldn't come in and Mabel stood behind Harold holding Nell in her arms as he told them the dreadful news.

'Mrs Wilmot passed away two hours ago,' he said.

Mabel's knees buckled and she sank onto her hall chair. Harold, too, was stunned into silence.

'Stay at home today, Goodman,' he went on. 'Wilmot has suspended operations. My office will send round messages.'

Harold stumbled over his words. 'Poor George, and .. and Miss Phoebe. I ... I don't know what to say.'

Mr Belfor seemed unmoved. 'This will change things for you, Goodman. Wilmot will be round to explain.'

'I don't understand, sir.'

'You will. Sit tight and wait for Wilmot to contact you.' With that, Mr Belfor tipped the brim of his hat to Mabel and walked away.

'But George will need us with him now,' Mabel argued.

'You heard the man, love. Best do as he says.'

'What did he mean "suspended operations"?' she asked.

'Stop trading, I suppose, until ... well, until after the funeral.'

'It'll be a big shock for a lot of folk. Most of 'em liked the Missus, in spite of the gossip.'

'She was generous.' Harold shook his head sadly. 'I ... I can't believe she's gone.'

'Me neither. Here, take Nell for me while I close the curtains in the front rooms.'

The hours dragged by. They reminisced about the past and speculated on how 'things will change' in the future. Mabel thought a few days' rest from the brewery would be good for Harold because he had been looking very tired lately. But his brow seemed to crease more as the day wore on.

They had tea, played with Nell and put her to bed, added coal to the front-room fire and tried to settle with a glass of barley wine. Harold lit the gaslights. Mabel suggested she read him one of the Dickens stories from their bookshelf and settled with it beside him on the sofa. Then George arrived. He was, as they expected, distressed; agitated, too. He refused to take off his coat and kept turning the brim of his hat round in his fingers. Mabel and Harold began to offer their condolences but he interrupted them.

'Yes, yes. Thank you but this is business, Goodman,' he said briskly. 'Mabel's presence is not necessary.'

Mabel looked at Harold with surprise. George wasn't himself at all. Harold took her hand and replied, 'Any changes will affect Mabel as much as me.'

'She doesn't need to hear this, Harold,' George

said in a more kindly fashion. He continued to turn his hat in his hands.

'Shall I make coffee?' Mabel suggested.

'Good idea, love,' Harold said. 'Why don't you take off your coat and sit down, George?'

As Mabel closed the door, she heard George say, 'It's bad news, I'm afraid.'

She put her ear to the crack and listened. 'I don't know how to tell you this,' George began, 'but, you see, all the Missus's properties were held in trust. She had the income while she was alive and now she's gone, the money's gone with her. Her rents were paying off the bankers for the new building, so now they'll foreclose on us. The brewery is bankrupt.'

Harold did not normally raise his voice but it came loud and clear through the woodwork. 'It can't be! What about my investment? And all profits from the ale? I do the deliveries. I know how much we sell.'

'It goes as soon as it's in the bank. Your shires, more men working for you and Sid, and all the improvements on the house for the Missus. You know how she likes to spend.'

'You can't have spent it all!' Harold argued. 'I've put by a small fortune.'

'Oh, that,' George responded. 'I need that to pay off creditors.'

'Well, you can't have it. I have a wife and child to support.'

'You can't stop me. I'm your guarantor and trustee until you are twenty-one. Be sensible, Harold. You're a partner in a bankrupt brewery; you don't want to end up in the debtors' prison, do you?'

'You're lying! This is a trick! You're going to take all my money and you're nothing more than a crook!'

George interrupted. 'Hey, steady on with your accusations. I know this is a shock but listen, I can buy you out of the brewery and it'll leave you enough to start up again as a carter.'

'And why would you want to buy my share of a bankrupt business?'

Mabel wanted to hear the answer to this, as well. She was rooted to the spot and the coffee was forgotten. But the room stayed silent. Mabel hesitated for a few moments and then opened the door and crept softly back into the room. The two men were standing in the middle of the floor staring angrily at each other. If they noticed her they did not acknowledge her.

'Well, you had better answer me,' Harold challenged.

George looked away and muttered, 'I told Belfor you wouldn't wear it.'

Harold glared at him. 'This is a swindle, isn't it? You want all my money and my share of the brewery as well!'

George grimaced. 'Well, who are you anyway? Just some farmer's boy. You're a good worker and if you do as I say you'll be all right as a carter.'

Harold laughed harshly, but his laugh turned into a choking sound. 'I'm not standing for this,' he croaked. 'I'll get the law on you, I'll– Argh.' Harold's eyes rolled and he clutched at his chest.

Mabel watched in horror as he staggered, bumped against the sofa and crumpled to the floor. She dashed forward and fell to her knees beside him. 'Harold? Harold? Are you all right?' He cried out in pain. The sound turned into a gurgling in his throat and his eyes stared at her. Then he was still. She panicked and shook him vigorously. 'Speak to me, Harold,' she begged, but his eyes continued to stare at her.

She turned to George and yelled, 'What have you done? Fetch the doctor! Run and fetch the doctor for him!'

PART 2

Wilmot's Brewery, South Riding, Yorkshire, 1910

Chapter 8

'Nell! Nell Goodman! Your ma's here again.'

'Oh no,' Nell groaned. She turned to her friend on bottle-washing. 'I'll have to take her back home. Tell the charge-hand for me, will you?'

Her friend grimaced. The charge-hand was new and much stricter than the old one.

'Mr Wilmot said I could,' Nell pleaded. That was two years ago, when George Wilmot visited his brewery every day, but Nell didn't have time to explain. She hurried over to the clerk waiting by the door.

'You'll have to do something about her,' he said. 'Miss Wilmot won't stand for it now she runs the show.'

'I'm sorry. If only Mr Wilmot was here. He'd see her and then she'd go away.'

The young man let out a guffaw. 'Don't be daft.'

Nell didn't respond. He didn't know the half of it, and neither did Miss Wilmot. Her mother called Mr Wilmot 'George' and maintained he'd once said he'd marry her. Nell chewed her lip, not sure herself how much of her mother's ramblings was the truth and how much was wishful thinking. She felt guilty for doubting her mother but nobody else ever listened to Mabel Goodman's claims.

'Get a move on,' the clerk urged. 'I've got work to do.'

Nell tore off her brown rubber gauntlets and

apron, and felt her brown cotton cap go askew. She hurriedly straightened it, smoothed down her brown drill overall and trotted after the clerk across the cobbled brewery yard. The dray was in and a couple of hefty fellows were loading barrels of Wilmot's Ale while two heavy horses waited patiently in the shafts. Their fetlock feathers were pristine white and their leather and brass harnesses shone.

'She's gone upstairs already,' the clerk called over his shoulder.

Nell followed him into the wood-panelled reception area and through the door taking her beyond the half-glazed partition. A young woman in a dark skirt and cream blouse sat at a typewriter and clacked away as Nell walked by. The lady clerk's fair hair was elegantly dressed in swathes and twists and Nell felt dowdy and grubby in comparison. She fingered a lock of her own hair that had escaped from her cap. It was a similar colour but plainly coiled into a bun at the nape of her neck. As she approached the door at the far end of the room she heard her mother's voice.

'Where is he? He's to blame, you know! It was all his fault!' Her cries carried down the staircase followed by irate tones from Miss Wilmot.

'Mrs Goodman, if you do not leave this minute I shall call the sergeant.'

Nell pushed past the office clerk and ran up the staircase to the administration centre of Wilmot's Brewery. 'It's all right, Miss Wilmot,' she called, 'there's no need to do that. I'll take her home with me.'

The upstairs offices were plush. The waiting area

had a square of expensive Turkish carpet on the floorboards. It had similar dark wooden panelling to downstairs but was furnished with mahogany chairs comfortably upholstered in maroon velvet. Mabel Goodman sat with a straight back in one of them. She wore a faded blue two-piece costume with a bustled skirt that was old but well cared for, and an ornate matching hat decorated by a drooping ostrich feather. It was her Sunday-best outfit and her boots were newly polished. Nell could see that her mother had dressed especially to come here today. She was nearly forty but still remarkably pretty.

'I'm not leaving until he sees me,' Mabel declared.

'I've already told you he's not here,' Miss Wilmot snapped.

Nell went to sit in the chair next to her mother. 'He won't be back today, Mother,' she explained quietly. 'He's away all day. Miss Wilmot is in charge now and she is very busy.' Nell had no idea whether this was true or not but Mother appeared to believe her.

'He's always out. Why is he always out?' Mabel frowned.

'He didn't know you were calling. You do look nice this morning. Why don't we walk to the draper's in the high street? I hear they have some lace gloves in the window.'

Mabel's eyes lit up. 'Lace gloves? Are they Nottingham lace, do you think?'

'I don't know. Shall we go and ask?'

'Well, if George isn't here, I suppose we must.' Mabel stood up gracefully and turned to Miss

Wilmot. 'Tell your father that I came to see him and he may return my call when my daughter is at home.'

Miss Wilmot gave an impatient gasp and disappeared into her office.

'Come along, Mother.' Nell took Mabel's hand and led her down the staircase where the office clerk stood with the door to the outside open. This was the main entrance at the front of the imposing stone building and it led directly out to the street. They stepped out into the sunshine. The brewery was out of town by the canal. The oldest of the buildings had once been an inn but that was now the head brewer's home with a little garden for his children. As they walked into town Mabel forgot about the gloves and urged Nell to take her past 'the house' instead.

'There isn't time,' Nell protested gently. 'I have to go back to work.'

'No you don't. You're the boss's daughter,' Mabel argued.

Nell suppressed a sigh and an inclination to say, *Not that again*. Walking past the house wouldn't help either, because it always brought back memories for her mother and the jumbled tales of what should have been their life. Nell had believed them all as a child, but then children do believe what their parents tell them. Now, at twenty-one, she took a more realistic view of her mother's flights of fancy. They were becoming more frequent these days – and more so around any anniversary connected with her late husband.

The house was lovely. Built of mellowing stone

with a front door flanked by bay windows, it looked out onto a street much busier than when Nell was born. Horse-drawn carts and carriages rattled past them delivering garden produce for the market. Occasionally, a motor wagon loaded with coal or bricks rumbled by.

'Did I tell you that we used to live here?' Mabel said.

Every time we walk down here, Nell answered silently. She said, 'The house would be far too big for us to live in now. We'd need two maids at least and think of the coal bills.'

Her mother appeared not to hear her. 'Your father was so proud of you,' she said, then lapsed into silence.

Black wrought-iron railings separated the house frontage from the street except for where a short flight of stone steps led to the door. Mabel stopped walking suddenly. 'Shall we go in?' she suggested brightly.

'We can't. We don't know the people who live there now,' Nell explained.

'They'll know *us*. Your father owns the brewery.'

'Father died, Mother,' Nell said gently. It had all happened a long time ago, but sometimes Mother forgot the years in between. It had been a difficult time for her and eventually her grieving had given way to a sense of injustice towards those she believed had wronged her husband and caused his death. Local folk had told her, in quite a kindly way, that Mother had had some kind of breakdown and had never really been the same since.

'It was George Wilmot's fault, you know. He killed your father. And then he said he'd look after us.'

'Well, he gave us a cottage to live in.' While he moved in here, Nell thought, taking in the size of the house they were passing.

Their cottage was small, in a terrace of similar dwellings all owned by Wilmot's. And the brewery had made so much money over the years that the Wilmots had ultimately moved to a manor house outside town and surrounded by acres of parkland. George Wilmot was gentry now and he spent much of his time playing the part of a country gentleman while his daughter looked after the brewery for him. Nell tugged on her mother's arm and eventually they left the house behind.

Mother and daughter walked on in silence until they reached the high street draper's with its double-fronted display windows. 'Oh, aren't they beautiful, Nell?' Mabel exclaimed.

A selection of Whitby jet adornments was laid out on a white linen cloth. Nell thought that black jet was old-fashioned but it was still favoured by the better-off matrons in the town. 'Do you think one would look nice in my hair?' Mabel asked.

'I'm sure it would,' Nell assured her. Everything Mother wore seemed to enhance her good bone structure and ivory skin.

'I shall wear it when George calls. Buy it for me, love.'

'I can't afford it, Mother. Besides, I'm sure you already have something similar in your jewellery box. Shall we go home and look?'

Mabel was distracted by this suggestion. She walked by the lace glove display without a second glance and onwards towards home.

Nell left her mother in the front bedroom of their small neat house deciding on how she would dress and decorate her hair for when George called. He wouldn't call, of course, but Nell hadn't the heart to discourage her and at least Mother would be occupied for the remainder of the day. Nell closed the front door softly and hurried back to work.

But she didn't even get as far as donning her rubber apron.

'That was your last chance, my girl,' the charge-hand barked. 'I'm not having you walk off when the fancy takes you. What if all my lasses did that? Where would I be then?'

'I'll make up the time, sir.' The charge-hand was new to Wilmot's and, although she had already told him, she repeated, 'Mr Wilmot said it was all right for me to see to Mother provided I made up the lost time. That's why I moved to bottle-washing from order-checking. As long as I do my hours—'

'Well, Miss Wilmot never agreed to that,' he interrupted, 'and she's in the office now so clear off out of here and don't come back. Your wages'll be ready by the end of next week.'

'But I need this job! I'm the breadwinner in our house,' Nell cried.

'Not my problem, lass. Now shift yourself.' The charge-hand took hold of her arm and man-handled her out of the nearest door.

'You can't do this without asking Mr Wilmot,' Nell protested.

'Yes, I can. I'm your boss down here,' he responded as he slammed and bolted the door behind her.

Nell was at the back of the building near to the canal and the rarely used lock gates. She sat down angrily on the broad wooden arm of the gate. It wasn't fair! She had worked at Wilmot's since she was fourteen: George Wilmot himself had given her the job. She always did her hours, even if it meant coming in early the following day to do a double shift. The old charge-hand had always been pleased with her work and had talked of promoting her to bottle inspection.

All right, Nell agreed, the incidents had increased in frequency lately but only since the recent anniversary of Father's death had unsettled Mabel more than usual.

'I'm not standing for this,' she said out loud and stood up, smoothing down her skirt. It was true that George Wilmot didn't come into the brewery every day now, not since his daughter had taken over the office. She was his eldest child – the product of his first marriage, which had ended abruptly and tragically. His wife had been taken shortly after the birth of their son, who had also died, when Miss Wilmot was a toddler.

Nell often considered this unfortunate start in life whenever Miss Wilmot became particularly trying at the brewery. Well, Nell's life hadn't been easy either, when her father had died suddenly. It was well known that George and Phoebe Wilmot had been left well provided for by his first wife, who had owned the original inn and adjoining brewhouse and stabling, as well as extensive property in town.

Nell pursed her lips and marched back through

the cobbled loading yard and into the office reception. 'I'm here to see Miss Wilmot,' she stated and swept by the girl at the typewriting machine.

The male clerk rose to his feet. 'You can't go up there. You haven't got an appointment,' he said.

Nell ignored him. She was through the door and climbing the staircase before he could stop her. She knew which of the upstairs offices was Miss Wilmot's and rapped firmly on the door.

'What is it now?' Miss Wilmot sounded impatient.

'It's Nell Goodman, Miss Wilmot,' she said as she walked in.

'I did not give you permission to enter. Wait outside.'

'This won't take long.'

Nell closed the door behind her. A few seconds later it opened again and the young clerk entered, apologising breathlessly to Miss Wilmot.

'I should think so too,' Miss Wilmot snapped. 'Take her out of here.'

The clerk took hold of her arm but Nell shook him off. He was just a spindly grammar school lad who sat at a desk all day and Nell had worked on bottle-washing for two years and scrubbed out her house and back yard every Saturday afternoon. She turned and bundled him out of the room, closed the door and turned the key. The doorknob rattled a few times and then went quiet. 'I'll fetch the sergeant, Miss Wilmot,' the clerk called through the door.

Miss Wilmot smiled triumphantly at Nell and said, 'I shall have you arrested.'

'Do your worst, ma'am. I shall be gone before

he arrives but you will hear what I've got to say first.' She took a deep breath. 'Your charge-hand has just got rid of me.'

'Yes. I told him to.'

'You ... you did?' For a moment Nell felt deflated. She had been so sure that Miss Wilmot did not know about the charge-hand's actions.

'But your father took me on here. He promised Mother I should always have a job.'

'I run the brewery now.'

It was the first Nell had heard of that. Although George Wilmot spent less and less time on the brewery premises everyone thought he was still in charge and that his daughter was just her father's dogsbody.

'I am a good worker!'

'Your mother is an embarrassment and her disruptions are becoming more frequent.'

Nell couldn't deny that. Her mother was confused, and she attempted to explain: 'She's been remembering the years before my father died and it has upset her! Her mood will pass.'

'Until the next time she takes it into her deranged head that Wilmot's Brewery owes her a living!' Miss Wilmot rose to her feet. She was a buxom woman with a pasty face that might be pleasant if she smiled more. A constant sour expression reflected an equally sour nature. Her father was known for his sunny disposition, which made Nell think that Phoebe Wilmot must take after her late mother, someone her own mother was never very complimentary about. 'Too rough and ready for me,' Mother once said. 'She'd never scrubbed in the corners.'

Nell sighed inwardly. If the order for her summary dismissal had come from Miss Wilmot then she was wasting her breath. Miss Wilmot was not going to change her mind and Nell was mindful of the sergeant on his way with the clerk.

'Your father will listen to me,' Nell stated. 'I shall speak to him about this.' She let herself out of the office with as much dignity as she could muster and glanced back as she closed the door: Miss Wilmot was sitting at her desk with a smug expression on her face.

Nell blew out her cheeks. This was a disaster for her as her wage was the only one coming in. As far as she knew, Mother had never worked and Nell had no idea how she had managed after Father had died, except that they had been obliged to move out of the big house.

Nell had been very young and had no memories of the time. But she did remember as a toddler the whiskered gentleman – George Wilmot – being kind to them both. And she was aware that Mother had hoped he might marry her and that they would move back into the big house. But George Wilmot was a wealthy man by then and had his sights set on breeding rather than beauty for his second choice.

Nell avoided the front entrance of the brewery – and possibly the sergeant – and left by the back door and the towpath. The tranquil sounds of birds and buzzing bees calmed her. She was confident that George Wilmot would listen to her and not uphold his daughter's actions.

Mother was watching for her from the front bedroom window and called from the top of the stairs. 'Come and tell me what you think, Nell.' She sounded pleased with herself, which cheered Nell.

Mabel had laid out her good skirt and a blouse on a piece of calico covering the counterpane. The blouse had tiny pleats and lace trims over the bust and had seen better days but it was clean and well pressed. She beamed at Nell. 'I shall wear this to receive George when he calls. When do you think that will be?'

'Oh, it might be a while yet. He's a very busy gentleman.'

'I expect he will tell you when and we can prepare tea for him.' Mabel's eyes suddenly opened wide with alarm. 'It will be half past six and he'll have had afternoon tea at five, what shall I do?'

'He won't expect to have tea with you, Mother. He'll be having a proper dinner with Lady Clarissa later on. We have some sherry left over from Christmas. You can offer him a glass of that.'

Mabel beamed. 'You are so clever, my Nell. Get the best glasses from the top shelf.'

'I'll find them when I go downstairs. I expect they'll need washing.'

Mabel nodded in agreement and seemed calmer.

Nell began to wrap the calico around the garments. 'I'll just put these back in the closet,' she said. 'Shall we have a little talk before our tea?'

'Oh, yes please. Who shall we talk about?' Mabel sat in a small upholstered chair beside her unlit fire.

Nell closed the closet door and brought the dressing-table stool to sit near her. 'How well did you know Mr Wilmot before you met Father?' she asked.

'George? He lived at the inn when I worked there as a housemaid. I wanted to do better but...' Mabel's voice trailed away. She frowned and seemed to shrink in her chair. 'I wasn't bad at reading and writing or at my sums, you know, but the teacher was harsh. He had a cane and he wasn't supposed to hit the girls...'

Talking about her childhood in the workhouse upset her mother and Nell knew she ought not to let her continue. She leaned forward to hold her hands. 'Tell me about the inn, Mother,' she said brightly.

'Mucky hole, it was,' she replied, 'until I cleaned it up for her. That landlady was a lazy trollop. She never had to lift a finger. Sid made the ale for her, what's-her-name did the cooking and I did the cleaning.' Mabel stared at the window. 'It was all left to her by her father. I never had a father, or a mother, come to that.'

'You've got me now,' Nell reassured her.

Mabel turned suddenly. 'Harold?' She looked around the room. 'Where's Harold?'

'Harold died, Mother, a long time ago.'

Tears filled Mabel's eyes. 'It was all George's fault; he knew it was.' She sniffed and straightened her back. 'He said he'd marry me, you know. He said I was the prettiest maid he knew.'

Nell realised that mother must be referring to before she married Father. Even so, George Wilmot must have been a dozen years older than her mother. A journalist at the *Chronicle* had written a piece about him when Nell was still at school.

The article had presented him as a local hero, building the brewery from a simple brewhouse in the back yard. At the time, Mother had been furious that there had been no mention of her husband. According to her, Harold Goodman had delivered the sacks of malted barley and hops and it was his grandmother's recipe for barley wine that had turned round the fortunes of the brewhouse. 'It should be Goodman's Barley Wine not Wilmot's!' Mabel had protested.

'You are still very pretty, Mother,' Nell reminded her now.

'Your father was a handsome fellow,' Mabel murmured. 'I was the envy of every girl in church when he married me.' She smiled dreamily and stared at the unlit sticks and coal in the fire grate.

'I wish I'd known him,' Nell said. She had no memory of her father and if she was honest with herself she couldn't even recognise his face. A faded, framed photograph of him and Mother standing in the brewery yard stood on the sideboard in the front room and that was all Nell had. He was indeed handsome: tall and straight, looking a little scared with a serious stare on his face. In contrast, Mother seemed ethereal, a sweet slip of a girl and so much smaller than father. 'What was Father like?' Nell asked.

Mabel did not appear to hear her. She was lost in her own world and said, quite suddenly, 'He still wanted to marry me, you know, after your father died. He was responsible, you see.'

Nell realised her mother's mind had reverted to George Wilmot. 'Why was that, Mother?' she asked.

Mabel continued to stare at the lifeless fire and went on, 'Because he was, so it was right that he should wed me.'

'But he married Lady Clarissa,' Nell pointed out.

George Wilmot was moving in grander circles by then, Nell thought. His present wife was an unattractive woman and, although well connected, she had no money of her own. She was the niece of an ageing dowager countess, also penniless, who depended on a distant male relative for a home. When the dowager died, the niece became homeless and George's mounting wealth provided a solution for everybody. Lady Clarissa gave George Wilmot the social standing he craved and access to the gentrified life he now led.

Nell's reflections were interrupted by a rapping at the front door. Mabel jumped, startled, and cried, 'He's here already! I'm not dressed yet!'

Nell crossed the bedroom to the window and saw the sergeant waiting on the step. 'It's not Mr Wilmot. It's the sergeant. You stay up here and I'll get rid of him.' And she hurried down the stairs to let him in. 'Nell Goodman; my, you're a sight for sore eyes these days,' he said. 'Can I come in? The kitchen will do for me.'

He didn't sound threatening and Nell's tense anticipation eased. 'Would you like a cup of tea, sir?' she asked.

'No, ta.' He pulled out a carver chair and added, 'I'll sit down if I may. My feet are killing me. You know why I'm here?'

'Has Miss Wilmot sent you?'

'Well, yes and no. I managed to persuade her

not to take the incident any further. We don't want you in the cells, do we? Who'd look after your ma?'

Who indeed? Nell thought.

'It's your ma I want to talk to you about, Nell. I've known her since I came here as a young constable before you were born, and she's a good woman. But I've been called to several incidents with her in town which haven't been easy for me.'

'She hasn't told me about any of them, sir, but she is forgetful these days.'

'I'll be straight with you, lass. Your ma's been trying to take stuff without paying for it.'

Chapter 9

Nell's short-lived ease disappeared and her body became rigid. 'You don't mean she's been stealing?' The sergeant nodded and she added, 'You didn't arrest her, did you?'

'Your ma's well known in these parts and she has some sympathetic friends, so no I didn't. She'd told one shopkeeper to put it on your account and you would pay at the end of the month.'

'I'm so sorry, Sergeant. I had no idea. Why didn't somebody tell me?'

'Well, I expect they didn't want to worry you, but I'm telling you now, lass.' His gaze wandered around their clean and tidy kitchen. 'You look as though you're managing all right on your money from the brewery.'

'We do, sir.' But only because we're living rent free in a brewery house, Nell thought. If I've no job at the brewery, I've no home here. She felt a sudden desire to talk to George Wilmot immediately about his daughter's cruel actions.

The sergeant went on, 'Why don't you take your ma to the market on a Saturday afternoon when you've got your wages, and buy her a few trinkets? It'll give her something to look forward to every week.'

'I'll certainly give it a try, sir.'

He stood up. 'Good lass. I'll keep an eye out for her in the week – and most of the shopkeepers are wise to her ways by now.'

Nell showed him to the front door and thanked him as he left. Mother was lucky that she had lived in this town for so many years. A newcomer might not have got off so lightly. She turned to call up the stairs, 'He's gone, Mother. You can come down now.'

Mabel appeared on the top step. 'What did he want?'

'Nothing much.' Nell considered not saying anything at all to her at first. But she couldn't ignore Mabel's increasingly erratic behaviour any more. 'The brewery sent him. You can't keep going into the offices to find Mr Wilmot. His daughter doesn't like it.'

'Miss Sourpuss never likes anything. I don't believe she's George's daughter at all.'

'You mustn't say things like that. It casts aspersions on Miss Wilmot and her mother.'

Mabel appeared not to hear. 'What are we having for tea today?' she asked.

She followed Nell into the back kitchen. This was their living room as the front room was kept for Sundays and visitors. Nell decided not to tell her mother she had lost her job as she was confident that, once he heard about her plight, George Wilmot would reinstate her. She would have to speak to him as soon as she could, she decided, and the best place to find him these days was at home in Wilmot Grange.

Nell rose early the following morning, got the range fire going and made porridge, then washed some potatoes in the scullery for her mother to peel later. She left the house at her usual time so as not to raise any suspicion in Mabel. She had to wear her workaday skirt but chose one of her pretty lace blouses, covering it with a long jacket in case Mother was at the window when she left. She pinned on a neat straw hat and checked her appearance in the hall mirror. Tidy but dull, she thought, and resolved to carry the jacket over her arm when she arrived at Wilmot Grange.

She took the omnibus out of town as far as the terminus and set off to walk the remaining few miles to the Grange. She enjoyed the fresh air. It was a fine day, breezy yet warm, but it was a long way. She hoped a delivery cart would overtake her and she could hail a lift, but after an hour she guessed she was out of luck and plodded on.

Wilmot Grange used to be called Fitzkeppel Hall and it had had a couple of scandals associated with it over the years. Years ago the lady of the house had run off with an Italian artist and, later, when her son had inherited at twenty-one, a young man had been murdered by his father in one of the gamekeepers' huts. There were scurrilous rumours that the Fitzkeppel heir had been over-friendly with this young man and implicated in the killing. Shortly after, the son and daughter joined their mother in Italy and never came back. Fitzkeppel Hall lay empty and decaying with this stigma attached until George Wilmot bought it and set about making it into a fine country residence for his lady wife.

Nell followed the curve of the renovated stone walls until she reached the huge ornate Wilmot Gates. They had been specially commissioned from Daniel Thorpe & Sons at Bowes steel works and travellers often came to the area for the sole purpose of viewing them. A photograph of them had once appeared in an architects' journal.

The gates were just one example of George Wilmot's show of wealth, which seemed to multiply year on year. Lady Clarissa had what Riding folk called 'breeding' and her uncle's family had always lived in grand houses. But, like all daughters, she had had to find herself a husband and she wasn't at all pretty. Large-boned and with a long face, she was known unkindly at the brewery as 'The Cart Horse'. She had not had a dowry either, but George Wilmot had been proud to marry her and provide her with the kind of home she wanted.

The huge wrought-iron gates were flanked by two smaller versions for horseriders or those on foot. Nell turned the heavy ring to lift the latch on one of these and the hinges squeaked as the gate swung open. She couldn't even see the Grange yet and she retreated to the shade of nearby trees for a moment's rest. She leaned

111

against an oak and closed her eyes, only opening them again when she heard the whine of gate hinges. She craned her neck to see who it was.

An older man was leading a pony drawing a small open carriage. When he closed the gates and climbed into the driver's seat she recognised him as Mr Belfor, the best-known solicitor in town. He called at the brewery on business from time to time, dressed in his formal business attire. Today he wore the same sober suit of clothes and tall hat, so Nell reckoned this wasn't a social call. She hid from view as Mr Belfor drove by. His presence reassured her that George Wilmot would be home and she hoped he wouldn't be too busy to see her. Refreshed, she set off along the metalled track towards the Grange. Surely the house would come into view after the next clump of trees?

Nell had been to the Grange once every summer until recently, to attend the Wilmots' annual summer fête for the brewery workers. But for the last two years they had hired a charabanc to take them all to the seaside. The excursions had proved to be much more popular with everyone. They had been to Cleethorpes and Filey and this year it was going to be Bridlington. They actually spent more time in the charabanc than by the sea but it was fun all the same because they had sing-songs on the way home until everyone fell asleep. They would have a grand day out in Bridlington, Nell thought, and smiled to herself; if she was still working for Wilmot's, of course. She quickened her step.

A moment or two later she became aware of the rumbling of machinery – the kind of sound that charabancs made, and threshers at harvest time, although it was too early in the year for the harvest. The noise was getting louder and it was coming from behind her. She turned to look and, in some surprise, stepped off the roadway onto the grass. A horseless carriage was trundling along the roadway, weaving from side to side, and accompanied by shouting and laughter from the two gentlemen occupants. They were muffled up in tweed hats, dust-coats and driving gauntlets, their faces obscured by goggles. The carriage was very much like a horse-drawn phaeton with a motor engine installed on the front and a large wheel for the driver to steer instead of reins for the horses. Nell watched in awe.

The gentleman in the rear waved a bottle in the air and yelled, 'Stay on the road, Cyril! I shan't let you drive it again if you can't steer.'

The gentleman at the steering wheel responded by squeezing the bulb on a klaxon and a raucous alarm split the air. Nell jumped and let out an involuntary squeal. Both men laughed helplessly and Nell realised they were drunk. She began to back away from the road but the passenger spotted her before she reached the shrubbery. 'A wench!' he yelled.

'A fine-looking one, too,' his friend responded. 'I shall stop the vehi ... vehi ... veh-i-cle!'

'You haven't time, old boy. My father is expecting us at the Grange.'

'Mine too,' the driver said. 'They can wait.' He leaned forward to crank a lever beside him.

The carriage stopped and the engine rattled into silence. The passenger stared at Nell for a

113

moment then said, 'I know you, don't I? You're from the brewery.'

His speech was slurred and Nell considered running. However, from their conversation, she realised that this gentleman was very likely to be Devlin Wilmot. He climbed down through a small gate at the rear and walked towards her. As he closed in on her, he pushed his grimy goggles on top of his tweed hat and she recognised him. He had grown taller in his years away, but his stormy grey eyes fringed with black and his perfectly straight nose had not changed.

George Wilmot and Lady Clarissa were very proud of their adopted son, Devlin. Mr Wilmot had spared no expense on his education and, Nell acknowledged, Devlin was certainly a handsome fellow – clever, too. He had absorbed some of his father's sunny disposition as he grew up and was popular at the brewery. Nell guessed he was about the same age as her, maybe a year or so older. From a young age he had shown an interest in brewing, working there during his school holidays. He had been willing to do menial tasks, gaining the respect of his father's loyal employees and the adoration of all the young women and girls, including Nell. Nell had worked in the office in those days and Devlin used to seek her out and delay her with his questions when she took the order book over to the head brewer.

The head brewer lived in a large house with a small garden at the brewery. He was a bookish man who knew all there was to learn about his trade. He had captured Devlin Wilmot's imagination and fuelled the boy's quest for knowledge.

But Nell had not seen Devlin at the brewery since he went away to the university. Now he was back, it seemed, and as handsome as ever, although Nell did not think she cared for the man he had grown into.

'I do believe it is Miss Goodman who stands before me,' he declared now. Swaying a little, he gave her an exaggerated bow. 'Miss Goodman,' he said, 'would you care to ride in my motor carriage?'

Nell would have loved to ride in a horseless carriage, but not with two gentlemen – if they could be described as such – who were clearly the worse for drink. 'No thank you, sir,' she replied. 'I prefer the safety of my own two legs.'

The other gentleman – Devlin had addressed him as Cyril – had climbed down too and removed his gauntlets and goggles. He appeared beside his friend. 'Dev, old boy, she prefers her legs to your new carriage,' he said. His words were very carefully delivered, but slightly slurred. And now she knew who Cyril was. She had seen his father arrive earlier in the pony and trap. Cyril Belfor was home as well, presumably to join his father as a lawyer in town.

Devlin grinned at Nell and said, 'They must be very special legs.'

'Well, shall we look for ourselves?'

Horrified, Nell froze for a moment. 'You most certainly will not,' she said clearly and began to walk away with determined strides.

'Hey, wench, don't you turn away from me!'

A heavy hand landed on her shoulder and a shiver of fear ran through her. This was no longer light-hearted fun. There were two of them and

115

they were drunk. Young bloods with more money than sense, out looking for sport. She glanced around for a source of help. The roadway was empty apart from their carriage. She was out of sight of the gates and the Grange. Even the sheep had deserted her!

She had noticed a thick shrubbery a few yards behind her that might provide cover if she ran. With a sickening feeling she realised it might also hide any attack on her from the road. Her fear mounted and she felt her heart thumping.

'Let go of me!' She tried to pull off his hand but he had a firm grip. Then she thought she might bite it but her mouth wouldn't reach that far. Another heavy hand landed on her other shoulder.

'I've got her, Dev!' Cyril cried. He had her arms pinned by her side. 'She can't get away.'

Devlin Wilmot staggered towards her with a broad grin on his face. She struck out at him with one of her boots, missed and lost her balance. Cyril lifted her bodily, clear off the ground, so she kicked out at Devlin with both her feet. He laughed and grabbed one of her ankles and then the other, until she was suspended between the two men like a hammock, helpless to kick or even struggle. Her skirt fell back to her knees, exposing black stockings.

Nell spluttered and choked with uncontrollable anger.

'You despicable louts! Put me down!'

Ignoring her, Cyril said, 'What do think, Dev, shapely or not?'

'Shapely, I'd say, as far as I can see.'

'Shall we look further?' Cyril swung her from side to side until the edge of her skirts exposed her blue and white garters. Another inch and her flesh would be exposed.

What were they going to do to her? 'Put me down,' she begged. Her distress and fear erupted into tears and she could not stop them. Frightened, she appealed to any better nature Devlin might still have, stared directly into his eyes and pleaded, 'Don't.'

His laughter waned to a grin. 'Do as she asks, Cyril,' he said, letting go of her legs. Her boots hit the ground and her skirts fell back to her ankles.

But Cyril kept a firm grip on her arms and replied, 'No fear, old boy. She's an angel sent from heaven and a pretty one, too.' He bent down and whispered in her ear, 'You like a bit of fun, don't you, wench?'

'No, I do not.' Again, she appealed to Devlin with frightened eyes.

'You heard her,' Devlin said. He fished his driving goggles out of his dust-coat pocket and added, 'Come on, we're late.' Then he turned and walked away.

But Cyril did not heed him and gripped Nell even tighter. 'Let go of my arms,' she spat out at him.

But instead he hoisted her up like a sack and grabbed her around the waist with both hands. He kept hold of her with one arm and explored the contours of her body with the other. When his hands lingered over her breasts she screamed at him, 'Take your filthy hands off me!'

Devlin whirled round as Cyril's fondling con-

117

tinued and shouted at him, 'I said leave her be! She doesn't want to play.'

'Not like Lottie, eh?' Cyril replied and guffawed. But he released his hold on her. Her knees buckled and she sank to the ground where he had dropped her. She was so relieved that she just stayed there trying to stifle her threatening sobs as the two young men returned to their carriage. She heard the machinery crank twice, shudder noisily into life and eventually rumble away towards the Grange.

Nell sat on the grass for a long time trying to compose herself and wondering whether she could continue on to the Grange. But she had come too far to turn back and anyway, shouldn't she tell George Wilmot about his son's despicable behaviour? He'd always had strict rules at the brewery about what he described as 'lewdness in any form', which extended to his employees' private lives.

She wrestled with this dilemma until she came to the conclusion that keeping her job was the most important task at present and so, reluctantly, she decided to keep quiet about the incident. Nevertheless, it had angered her and coloured her opinion of Devlin Wilmot. A few years ago she had thought they were friends. She ought to have known better. He was gentry and gentry behaved as they pleased.

Nell trudged on, taking deep breaths to quell her fury. It was difficult to suppress and she noticed her hands were shaking. Finally the Grange came into view. It was a fine house in mellow stone over three floors, with elegant sash windows and a portico that hid the attic dormers of the servants' rooms. Nell had not taken much notice of it before. She had usually been enjoying the summer fete too much and the best part – the tea – had always been served in a big tent.

Devlin Wilmot's horseless phaeton stood at the foot of a wide flight of steps that led up to the front door. Nearby was Mr Belfor's carriage but the horse was still hitched, implying he didn't plan to stay long. Nell marched up the steps and tugged on the iron ring. A butler in purple livery with gold braiding opened the door. He was a large man, tall not fat, and immaculately dressed. Nell hadn't expected such grand formality and was momentarily speechless.

'Can I help you, miss?' The butler looked over her seriously and added, 'Is Her Ladyship expecting you?'

Guessing that he meant Lady Clarissa, she pulled herself together and answered, 'I've come to see Mr Wilmot. I'm from the brewery.'

The butler's facial expression barely changed, but he began to close the door. 'Tradesmen and servants round the back, if you please.'

'No, wait!' But she was speaking to the closed door and she had no alternative but to go in search of the servants' entrance. She followed a gravel path that disappeared under an archway and found herself in a quadrangle enclosed by long, low stable buildings with dormers at intervals in the slate roofs. It was rather pretty as the many windows were made up of small panes of glass and the numerous glazing bars were painted white. A young lad was rubbing down a sleek chestnut horse. She walked over to him and asked, 'Is this the way in for the servants?'

'Are you the new housemaid?'

She shook her head. 'Just visiting ... er ... someone.'

'Oh, right. See those railings by the house? Go down the steps behind them and in through the door at the bottom. Report to the housekeeper first. Her room is on the left.'

'Thank you.'

She followed these directions but hesitated once inside the dimly lit stone-flagged passage. It was lined with wood and glass partitions, rather like the brewery offices. Kitchens and sculleries were on one side and housekeeper and linen rooms on the other. At the far end of the passage she saw the butler come out of a preparation room carrying a laden tray, walk up a flight of stone steps and push his way through a wide door. She caught a glimpse of wood-panelled walls before the door swung shut again and the smell of coffee wafted down the passage. If she followed the coffee no doubt she would find Mr Wilmot on the receiving end of it, she thought, and walked purposefully towards the steps. One or two maids dressed in grey cotton frocks covered by white aprons raised their eyebrows as she passed, but no one challenged her.

The swing door was covered in thick green felt held in place by a diamond pattern of brass studs. It opened into a dark corner beneath a wide staircase rising from a marble-floored reception hall. Gilt-framed portraits and hunting scenes hung around the walls between large panelled doors. Emerging from the darkness, Nell gazed in amazement. The front door was opposite the stairs. A huge crystal chandelier hung from a high, ornately plastered ceiling. She'd had no idea that George Wilmot's home was so glittery and grand.

She heard footsteps on the stairs above her head and shrank back into the shadows. One of the doors opened and a loud voice called, 'Paget, where is my son?'

'He's washing, sir. The motor car journey was dusty and he is a little ... a little tired. I have taken him and Master Cyril some coffee to revive them.'

'Well, get back up there and hurry them along.'

Nell recognised George Wilmot's voice and she peeped out from her corner. He was alone, except for the man Paget, who was on the stairs. This was her chance. She stepped out into the light. 'Mr Wilmot! Sir! Please may I have a word with you?'

Wilmot's head turned in her direction. 'Who's that? What are you doing lurking in the shadows? Show yourself.'

Nell stepped into the light and George Wilmot added, 'Did those boys bring you? I'll have none of that here, you know.'

Chapter 10

Paget came running down the stairs again. Nell recognised him as the butler who had closed the front door in her face. As soon as he saw her he said, 'I'm very sorry, Mr Wilmot. I don't know who this young woman is. She must have sneaked in through the servants' entrance. I'll get rid of her immediately.'

'Wait a minute.' George Wilmot took a step closer to Nell. 'I know you. Come over here, where I can get a proper look at you.'

Nell obeyed and Paget scowled.

'I'm Nell Goodman, sir, from the brewery. I really need to speak to you.'

George Wilmot peered at her. 'Are you Mabel's lass?' He looked her over with interest. 'You are, aren't you? You've grown some since I last saw you. What do you want with me? Our Phoebe runs the brewery now.'

Nell glanced at Paget and said, 'It's a private matter, sir.'

Paget said, 'I'll make sure she leaves forthwith, sir.'

George Wilmot frowned at his butler. 'You'll make sure those boys get a move on. I'll take this one into the library. Come and get me when my son is ready.'

'Very good, sir.'

Paget walked over to the library and held open the door. Nell walked past him with her head held high and a serious expression on her face. She stood in the middle of the carpet and gazed at the bookcases that stretched from floor to ceiling and filled the walls between door and windows. They were full to bursting with leather-bound volumes. George Wilmot sat in a comfortable chair by the fireplace and indicated to Nell to sit opposite him.

'How did you get here, Nell?'

'I took the early omnibus to the village and

walked the rest of the way.'

'Well, I haven't much time, so get on with it.'

George Wilmot was known in the town as a rough diamond and in these opulent surroundings Nell realised what this meant. His first marriage and the brewery had made him a wealthy man, but he still had a few rough edges that needed polishing away. His aristocratic second wife had been some help in this respect, but George Wilmot still had a long way to go to measure up to Lady Clarissa's standards.

'I've got to leave the brewery, sir.'

'I thought you were suited there.'

'It's Miss Wilmot, sir. She told me to leave.'

'Our Phoebe's got rid of you? Why did she do that?'

Nell hesitated for a few seconds only.

'I haven't got all day, lass. Spit it out.'

'It's Mother, sir.'

'Mabel? Has she been taken bad?'

'Not really. Well, yes, in a way. She keeps turning up at the brewery office and disturbing Miss Wilmot.'

'Does she now? What does your ma want with our Phoebe?'

'Nothing, sir. It's you she keeps asking for. You see, she's not herself these days. She's remembering things from years ago and it upsets her so she goes on about it. If I distract her she soon quietens down, but not before she's upset Miss Wilmot as well.'

George Wilmot's genial face darkened and his features set into a frown. 'You mean Mabel's been turning up at the brewery and saying things about

123

the past?'

Nell nodded reluctantly.

'Well, what's she been saying?'

'Nobody believes her, sir. She's always been a bit fanciful, but just lately... Oh, I don't know...'

George Wilmot raised his voice. 'What's she been saying, Nell?'

Nell knew she had to be honest with him and swallowed. 'She says it was your fault that father died and because of that you promised to marry her. Yesterday she sat outside Miss Wilmot's office waiting for you. I had to take her home.' Nell was flushed with embarrassment and went on too quickly, 'I'm ever so sorry, sir. I'll make up the time. I always do.'

George Wilmot turned down the corners of his mouth, indicating his displeasure. He stood up quickly and walked over to the window.

Nell was unsure what to do next. She twisted in her chair to face him but he had his back to her. Nevertheless, she went on, 'Miss Wilmot called the sergeant and he came to the house last night, which gave me quite a scare.'

Still, he didn't say anything, so she added, 'I was hoping you'd talk to her, sir – to Miss Wilmot, I mean. I can't afford to leave, with only my wages coming in.'

She couldn't think of anything else to say and lapsed into silence, broken only by Paget coming back. He announced, 'Master Devlin and Master Cyril are waiting in the drawing room, sir, with Mr Belfor.'

An expression of displeasure had stayed on George Wilmot's face. He spoke to Paget. 'Look after her and see she gets some food.'

'Shall I arrange transport back to town for her, sir?'

'Not yet.'

Nell rose to her feet. 'What about my job, sir?'

'Wait in the servants' hall.' He went out of the room leaving her with Paget.

'Follow me,' the butler said. 'And I don't want any trouble.' He led the way back through the green baize door and down the stone steps into the dark passage.

'Servants are the second door on the right. Downstairs maids have their dinner at half past eleven,' he said briskly.

'Thank you, Paget,' she answered.

'It's Mr Paget to you,' he grunted and disappeared into one of the kitchen rooms on the left. Appetising cooking smells seeped into the passage and Nell's mouth watered.

She knew George Wilmot would listen to her because he had always done so in the past. She still didn't know about her job at the brewery but felt hopeful. Nonetheless, she wondered what she would do if he decided she couldn't go back.

The servants' hall was comfortable and cosy for such a big room. There was a fireplace with a fire going even though it was summer and a few fireside chairs as well as a long scrubbed wooden dining table already set with knives and forks for dinner. No one else was in the room so she sat by the fire and waited.

Eventually, a couple of young housemaids came in and were about to sit at the table when one of them noticed her and said, 'I saw you in the passage earlier. Have you come for a position?'

'If you have, you'd best move yourself,' the other girl added. 'That chair is for when Cook comes in here.'

'I didn't know.' Nell stood up immediately.

'Well, the kitchen maids'll be in with dinner in a minute and they'll tell her.'

Nell went to sit next to the housemaids at the table. Very soon the empty chairs filled with other maids and an assortment of lively young male servants and gardeners. They were ill-disciplined until the food arrived and an older man came in to carve the boiled mutton.

'Who's that?' she whispered.

'He's the head footman.'

If he noticed Nell, he didn't acknowledge her and she assumed Mr Paget had told him about her. Very soon, the only sounds were of cutlery on plates, quiet requests to pass the potatoes or salt and pepper, and the occasional muted belch followed by a stifled giggle. The food was good and plentiful. Nell would have liked to take some home for Mother, who would welcome a change from their usual scrag-end stew. A steaming jam roly-poly and a jug of Bird's patent custard arrived for pudding. Two of the maids cleared away the dirty pots and brought in an enormous brown enamel teapot and a tray of cups and saucers. Conversation resumed when the head footman left the table with his cup of tea and went to sit in a fireside chair.

The girl next to Nell asked, 'Are you an upstairs maid? Our head parlourmaid said we needed another one now that she's Miss Phoebe's personal maid.'

'I'm a bottle-washer at the brewery,' Nell answered.

'Ugh, I wouldn't like that. You have to wear a brown overall, don't you? Is that why you want to come here?'

'I don't want to come here. I came to see Mr Wilmot and he's asked me to wait.'

'Oh.'

'The upstairs maids'll be here in a minute. They have dinner with Mr Paget and Mrs Quimby, so they won't want a bottle-washer hanging about.'

'Where shall I go?'

'I dunno. I've got some more polishing to do for tonight's dinner. Her Ladyship's having guests for a celebration. Master Devlin is coming home for good this afternoon.'

'He's here already.'

'How do you know that?'

'He drove past me in his horseless carriage on the way here.' Nell felt a blush rise in her cheeks as she remembered the incident, and she looked away. When she turned back the maids had gone. All the young servants were filing out of the door and back to their work except one who was laying up the dinner table for the second sitting. The head footman was reading a newspaper. Nell stood up, went over to the far corner of the room and sat on a stool in front of an upright piano. It was next to a small wooden table and a spotty cheval mirror that had seen better days.

Eventually Mr Paget came in with a mature woman in a plain black gown. Nell assumed she

127

was the housekeeper, Mrs Quimby. She went to check the table layout while Mr Paget talked to his head footman, who rose to his feet as soon as the butler approached him. Their deep voices carried well.

'Anything to report?'

'No, Mr Paget.'

'See that nobody steps out of line today. Her Ladyship has the Lord Lieutenant here later so I don't want any hitches. Mr Wilmot was fine until that lass arrived from the brewery. I don't know what she said to him but it put him right out of sorts. The young master's had an earful from him already.'

Nell experienced a sense of satisfaction from overhearing the latter. Master Devlin deserves a telling-off, whatever the reason, she thought. Clearly, George Wilmot wasn't pleased with him.

'What have you done with her?' Mr Paget went on.

'The brewery lass?' The head footman inclined his head. 'She's over by the piano.'

Mr Paget glanced in her direction. 'Well, she can't stay there while we're having our dinner and he won't see her until after he's spoken to Miss Phoebe.'

'I'll stick her in the boot room for now.' The footman called over to her. 'You. What's your name?'

Nell hurried towards him. 'Nell Goodman.'

'Come with me, Goodman.' She hurried after him as he swept through the door.

The boot room smelled of leather and saddle soap. There was a low stone sink at one end with a brass water tap in the wall. Two pairs of muddied riding boots were drying out on the red quarry-tile floor. Most of the room space was filled by a large old wooden table holding boots in various stages of cleaning and polishing. They stood like soldiers, erect on their wooden boot trees, lined up under nameplates on the wall. 'Wait there until someone fetches you,' the footman ordered and promptly disappeared.

There was nowhere to sit so Nell occupied herself by counting the boots. Lady Clarissa's were made of especially fine leather but Nell wondered why she would need five pairs for riding, all identical in colour and style. Miss Phoebe, as she was called here, had three pairs, which seemed more than enough to Nell. She grasped her skirt and lifted it a few inches to expose her plain black boots laced to just above her ankle. They had been clean when she set out this morning but were dusty now. She picked up a brush and bent down to buff them.

'Who are you and what are you doing in my boot room?'

Startled, she straightened and the young voice continued, 'Oh, are you the new housemaid?'

Nell relaxed and smiled. The boy couldn't be any older than fourteen. In fact, he looked and sounded more like twelve to her. 'The head footman told me to wait here until I'm called,' she said. 'You must be the boot boy.'

'That's me,' he answered proudly. 'But I've got to help out in the stables today, 'cos Mr Paget says Her Ladyship is expecting guests.'

'I see.' Nell held up the buffing brush. 'I promise I'll put it back where I found it.'

'You'd better.' He set about putting dubbin, saddle soap, cloths and brushes into a box then called 'Ta-ra' over his shoulder and skipped away.

Nell returned her concentration to her own boots until she was disturbed by a much stronger male voice. It was Cyril Belfor. He was dangling a pair of dusty gentlemen's day shoes above the table top and he called out, 'These need doing now.'

He looked at her expectantly without registering any recognition. Why would he? He had been the worse for drink and she'd just been an anonymous country wench, presumably as this 'Lottie' was at first. Nell put down the buffing brush and said, 'I'm not the boot boy, sir.'

'Obviously not. Where is he?'

'Helping out in the stables, sir.'

'Oh. Well, all servants know how to clean boots so you'll have to do them.'

'I don't work here, sir. I'm only visiting.'

Nell heard the dulled sound of a reverberating gong in the distance.

'Hear that? That's for sherry in the drawing room, so see they get done and look sharp about it. I'll collect them in fifteen minutes.' He placed the shoes on the table and left.

She supposed that somebody would be in trouble if the shoes weren't cleaned and it would most likely be the poor boot boy. She went out into the dim passage to look for one of the other servants. It was empty. She guessed that everyone was busy with preparations for luncheon. She found one of the kitchen maids at the scullery sink and explained.

'Well, by rights a valet should do it but they're all helping the footmen with luncheon,' the maid said. 'The housemaids won't touch 'em, so that leaves one of us in the scullery. Pass me that towel, will you, and pray that Cook doesn't find out. At least the washing-up will get the blacking off my hands.'

'Oh, don't stop what you're doing,' Nell responded. 'I've got nothing else to do and I'm stuck down there until Mr Wilmot will see me.' Nell was beginning to wonder if he would actually see her again. It was clearly a very busy day for him with business talk over luncheon and guests arriving for a banquet tonight. If the Lord Lieutenant was coming Lady Clarissa would wish to impress.

Nell was happy to help out the scullery maid, if only to relieve her boredom, and she cleaned the beautifully crafted leather shoes with a good heart. They were new and the craftsman's name in gold tooling was still readable on a sliver of leather sewn into the sock: *Wainwright's*. It sounded vaguely familiar but there wasn't a bespoke shoemaker in town any more so perhaps she'd read about them in the paper. The shoes didn't take her very long to clean because they weren't really dirty, not even muddy. But motoring was a dusty way to travel, although not as bad as the railway train, which puffed out sooty smoke that left black spots on your face and clothes.

She left the shoes on the table and retreated to the back corner of the room where she'd noticed some wooden boxes out of sight in an alcove. She guessed they contained wooden lasts and trees for reshaping wet footwear but they provided a temporary resting place while she waited. She leaned her head against the wall and closed her eyes, feeling sleepy. She was not used to such a heavy dinner at midday, not even on a Sunday. But she opened her eyes quickly and stared at the whitewashed brick wall when she heard the gentleman approach again. This time he wasn't alone and he sounded really anxious.

'Come on, Dev. The second gong is due any minute. Pater will be furious.'

'Not as angry as my father will be if I go into luncheon looking less than perfect. He is not in a good humour today and the Lord only knows why.'

'It could be something to do with you arriving late – and drunk.'

'I'm celebrating! For God's sake, Father owns a brewery and he expects it of me. No, it's not me; something else has rattled him this morning.'

Nell heard him inhale deeply. 'Ah, the smell of leather and wax. It takes me back to when I was a lad. I used to love it down here. I could sneak out of the servants' entrance and explore the old dairy and the game larder; and in heatwaves, I'd go and sit in the ice house until my backside froze.'

'Come *on*, Dev.'

'All right, all right; don't be such an old crone, Cyril. If my luggage had arrived before me as it should have, I'd have half a dozen pairs of shoes to wear at luncheon.'

The voices faded as Nell stood up. The shoes had gone and she realised that they had not belonged to Cyril, but to Devlin. This irked her more than she cared to admit. She was not his servant. She wasn't anybody's servant and she considered walking out there and then. But she couldn't. She needed her job at the brewery and anyway she couldn't go home before half past six without worrying Mother. Yesterday's visit from the sergeant meant that Miss Wilmot had been serious in her decision and was not likely to change her mind. Only George Wilmot could overrule her. Nell was distracted from her anxieties by a commotion down the passage and she went to investigate.

A kitchen maid was complaining vociferously that carters had arrived at her kitchen door and Paget should be dealing with them. All the footmen were busy upstairs in the hall and dining room. Consequently, the carters' men simply deposited trunks and valises outside the kitchen, cluttering up the passage. The carters ignored the maid's protests and piled up the pieces of monogrammed luggage at the base of the stone steps as they had been instructed by 'the young master'. On top of the largest trunk was a fishing basket and rods, two gun slips containing his shotguns and a leather cartridge bag, all identified by the initials D H W. Nell wondered what the H stood for.

The maid caught sight of her and barked, 'You over there, go and find a footman to shift this lot. There'll be hell to pay if Cook finds it here.'

Nell hesitated. The maid ought to know Nell wasn't a servant here, but that didn't seem to concern her. She was red-faced from the heat in the kitchen and went on, 'Well, go on then and hurry!'

Nell took the stone steps two at a time, stopping to compose herself at the green baize door. She pushed it open and stepped into the hall just in time to hear Mr Paget announce Miss Phoebe and see her stride into the drawing room. The head footman was nearby, standing to attention.

He caught sight of her and hissed, 'Get out of here.'

'The kitchen sent me. Master Devlin's luggage is in their way,' she said.

The head footman clicked his tongue and rolled his eyes upwards. He held his right hand aloft and snapped his fingers. 'Go and see what she wants,' he said.

Two junior footmen appeared from the other side of the hall and pushed past her. She was about to follow them when the head footman called, 'Goodman, hold this door open for them.'

She had not noticed it before, but there was a small door cut into the wood panelling opposite. It led into a lobby at the foot of a narrow uncarpeted staircase that wound round and round until it disappeared into the gloom, way above her head. The footmen took off their white gloves and gave them to her while they carried the luggage and stacked it at the bottom of these stairs. She watched them with interest, noting that all the footmen here were, on the whole, tall young men, and these two seemed to be as strong as the draymen at the brewery. When they had finished they dusted down their livery, replaced their gloves and went back to their positions. One of them thanked her and smiled. Nell thought he would have lingered because he said, 'Luncheon is late already,' as though excusing himself as he rushed away.

Nell went back to the boot room, which seemed a haven of peace and quiet away from the kitchen and sculleries during luncheon. She thought that the footman who had spoken to her was a very nice young man, well spoken and not coarse like the draymen at the brewery. She wondered what his name was. She found a pile of old newspapers and occupied herself by reading them between dozing until Mr Paget himself came to find her. She stood up immediately.

'Mr Wilmot is waiting in his library,' he said.

Chapter 11

'When he's finished with you,' Paget went on, 'one of the stable lads will take you in the dog cart to the terminus for the omnibus.' He scrutinised her appearance and muttered, 'I suppose you'll do.'

Miss Wilmot was in the library with her father. They were sitting either side of the fireplace and half turned to face the centre of the room where Mr Paget had left Nell. She felt exposed and vulnerable in these strange surroundings, but at least George Wilmot was smiling and this gave her hope.

'Now then, Nell,' George Wilmot began, 'let's get this business of your mother sorted out once and for all. The sergeant has told our Phoebe about calling on you. Phoebe, tell Nell what he said to you.'

Phoebe Wilmot looked pleased with herself, which Nell did not find comforting.

'He agreed with me,' Miss Wilmot said. 'You cannot allow your mother to roam around town creating havoc. The sergeant informed me of her visits to the high street shops.' Miss Wilmot's tone was not kindly. She raised her voice as she went on, 'And the things she's been saying. Something has to be done about that loose tongue of hers.'

Nell's heart began to thump. She could only guess at what Mother had been saying. 'She doesn't mean any of it. It's just that, sometimes, she gets confused.'

George Wilmot's mouth turned down at the corners. Nell realised that this was his look of displeasure. 'When we spoke earlier, you didn't tell me about her gossiping around the town. I had to find out about that from our Phoebe.'

'I didn't know myself until last night, sir.' Besides, Nell thought, it wasn't what Mother had said that worried her. But, clearly, that was not the case for George Wilmot and his daughter.

Phoebe interrupted impatiently. 'Father, do get on with this. We can't have some old biddy spreading scurrilous lies about you up and down the high street.'

Oh dear Lord, what had Mother been saying to the shopkeepers? 'I did warn her about that,' Nell said. 'I'm sure she won't do it again.'

'Well, I'm not,' Phoebe stated.

'You've got to agree with us, Nell lass. Your mother isn't safe to be out on her own. You don't want her to end up in front of the magistrate, do you?'

That was more or less what the sergeant had said to Nell and she was forced to agree. 'No, sir, of course I don't.'

'She needs proper looking after.'

'Oh, I can look after her, sir.'

'Not while you're working at the brewery, you can't,' George Wilmot argued.

'She doesn't work there any more, Father,' Phoebe pointed out.

Nell took up this cue to state her case to George Wilmot. 'That is why I came here today, Mr Wilmot. You said there'd always be a job for me at the brewery. You promised Mother.'

Phoebe looked cross and her father seemed uncomfortable. 'Yes, I did and I meant it. But you can't look after your ma if you stay on at the brewery, can you? The sergeant saw that, which is why he has suggested a solution.'

'I'm going to take her to the market every Saturday,' Nell volunteered hopefully.

'I'm not talking about taking her shopping. She's got to be looked after and it's best that you agree with us. You don't want to be forced into it by the corporation, do you?'

'What has the town corporation to do with my mother?'

'Well, for a start, the ratepayers will be paying for her,' Phoebe explained.

'Paying for what?'

'The infirmary lass. That's where Mabel needs to be.'

'She doesn't need to be in hospital. She isn't ill.'

'Her constitution is strong, I grant you. But you have to admit that, with what she's been saying, she's not right in the head. The infirmary is used to dealing with folk like her.'

Nell was horrified by his implication. A cold fear crept over her. 'You can't mean the lunatic asylum?' she said. 'You can't. She's not insane.'

'Nay, lass, not that infirmary. I mean the one for old folk in the ... in the...'

The chill creeping down Nell's back turned to ice. The alternative was even worse. 'You want me to send her to the workhouse?'

'They'll take care of her for you.'

'I don't need them to do that. I can look after her.'

'Nonsense! You have to earn a living.' Miss Wilmot shrugged.

'It's the only way, Nell lass,' George argued. 'Then you'll be able to come back to the brewery in the office where you belong.'

Phoebe looked aghast at this statement and protested, 'I don't have a vacancy. And I need her cottage for my accounts clerk.'

The coldness of her tone sent a shiver through Nell. So that's what this was about as far as Phoebe Wilmot was concerned. She turned on her angrily. 'You want us out so you can give our home to one of your favourites?'

'There are plenty of domestic posts to suit you until you marry,' Miss Wilmot stated. 'It will be easier for you to find a position, or indeed a husband, with your mother out of the way.'

Her matter-of-fact response astounded Nell. She repeated, 'My mother does not need to be in the workhouse. She has a home and someone to look after her.'

'She has neither,' Miss Wilmot responded. 'Her home belongs to the brewery and as you no longer work for us she may not live there. My clerk can marry as soon as he has a house–'

'Phoebe, that's enough,' George Wilmot interrupted. His daughter closed her mouth and frowned.

Nell turned to George Wilmot. 'Is this about my mother, or the house she lives in, sir?'

Why didn't he say something? He had always seemed such a genial, reasonable man and yet he was letting his daughter turn her out of her home! 'Mr Wilmot,' she pleaded, 'you promised Mother she'd always have a home. You promised.'

He pulled a face, clasped and unclasped his hands in front of his silk waistcoat and then replied, 'That was all a long time ago. I can't have your ma spreading lies about me. My name is well respected in the Riding and I aim to keep it that way.'

'But nobody believes Mother's ramblings,' Nell protested. She was met with blank stares and broke the ensuing silence by adding pointedly, 'Do they?'

Neither father nor daughter replied to her. Nell thought George Wilmot was embarrassed because he gazed out of the window instead of looking at her and muttered, 'Our Phoebe's right. The infirmary is the best place for your ma now.'

Nell's hopes of appealing to his genial nature drained away. George Wilmot was not going to reverse his daughter's decision. Nell had wasted her time coming here, time she ought to have spent looking for another position.

She was angry and responded, 'If you mean the workhouse, Mr Wilmot, then why don't you say so?'

'Now then, lass, you don't have to take that tone with me. I'm only thinking of the future. What sort of life will it be for you looking after Mabel? A pretty young thing like you, tied to being nursemaid to a dotty old lady?'

'She is my mother! And she is not old!'

'But she is dotty, even you have to admit that,' Miss Wilmot said.

'Be quiet now, Phoebe,' her father snapped. 'You've said your piece. I'll handle this from here. Nell lass, you have to accept it. If you agree to ... to what the *sergeant* has suggested you do with your mother, you can come back to your job at the brewery.'

Nell didn't believe the sergeant had suggested the workhouse. She reckoned that the idea had come from Miss Wilmot, who wanted Mother's house for her pimply obsequious clerk in the office. And her father, to Nell's crushing disappointment, had readily agreed.

'Well, what do you say, lass?' George Wilmot prompted.

'I say keep your brewery job. I'd rather take in washing.'

'How will you do that without a wash house and a back yard?' Phoebe challenged.

'I shan't tell you again, Phoebe!' George Wilmot softened his tone for Nell. 'You can't stay in the house without your job at the brewery. You'll be in the workhouse yourself, lass, if you don't do as we ask.'

'Neither of us is going in the workhouse. This is the twentieth century and young women can find work just the same as young men. I started at the brewery in ordering, if you remember.' Nell appealed to George Wilmot's obvious discomfort at her resistance. 'You will surely give me a testimonial so that I may find another position and rooms to rent?'

'Certainly not, you were dismissed!' Miss Wilmot responded.

George Wilmot stood up. 'I haven't got time for all this today. My God, you women! You give them what they want and then they only ask for something different. Well, I've got my lawyer waiting and papers to read and sign. This interview is at an end. Phoebe, go back to your mother and our guests.'

Miss Wilmot left with some reluctance, as though she did not trust her father to keep his word. George Wilmot appealed to Nell. 'You've got to see sense. Your ma is an embarrassment.'

'Not to me, sir; nor to others who know her well.'

He shook his head slowly. 'Don't make me send in the bailiffs,' he said, then stood up and pressed a bell-push by the fireplace.

It was his last word. He was siding with his daughter. Nell should have guessed that he would. Blood is thicker than water. His earlier promises to her and Mother meant nothing now. Mr Paget came in and led her away, through the green baize door and down the stone staircase.

'I hope you're satisfied,' he said sourly as he held open the back door at the end of the passage. 'We've got enough on our plates today without you making things worse. The dog cart's waiting for you.'

'I'd rather walk,' she said. That wasn't actually true but her pride had been hurt. She had been humiliated after being so sure that George Wilmot would support her.

'Suit yourself,' Mr Paget replied and closed the door, leaving her standing on the outside looking up at the black iron railings. At the top of the steps she could see the boot boy sitting up front of the cart and holding the pony's reins. 'Hurry up,' he called. 'You don't want to miss your 'bus.'

No, she didn't. She had an urgent need to find a job and somewhere to live. And how was she going to explain everything to Mother when she got home?

'I heard about you cleaning Master Devlin's shoes,' the boy said when they were on their way. 'I owe you a favour for that. He told Mr Paget he was pleased with them so I'm in his good books.'

Nell wished she could have said 'Happy to oblige' but the words stuck in her throat. It wasn't the boy's fault, and the knowledge made her even more cross so she stayed silent and scowled.

'I mean it,' he said. 'If there's ever owt you want.'

'How about a job and a home,' she responded and immediately regretted her words. But the boy didn't pick up on her irony, which gave her some relief. He had not done anything wrong to her; quite the opposite.

'I can ask my mam and dad when I go home for

142

Sunday tea.'

Nell looked at him. He was serious. 'Would you?'

'Course I would,' he answered cheerily. 'My dad says us ordinary folk have to look out for each other.'

'Yes indeed,' Nell agreed. She asked him his name – Eddie – and she gave him hers. His family lived in Keppel village, which was on the other side of the estate and not on the 'bus route. There was no point in masons building terraces for labourers there if they couldn't catch an omnibus to work and so its prosperity had declined along with Fitzkeppel Hall.

Before the dog cart reached the estate boundary, it was overtaken by Mr Belfor in his carriage being driven by his son. Both gentlemen appeared to have enjoyed their luncheon and were in good humour. Cyril Belfor stared at Nell as he urged his horse onwards but did not acknowledge her in any way. Not long after, Nell heard the rumble of Master Devlin's horseless carriage. They were approaching the ornate gates, which had been left open by Master Cyril. The motor didn't roar by as Nell expected but trundled behind them until they stopped the other side while Eddie climbed down to shut the gates.

Devlin Wilmot drove around Nell, sitting primly in the back of the dog cart, and shuddered to a halt in front of her. He got out and walked towards her. He wore his long dust-coat and a soft chequered cap. As he pushed his driving goggles onto his forehead, Nell noticed that his face was flushed and grinning. 'When is your half

143

day, Nell?' he asked.

He thought she was a servant at the Grange! She didn't deny it. Let him believe what he likes, she thought.

He went on, 'The offer to ride in my motor car still stands.'

She was reminded of his earlier behaviour and became nervous. But this time he was on his own and she was in full view of Eddie. She glanced over at the lad closing the second gate. They would soon be on their way.

'No thank you, sir.' She didn't like the conditions that the Wilmots attached to their favours and she had a clear idea of what Devlin Wilmot would want in return. In a flash of pique she added, 'However, I'm sure Lottie can oblige you well enough.'

He didn't expect her barbed response and, frankly, Nell had surprised herself with it. But he was a Wilmot and they did what they wanted, took what they wanted, and never mind the effect on other folk. How dare George Wilmot suggest that she send her mother to the workhouse! She watched with pleasure as Devlin Wilmot's grin faded and he said, 'I thought we were friends.'

'So did I until—'

She stopped speaking. Eddie had returned and was waiting for Devlin to leave before climbing into the cart.

'Some other time,' he commented and went back to his motor car.

'Not if I've got anything to do with it,' she muttered.

'You do know that was Master Devlin, don't

you?' Eddie said.

'So?'

'My mam says it doesn't do to make enemies of your masters.'

'He's not my master.'

Eddie shrugged, flicked the reins and they followed the cloud of dust and fumes left by the motor car.

Noisy, dirty contraption, Nell thought. Give me a horse any day.

After a while, her anger receded and she realised she ought to apologise to Eddie. It wasn't his fault she had lost her job, and luckily, he wasn't upset. He was wise for his years, she considered. He suggested she look out for his mother in the market on Saturday. She ran the second-hand boot and shoe stall and Nell knew her by sight.

Chapter 12

Nell explained to her mother that she was leaving the brewery because George Wilmot was no longer in charge and Miss Wilmot was making changes. Mabel didn't make the connection with her own visits, or the sergeant's, but was taken up by Nell's decision.

'You do right, my love,' she said. 'She's a proper sourpuss, that one. Her mother wasn't, mind, but she let other folk look after Phoebe right from being born.'

Nell was surprised by her mother's reaction and considered it was best to tell her everything now. She said, 'It means we'll have to move from here.'

'Will we? Oh good, can we have a little garden with roses in it? I always wanted roses. Your father promised to grow them for me.'

Nell didn't know whether to be pleased that Mother had, it seemed, taken the news well, or worried that she couldn't afford to rent a house with a garden. In fact, until she had a job, she would have to take rooms or lodgings for them. A job was her priority. She had started as a junior in the office at Wilmot's and that must count for something. But only if she had a testimonial, she realised. Oh Lord, would she have to go back cap in hand to Wilmot's and eat humble pie? Miss Wilmot would laugh in her face.

'I'll start looking tomorrow,' Nell said. 'While I'm out you can turn out all the cupboards and see what we can sell to the rag and bone man.'

Mabel's face lit up at this prospect. 'He used to give us ribbons. Do you think he'll have velvet?'

'I expect so. Have you done the potatoes for tea?'

Over the next two days Nell tried several offices in town for a job but they all wanted a testimonial from Wilmot's, even those who recognised her. Then she tried the high street shops where she was better known. Unfortunately, so was her mother and, although they were kind in their rejections, Nell knew they didn't want the risk of Mabel's unpredictable behaviour disturbing their customers.

146

In the draper's, one of the junior assistants came after her and mentioned that one or two better-off customers, who lived in the big houses out on the Moorgate Road, were always complaining about their servants. 'They're always looking for a hardworking girl,' she said, then hesitated. 'I ... I used to work for one of them.'

'But you don't any more,' Nell prompted.

'The mistress expected too much from me; housemaid and parlourmaid and she didn't keep a cook either. It was a long day. I was up at half past five and still on the go at ten at night.'

'I see,' Nell replied. 'Thank you for telling me.' She thought, but didn't say, I'd rather work in the bottle factory.

After two days she realised that it would have to be the factory if she wanted to stay in town. She could find a position as a buffer girl for a Sheffield cutler, or a pit head lass at a village coal mine, but both were notoriously dirty jobs and both would mean moving Mother to live among people she didn't know, who wouldn't be as understanding as the locals here. She tried the smaller shops. They were mostly run by families who didn't take on help they had to pay. The money went the other way for workshops, where the tradesmen were paid by parents to take on their offspring as apprentices.

This realisation reminded her of Eddie whose mother ran the boot and shoe stall on the market. Cheered by this option, she put the bottle factory out of her mind and bought a whole bag of end-of-the-day bargain bits from the cooked meat shop.

Nell hurried home with the hot meat and was tired when she arrived. Mabel came running down the stairs, wearing a gown that Nell had not seen for years. 'I've been waiting for you,' she cried. 'Look what I've found.' She stood in the middle of the kitchen and twirled around. The gown was tight-waisted with a low neckline and very full skirts. Mabel went on, 'I've put on all your petticoats. How do I look?' She twirled again.

Nell's cheeriness deserted her. She had expected Mother to turn out the cupboards in the scullery and kitchen. But this gown was out of the old travelling trunk at the back of the closet on the landing. It was an old-fashioned style and needed an old-fashioned corset underneath it. The satin had been good quality and a pretty blue but now it was worn and faded in places.

'You look lovely, Mother,' Nell replied.

'Your father liked me in this.' Her expression saddened and then set into a frown. 'George killed him, you know. That's why he said he'd marry me.'

Nell saw tears welling in her mother's eyes. She said quickly, 'Show me what else you found in the trunk.'

'We were so happy in the big house,' Mabel said. Her lip trembled and Nell knew she was thinking of Father.

'Upstairs in the trunk?' Nell urged brightly. 'Shall we go and look?'

'Oh yes,' Mabel remembered. 'I turned out the closet. Come and see.' She turned and went back upstairs.

Nell placed her warm parcel in the range oven

and followed her mother. She found their small landing between the front and back bedrooms strewn with an assortment of clothing and footwear. Some of the items were normally taken out and worn in the winter but most of them had been packed in the trunk or wrapped in old calico and pushed to the back of the closet. The doors to both bedrooms were open and items spilled over the thresholds. Nell was hungry for her tea but thought she ought to make some sense of this chaos first.

She bent to pick up a few items of her own and said, 'Decide what you want to keep and put them on your bed. I'll see if I can sell the rest.'

'I want to keep all of them!' Mabel cried.

'We won't have room when we move,' Nell explained gently. They would probably have to share a bedroom, but she did not say so.

'I want all my shoes and frocks.' Mabel pouted.

Nell took hold of a set of metal crinoline hoops leaning against the wall and rolled them back into the closet. 'Well, you won't be wearing these again, will you? We'll look again tomorrow and see what else we don't need.' She changed the subject. 'Are you hungry?'

Mabel sniffed the air. 'Why? What's for tea?'

'Roast pork. It's still warm. I thought I'd make bread-cakes like he does in the shop in town.'

It was a feast. The shopkeeper had put in bits of crackling and stuffing and Nell opened a jar of apple cheese she'd made from windfalls last autumn. They drank a huge pot of tea between them and finished with jam tarts from the pantry. Mabel forgot about her frocks and insisted she washed the pots afterwards. While she was in the scullery Nell went upstairs to tackle the chaos on the landing.

She pushed everything back in the closet as quickly as she could. Nell didn't want to cause Mabel any more distress. Rooting through possessions brought back old memories for her mother and these days they all seemed to be unhappy ones. For the first time Nell wondered if moving Mother away from reminders of her past life might be the best way forward for both of them.

When they set off for market the next day, Nell had gathered quite a bundle of garments and boots that neither she nor Mabel wore. The second-hand clothes stall gave her several shillings and, although Mabel wanted to buy a coat that caught her eye, she didn't need one and Nell persuaded her to choose the meat for Sunday dinner instead. Her shopping basket, with her old school boots still attached by their laces, was full when she approached the second-hand boot and shoe stall run by the formidable Mrs Wainwright. She was well known for never bargaining. Her price was the price, it was fair and she expected it.

Nell had always assumed Mrs Wainwright's husband was a cobbler because you could leave your boots with her for mending and collect them repaired and polished – always beautifully polished – a week later. Now she made the connection with the label inside Devlin Wilmot's shoes at the Grange. Mr Wainwright was a shoemaker as well as a cobbler and some of the worn footwear on display was his own work. Nell glanced over the neat rows of black and brown workaday boots

150

while Mabel's attention was taken by a pair of soft kidskin summer shoes with heels.

Mrs Wainwright examined Nell's boots and nodded. 'Anything on here take your fancy in exchange?'

'I'll take the money, if you please.'

'You get better value in goods, miss.'

Mabel appeared at Nell's side with the kid shoes in her hand. 'Aren't they pretty?' she said, 'I'll take them.'

'They'll cost you another two shillings,' Mrs Wainwright said.

Nell tried not to react. She didn't want to upset her mother by refusing and they had already had one tussle, over the coat. 'Have you tried them on, Mother?' she asked.

'Oh.' Mabel looked confused.

'There's a stool round the side, dear,' Mrs Wainwright added and came out from behind her stall to help her.

Nell shook her head and whispered, 'I'm not taking them,' but Mrs Wainwright didn't hear her.

Fortunately the shoes were too big. 'Never mind, Mrs Goodman, come back next week.' Mrs Wainwright smiled at Nell. 'I'll give you the money for your boots.'

Nell was relieved. 'Thank you. Do you know my mother?'

'I had to call the sergeant on her one day, but he knows her and it was all sorted.'

'I'm so sorry.'

'She's harmless enough but you have to keep an eye on her. Not everybody is sympathetic.'

'I know. I'm sorry.' She took the coins from the

older woman's hand. 'Thank you. I met your son Eddie up at Wilmot Grange the other day. I'm looking for work and he said you might know of something.'

'What can you do?'

'Reckoning up; I used to be in ordering at the brewery and I have neat handwriting.'

'Have you tried the high street shops?'

Nell nodded. 'And the offices, but they want typewriting nowadays.'

'Was there nothing at the Grange? They've got house parties for the rest of the summer and then there's the shooting. Cook is crying out for help.'

'Oh, I ... I didn't ask. But, well, the thing is, I can't really go there.'

'Why not?'

Nell heaved a sigh. There was no point in hiding the truth. 'I had to leave Wilmot's Brewery because ... because I took time off to see to Mother.'

'Oh, I see. That Miss Phoebe is making her presence felt, then.'

'I'm afraid so.'

'Well, she got nowhere trying to be lady of the house at the Grange. When she started pushing the servants around, Lady Clarissa soon put her right.'

'Is it time for dinner, yet?' Mabel asked. She sniffed the air, full of good smells wafting over from the hot food stalls.

Nell counted out some coins and handed them to Mabel. 'Go and fetch us a hot pie each, mutton if they've got them.' She watched her walk in the direction of the pie stall and turned back to Mrs Wainwright, who was serving a customer.

When she was free, Nell carried on their conversation. 'One of the shop girls suggested going into service although it doesn't pay as much as the bottle factory.'

'It's up to you, ducks. But Lady Clarissa knows what she's doing and lasses who land positions at the Grange stay there. They can always land jobs going at the factories in town so ask yourself why. That Lady Clarissa has been a godsend for our village.'

Another of her customers distracted Mrs Wainwright and Nell lost her attention. She went off in search of her mother at the crowded hot pie stall and experienced a moment of panic when she couldn't see her. Please God, she thought, don't let her have bought that coat!

She heard raised voices at the roast pork stand. It was run by the same man who had the shop in town and he brought out wooden trays of warm bread-cakes filled with hot cooked meat. He usually had a queue and always sold every last crumb, even though they were dearer than pies.

'I've already paid you!' she heard her mother cry.

'It's not enough for two. Give me one back!' The man sounded angry.

Nell hurried forward, pushing her way through the gathering onlookers. 'Mother!' she called. 'What are you doing?'

'She's trying to get something for nothing, that's what she's doing!' The cooked meat man recognised Nell and added, 'Oh, it's you. It's your ma again.'

'I'm sorry, sir,' Nell said. 'She only had enough

for meat pies.' She opened her purse, took out more money and raised a smile. 'Mother enjoyed your pork so much the other night she must have decided to have it today as well.'

'That's all right, then,' he said, accepting the coins.

Nell took one of the bread-cakes and someone in the queue said, 'G'morning, Mrs Goodman, how are you today?' Mabel recognised her and went over to chat. She was a neighbour, but as soon as she'd been served she hurried off home with her bread-cakes. Nell led Mabel over to a low wall and they sat down to eat their dinner.

Afterwards, Nell wanted to talk to Mrs Wainwright again but Mother looked tired. 'Shall we go home for a cup of tea?' she suggested.

'Yes, please, love,' Mabel answered readily. 'That man was nasty to me.'

'It wasn't your fault, Mother. It was mine because I didn't give you enough money. He was all right with you in the end, wasn't he?'

Mabel was upset and didn't reply. However, the incident was forgotten by the time they reached home. Nell had already decided that, once Mother was settled by the range with a cup of tea, she would go back to the market with some more clothes for the second-hand stall and another chat with Mrs Wainwright.

Stall holders called out to each other as they packed away. It had been a good day and they were tired. Most had handcarts and were helped by children: sons and daughters or younger brothers and sisters, fractious and hungry for their tea. A few local lads hung around to earn sixpence from the likes of Mrs Wainwright, who was on her own until her eldest arrived with his horse and cart.

'Oh, it's you again,' the older lady said. 'Have you found anything yet?'

Nell shook her head. 'Would I have to have proper training for Wilmot Grange?'

Mrs Wainwright stopped stacking boots into an old tea chest. 'You would if you want to be a parlourmaid. The housekeeper is very fussy. Cook is just as particular but she likes her kitchen maids trained in her ways. If you've got gumption and show promise, she'll take you on and Lady Clarissa won't argue with her. Even the butler doesn't cross swords with Cook.'

Nell remembered how the maid had been terrified of Cook's reaction when she had been faced with Master Devlin's luggage. Also, the mention of George Wilmot's butler caused Nell to waver. Mr Paget had already taken against her. She wondered how long she would last when Mr Paget found out about her, assuming Cook took her on in the first place. However, the notion that Cook would give her proper training appealed to Nell. Given her present situation, she had little choice anyway. If the work was there and she could do it, why not try? Eddie Wainwright was in a very lowly position at the Grange and he seemed happy enough.

'The thing is,' Nell said, 'I couldn't live in. I can't leave Mother, you see.'

'Yes, I do see that. If you want work at the Grange you'd have to live nearer than in town.'

'We're in a brewery house at the moment, so

we've got to get out anyway.' Nell noticed Mrs Wainwright frown but didn't stop to explain further. She went on, 'I've thought about it already. If I find rooms for us near the omnibus, I'd only have the walk at the end.' It was a long way in all weathers but at least she might hitch a ride with an early-morning carter.

Mrs Wainwright shook her head. 'The first omnibus is for taking folk into town to the factories, not bringing them out to the Grange. You won't get there for six in the morning.'

No wonder Cook was desperate, Nell thought. And now, so was she. Her face fell. 'Oh,' she responded, 'I'll have to try for a maid's position on the Moorgate Road instead.' She wasn't very hopeful. If she couldn't live in she'd just be offered the 'rough work' on a daily basis. That meant cleaning out fire grates and scrubbing floors.

Mrs Wainwright continued, 'You could try nearer us for somewhere to live. In my grandmother's day, it was always Keppel village that provided extra hands in the big house when they needed them. So when Fitzkeppel Hall went to rack and ruin so did our village. We're the wrong side of the estate for the new terraces and the omnibus. All the young men left to find homes nearer the pits and steel works and the girls followed them. So, if it is rooms you're after, there's plenty'll be pleased to have you in Keppel.'

'Keppel? That's a long way from town. I don't know what Mother would say to that. She likes coming in to the high street for the shops.'

'Yes, well, you'll have to stop her doing that, won't you? Before the magistrate does.'

156

Nell blinked. Mrs Wainwright didn't mince her words. She was right, of course, but what would Mother do all day on her own with nowhere to go?

'It won't work,' Nell said. 'She'll come looking for me at the Grange.'

'The vicar's wife can keep her occupied, that's if you're church? We haven't a chapel in our village. You'd have to walk to–'

'We're church,' Nell interrupted. 'Mother looks forward to putting on her best frock and going to the morning service on Sundays.' She'd meet new friends, Nell thought, and be well away from the high street shops and the sergeant. Understanding as he was, he couldn't ignore her behaviour for ever; and neither could Nell. This might be the answer for her! She experienced a shiver of anticipation and said, 'Perhaps I ought to ask if Cook will see me first.'

'She generally comes into Keppel of a Wednesday afternoon and has a cuppa at the tearooms before she goes back. Can you get over there?'

'Yes,' Nell answered without hesitation, although she had no idea how.

'I'll leave a couple of addresses for lodgings with Mr Wainwright. If you bring your mother with you on Wednesday, you could take a look. My lad will bring you back when he comes for me at the market.'

'Oh, thank you.'

'It's no trouble, lass. We could do with one or two new faces around. Bring your testimonial.' Mrs Wainwright raised her head and called to her son, 'This lot is ready to load.'

Their conversation was at an end, giving Nell much to think about. Of course, Cook might not want her and if she did, what would happen when Mr Paget found out, or Miss Phoebe? But it was surely worth a try and Nell had to do something quickly. One thing she was certain of was that Mother would not end up in the asylum or the workhouse while she had breath in her body. Every time she thought of it she went cold all over. How dare they even suggest it?

She bought sausages for tea and crossed the town square to go home. Ahead of her, Devlin Wilmot's motor car stood outside Mr Belfor's office. Mr Belfor was a powerful man in this town and he practised his profession from one of the finest stone buildings on the square. A young fellow in a dark suit and stiff white collar was taking a keen interest in the vehicle. Another man joined him and they began talking. Before she reached them, Devlin and Cyril came out of the office building and greeted the other gentlemen. Their attention was taken up by a close examination of every aspect of the motor vehicle and none noticed her approach.

As she walked by, Cyril glanced up to wave to his father, who was looking out of his office window on the first floor. He saw Nell, recognised her and detached himself from the others. 'Not so fast, you!' He caught up with her, grabbed her hand and added, 'Tell me your name.'

Chapter 13

Nell did not wish to speak to Cyril Belfor. His behaviour towards her at the Grange had been abominable and being drunk was no excuse. He had had a chance to apologise later in the day in the boot room and when he had driven past in his father's carriage, but he had chosen to ignore her.

She glanced around. Devlin and his friends were engrossed in the workings of the motor car engine, but Cyril's father seemed to be watching them. She felt like shouting at Cyril to stay away from her, but she did not want to make a scene in the middle of town on market day. None-theless, she ignored his question and tugged at her hand to move on.

He tightened his grip. 'Oh come on, I mean you no harm. Tell me your name.'

'What do you want, Mr Belfor?' she responded.

He grinned at her. 'Meet me in the Green Dragon tonight and I'll tell you.'

She hitched her basket onto her forearm. 'I'm in a hurry, sir.' She noticed, over his shoulder, that Devlin had straightened up and was looking in their direction.

'Cyril,' he called, 'do you want to see this or not?'

'Eight o'clock,' Cyril urged her.

'No thank you,' she said. Devlin had taken a few

steps towards them so she added, 'Your friends are waiting for you.'

'Don't be late,' Cyril persisted.

No thank you, Nell repeated silently to herself. Devlin avoided her eyes but she heard him say, 'What did Nell Goodman want?'

To her astonishment, Cyril replied, 'Me, old boy.'

She didn't hear any more as she quickened her pace, shaking her head unconsciously. She admitted to not having much personal experience of young men and their ways. Her life away from the brewery was taken up by coping with Mother and their home. One or two fellows at the brewery had shown an interest in her, but she hadn't been inspired by them and they soon gave up on her.When she moved to bottle-washing, she listened to the women and girls chattering about their husbands or sweethearts and had to deal with some light-hearted ribaldry from the dray-men. But now that Mother had become more of a problem, few ventured further with her.

Nell supposed that Cyril Belfor was considered 'a good catch' in the marriage market. His father, no doubt, would have big plans for his future and they would not include someone like her as his wife so she could only conclude that his interest in her was immoral. His previous behaviour towards her certainly pointed to that. He wanted a handy plaything – perhaps several – until he settled down with a well-connected and wealthy wife chosen by his powerful father.

There had been stories at school of housemaids who took up with the sons of the household. One became with child and the father wed her. She and her baby had been welcomed into the family. But another one had been shunned and turned out, her lover had no money to take care of her and she had ended up in the workhouse.

It was not a direction that Nell would ever consider, even if it meant remaining a spinster and dying an old maid. There were women living in town who had chosen not to marry but they had private incomes or expensive educations that enabled them to earn a good living. Or, like her, they were prepared to work long hours at anything they could turn their hands to.

As she hurried home she realised that this future was a distinct possibility for her. She could not leave Mother or give a husband the attention he expected, and unless he was established in a trade, he would not be able to afford to keep them both. She was already past the age when many of her contemporaries were settled with husbands, fiancés or sweethearts. She had to find a position.

Nell hurried on, wondering how long it would take her to walk to Keppel on Wednesday. It wasn't even near to a railway station. The only way to get there was by horse or ... one of the young men who had been admiring Devlin Wilmot's car whizzed by on his bicycle. A bicycle! Perhaps she could borrow one? But not many girls she knew owned them as they were expensive to buy.

She overtook a neighbour and exchanged a greeting and a word about the market.

'Did your mother find you all right?' the neighbour asked.

'Find me?' Nell queried.

'About half an hour ago,' her neighbour went on. 'She said she was going to look for you in the market.'

Nell frowned. 'How on earth did I miss her?' She craned her neck and scanned the knots of people making their way home. She began to retrace her steps and broke into a run when she saw Mabel walking towards her on the arm of a tall, broad-shouldered young man that she did not recognise.

'Thank you, Mr...?' she said.

'Joe Wainwright,' he said, and she saw immediately that he had his mother's shrewd brown eyes. He smiled at her and inclined his head in a courteous acknowledgement.

'Nice man,' Mabel commented after he had returned to his mother. 'He reminded me of your father. He was a nice man too.' She went quiet and Nell realised that her mother was tired. She leaned heavily on Nell's arm as they walked. Nell slowed her pace. The sun had set but it wasn't yet dark, although clouds were gathering and Nell wanted them both to be indoors before it started to rain. She patted her mother's hand and said, 'He lives in Keppel. We're going to look at a house there next week.'

'Has it got a garden?'

'I don't know until we see it.' And how are we going to get there? she wondered. Even if she could borrow a bicycle, it wasn't an option for Mother. 'It's not in town, so I expect it has,' she answered.

'Is it in the country? All the best people move

to the country.'

'Would you like that, Mother?'

'Oh yes, as long as the coal man goes there.'

The coal man! Of course! The coal man went everywhere because everybody needed coal. He was bound to go out to Keppel with his big shire horse and cart. However, she couldn't imagine Mabel taking kindly to being asked to sit on a pile of coal sacks in her best frock. And what colour would her skirt be when she arrived to talk to the cook from the Grange?

The first drops of rain fell on her head. She took off her shawl and wrapped it around her mother's head and shoulders. 'Can you hurry, Mother? We'll shelter under the chestnut tree at the cross-roads if it gets any worse.' Nell bowed her head ineffectually against the shower and, as she did, she heard the rumble of a motor vehicle behind her and turned to see Devlin Wilmot's phaeton. 'Best stand well back against the hedge, Mother,' she said. 'We don't want to get splashed.' They huddled together as the vehicle approached.

'I saw that earlier in the town square,' Mabel commented and watched it rumble along the road.

It was an attractive vehicle with dark green coachwork and two enormous lamps at the front, but Nell kept her eyes lowered so as not to make any sign of contact with the driver.

'Can you see who it is, Nell?' Mabel asked, stepping forward.

Nell pulled her back. 'Be careful, Mother.'

'Well, he's all muffled up,' Mabel muttered. 'I can't see who it is. Oh look, he's stopping.'

The vehicle drew to a halt but the engine rumbled on and the driver had to raise his voice above the noise. 'Good evening, Nell,' he said. 'Although I'm afraid it is not. You will surely not refuse a ride in my motor now? I have an umbrella you can use.'

Nell's immediate response was to send him on his way as she had done before, but she had Mother with her now and the rain was getting worse. She replied, 'My mother would be very grateful for a loan of your umbrella, sir.'

He climbed down from the driving seat and walked to the back of the motor car, where he opened the small gate and let down the step. 'I should be very happy to take you and your mother wherever you wish to go.'

'Oh yes, please do, young man,' Mabel answered and walked towards him.

Devlin Wilmot was helping her to climb in before Nell could stop either of them. When Mother was settled and holding the umbrella, he reached out a gauntlet-covered hand towards Nell. She remained where she was, feeling cornered and irritated by his actions.

He gazed directly at her and said, 'I was celebrating and the worse for drink. I behaved badly and should like to make it up to you.' He stretched his extended arm further.

She stood perfectly still. Did he think that giving her a ride in his motor carriage made up for humiliating and frightening her?

He added, 'I am also getting wet, as indeed you are, too.'

'Hurry up, Nell,' her mother called.

'Very well,' she muttered. She allowed Devlin to help her up the steps and close the gate behind her.

'Where to?' he asked as he climbed into the driving seat.

She gave him their address. Mabel had already found another umbrella and Nell put it up against the rain. Devlin Wilmot squeezed his klaxon and the motor carriage jolted forward.

Nell thought her mother would be frightened, but she was quite the opposite and her eyes shone with excitement. When they arrived home, a few net curtains twitched and a neighbour actually came out of his house in an oilskin to watch as Devlin Wilmot helped them down. He had taken off his gauntlets and goggles and his face glowed from exposure to the cold rain. Nell wondered if hers looked the same.

Mabel, whose skin remained as pale as porcelain whatever the weather, was extremely reluctant to climb down. She sat, prettily and proudly, clutching the umbrella and said, 'Isn't this lovely, Nell?'

'It is, Mother, but we must go in for our tea now.'

Devlin Wilmot stood on the motor carriage step to help Mabel down. 'Would you like to go for a drive in the country one day, Mrs Goodman?' he asked, adding, 'When the weather is more clement.'

'Why, that is very kind of you, sir. Isn't that kind of the gentleman, Nell?' Mabel allowed him to take the umbrella and help her down.

Nell was cross. Clearly, Mabel did not know

165

who he was and he had used her mother's innocence to take advantage of the situation. Nell thought it best if Mabel did not know he was a Wilmot and replied, 'It is, Mother, but the gentleman is far too busy–'

'Not at all, Nell, I am sure you will wish to accompany your mother.' He lowered his voice and leaned forward to whisper in Nell's ear. 'Please let me do this, by way of apology.'

Nell gritted her teeth. She would rather not be reminded of that unpleasant incident and remained silent. The delay was foolish because Mabel answered for her. 'We shall be pleased to accept, sir.'

'Mother!'

But Mabel was already walking to the front door and Devlin Wilmot followed her with the umbrella. Nell thought quickly. If this was simply a ruse to turn her into another Lottie, she was having none of it. But if he was truly sorry for his inexcusable behaviour, then there was hope for him yet and she could turn the offer to her advantage.

She unlocked the front door and let her mother inside before she said, 'Very well, sir. My mother and I should like to visit Keppel next Wednesday afternoon.'

He smiled at her and, close up to him, she noticed the crinkles at the corners of his hazel eyes and how white his teeth appeared against his reddened skin.

'I shall call for you at two o'clock. I have rugs for your knees but remember to bring scarves for your hats.' He hurried away through the rain and

Nell went indoors to dry out in the kitchen.

'Such a nice gentleman,' Mabel commented as she removed her wet shoes. 'He knew my name.'

'Yes,' Nell agreed automatically as she put the frying pan on the hotplate.

Over the next few days, Mabel occupied herself deciding on her dress for the motor carriage drive and, as the rain clouds didn't last, Nell cleared the wash house in the back yard. She found some workmen's tools that she sold to a neighbour but the wash-house tubs, dolly and mangle had to stay until they left.

During the day, Nell felt optimistic about the future. It was only at night that she lay awake worrying about how foolish she was even to think of working at the Grange, let alone living within a stone's throw. It occurred to her that when George Wilmot found out, as indeed he would, he would assume she was flaunting her situation in his face.

Perhaps she was, she reflected. She could have said no to Mrs Wainwright's idea, but why should she? She had to live and work somewhere or both she and Mother would be in the workhouse, so why not at the Grange if there was a position? Yet in the chill of the night before dawn started to break, she conceded to herself that she might be asking for more trouble.

In the morning she forgot her misgivings as she was more concerned about her lack of testimonial. She was too proud to ask Miss Wilmot at the brewery so she decided to show Cook her school-leaving report instead, which was good.

She did experience a pang of regret when she thought about her time at the brewery. She had enjoyed working in the office, and knew how most of Wilmot's operated. It seemed such a shame to waste all that.

However, she wasn't sorry to leave bottle-washing behind her, which, if she was honest, she had found boring even though she had made some good friends there. She missed them, she realised, and if she moved to Keppel it would be difficult to keep in touch. However, there would be new friends to be made at the Grange, she decided, and this cheered her.

Mabel's excitement at the prospect of a drive in a motor carriage grew more intense as the time drew near. When she was ready, in her best blue costume, with a muslin scarf tied under her chin to secure her best wide-brimmed hat, she sat in a chair by the front window. Nell locked up the back and checked she had everything in her small carpet bag. She had dressed carefully to impress the Grange cook and looked quite severe in a dark skirt, long jacket and white blouse with floppy bow at the high neck. She stood in the middle of the front parlour thinking that she looked more like a governess than a kitchen assistant.

'A nip of brandy,' Mabel stated. 'You have to have a nip of brandy before you leave to keep out the cold.'

'Well, *we* don't, Mother,' Nell responded with a smile. 'It's summer and anyway we shall not venture far.' Nonetheless, Nell could have downed a tot. She was feeling increasingly nervous as the clock on the mantelpiece ticked away the minutes. When she heard the rumble of the motor engine in the road, she experienced an unusual trembling in her throat. This is a mistake, she thought as the fluttering strengthened to a thumping in her chest.

Mabel was already opening the front door so Nell quelled her misgivings and determined that her mother, at least, would enjoy the afternoon. She realised quickly that Devlin Wilmot was of the same mind for he was so charming and attentive towards Mabel, she almost forgot his previous appalling behaviour, but not quite. Two sides of the same coin, she decided, as she watched him help Mother into the back of the phaeton and tuck a woollen rug around her knees.

He offered Nell a helping hand from aloft and half hoisted her aboard, seating her facing her mother and handing her a matching rug. 'Keppel, wasn't it, Nell?' he asked.

'That's right, sir,' she replied. 'I should like to be there for three o'clock.'

They didn't travel much faster than a horse and cart, although it was more comfortable, even when it jolted and went around corners. Nell moved across to sit next to her mother in case she fell over as she adjusted to the speed. However, Mabel was thoroughly enjoying herself, even more so because of the attention the vehicle received as they drove through the terraced streets towards the countryside. The motor carriage was able to deal with hills better than horses, Nell thought.

Devlin stopped at the crest of one climb, half turned and called to them, 'This is a fine view, don't you think? You can see the town parish church behind you and the spire of Keppel church through the trees ahead.' The engine juddered into silence and he lowered his voice. 'If you care to stretch your legs, you can see the Grange from that brow.'

Mabel sat up and twisted her head around. 'Where?' she demanded. 'Is that Wilmot Grange, where George lives? Can we drive there instead of Keppel? I want to speak to George.'

Devlin Wilmot pushed up his goggles. 'Do you know my father well?' he asked.

Nell interrupted swiftly. 'We haven't enough time today, Mother.' She had raised her voice unnecessarily and glanced at Devlin. 'Please take us straight to Keppel, sir.'

'But I wish to speak to George,' Mabel insisted.

'Another day, Mother. We are expected for tea in Keppel.'

'Are we? Who do we know in Keppel?'

'Mrs Wainwright from the market, from the boot and shoe stall.'

'Oh yes. Shall we have scones?'

'And jam. We may even have strawberry jam. The crop was good this year. Do you remember seeing them in the market?'

'Strawberry jam is my favourite.'

'Mine too.'

Devlin Wilmot had climbed down to crank the engine into life. When he was back in his driving seat he called over his shoulder, 'Keppel it is, Mrs Goodman. Off we go.'

The motor car jolted forward and it was too noisy to explain to Mother that Mrs Wainwright wouldn't be there for tea. Mabel was likely to forget anyway but Nell was sure she would enjoy her visit to the Keppel tearooms.

Chapter 14

The residents of Keppel took far less interest in the motor carriage than Nell's neighbours did. The village was larger and busier than Nell had imagined, with some fine villas on the outskirts, several shops and tradesmen on the main street and an old coaching inn built of mellowed stone. A butcher and game dealer, provisions merchant and draper were thriving.

As they motored through, towards Wainwright's, Nell noticed two bent old ladies come out of the small post office. All villages had post offices, not just for letters and parcels but to pay out the new old-age pension. It was five shillings a week once you'd reached seventy and had been going for over a year now. Well-off ratepayers moaned about the cost but Nell thought it was a good thing because it kept a lot of old folk out of the workhouse.

Wainwright's shop-front came into view next door to an ironmonger and forge.

'Mrs Wainwright's,' Devlin called over his shoulder and shuddered to a halt. As he helped Nell down he added, 'Will four o'clock give you enough time for tea?'

'You need not wait for us.'

'There is no omnibus,' he explained, 'and it is no trouble. I have business at the forge.'

'Thank you for your kindness, sir. I've made

arrangements for our return.'

'I see.' He frowned and added, 'We used to be friends, Nell. You know my name, so could you at least stop calling me "sir"?'

'I don't think so, sir.'

Devlin turned to help Mabel. When she was safely down, he bowed his head formally and added, 'It has been a pleasure. Good day, ladies.'

'Good day, sir,' Nell replied.

He walked in the direction of the forge. Nell was relieved their shared journey was at an end. She didn't want Mother to know who he really was and she didn't want to feel as though she owed him anything. She took her mother's arm and steered her towards Wainwright's.

'Who did you say he was?' Mabel asked. 'I've forgotten already.'

Nell distracted her by drawing attention to a burnished chestnut-coloured saddle that glowed in Wainwright's window. The shop was double fronted and a selection of boots and shoes was displayed in the other window. The inside smelled of leather and wax. Behind a wooden counter several shelves held pairs of worn, mended footwear. To one side there was a small display of new shoes and a worn velvet-upholstered chair. Nell rang a small brass bell on the counter and a middle-aged man in shirtsleeves, waistcoat and leather apron came through a door from the back. Nell introduced herself and he bent down to retrieve two folded sheets of paper from under the counter.

He handed them to her and said, 'Be here at half past four and our Joe will take you back to town in the wagon.'

'Thank you, Mr Wainwright. Can you tell me where the tearooms are?'

'Tearooms? Oh, you mean Miller's. They're in the back of the grocer's shop.'

One of the notes listed three addresses where she might find rooms. Nell decided to wait until after she had spoken to Cook from the Grange before she looked at them. The other was a letter of introduction 'to whom it may concern' vouching for Nell as known to Mrs Wainwright, which Nell thought was a really kind and thoughtful thing to do for her.

A shiver of anticipation ran through her. This really was a new direction in her life and, whatever the outcome, Nell felt confident that this was the right one for her.

Mabel was enchanted by the cottages in Keppel. Some were stone with thatched roofs and others were brick and slate terraces similar to their own. The difference here was that most had front gardens full of flowers and vegetables. There were large houses, too, double-fronted with wrought-iron railings and paved paths up to the front door.

Mabel wanted to go inside the draper's shop and Nell, too, was tempted by the cloth and notions displayed in his window. But she had no spare money to spend and was anxious not to miss meeting with Cook from the Grange.

'Miller & Son, Groceries and Provisions' shouted from a sign above the shop. The dim interior was lit by oil lamps and her footsteps echoed on a black and white tiled floor. Sure enough, a doorway on the left led to what must have once been a living room but was now furnished with a small tables and chairs. White cloths and pretty china gave the place a genteel ambience, which Mabel clearly adored. Two young women, dressed similarly in cotton dresses of light green, sat with their heads close together in whispered conversation. Nell recognised their uniform from the Grange.

She took a table near to them and a waitress about her own age came to take her order. However, Nell thought that the waitress didn't quite fit the atmosphere of quiet gentility. Her skirt, though black, was above her ankles, showing off white stockings and shoes with heels. She wore a fussy pleated white lace blouse with a low neck that showed off her ample bosom and was more suited for evening. Her fair hair was done up in swathes and coils with ringlets draping her neck and she had rouge on her lips. Nell thought that her frilly white apron seemed, somehow, out of place. If she was typical of Keppel, then it was certainly no backwater! It even crossed Nell's mind that the waitress resembled one of the ladies of the night that frequented the Crown on a Saturday night.

She was a touch off-hand when she took the order, as though she didn't want to serve them, but she had a pretty, if insincere, smile, and brought them strawberry jam for the scones. The tea was good, too. As Nell poured it, an older woman came in, acknowledged the two parlour maids with a nod and sat in the far corner. Nell leaned across to the young women.

'Excuse me,' she whispered to them, 'is that Cook from the Grange?'

They nodded and went back to their conversation. Cook's tray of tea appeared as if by magic and the contrast between her and the waitress was marked.

Cook was straight-backed and slender, in a dark blue silk afternoon dress and small blue felt hat. Her grey hair was drawn into a simple bun at the nape of her neck. She had a gracious air about her and could easily have been taken for a lady. Nell ate her cucumber sandwiches and gave her scone to Mabel. Then she took out her letter from Mrs Wainwright and went across to Cook's table.

'Excuse me, ma'am. I am told you might be looking for a kitchen assistant at the Grange.'

Cook sat back in her chair. 'I am. And you are?'

'Nell Goodman, ma'am. I am available for work and I have a letter of introduction.'

Cook did not take the sheet of paper from her. She said 'You are too old, Miss Goodman. I am looking for someone to train.'

'I am very willing to learn, ma'am, and I am a hard worker.'

'I do not doubt that and I am sure you have already learned a great deal, which is why you are not suitable.'

'But I haven't worked in service before,' Nell explained. 'I have done clerical work.'

Cook looked at her for a second. 'Well, that is in your favour, but I am offering an apprenticeship, Miss Goodman.'

Nell stared at her, unwilling to give up. An apprenticeship meant seven years learning the craft.

She would have to pay a premium and buy her uniforms. She would be nearly thirty before she earned a decent wage. She simply could not afford it.

'Oh, I see.'

Cook was very gracious with her. She said, 'I am sorry, Miss Goodman. I hope you find a position to suit you.'

At that moment the waitress came up to the table and said, 'Is this lady bothering you, Cook?'

Cook replied, 'No, Charlotte. Thank you.' She frowned slightly at the waitress and stared at her in silence until she moved away. Then she seemed to change her mind about Nell and took the papers from her. She glanced over them, 'If you really want to go into service I can pass these to the housekeeper at the Grange; with your permission, of course?'

'Oh yes, ma'am,' Nell agreed readily. 'Thank you, I am much obliged to you.' She went back to her table where Mabel was trying to decide which cake to eat from the selection in front of her.

'Which one are you having?' Mabel asked.

'You choose first, Mother,' Nell said and smiled.

'I can't,' Mabel wailed.

Nell selected a Viennese whirl for her mother and a lemon curd tart for herself.

She didn't hold out any hope for work at the Grange. Even if the housekeeper took her on, Mr Paget would soon spot her and have her out. But she liked Keppel; some of the houses reminded her of the properties on the Moorgate Road in town that kept live-in servants.

The draper's shop stocked cloth for uniforms, and Nell thought they might know of a vacancy. She left Mabel enjoying a fresh pot of tea for a few minutes to enquire, and came back with the name and address of a gentleman.

Mabel had let her tea go cold and nodded off in her chair. Nell chewed on her lip. She couldn't leave her here but Mother was clearly too tired to follow Nell around as she enquired about a position. She allowed her to slumber on while she waited for the waitress to appear with her bill.

The Grange parlour maids and Cook had left. Nell went to the open door at the back, said, 'Excuse me,' and peeped in. It was a large homely kitchen containing a pinewood table spread with the ingredients and utensils for making afternoon teas. A dresser holding the china filled one of the walls. Charlotte was standing by the cooking range at the far end engaged in an intimate conversation with a young man. Their heads were very close together as she whispered furiously.

The fellow was Devlin Wilmot and, as Nell took in the intimate scene, one or two pieces of information suddenly fell into place. She raised her voice and called, 'Excuse me, Lottie, may I have my bill?'

Devlin's head swivelled in her direction and his expression turned from surprise to discomfort. *Caught in the act,* she thought, and stifled a chuckle. 'I should like my bill now,' she repeated.

Charlotte stepped away from Devlin, smoothed down her bodice and apron and replied, 'Be with you in a minute, miss.'

Nell went back to her seat and roused Mabel, who blinked and drank her tepid cup of tea. When Charlotte came through she explained, 'Your bill has been settled, miss. We're closing now.'

Nell was astounded. A full afternoon tea with an extra pot on top! 'May I enquire who has paid it?' she asked.

'Oh, I can't say, miss. Does it matter?'

'Yes, it does. I am in someone's debt and I don't know who.' She had a good idea. But why would Devlin do that if he was canoodling with this Lottie? It didn't make sense to her, or any difference to her low opinion of him.

'Well, you can't pay the debt if you don't know, can you?' Charlotte shrugged.

Nell didn't argue with her logic. She replied, 'Then please thank the gentleman – or lady – for me.'

Charlotte held open the door for Nell and Mabel as they left, locked it after them and pulled down the blind. Her haste to close up made Nell chuckle again and this cheered Mabel as well, who had decided that the waitress was 'a right floozy'.

Mabel was too tired to traipse with Nell to a villa outside the village looking for a position, even though Nell knew she would enjoy visiting a big house. Anyway, she thought, I need my letter of introduction, and she hoped the housekeeper would post it to her soon.

They walked past the shops again and Mabel commented, 'This is a nice village, isn't it?' Nell agreed and decided to write to the gentleman about the position and secure a proper interview. The church clock chimed a quarter past the hour and she noticed a horse and cart being led from the track at the side of Wainwright's.

Joe Wainwright was dressed in shirtsleeves and waistcoat, dusty from a day's toiling in his father's workshop. He helped them into the cart where they sat beside wooden chests to carry home the boots and shoes, then he saw to the horse. Mabel moved into the corner, leaned back and closed her eyes. It had been an exciting day for her. Nell wrapped a rug around her knees and let her doze.

As they waited to move off, Nell heard the phaeton crank into life further up the street and a few minutes later it rumbled past with Cook from the Grange sitting upright and stately in the seat where Mabel had sat. Devlin glanced in their direction but that was all. Cook inclined her head in an acknowledgement as she rode by and Nell responded.

Joe noticed and commented, 'Ma told me why you were here. Any luck?'

'I'm afraid not. I'm too old for the position at the Grange, but the draper told me that a gentleman out on the Barnsley Road needs a housekeeper.'

'That must be old Ferguson again. Retired farmer, he is. You need a good heart to take him on. He worked his late wife into the ground and nobody stays with him longer than six months.'

'Why's that, then?'

Joe lifted the reins over the horse's neck, climbed up into the driving seat and answered cryptically: 'It's not for me to say.'

Nell's imagination ran riot. You heard all sorts

of stories about goings-on in isolated houses, and she had Mabel to think of as well. 'Oh, but you must tell me if it's something I should know. Mother will have to live there as well.'

Joe stared ahead and was silent for a couple of minutes, which seemed like a long time to Nell. 'I need to know, Joe,' she prompted.

He spoke at last. 'Well, he's mean, you see. He'll probably charge you for your mother's board and lodging, even if she helps out. He never believes what things cost these days and he ends up accusing his housekeepers of stealing from him. It's the same with all of 'em. That's why they leave.'

'Oh.' Keppel was not quite as idyllic as Nell had first thought. But she could keep proper accounts and if she lasted six months it was better than nothing. Except that there'd probably be no testimonial again and she really needed one.

'Will you drive by the house on your way to town?'

'Barnsley Road is the other way, miss. Sorry.' He flicked the reins and called to the horse to 'gee-up'. 'It's a pity about the Grange not working out. Mind you, even Lottie didn't get a look-in there.'

'Did she want the position with Cook?'

'Well, she already does baking for the tearooms and her father was prepared to pay the premium but my ma says Cook wouldn't touch her with a barge pole.'

Nell believed that. She remembered the frostiness between Cook and the waitress earlier. 'Anyway, her mother wants her in the tearooms,' Joe went on. 'We get the carriage trade out here, you know, well-off folk come a long way for a pair of my father's bespoke riding boots.'

But, Nell knew, ordinary mortals bought their boots and shoes ready made from a shop in town that had a small factory in its back yard. Or from Wainwright's market stall where a second-hand pair would be cheaper and last longer. 'Do you work with your father, Joe?' she asked.

'I'm a master craftsman and my kid brother is my apprentice.'

'That's not Eddie, is it?'

'No, not our Eddie. He started in the workshop but he wanted to be out rabbiting with his mates all the time. He's better off where he is.'

'He didn't seem to mind being sent over to the stables at the Grange when I was there.'

'Gets on with the animals, does our Eddie. I miss him looking after our Nellie.' He glanced sideways at Nell, and she noticed alarm in his eyes, and his mouth twitched. When he saw her smile, he smiled too and inclined his head towards the horse. 'This is our Nellie.'

'She's lovely,' Nell said. 'Have you got any sisters?'

'Two. They help Mother in the house now they've finished school. Have you got any brothers and sisters?'

'Sadly no. My father died when I was a baby and Mother never remarried.'

'I see.'

Nell wasn't sure what he saw, but he fell silent as the horse plodded on. He took them along a farm track to town, which was a short cut. Horseback riders used it and several men on bicycles. A bicycle! She remembered. That's what she needed if there wasn't an omnibus and wondered again how much they cost.

Market day was always busy and noisy and today was no exception. Carriages, carts and even motor wagons were entangled in the town square so Joe was late arriving at his mother's market stall. Nonetheless, he turned to Nell and said, 'Wait there. I'll just unload these boxes for Mother then I'll take you straight home.'

'You don't have to do that, Joe. We can walk from here?'

'Your mother is tired, Nell. Leave her be for a few more minutes.'

What a nice kind man, Nell thought. She watched him greeting his mother and exchanging a few words. He was an attractive man, too; strong as well as tall and with thick brown hair and regular features. Handsome, some might say. Mrs Wainwright waved an acknowledgement to Nell as Joe came back to the cart and then they trundled on to Nell's home.

When they were standing on their front doorstep and had thanked Joe for his generosity, he said, 'Did you like Keppel?'

'Oh yes,' Mabel answered. 'We're going to live there.'

'Only if I can get a position,' Nell explained to her.

'My mother will keep an eye out for something better than Ferguson's,' Joe went on. He paused a moment, then added, 'So will I.'

Mabel went indoors but Nell stayed on the front step until he had turned around his horse and cart and disappeared down the road. He has a lovely smile, she thought, and intriguing eyes. They were dark and deep set, giving him a mysterious air, and a shiver of excitement ran through her. No doubt she would run into him again sometime and she looked forward to that.

Nell wrote two letters: one to the housekeeper at the Grange apologising for wasting her time and requesting the return of her documents. The other was to Mr Ferguson, offering her services as his housekeeper. She gave brief details about herself, assuring him that, should he wish to interview her, she would furnish him with all the information he required.

She considered delivering the letters by hand, at least as far as Keppel village. Now she knew the short cut across the fields she wouldn't have to go into town and out again on the main roads. If she worked out a way through the sprawling brick terraces, she would surely find the track that Joe had used? Nonetheless, it was still several miles and she was reluctant to leave Mother for long. Instead, Nell suggested to Mabel that they walk into town at the end of next market day to pick up a few bargains and ask Mrs Wainwright to take the letters for her. And, Nell mused to herself, she might see Joe again. Meanwhile, there was much to do, clearing and cleaning cupboards and selling items they no longer needed. Mabel seemed much better now that Nell was home with her all the time. She was calmer and more cheerful, although she asked constantly when they were moving to 'that nice place with the tearoom'.

If the house was peaceful, Mabel was less forgetful and spoke quite rationally of her early years when Father was alive. Nell had heard these stories as a child and believed them to be true and, although she did not remember herself, she knew that Mother and Father had lived in the 'big house' when she was a baby. An elderly neighbour, now passed on, had confirmed this once to Nell when she was growing up. It seemed that George Wilmot had been involved with Father in some way and he had been helpful to Mabel and Nell over the years. So why did Mabel think the worst of him?

Chapter 15

They were sharing a pot of tea at the kitchen table when the sergeant called round at the back door. Concerned, Nell hurried to let him in.

'Is something wrong, sir?' she asked.

'Nay, lass. I'm just on my way home and I thought I'd drop in to see how you were getting on. I heard you'd left the brewery.'

'Miss Wilmot insisted.'

'Aye, strong-willed like her ma, that one is.'

'Would you like a cup of tea? I've just mashed it.'

'Don't mind if I do.' He took off his distinctive helmet exposing his thinning grey hair, undid the top two buttons of his tunic, and drew out a chair.

Mabel was pleased to see him. She had known him most of her life and for the first time Nell realised that the sergeant was several years older than Mother.

'Did you know Miss Wilmot's mother?' Nell queried.

'I knew all the ale-house keepers in those days,' he replied. 'Phoebe's ma inherited the inn and its brewhouse as a young woman. An old couple ran it for her and then she took on young Mabel from the workhouse.'

Nell's eyes swivelled to her mother. Mabel didn't care to be reminded of her workhouse days and looked alarmed. Nell quickly changed the subject: 'Pass the jam tarts to the sergeant, Mother. Do try one, sir,' she urged. 'Mother made them herself this afternoon.'

The sergeant bit into the delicate pastry and finished the tart in two mouthfuls. 'Very nice. You haven't lost your touch with pastry, Mabel.'

Mabel smiled. 'Harold liked my baking. George did, too. He said he'd marry me if it weren't for Harold.'

Nell's eyebrows went up and she exchanged a glance with the sergeant.

'George Wilmot lived in the inn at the time,' he explained. 'Your father was ten years younger than him but they struck up a partnership.'

'How well did you know my father, sir?' Nell asked.

'Harold? He was honest and hardworking, a well-respected carter. He started off with a donkey cart. Do you remember Harold's donkey, Mabel?'

Mabel did. 'Donkey? I could drive a donkey cart. Harold showed me. George was jealous of him because he was so handsome.'

'Aye,' the sergeant agreed, 'he was a fine-looking fellow.'

'George Wilmot killed him, you know. It was all his fault.'

Mabel didn't sound angry and Nell noticed her eyes were filling with tears.

'We had a lovely afternoon in Keppel recently, sir,' she said quickly. 'Mother, tell the sergeant about the tearoom in Keppel.' But Mabel looked puzzled so Nell went on, 'If I can find a domestic position there I think it would suit Mother to be away from town.'

The sergeant nodded in approval. 'It's a long way out, though, and no omnibus to get you to market.'

'There's a short cut across the fields and I'll save up for a bicycle.'

'Bicycle, eh? I hope you don't turn into one of them suffragettes. They're causing a right rumpus in Sheffield. Have you read about what they're doing?'

'No, I haven't. Do you think I should know?'

'Not if you're going to live in a nice little backwater like Keppel.'

'We had tea in Keppel,' Mabel said, 'with strawberry jam.'

'Yes we did.' Nell smiled, pleased that she had recalled it. She thought it strange that Mabel could remember details of her life over twenty years ago but forgot what she'd done last week.

The sergeant drained his cup and refused a top-up. 'My good lady will have tea waiting. I only dropped in to see how you were doing.'

Nell walked to the front door with him and

said, 'I should like to ask you more about my father if I may. I'm never really sure that what Mother says is ... is, well, always accurate.'

'Maybe it's best forgotten, lass,' the sergeant said and pulled on his helmet.

Best for whom? Nell wondered as she held open the front door. She considered that the sergeant knew much more about the early days of the inn and the brewhouse than he was prepared to divulge. And as some of it concerned her late father she wanted to know.

'I'll call again if you've no objection,' he added.

'None at all,' she answered, 'thank you, sir.'

Mother had come through to the front room. She stood at the window and watched the sergeant walk away. 'He came to the inn every night for a jar of ale,' Mabel said. 'He always asked me if I was all right.'

'Why? Did you have any trouble at that inn?'

'Only the Missus. She had stallions. I caught her at it one morning.'

Stallions? Nell was puzzled until it dawned on her what Mother was saying and her mouth opened. Then her eyes widened as Mabel went on, 'She was after Harold an' all, when he moved in.'

'Father lived at the inn?'

'She fell for George, though, and he wed her, thank goodness.' Mabel began to wave her hand in the air. 'What was her name, you know, the Missus, she had a fancy name, what was it?'

'Do you mean Phoebe's mother?'

'That's her! A right trollop she was; mucky an' all.'

'Mother!' Nell's exasperation was gentle. 'Don't

187

say things like that.'

'It's true! And they stole your father's barley wine. Oh, I enjoyed a glass of Harold's barley wine of an evening. Will you make me some, Nell love, in the wash house?' Mabel stood up and went into scullery. 'Where do you keep the stuff?'

Nell followed her. 'What stuff, Mother?'

'You know, the...' She waved her hands in the air. '...for brewing beer.'

'I've never made beer, Mother,' Nell explained.

'Not in the wash house?' Mabel was disappointed.

Nell shook her head. 'I can nip out to the Crown and buy you a bottle.'

'George stole it, you know. He stole it from us.'

Nell suppressed a sigh and put her arm around Mabel's shoulders. 'Let's have a look and see what we have in the pantry for supper, shall we?'

'I'm not hungry.'

Neither was Nell because she had eaten too many jam tarts with the sergeant, but Mabel was easily distracted.

The local mission hall had started to do a hot pie and pea dinner on two days a week for the old folk. They weren't free, but the mission ladies only charged for the cost of the food and most seventy-year-olds had a pension nowadays. They looked forward to the company and a neighbour suggested to Nell that Mabel might enjoy it, too. She offered to take her for dinner and then back to her own house for a cup of tea so that Nell could spend an afternoon in town without too much worry. Nell was grateful and Mabel dressed herself up for the occasion.

Nell set off for market with her letters and her shopping bag. She was disappointed she couldn't stay until the end of the day and see Joe, but at least she would have the chance to speak to Mrs Wainwright again.

Mrs Wainwright waved and beckoned her over as soon as she spotted her. Nell hurried over, reaching into her bag for the letters.

'I was hoping you'd be in town today,' the older lady began. 'The housekeeper from the Grange called into our shop about you.'

'I wasn't suitable for Cook but she took my papers away with her.'

'Yes,' she said. 'The housekeeper wanted to know more about you.'

'Did she? What did you tell her?'

'That you are a steady young woman, capable in a crisis. Don't look so surprised! Everybody says that about you and that they don't know how your mother would manage without you.'

'Thank you.'

'Well, she knows you don't want to live in, but she said that didn't matter. Anyway she's going to see you.' Mrs Wainwright seemed pleased about this.

'Oh.' Nell felt she couldn't now tell Mrs Wainwright there was no point as Mr Paget would never take her on. Her hand was still inside her shopping bag, clutching the letters. 'That's good,' she said, 'and I've written to Mr Ferguson as well.'

'Joe told me about that. Ferguson's a mean old skinflint. You don't want to go there.'

'I might have to,' Nell said with a frown, thinking, The Grange won't take me on when they know about me, and even if they do I shan't last long. At least Mr Ferguson can provide a roof over our heads.

'Well, talk to the Grange housekeeper first. She said she'd write to you.' Mrs Wainwright turned her attention to her customers.

Nell let go of her letters. She'd rather explain her situation to the housekeeper face to face – it was probably best that way – and invest in a stamp for Mr Ferguson's letter. She moved away from the stall and as she did Mrs Wainwright called after her, 'I'll tell my Joe you dropped by.'

Nell's worried face broke into an involuntary smile. She could put up with any number of Mr Fergusons if she had Joe as a friend in Keppel. She did her shopping in the market then gazed in the windows of the high street shops before it was time to go back for her mother. She put away the shopping and went round to her neighbour's for Mabel, who had enjoyed her afternoon and chattered on in a disjointed way as they walked the short distance home. Mabel wasn't hungry after her pie and pea dinner so Nell ate her own pie alone.

Sure enough, a letter from the Grange arrived asking Nell to present herself to the housekeeper on the following Wednesday afternoon with any testimonials in her possession. That'll settle it, Nell thought. She definitely won't take me on without a reference. The letter advised that a cart took maids on their day off to the omnibus terminus and it would carry her to the Grange on its return.

She explained to her mother that it was an inter-

190

view for a position but did not say where, and Mabel assumed it was in Keppel. Nell was forced to leave her for the day with some mending and furniture polishing, which Mabel enjoyed. She dressed in the same outfit that she'd worn to meet Cook and rehearsed her explanation as she bumped along in the omnibus. She was delighted to see Eddie driving the small horse and cart.

'Oh, it's you,' he said as she climbed up front beside him.

'No boots to clean this afternoon?' she queried.

'Mr Paget sends me to the stables when my work is done. I don't mind. I prefer the horses.'

'Yes, your Joe said you were good with them.'

'Our Joe's good with leather. He knows it better than his own skin, I reckon.'

'Is he in your father's workshop today?'

'He's gone out to the tannery. Father has a new order in from Lady Clarissa. She wants this mauve colour, the same as her gloves.'

Mauve leather gloves and shoes, Nell dreamed. How elegant.

'You're not saying much.'

'I'm thinking about what I shall be saying later.'

'Are you coming to work here, then?'

'I doubt that the housekeeper will take me on,' she replied. 'Not when I tell her about Miss Phoebe getting rid of me from the brewery. But your mother has been very helpful so I'm sure I'll find something.' She had already posted her letter to Mr Ferguson. 'Can you ride a bicycle, Eddie?' she asked.

'Aye. I haven't got one of my own yet, but one of the under-gardeners lets me have a lend of his.'

191

'Is it hard?'

'It is at first, but once you get used to it, it's easy. Fast an' all. The hardware shop in the village sometimes gets a second-hand one in if you're interested. Mind you, he doesn't get in many for girls. Do you know owt about them?'

'Not really.'

'You should find out if you're going to get one. Come to think of it, I don't know many lasses with bicycles. The maids at the Grange can usually get a lift in a cart if they're going anywhere. Besides, have you seen what some of them lady bicyclists wear?' Eddie laughed. 'Pantaloons, they call 'em.' He started giggling.

Nell had seen newspaper sketches and pictures that told her they were 'absolutely the thing' to wear when bicycling, but she hadn't actually seen any women wearing them.

Eddie continued chuckling. 'We had a group of them through the estate last Easter. They were teachers from Sheffield and they wrote to Lady Clarissa wanting permission to use the bridleways. Her Ladyship asked them to call on her and she gave 'em all tea in the drawing room!'

'Perhaps she thought Miss Phoebe might join them?' Nell suggested and burst out laughing at the image that sprang into her mind of strait-laced Miss Phoebe in pantaloons. When she had calmed down she asked Eddie to let her know if he heard of a second-hand ladies' bicycle for sale.

Wilmot Grange came into view. Eddie headed the horse off the main track towards the stables and domestic offices at the rear. Devlin Wilmot's motor car stood outside one of the carriage houses. Two men were standing next to it and as they drew closer, Nell realised it was Devlin Wilmot, casually clothed in corduroys and gaiters with a leather waistcoat over a countryman's checked shirt. He looked more like an ordinary mortal than one of the gentry. She liked what she saw and despite still being cross with him, her heart gave an annoying flutter. He was only interested in her in the same way as he was with Lottie.

The other man was older and dressed in similar country clothing. 'Who is Master Devlin talking to?'

'That's Lady Clarissa's gamekeeper. He wants one of them motor vehicle contraptions for taking the guns up to the moor.'

'I thought shooting didn't start until the autumn.'

'It's the middle of August for the grouse. Mr Paget reckons he'll soon have one house party after another until Christmas.'

Nell twisted in her seat to watch the two men until Eddie pulled up outside the steps to the kitchen. 'You know where to go, don't you?' he said as she climbed down.

'Yes, thanks. Give my regards to your mother when you see her.' She hesitated for a second then added, 'And to Joe.'

'Right you are. Cheerio, then.' He flicked the reins and moved off.

Nell stole one last glance at Devlin, engrossed in conversation on the other side of the courtyard, took a deep breath and walked down the steps.

Mrs Quimby, the Grange housekeeper, spoke

with a Scottish accent. Her manner was formal and brisk, as Nell had expected, but Nell wasn't nervous. She had come here in good faith.

Mrs Quimby invited Nell into her sitting room, a simply furnished room with easy chairs, a small table by the fire and bookshelves next to a writing table against one of the whitewashed walls. Framed photographs graced the mantelpiece – some of family groups dressed in kilts – and Nell recalled that a branch of Lady Clarissa's family lived in a castle in Scotland somewhere.

'Take a seat, Miss Goodman.' The housekeeper held out her open palm. 'I'll see your testimonials first.'

Nell remained standing. She was sure this would not take long. 'You have the only one in my possession, ma am.'

Mrs Quimby sat at her writing table, picked up a pen and dipped it in the inkwell. 'Then you will dictate to me the names and addresses of your previous mistresses.'

'There are none. I was employed at Wilmot's Brewery until ... until recently.'

The housekeeper placed her pen carefully in its cradle on the inkstand and stated, 'You have not worked in service before.'

'No, ma'am.' Nell saw her letter and school report on the writing table.

'Mrs Wainwright spoke well of you.'

'She is very kind, but I assure you that Miss Wilmot will not.'

'Miss Wilmot? Miss Phoebe Wilmot? What has Miss Phoebe to do with you?'

'She dismissed me from the brewery. I've no tes-

timonial, you see, and I came here to tell you this.'
Nell waited for a response but none came. She
added, 'And to ask for the return of my report.'

Mrs Quimby drew Nell's paper in front of her.
'But this indicates much promise, Miss Goodman, and your handwriting is excellent. What
were your duties at the brewery?'

'It doesn't matter now. I'm not suitable for a
position here.' The housekeeper frowned at her.
Nell went on, 'I apologise for wasting your time.
As you were kind enough to interview me, I
wanted to explain to you in person.'

'Kindness doesn't come into it, lassie. I need
another pair of hands for the grouse season. You
have delayed me in that process by coming here
under false pretences.' Nell opened her mouth to
repeat her apology but Mrs Quimby went on, 'I
don't want another child from the workhouse
who can barely write her own name. You are capable and sensible. Cook could see this as soon as
she met you. Now, sit down and tell me what
your duties were at the brewery?'

Nell realised she would have to tell the whole
story so she explained about her mother and
their enforced move but stopped short of de-
scribing her previous visit to the Grange.

Mrs Quimby made a few notes and, when Nell
had finished, she said, 'Yes, I see your difficulties.
That is a pity. You are literate and numerate, and
just what I am looking for to work in my linen
room. You would have suited the position well.'
She stood up, holding Nell's papers and her notes.

'May I have those back now, ma'am.'

'Oh, very well.' She handed over Nell's school

report and placed the others on her writing table. 'If you go over to the stables someone will take you back to the terminus. Good day.'

'Thank you.' Nell glanced at the mantelpiece clock and did not linger. There was an omnibus at half past one to take the two o'clock shift workers into town. Devlin's motor car was still in the courtyard, Eddie's horse and cart too, but there was no sign of Eddie. She called his name. A moment later she tried again and the gamekeeper emerged from one of the carriage houses.

'Eddie's not here. Be on your way.'

'Mrs Quimby said someone would take me to catch the omnibus for town.'

'Go over to the stables on yon side. You'll find somebody there.'

As the gamekeeper spoke to her Devlin came out of the same carriage house and said, 'Why don't you take her in my phaeton?'

Surprised, Nell's eyes swivelled around to him but he was looking at the gamekeeper.

'Me, sir?' the keeper replied.

'You know how to drive it, don't you?'

'Yes, sir.'

'Then you'd better get in some practice if you're having a shooting brake for this season.'

The gamekeeper nodded. 'Certainly, sir. Get in, miss.' He took out the crank handle and went round to the front of the car.

Devlin opened the rear gate of the passenger seats and stood back. 'Can you manage?'

'Yes, thank you.' Nell glanced at his face. He stared over her head. She stumbled up the steps and sat down quickly. As she did, he asked, 'Are you coming to work here?'

She opened her mouth to answer but the motor engine rumbled into life. Rather than raise her voice to be heard she opted to stay silent. It was no business of his anyway. She pulled one of the rugs onto her lap. It wasn't cold and she didn't need it but it gave her something to do so she needn't look at him.

The gamekeeper put the cranking handle back under the driving seat, climbed in and they were on their way. He drove out of the stables under the clock tower and turned sharply down the track so that Nell had a view of the carriage houses. Devlin had disappeared. She was annoyed with herself for feeling disappointed. But at least he had finally got her message of rejection now, loud and clear.

I ought to be pleased, she thought, so why am I not?

Chapter 16

At home, Nell received two more letters. The first she was expecting, for it was her reply from Mr Ferguson in Keppel. At least, it was from a Mrs Ferguson who said she was his daughter-in-law and writing on his behalf. The letter was brief to the point of curt and stated that Mr Ferguson had no need of a housekeeper. Was it to be the bottle factory for her after all? Disappointed, Nell opened her second letter apprehensively.

The envelope carried the Belfors' crest and she guessed rightly that it was to confirm her eviction from the house.

In fact, it was from the younger Mr Belfor and kindly in its tone. He asked her to call at his father's offices in town at the close of business to finalise the termination of her tenancy and discuss how he might help her. Nell thought that Mr Belfor should be writing to Mabel and not her, but was in fact grateful that he had not involved Mother. It showed an understanding of her position.

She wondered how he might be able to help her. Perhaps he knew of a position or even rooms to let? She had nowhere to go yet and could not afford to ignore any opportunity. Then she realised that the Belfors were the Wilmots' lawyers who charged fees for their advice – very large fees – and she had no money. But Mr Belfor would be aware of her situation so perhaps he had more of a conscience than Miss Wilmot about her dismissal?

Nell often went to market at the end of the day to pick up bargains so she took her basket with her and presented herself at Septimus Belfor's offices. It was a fine stone building with three steps up to the front door. The brass plaque on the wall was new and bore the name 'Belfor & Belfor'. Cyril Belfor had recently joined his father's practice, and Nell wondered if working alongside his father might improve the young man's behaviour outside the office?

She pulled on the bell and waited, stepping back onto the pavement to look in the windows.

The shutters were already closed, indicating that the clerks had left for home. The letter did say at closing time so she pulled at the bell again and a moment later, she heard the key turn in the lock and the grating of a bolt. Cyril Belfor opened the door.

'Oh!' she exclaimed, 'I'm here to see your father.'

He's the image of him, she thought. Younger, of course, but it was mainly his formal clothes of black suit and a white shirt with a high stiff collar and black silk tie. His footwear, too, was black and highly polished. He seemed to be much older than she as he stared down at her and examined her appearance. He was not handsome and his small dark eyes were beady, like the button ones sewn onto toy bears. They didn't change as he smiled. It was a crooked smile and she felt the first pang of unease about this visit.

'Nell Goodman. Phoebe told me about your visit to her father. You've got yourself into a bit of a pickle, haven't you?'

His use of Phoebe's name rather than 'Miss Wilmot' or even 'Miss Phoebe' made Nell realise that she was more than a client to him and misgivings about any help he might offer her mounted. She said, 'Mother and I shall soon be settled elsewhere, Mr Belfor. Will this take long?'

He stood back and gestured with his arm. 'You'd better come in. My office is upstairs. My name is on the door.'

She stepped into the dim interior of wood-panelled walls and dark staircase. 'Go on up then,' he said, turning the key in the lock. 'The clerks have gone and it's market day so I can't be too careful.'

Nell hesitated, thinking she would wait for him to go first but he simply stood there until she moved towards the staircase. She walked up slowly and stopped when she heard the key and bolts grating behind her. Of course it was a perfectly sensible thing to do but it was the fact that everyone else had gone home that worried her. She had not forgotten that his behaviour had been as bad as Devlin's that day at the Grange. In fact, when she thought about it, he had been worse. It had been his idea to lift her skirts and Devlin's to put her down. But Cyril was sober now, they were in his formal offices and they had business to conduct.

She continued her journey to the landing and waited outside his door. The one next to it had a nameplate for his father Septimus. 'Is your father working late as well?' she asked lightly as he approached her.

He didn't answer and opened the door into a beautiful square room with large sash windows overlooking the street. The shutters were open, letting in the late-afternoon light. A large desk dominated the room but it was completely clear of documents.

'This is about ending my mother's tenancy, isn't it, Mr Belfor?'

'In a manner of speaking.' He smiled, adding, 'Sit down.' He went round the desk and sat on the opposite side.

'I don't think I can sign anything on her behalf.'

'There's nothing to sign. It's a tied cottage. No

200

job, no house, it's as simple as that.'

'Then why am I here?'

He leaned back in his chair. It was one of those leather, button-backed affairs that swivelled round and round, and Cyril pushed it from side to side as he stroked his chin.

'What are you going to do?' he asked.

'Find somewhere else to live.'

'That won't be easy with no job and your mother to accommodate as well.'

'I'm sure I'll find something. I have friends who are helping me.'

'Not any that will give you an income and a roof over your head in the way that I can.'

Nell's heart leaped. Septimus Belfor was hugely influential in town and now Cyril had joined him in his law firm he would enjoy the same attention. She said, 'I am experienced at clerical work. I did several years in ordering for Wilmot's.'

'I was thinking of something more on the domestic front.'

'Oh.' This was a disappointment, but she had reached the same conclusion for her future and at least he had established that this meeting was about helping her. She responded, 'Well, I have been considering domestic positions. Do you know of any? I have been looking out of town as I have Mother to think of, too. She is quite taken with Keppel and there is domestic work available there.'

He seemed pleased. 'Indeed there is.'

'Mother will fare better away from the temptations of the high street and the market,' Nell added.

201

'So what exactly are you thinking of doing with her?'

'Doing with her? I don't know what you mean. When I have a position, if we cannot live in I shall find rooms for us both nearby.'

'The sergeant has reached the conclusion that your mother ought to be in the workhouse.'

Nell felt her heart constrict in anger. His show of friendliness was no more than a cover. 'No, sir,' she replied. 'It is Miss Wilmot and her father who have decided that. If this is another attempt to persuade me to agree with them then you are wasting your time.' She stood up. 'I should have guessed that you are speaking to me on behalf of the Wilmots. You are no more interested in my mother's welfare than they are. Good evening, sir.'

He was on his feet and round the desk in a second. 'Sit down, Nell. You've not heard my offer yet.'

'I do not want to hear it.' She walked to the door with her heart thumping in her throat.

He caught hold of her hand to still her progress and said, 'Don't leave. Not yet.' His voice was surprisingly soft and he had moved too close to her. It suggested intimacy and she recoiled at the notion, but this made him grip her hand more tightly. 'I can help you,' he said.

She stepped back immediately. But not before she had caught a whiff of his eau de cologne. He did not let go of her hand and tugged on it gently. She resisted. Her heart was still thumping and she noticed his chest rising and falling beneath his waistcoat.

'The Wilmots have nothing to do with my offer,'

he said, 'except perhaps Devlin. He sees your virtue as well as I do.'

'My virtue? What does Devlin Wilmot know of my virtue?'

Cyril gave an easy, good-natured shrug. 'The same as any man can see. Your virtue is still intact. You've never had a sweetheart because your life has been taken up by looking after your mother.'

Nell was speechless with indignation. Even if what he said was true, she was embarrassed that they had talked about her in such a way. Did everyone think that of her? She felt obliged to defend herself and retaliated, 'I am not ashamed of my single status.'

'But you don't see what is so clear to everyone else. You are one and twenty and without a sweetheart. You've missed the boat, so to speak, my dear. If you want a husband, you'll have to wait for the widowers now.'

'What nonsense!' But she knew that, for her, there was a vestige of truth in what he said. This was a small town with very few women like Miss Wilmot, who did jobs normally undertaken by men. Hardly any ordinary working women of her age were unmarried and there were not many men she knew who were not married or betrothed. Nonetheless, she added, for good measure, 'Devlin Wilmot knows nothing about me.'

'He knows you don't like him.'

Nell could well imagine how he had got that idea and experienced a mingled sensation of satisfaction and resentment.

Cyril continued, 'I hope you do not still think ill of me, because I am not Devlin.'

She stared at him, not quite sure what to make of him. He fingered her hand gently. They were softer since she'd given up the bottle-washing and had more time to care for them.

'You are a fine-looking woman, Nell,' he said quietly.

First he insults me and then he flatters me, she thought. None of this made any sense to her and, lawyer or not, she did not trust him. But then he really surprised her by lifting her hand and caressing the back of it with his lips. 'It's a shame to waste such beauty,' he murmured.

Dear heaven, he cannot mean it! A gentleman of his standing cannot seriously be proposing courtship to her. She stayed very still, not knowing how to react. He seemed to be sincere yet, underneath, her instincts told her to be wary.

She said, 'As you have pointed out so well, sir, I am not a naive sixteen-year-old. I should prefer you to be clear about your intentions.'

He pursed his lips for a second. His romantic gesture was over. He placed her hand by her side and walked over to a small sideboard. It held two decanters and several glasses on a silver tray. 'Very well, Nell. Sit down and take a drink with me.' She heard the chink of the glass stopper as he placed it on the tray. 'I meant what I said,' he added.

She was puzzled. Surely he was not seriously interested in courting her? His father was known to be a snob and Cyril had been at Cambridge with the son of local gentry.

'I thought your taste was more for Lottie from the Keppel tearooms,' she said.

Her response was barbed and reminded them both of his loutish behaviour. His lips compressed again. She thought briefly that if he had been holding a torch for her she had surely extinguished it now.

'Charlotte has Devlin in her sights,' he stated. 'Besides, she is far too coarse for me. I prefer a little more discretion. Sherry?' He handed her a glass of amber fluid. 'I want us to be friends, Nell.'

She took the drink and sipped, wondering if he had colluded with Devlin and this was Cyril's way of apologising for the appalling way he had treated her. She still smarted when she thought about it. The sherry was lovely. It relaxed and warmed her. But she noticed that he held a whisky tumbler that was half full.

His office chair moved on castors. He wheeled it around to her side of the desk and sat down. 'You want to live out of town for your mother's sake?'

'I do and your letter said you may be able to help. If you cannot, then please say so and I shall leave.'

'I can help you, Nell, if only you will allow me to. What are you looking for? A pretty little cottage and garden situated not too far from Keppel village?'

'I doubt I could afford the rent on such a place, sir.'

He finished his whisky and got up to pour another. 'Of course there is work involved. A domestic position, you said.'

Nell's eyes widened. 'Work in this cottage? Do

you know of something? Will they take Mother as well?'

'That might be difficult.'

'Oh.' Nell had thought this sounded too good to be true.

'But you like the idea, do you?'

'Well, yes, sir. However, let us be clear that I shall not abandon my mother.'

'I have considered Mrs Goodman, if you are willing to let her lodge in the village. A friend of her own age may be what she – and you – need.'

'She is very dependent on me, sir.'

'Ah yes, but that is because she only has you. A little company of her own age will give her a new interest.'

Nell regarded Cyril with fresh eyes. This was similar to what Mrs Wainwright had advised and what appealed to Nell about Keppel. It made sense to her and her expression brightened.

'I can see you like my idea,' he went on. 'You see, my father is a trustee for several lonely old ladies who are living out their last years in large empty villas. He has passed over to me the task of overseeing one such lady of means in Keppel. It is my considered opinion that she would benefit from a companion.'

A companion? Nell frowned. She was doubtful because it sounded like one of Mabel's own fanciful ideas and she said, 'I don't know how Mother would cope with the responsibilities.'

'The lady I have in mind has a daily woman for domestic duties. She keeps an eye on things for my father. She was his choice and is loyal.'

Nell thought about this for a minute and murmured, 'I really don't know if Mother would like living away from me. She often came looking for me at the brewery.'

'But she didn't have anyone to talk to at home then,' Cyril argued, 'and you wouldn't be too far away to visit her.'

He was very convincing and it did seem like a solution worth trying. Mother would adore living in a big house again. 'What would be her duties as a companion?' Nell asked.

Cyril seemed mildly irritated by her question. 'To provide companionship,' he replied. 'It's what women do, isn't it?'

Nell thought that he was losing patience with her. But it would be a big change for Mabel and one that needed some thought. After a pause, Cyril regained his persuasive tone and added, 'My father will draw up a simple agreement with a stipend.'

'A stipend? Mother will be paid?'

He nodded. 'As I said, this lady has a trust fund and a companion must dress well to accompany her mistress on outings.'

Mother would adore outings with a lady of her own age, Nell thought. 'Mother is very particular about her appearance,' she murmured.

'So you think your mother will do it?'

'I can't make promises on her behalf but I shall certainly discuss it with her.' Actually, she knew that Mabel would say yes straightaway, but Nell wanted to know more about the lady herself. However, there was time for that, she decided. She only had to go to the market when Mrs Wainwright's stall was there. Mrs Wainwright knew everyone in Keppel.

Nell finished her sherry and went on, 'It really is very kind of you to help me in this way, sir.'

Cyril took the empty glass from her. 'Another sherry?'

She stood up. 'Thank you, no. I need to speak with Mother.' In fact, she wanted to get back to Mother. Time was getting on and it was growing dark. Nell didn't want Mabel to come out looking for her. She went on, 'Would you be good enough to ask your father to let me have sight of the agreement?'

'Actually, Father has handed over the lady's affairs for me to manage. He has to sign the authorities and cheques but he will agree to anything I put in front of him.' Cyril smiled at her. 'So you see, we can decide between us.'

It seemed conspiratorial to Nell and she felt uneasy. 'But your father is the trustee.'

His impatience returned. 'And I am his associate. He has a cupboard full of trusteeships and you'd be surprised how long some of these old ladies last when they have an income. Now sit down and have another sherry.'

He had drained his whisky glass again so he got up, poured drinks for them both and returned to his seat. 'You haven't heard your part of the bargain yet.'

Chapter 17

She hadn't thought of it in those terms but said, 'I imagine this offer is conditional upon my taking up the domestic position you mentioned?' It occurred to her that it might be with Mr Ferguson but Cyril had talked of a cottage and Mr Ferguson lived in a larger house.

'Don't you wish to know the details?'

'I'm sure I can cope with a domestic position well enough. It's getting late and Mother will be wondering where I am. Do I have to know the details tonight?'

He gave a low laugh that rumbled in his throat. 'Yes, you do, Nell.' His tone made her nervous and his crooked grin seemed to sneer at her.

She felt apprehensive. This was supposed to be a business meeting in a formal office but somehow Cyril was turning it into a kind of assignation; the sherry, the compliments, and now his triumphant grin that seemed to say it all. She half expected him to lick his lips as he looked at her. Dear God, did he expect some personal favour from her in return for getting her this position? She stiffened in her chair and muttered, 'What do you want from me?'

'I want you, Nell. Have I not made that clear enough? In return I shall provide a cottage not far from Keppel and a regular income for your good self.'

'What are you suggesting?' But Nell was already pretty sure what he had in mind. Surely he was not serious?

'Don't be naive, Nell. You'll be left on the shelf in a year or so and still have Mabel to look after. Without a husband you need a patron otherwise you'll follow your mother into the workhouse.'

'My mother is not going to the workhouse.'

'If you haven't any means of supporting her, you won't be able to stop them taking her.'

Nell feared that was true. But this? He was asking her to sell herself like a common prostitute. It was an appalling suggestion.

'I'll find a way,' she responded.

'See sense, Nell. You don't have to look any further. I liked what I saw of you out on the Grange estate that day. You'll suit me perfectly.' He moved his chair closer to hers and gave her another of his crooked smiles.' You know how these things are. Father has plans for my future. Well, I want some of my own. Don't you want a comfortable home with nice clothes and a pony and trap for shopping?'

She couldn't deny that, but not at this price. 'You want me to be a kept woman,' she stated.

'What were you at the brewery? It's just a different way of earning your living. A mistress is a requirement for a gentleman these days. Face facts, Nell, your future is bleak. A woman of your background could never be the *wife* of a gentleman. If you are lucky enough to land a husband at all, he'll be a factory hand or a tradesman. You'll be living in a crowded terrace with a tribe of children around your skirts.' He stopped for a

210

moment, then added, 'Not that you've much chance of anyone marrying you with that mother of yours always in the picture.'

Sadly Nell had reached similar conclusions herself and it was something she didn't care to dwell on. Offers to walk out on Sunday afternoons or go to a concert at the Institute had waned. But she had learned to live with it. Her first duty was to her mother for as long as she needed her.

'I know of a lovely little property that is vacant now and will be ready for occupation soon. It's nice and isolated, but not too far from Keppel with a pony and trap. I even thought of a cover story for you.'

'Just how long have you been planning this, Cyril?' Nell demanded.

'I've thought about you a lot since that day at the Grange. I couldn't get you out of my mind, even when I sobered up. I want you, Nell, and I shan't ask you to put your mother in the workhouse. A husband wouldn't even bother to ask you, he'd just do it.'

'But to become your mistress! It's immoral! I don't understand how you could be so disloyal to your future wife? I won't do it. I couldn't. My mother would be devastated if she ever found out.'

'She won't. I'm taking over all Father's clients in Keppel. I shall have numerous reasons to ride over there.'

'And how should I explain to people how I pay my rent?' It was a hypothetical question and within seconds Nell wished she hadn't asked it. She meant it as another argument against this absurd idea, but Cyril viewed it as a sign of her submission. He stood up, took both her hands and pulled her towards him.

'Oh God, you agree. Come here.'

His arms snaked around her back until she was pressed up against him and he began kissing her forehead and then her eyes.

'Stop this at once, I–' Her words were stifled as his mouth covered hers and his tongue searched for hers.

She tried to push him away but he overwhelmed her, forcing his kisses on her and exploring every curve of her body with his fingers. When he stopped for air, he breathed in her ear, 'God, I've ached to do that ever since that day. Let me show you how much I want you.'

Nell tried to keep calm. 'Cyril, stop it. I don't want you.'

'You will.' He bent down to grasp the fabric of her skirt, bunch it up and explore underneath. 'Come on, Nell. You don't know what you're missing.' He was already grasping the flesh of her thigh and pushing his body against her.

Good God, he really meant it! She could feel the hardening of his masculine desire through his clothes and his hands continued their persistent search. For the first time a genuine fear clutched at her heart. 'Didn't you hear me?' she cried, 'I said *stop it*.'

'You don't mean that,' he murmured. He tried to kiss her again but she turned her head away.

'Yes, I do. This isn't right.'

Despite her efforts to push him away, his hand had reached her drawers and slid underneath them with probing fingers. 'Don't be a prude, Nell,' he breathed. 'All young women do this nowadays.'

'If you don't stop I shall scream for your father.'

The mention of his father cooled his ardour. He removed his hand, allowing her skirt edge to drop to the floor. Nell went hot and cold with embarrassment as she realised that Septimus Belfor actually was working in the adjacent room. How on earth had she allowed herself to get into this mess? A clock chimed somewhere close by.

'Lord, is that the time?' Cyril said. 'I've got a charity supper tonight. You'll have to go now. Look here, I'll see you on Sunday afternoon. The cottage isn't ready yet but I'll take you and your mother to meet the old lady.'

It took Nell a few seconds to recover her composure. He obviously had not believed any of her protestations. When her breathing had subsided and she felt calmer, she said, 'I'm not doing it, Cyril, and I don't know what possessed you to ever think that I would.'

He gave her a surprised stare as though he still did not believe her. 'What options have you got? I've made you a good offer,' he said. 'Talk to your mother about it before Sunday.'

Nell had no intention of mentioning any of this to Mother and marched to the door decisively. She said, 'I shan't change my mind. Goodnight, Mr Belfor.' She meant to close the door firmly but it slammed instead and she jumped, stared at the adjacent door for a second and ran down the stairs.

The more she thought about it, the more she queried whether she had really understood Cyril

213

Belfor's intentions correctly. But there was no other interpretation, she concluded. This shocked her so much that she hardly noticed the walk home. The house was in darkness and when Nell let herself in there was no sign of Mabel. Any concerns about Cyril Belfor drained away as she panicked about her mother.

She went to the neighbours and they hadn't seen her. She went up and down the street and then further afield. The gas lamps were lit and a few people were trudging home from their labours. She stopped one or two and asked if they had seen her mother. A middle-aged woman told her she had seen a woman answering Mabel's description knocking ceaselessly on the front door of a big house on the Valley Road.

Dear God, please no! The Valley Road was where Mabel had lived when she was first married. She had gone to 'the house'! Relieved that at least she knew where her mother was, Nell headed off in that direction. But her relief turned to anxiety as she wondered what scene she would encounter when she arrived.

A street lamp illuminated the clump of people arguing on the pavement. A sprinkling of inquisitive passers-by or neighbours ogled on the periphery. In the pool of gaslight a well-dressed gentleman surrounded by a family group was arguing with the sergeant.

'She is trespassing in my house,' the gentleman shouted.

'Did she break in, sir?' the sergeant asked.

'No, my elder daughter let her in. She gave her some cock-and-bull story about it being her house and she was moving in to live here.' The gentleman turned to his daughter who was weeping into her mother's bosom. 'It's all right, Maude,' he soothed, 'it's not your fault.' Three other children of varying ages were hovering behind their mother and an older woman holding a baby was watching from the open front door.

'Where is she now?' the sergeant went on.

'She has installed herself in my front room.'

'Is the lady a relative of yours?'

'No, she is not! I have asked her to leave umpteen times and she won't. Just get in there and arrest her. She needs locking up, she does. She's got bats in her belfry.' He made a circular motion with his forefinger at the side of his head.

Nell was half sobbing as she reached the group. She was out of breath and shaking uncontrollably. 'Please don't arrest her, sir!' she cried.

The sergeant recognised Nell immediately and his face broke into a smile. 'Oh, it must be Mabel Goodman you've got in there. She's harmless, sir.'

'She most certainly is not!' The gentleman turned his venom on Nell. 'Do you know this woman?'

'She's my mother.'

'Well, do something about her. She's not safe to be let out on her own, terrorising my family like this.'

'She used to live here, sir.'

'Well, she doesn't now.' He addressed the woman with the baby in the doorway. 'Take young Charlie upstairs, Ma. The sergeant is coming indoors.'

Nell went to look in the front window and, sure enough, Mabel was sitting in isolated splendour in the middle of a chaise longue in front of the drawing-room fire. The gaslights on the wall were lit and Mabel seemed totally at home and unconcerned. Nell saw the sergeant go in and talk to her for a few minutes and eventually Mabel stood up and walked out with him.

'She was waiting for you, Nell,' the sergeant said as he handed her over. Then he addressed the amused onlookers. 'Show's over, folks. Go back to your own firesides.'

Weary with anxiety, Nell thanked him for not arresting her mother and apologised to the gentleman once again. Mabel was shivering in the night air so Nell took off her jacket and put it around her shoulders. There was no point in chastising her mother and even if she did, Mabel would have forgotten about it in the morning.

'When are we going to live there?' Mabel asked.

'I've already explained to you that we can't. That gentleman and his family live there now.'

'Well, I told him about George and how he killed your father and took his half of the brewery.'

Nell's spirits sank even further but she could not let that pass. 'Mother, you really mustn't say that. Mr Wilmot did nothing of the sort.'

'Yes, he did; it was his fault. He stole all our money.'

This was a new slander to Nell's ears and she despaired. The house must have stimulated more memories of the past. She patted Mabel's hand tucked into her arm and tried to reassure her. 'We don't want to live in that house anyway

216

because we are going to live in the country as soon as I can arrange it.' It might hold a better prospect for Mabel, she reflected uneasily, but not for her.

Mabel put Nell's jacket on properly and snuggled into her daughter's side as they trudged on in silence. Nell felt at the end of her tether. Nothing seemed to be working out for her and she couldn't go on just hoping for things to improve. She wondered how much influence the Belfors had on folk living in the spacious villas in Keppel.

The sergeant caught up with them and escorted them all the way home, which Nell thought was very kind of him. But his message wasn't quite so benevolent. 'That's the last time I can bail her out for you, Nell lass. Word about your ma has got as far as my inspector's ears and he'll do something about her if I don't. That gentleman is high up in the municipal offices. He knows what's what and he'll ask questions about her so I'll have to write a report.'

They continued in silence until the sergeant prompted, 'What shall I say you're going to do with her?' Nell realised he meant well but he made Mabel sound like a stray dog. He went on, 'If you don't decide, my inspector will do it for you and you know what that means.'

Nell wanted to sink to the pavement and weep. She plodded on, not knowing what to say.

'I'll have to write something,' the sergeant pressed.

Nell took a deep breath. 'We're going to live in Keppel,' she said. 'I've been offered a position there and somewhere for us both to live.' It was the truth, even though she had turned it down. Nell hated even voicing Cyril's abhorrent idea and was horrified that it was going to be written down in a policeman's report. She prayed that he would not question her about it.

She heard the sergeant heave a sigh. With relief, presumably, because he said, 'Nell lass, that's grand. It's the best news I've heard all week.' He sounded quite cheerful. Why shouldn't he? He had one less problem to deal with now.

Mabel was tired and went straight to bed. Nell made cocoa and took her mother's up to her bedroom. She sat on the bed while she drank it.

'When are we moving?' Mabel asked.

'Soon.' Nell felt her eyelids closing and her head drooping.

'But when? Tell me when. I want to know when before I go to sleep.'

She had to give Mother an answer and said, 'We'll have a look next week, shall we?'

'Next week,' Mabel repeated. She yawned, slid under the bedcovers and drifted into sleep.

Nell took the empty mug and went downstairs for her own drink, which was keeping warm on the range. When she had finished, she sat with her arms on the kitchen table and her head resting on her arms and wept. She cried until all her anguish was out of her and hoped she would feel better. She didn't. She came to the conclusion that she had to start looking for a position all over again, and she had no idea how to explain to Mabel that they were not going to live in Keppel after all.

For two days, Nell was so reluctant to leave

Mabel alone that she hardly went out of the house except to the horse and cart that doled out fresh milk from churns. On Saturday she planned to take Mother to the market to do the shopping and they rose early. Mabel liked to take her time to dress as she wanted to look her best for town. Nell locked the back door and waited in the front room with her shopping baskets.

She watched idly through the window as neighbours came and went about their business and was intrigued when she saw a carriage and pair coming down the street. She recognised it as the Belfors', for she had seen it twice on the day she first went to the Grange. She rose to her feet, startled, as it drew up outside their house and Septimus Belfor climbed down from the driving seat. She was even more shocked to see George Wilmot step out of the carriage.

Chapter 18

Nell blew out her cheeks. What on earth could they want with her now? She stood behind the front door for a full minute before she heard one of them knock and took a deep breath before opening it.

'Good morning, gentlemen,' she said.

'Good morning, Miss Goodman,' Septimus Belfor replied. 'May we crave a few minutes of your time?'

'I am just leaving for market.'

'This is important, my dear,' he said.

George Wilmot added, 'It's about Mabel.'

'Oh.' Nell stood back and held open the door. 'You had best come in then.' She showed them into the front room and offered them tea.

Septimus answered. 'Thank you no, dear. Is your mother in?'

'She's upstairs getting ready to go out. Why are you here, sir?'

'It's about the incident the other evening and what you are going to do about her.'

'Well, I'm not sending her to the workhouse,' Nell said.

'Yes, I understand that but we cannot have her going around slandering Mr Wilmot, can we? The police sergeant tells me you are moving to Keppel. Will she ruin his good name there as well?'

Nell didn't say anything for a moment. She felt intimidated by these two powerful gentlemen sitting authoritatively in their fine clothes and filling the front room. 'Actually, I was thinking of moving even further field. There are more opportunities in Sheffield. I can easily get a job as a buffer girl for one of the master cutlers.'

'And what will your mother do all day? Sit quietly at home, in your one room at a lodging house? Or will she occupy herself with petty pilfering? It won't do, Miss Goodman, and you know that as well as I do.'

'You're not taking her away from me,' she said stubbornly.

'If there are any more incidents like the other evening you will not have a say in the matter, my dear.' Septimus Belfor glared at her.

Nell swallowed. She didn't really have an answer. She glanced at Mr Wilmot who had been staring at his gloved hands resting on top of his walking cane. He looked up at her, gave her a small smile and said, 'I want to help you, Nell. You know I do. Mabel needs someone to keep an eye on her all the time.'

He was right, of course. Cyril Belfor had said more or less the same thing and his solution might have worked were it not for his outrageous demands on Nell. She could hardly tell these two gentlemen about that.

'I can take Mabel in at the Grange to keep her out of harm's way,' Mr Wilmot continued. 'What do you say to that?'

'I ... I don't know what to say, except that surely Miss Phoebe will not approve, and ... and, well, Mother will not be happy away from me.'

Mr Belfor placed his hand on George's arm, which Nell realised was in order to silence him, and took over the conversation. 'You will come too and be given work in the servants' hall. Mrs Goodman will be kept occupied by Her Lady-ship's former governess.'

Nell expressed surprise. She had many ques-tions to ask as it sounded, again, too good to be true – and she wondered what price she would have to pay this time.

'That is very generous, Mr Wilmot–'

Mr Belfor interrupted. 'Indeed it is, my girl. Take heed.' After a short silence, he added, 'If you are in agreement, I shall finalise the details today.'

Nell blinked, hardly able to believe her own ears. Move into the Grange? It didn't seem possible. She was sure there would be strings attached, but whatever they were, they could not be as monstrous as Cyril Belfor's, and Mother had frequently announced that George Wilmot 'owed them'. Perhaps he did? He seemed to want to help her and was being held back in his kindness by his lawyer. Perhaps there was some truth in Mabel's ramblings after all?

'I want your answer now, Miss Goodman, if you please?' Septimus Belfor prompted. 'Mr Wilmot is a busy man.'

At that moment, both gentlemen rose to their feet as Mabel entered the room. Nell noticed that she had stopped in the hall to pin on her hat and she did look very fetching.

Mabel said, 'Dear me. George Wilmot. You have taken your time to return my visit.' In the next breath, she added, 'Why are you calling at this hour of the morning? I am just going out.' She stretched out her hand to be kissed. Both gentlemen simply nodded in response, murmured, 'Mrs Goodman,' and remained standing. 'These gentlemen are just leaving, Mother,' Nell said and went to stand by the open door.

'Your answer, Miss Goodman?' Mr Belfor repeated.

As if I have a choice! she thought. A position at the Grange presented nothing but difficulty for her. She had already upset Mr Paget the butler and Mrs Quimby the housekeeper, the two most powerful people below stairs. But her hardships were of no consequence if Mother was safe from harm. She wondered what Lady Clarissa's former governess was like and decided that she

222

must come from a respectable background, which would impress Mabel. Anyway, at present, there was no other option for her and she *was* fearful of the alternative. She could not allow Mother to be evicted onto the streets, for that would surely seal her fate in the workhouse. Cyril Belfor had known that and exploited her predicament with his shameful proposition. It disturbed her to remember it and she felt a blush rising in her cheeks.

George continued to look down at his hands, but Mr Belfor's enquiring gaze demanded her decision. Despite the fact that George Wilmot seemed unwilling to meet her eyes, Nell addressed him with her answer. She said, 'Thank you, Mr Wilmot, I am grateful for your kindness. My mother and I are pleased to accept.' Still he did not look up.

'A wise decision, if I may say so,' the lawyer responded briskly. 'Good day, ladies.' He bowed his head and moved to the door.

George Wilmot followed him without taking his leave or looking at either of them. He seemed in a hurry to get out of the house. If Mother was such an embarrassment to him, why had he suggested they go to the Grange? Perhaps he hadn't. Perhaps it was all Septimus Belfor's idea and she wondered how much he knew of the truth.

Mr Belfor paused on the threshold of the front door and said, 'You are lucky that Mr Wilmot is so understanding. My son will make the arrangements for your removal.'

Nell had no wish to set eyes on Cyril Belfor ever again. She would have preferred to hire Joe

223

Wainwright and his horse and cart, but had no chance to say so. She closed the front door and went back into the front room. Mabel was watching the gentlemen climb into the carriage and she said, 'Did he come here to give back your father's money?'

'Not exactly, Mother. But he has asked you to go and live at the Grange.'

'Live with him at the Grange? How dare he? He's a married man!'

'No, Mother, not in that way...'

But Mabel wasn't listening. 'Well, I'm not going,' she continued. 'I am not a trollop and I shall go out there this minute and tell him as much.'

Nell barred her way. She took her mother's hand and led her to a chair. 'No, Mother, he didn't mean that at all.' She sighed. 'Come and sit down for a minute and let me explain.'

In fact, there was little that Nell could tell her because she didn't know what to expect herself. But hopefully, Mother would be pleasantly occupied and that was more important to Nell. They enjoyed their subsequent trip to market. Nell kept a firm hold on Mabel's arm and they stopped at Mrs Wainwright's boot and shoe stall. She was very busy as it was Saturday and Nell had to wait for a lull.

'I'm going to the Grange,' she told her at last.

'Well done, lass. I'll tell my Joe. He'll be pleased for you, too.'

Nell felt a flush of pleasure wash over her and looked forward to seeing more of him.

'Mother is coming too. She's going to help

Lady Clarissa's old governess.'

'That's nice,' Mrs Wainwright answered. 'We might see you in church on a Sunday, then.'

'I hope so,' Nell said with a smile.

Mrs Wainwright went back to her customers and Nell's warm feeling continued. Things were working out for her at last. She celebrated by suggesting they have dinner in town and bought bread-cakes filled with hot roast pork, sage-and-onion stuffing and apple sauce from the cooked meat shop. They ate them sitting on one of the new municipal seats, and washed them down with glasses of ale from the off-sales window at the Crown.

Mabel wanted to go to the draper's in the high street for feathers and lace to trim her hats and gowns 'for the Grange'. Nell thought this was a good idea until she saw the phaeton pulling up on a side road that led to the high street. Devlin Wilmot climbed out, helped his sister Phoebe from the rear and walked off towards the shops. How would Miss Phoebe react to Mabel and Nell being in residence at the Grange? Nell wondered. And Devlin, she knew from bitter experience, was cut from the same cloth as Cyril Belfor and not to be trusted.

Life at the Grange is not going to be easy for me, she thought.

Nell turned to her mother and said, 'Why don't we wait until we can walk into Keppel to that lovely draper's shop there? We can meet others from the village and have tea in the tearooms.' Mabel agreed, much to Nell's relief.

Septimus Belfor sent a formal letter setting out

the removal date and confirming her employment at the Grange. Nell's heart sank when she read the last sentence, which passed all further dealings on the matter to his son. But this was tempered by a later note from Cyril informing her that Joe Wainwright would be responsible for transferring their belongings to the Grange.

On the appointed day, Eddie arrived with his brother Joe and stacked the few pieces of furniture they were taking onto the cart, along with the old tin trunk for their clothes and a borrowed tea chest full of items they had spent hours wrapping carefully in old newspapers. Mabel was excited to be moving but Nell felt sad. She had grown up in this little house and it held many memories for her.

'Joe's ready for the off.' Eddie came into the hall where Mabel was hovering anxiously.

Nell came forward from the kitchen. 'Thank you. Will you ride in the back with me so that Mother can sit up front with Joe?' she asked.

'We're not taking you,' Eddie replied. 'Just the house stuff, Mr Belfor said. He's coming for you two in his carriage.'

'Oh, I'd rather go with you and Joe.'

'Well, I wouldn't,' Mabel said, 'not if we can ride in a carriage.'

'Your ma's right,' Eddie said. 'It'll be much more comfy for her.'

Nell hurried outside to thank Joe and say goodbye, but he was already turning around his heavy horse and laden cart. He waved at her and called, 'Mr Belfor is on his way for you.' Eddie skipped across the road and climbed up beside him.

Mabel and Nell loitered in the road for a few minutes then went inside to wait. It seemed a long time before Cyril arrived and Nell was becoming anxious about Mother who was ready to set off walking to town. She was apprehensive, too, about seeing Cyril again after their last encounter at his office.

He was all broad smiles and pleasantries when he finally arrived and said, 'Well, this is working out fine for you, after all. Your mother will be taken care of and you have a secure domestic position.'

'We don't know that yet, sir,' Nell replied. 'But Mother and I are grateful for your help this morning.'

'So you should be. I'm your only friend at the moment. I'm the one you come to if you're not happy about anything.'

I'm not happy about any of this, Nell thought, and you're the last person I'd go to for help. The only man she really trusted had just driven away with her belongings. She didn't reply to him and she must have been frowning because he went on, 'Don't cross me, Nell. I'm as much a part of the family at the Grange as Master Devlin. I can make life hell for you if I want.' She was thinking that he'd made a good stab at that already until he added, 'And for your mother, don't forget.'

'I understand you perfectly, Mr Belfor,' she said and resolved to keep out of his way as much a possible.

'Get in then.'

Nell helped her mother into the small open carriage. It was very comfortable, with padded, leather seats and fur knee rugs, and well sprung to cope with the uneven roads. They went into town and then took the track across the fields to Keppel where Cyril stopped outside the vicarage, braked the carriage and climbed down.

'This is just your mother, Nell. The vicar's wife gets the spinsters and widows together once a week for dinner and a whist drive. Lady Clarissa's old governess will be here.'

Mabel got up eagerly and went off with a kindly-looking lady.

'Will you come back for her?' Nell asked Cyril.

'She'll go back to the Grange with the others.'

Nell felt comfortable about that and she would have time to organise their room for her. She didn't know what to expect but she supposed they would have a room somewhere near the other servants. She sat back expecting to drive directly to the Grange. Outside the village, Cyril turned off the road down a track through the trees.

'Where are we going?' she called.

'A picnic spot I know. You're hungry, aren't you?'

'I am expected at the Grange.'

He ignored her comment. The track went deeper and deeper into the trees until they reached a clearing in a sudden pool of sunlight. A small deserted cottage stood to one side and at the other was the remains of a charcoal burner's firepit, clearly unused for years. Yet the smell of charred wood still pervaded the atmosphere. It was pleasant at first but grew sharper and more acrid as they neared the blackened heap.

Cyril tethered the horse, opened the carriage door for Nell and let down the steps. Then he took a large wickerwork basket from under the driver's seat and said, 'Come on, I'll show you inside.'

'Where is this?' she asked.

'Keppel Woods.'

'The bluebell wood!' she exclaimed. The wonderfully scented flowers were over now but were beautiful in early spring and a delight for Sunday-afternoon walkers. 'Is this the old charcoal burner's cottage?' she added.

'It's mine now. I'm waiting for the builder to put in a water tank.' He took a large iron key out of his pocket and unlocked the front door. 'Come inside.'

Nell was curious but as soon as she stepped over the threshold she realised to her regret that this must be the cottage Cyril was preparing for the planned assignations with his mistress. 'It's very pretty,' she said and turned to leave, adding, 'I'll wait for you in the carriage.'

'Oh no you don't.' He grabbed her arm and wrenched her back into the tiny entrance hall. 'I haven't brought you all this way for nothing.' He quickly locked the front door and pocketed the key. 'I can get around Father's arrangements well enough.'

'But I gave you my answer!' she cried.

'Do you think that's going to stop me? We should have been here on Sunday, together, as I planned.'

'I said no to you, Cyril. No!'

'You won't be saying that after you've had a taste of pleasure. Come here.'

Chapter 19

He overwhelmed her with his size and strength, first pulling her towards him and kissing her mouth savagely, then pulling aside the neckline of her best blouse and descending to the swell of her breasts. He had backed her against the cold plastered wall and with one hand he reached to push open an adjacent door.

She resisted his tugging and shoving with little effect and he slammed the door shut with a kick. She found herself in a small room that contained items of furniture covered in dust sheets. There was a fire laid in the hearth and a rug spread on the floorboards in front of it. He pushed her backwards and she stumbled, the backs of her knees connecting with a couch of some sort. She fell back onto it and he was beside her immediately, pinning her down.

Her heart began to thump. He'd done this before! More than once, she guessed, and a vision of Charlotte Miller flashed across her mind.

'I'm not Lottie!' she protested.

'I know that,' he laughed. 'You're much prettier and have more spirit.'

She made a superhuman effort to push him off. He laughed again, because she was unable to budge him and, more than that, he enjoyed her ineffectual struggle. He pushed her sideways so that she was half lying on the couch and half covered her with his body. Fear gathered in her chest, making her feel queasy with a dreadful foreboding. He was not going to stop. He did not care about her wishes or her feelings. His concern was only for what he wanted, right now, and by God, he was determined to get it. Her heart thumped loudly in her ears.

She remembered, in his office, the mention of his father had cooled his passion and cried, 'I shall tell your father about your despicable behaviour!'

This time he did stop for a moment, although she was still unable to move from under him. 'No, you won't,' he said, 'because I shall inform him you're just a trollop that flaunted yourself at me and you're not the kind of woman to be given a position at the Grange.'

'But that's not true!'

He just grinned. She hated that crooked grin of his with a vengeance. He did not say any more. He forced her lips open with his and pressed his tongue on hers. One of his hands reached under her skirt and traced a line up her leg to her thigh and higher. She snapped her legs together but he grasped the top of her drawers and pulled them down to her knees.

She screamed out and tried to kick him. But her boots hindered her drawers, tangling them around her ankles. She punched at his head with her fists, and succeeding only in hurting her own knuckles. His hand was between her legs, his fingers probing. Dear God no! Surely this was not happening to her? Well, she would not give up her virtue to this atrocious excuse for a man without a fight.

She bit him. She tried to reach his ear and her teeth latched onto the flesh over his jaw bone. He yelped and laughed again, raising his head whilst keeping one arm pinned across her chest.

'Stop it, Cyril!' she yelled. 'I don't want you!'

'Yes you do.' He stared into her eyes as his probing fingers invaded her. She struggled to stop him but he just laughed at her. 'I don't,' she protested. She meant it. 'Get off me!'

He shook his head and started to fumble with his own clothing. Exhausted from her efforts, she had only words left as her weapons. 'Don't do this to me,' she appealed. 'It will only make me hate you even more.'

If he heard her he did not acknowledge her. He was more concerned with his open trousers and what lay inside them. She could feel it against her thigh and felt her tears rise and begin to spill. She was unable to stop him. She didn't know how to and she feared that he would hurt her. 'Please don't,' she begged. 'Not like this. I haven't done anything to you to deserve it.'

For a second she thought he had listened because suddenly his weight was off her. His eyes were not smiling. They had become dark and brooding and seemed not to see her. She wished she had reacted a little more quickly but before she could lever herself to sitting, he had dragged her off the couch and over to the rug. She bent her knees and pushed against the floor to try to stand up. It was a futile effort that he ignored as he pushed his trousers and under-drawers down and lowered his body over hers. She had not seen a man in this state of undress before and froze at the sight of his dark and swollen private parts. Nor had she seen this expression of unconscious purpose on a man's face before. It was as though nothing existed except the act he was determined to perform.

He tugged her drawers free of her boots and pushed her flimsy skirt up to her waist. She kept her legs pressed together and pushed her bottom into the floor away from his probing. But she was weeping and murmuring 'no' over and over again.

A heavy knee forced its way between hers, pushing them wide apart, and his fingers resumed their exploration. Beating his shoulders with her fists made no impression. He entered her quickly with a groan and started his onslaught, pumping away at her for what seemed like an age. His face against hers began to sweat and still he went on.

She felt nothing except the physical pain he caused her, forcing his way into her, pushing at her soft tissues and pounding her body. He was heavy and he was strong. And then it became worse because he began to gasp and increase his thrusting. The sweat dripped off him onto her cheeks, mixing with her tears and tasting of salt on her lips. Suddenly he stopped, reared up on her and cried out like an animal in pain. He flopped back on top of her. She felt him pulse inside her and realised that it was over. He lay perfectly still for while, squeezing the breath out of her, then turned over onto his back on the dusty floor, leaving himself exposed.

Nell rolled away from him, curled herself into a ball and wept softly. She felt dirty, soiled and sticky and she understood what it was like to want to kill someone. But she had no fight left in her. Her mind and body were numb. She could scarcely move her limbs. Gradually her senses returned, and with them the pain. Her head ached. She was raw and sore where he had invaded her. Her back hurt where it had been pressed against the hard floor. She brought her knees up tightly to her breast and hugged them with her arms. More than anything she wanted to go home, to her little bedroom in town, to wash away the stench of this man and hide herself completely in the bedclothes.

It was difficult to stem her tears but eventually she hiccupped herself to a standstill. She heard him moving about and then the distant whine and creak of a water pump and the sluicing of water. She imagined the cold cleansing effect of fresh water on her face and rolled back to a sitting position. The cottage was quiet. Had he gone outside? She considered escaping and running. She had no idea where she was but surely she could not be too far from the Grange.

She stood up gingerly, in no fit state to run. Her joints were stiff from their lengthy enforced position and she went in search of the scullery. It had an iron water pump beside a stone sink containing a chipped enamel bowl. There was dirty water in the bowl. She tipped it into a pail underneath the sink and pumped fresh. She found a handkerchief to use as a sponge and squeezed the icy water over her face and neck. Then she washed the sore areas between her legs and dried them with her petticoat.

The grating sound of a key in the front door jangled her nerves and she stiffened. He had returned and locked the door again.

'Come back in here and eat,' he called. 'I'm starving.'

It was as though nothing was different for him.

The water had revived her and she went to stand at the open door of the front parlour. He had dragged off some of the dust sheets and was standing at a table in front of a small basket with his back to her. 'Pork pie and a glass of barley wine?' he asked.

'No thank you,' she replied. 'Will you let me out, please? I'll walk the rest of the way to the Grange.'

'Don't be ridiculous.' He turned around, sinking his teeth into a pork pie. His face was flushed and his hair slicked back and damp. 'I'm taking you.'

'But I'll be late. Someone must be expecting me.'

'You'll arrive when I say so.' He waved a bottle in the air. 'Drink?'

Her mouth tasted of ashes and a glass of barley wine might calm her fractured nerves. She nodded briefly.

'Well, come in then.'

She stepped inside the room. Her eyes were drawn to the crumpled rug in front of the hearth and he followed her gaze.

'Here. You have this one.' He handed her the opened bottle and unscrewed the stopper from another in the basket. 'Bit of a jolt for you, was it? You'll get used to it and then it'll be more fun for both of us.'

'It won't happen again.' She wiped the top of the bottle with her hand and took an unladylike swig.

'Of course it will. You're my mistress now.' He sounded as though he was proud of this achievement. 'You belong to me; me alone,' he repeated. 'And you'd better keep it that way, if you know what's good for you.'

'I don't belong to anyone.'

'Well, no self-respecting fellow will want you when I explain our arrangement to them.'

'We haven't got an arrangement!' She was filled with dread that somebody would find out about this shameful encounter. 'And I shall tell them you forced me!'

'Why would I have to do that? I'm a respectable lawyer and you are desperate to keep your mother out of the workhouse. You'll do as I say or you and your ma will both end up there.'

He was a truly cruel and selfish man and she hated him. She sank onto a nearby chair and argued, 'Well, I shan't have any time for you once I start work at the Grange.'

'I'll find a way,' he said airily. 'I'm a favourite at the Grange.' His tone became threatening. 'I hope you know that you'll have to watch your step there,' he warned. 'Lady Clarissa's a tartar and I am your only friend. You make sure you're nice to me or I'll make sure you and your ma suffer.'

'But it was Mr Wilmot offered me the position,' she protested.

'George Wilmot is only doing what my father tells him. Your mother is spreading some dangerous rumours and the best thing to do is to put her out of harm's way in the attics at the Grange with the batty old nanny.'

'Do you mean he will lock her up?'

He drank copiously from his bottle. 'Keep an eye on her, that's all.'

Alarmed that she wouldn't be with Mabel when she arrived at the Grange, she said, 'I must speak with my mother. May we leave now?'

'When I'm ready,' he answered. He drained his bottle of barley wine, reached for another and unscrewed the stopper. He waved it in her face and grinned. 'Drink up. You look as though you need it.'

Nell drank again too and muttered, 'I should have known George Wilmot was only thinking about himself again.' But she wondered why George Wilmot would do as Septimus Belfor told him. And why would both of them be so concerned about her mother's ramblings? She felt the fortifying effect of strong ale spreading through her veins and stood up. 'I am ready to leave now,' she stated, 'and if you want to remain a favourite at the Grange you had better get me there quickly.'

He laughed. 'Or else?'

'Or else I shall tell the housekeeper about you and she will know what to do. I bet I'm not the first maid you've interfered with and I'm sure Lady Clarissa does not tolerate such behaviour in her guests any more than in her own family and servants.'

His face changed within seconds and took on an angry scowl. He stood up as well and put his face very close to hers. 'You will not breathe a word about me to anyone at the Grange! Do you hear me? I can have your mother in jail for her stealing and that'll be far worse than the workhouse.'

He was so agitated that she thought he might strike her and turned away from the stench of drink on his breath. He grasped her head, twisted it back and lowered his open lips over hers. He kissed her painfully and savagely, as though this was punishment, and she realised that it was and that he was going to take her again.

She struggled, tearing her mouth away and cried, 'Is this what you want? A woman who hates you and whom you have to rape to gain your satisfaction! You are not fit to call yourself a gentleman.' She still held the bottle in her hand and considered smashing it against the edge of the table and brandishing it as weapon. But she knew he had strength enough to overcome her and – heaven forbid – use it against her. Instead, she glared into his eyes at very close range and hissed, 'Somebody will believe me. There's never any smoke without fire.'

He snarled like an animal and turned it into a mocking laugh. But he moved away from her, picked up the picnic basket and said, 'I'll be in the carriage. Get this room tidied up and lock the front door behind you.'

Nell held her breath until he had left the cottage and then let out a long shuddering sigh. Her hands were shaking but her choice of words had saved her from further humiliation. It seemed that the mention of Lady Clarissa had a more marked effect on him than the threat of his father. Nell ignored his orders, she was not his servant, but lingered until her trembling had subsided, wondering how far they were from the Grange. She was worried about Mother and realised she would have to trust Cyril Belfor to take her there. She straightened her clothing and walked out into the fresh air.

'Bring the key,' he called.

She obeyed him this time and locked the door behind her, handing it over to him without a word. He, too, was silent as they emerged from the other side of the woods to see the Grange boundary wall ahead of them. He drove the carriage to the servants' entrance. A line of carriages occupied one side of the courtyard. Several stable doors were open as visiting coachmen tended their horses or sat in the sunlight polishing harnesses.

He stopped the carriage at the basement steps, climbed down from the driver's seat and walked off towards the coach houses, leaving his horse untethered until a groom came running over. Nell hoped fervently that she had seen the last of Cyril Belfor.

The kitchens were busy. Nell stopped a footman in the passage to introduce herself. He simply yelled out 'Madge!' and disappeared up the stone steps towards the green baize door. A harassed, middle-aged woman came out from a scullery with reddened wet hands. 'Where've you been?' she demanded. 'I'm on my own in there! Follow me.'

Madge took the stone steps two at a time and crossed the rear of the magnificent reception hall in a trice. 'Keep up,' she called as she ran up the narrow wooden stairway.

Nell hurried after her to the very top and they were both out of breath as they went through a small door into a corridor under the eaves, and then into a small room with sloping ceilings.

Madge pointed to one of the iron bedsteads. 'You're over there, and don't be long,' she said.

'Oh, but I have to–' Nell was speaking to an empty room. She blew out her cheeks. She had to find out what had happened to her mother first.

The attic had four iron bedsteads, three of which were made up very neatly. Hers had a pile of folded bedding on it next to a plain grey cambric dress, similar to Madge's. Some calico caps and aprons were on top of it. She put the uniform on a rickety chair, quickly made up the bed, then changed using a spotted mirror on the wall to arrange the plain bonnet-style cap. It covered all her hair and had no decorative embellishments whatsoever. She looked – and felt – plain and dowdy. She wasn't a kitchen maid, she thought, because they wore grey and white stripes under their aprons.

She wished her tin trunk were here so that she could, at least, change her underclothes and wash away all reminders of the afternoon. When she thought about it she felt her colour rising and wondered how long it would be before that stopped. Best to take her mind off it, she decided, and went in search of the old governess and her mother.

Her footsteps echoed on the wooden floorboards and the attic corridor was quiet so she was startled when a door was flung open.

'What are you doing up here? Are you ill?' The woman wore a green parlourmaid's dress open at the neck. She had her lacy cap and apron in her hand. 'Are you the new scullery maid?' she added.

Nell supposed she must be. 'I'm looking for my–' she began.

'I don't care what you're looking for you shouldn't be up here at this time of day. Get off downstairs or I'll report you before you've even started and you'll be carrying slops to the laundry instead.' She glared at Nell, stepped into the middle of the corridor and barred her progress. 'Go on then,' she added and stood there until Nell had retreated to the stairs at the end of the corridor.

Nell guessed there was no one else up there anyway. Governesses were not classed as servants as they were usually from good, if impoverished, families, so Lady Clarissa's old governess would not be housed in a servants' attic. Madge would know where to find her, Nell realised, and hurried down to the sculleries.

They were easy to find as they had glass partitions separating them from the passage. Madge was bending over a wooden sink, up to her elbows in soapy water as she washed the finely decorated china. She placed each piece carefully in a second sink full of clear water.

'What shall I do?' Nell said to her back.

Madge didn't look up. 'Next door,' she said with a jerk of her head. 'Stoke up the fire under the copper and get stuck into that lot in there.'

'Very well,' she replied. 'But please can you tell

me where the governess's room is first?'

'No I can't! Save your chit-chat for teatime; and I want at least half of them pans done by then.'

Chapter 20

The brick-encased copper was in the corner. It had a large brass tap for drawing off the hot water and, underneath it, a small cast-iron door housing the fire pit. Modern kitchen coppers in town had gas to heat them now, Nell thought, as she shovelled in coal and took off the copper's large round lid to test the temperature. It was steaming gently.

This scullery had two deep stone sinks that were piled high with greasy cooking pots and pans. The sinks were linked by a grooved wooden draining board. A stained, worn kitchen table held a selection of scrubbing brushes and two large stone jars of soda. Hessian aprons hung from a wooden peg on the wall. Nell took off her calico, replaced it with hessian and emptied one of the sinks. Then she picked up a large brass pitcher and filled it with hot water. It took ten jugfuls for one sink. She added two handfuls of soda and dropped in the worst of the roasting and baking trays to soak while she tackled the other sink.

That took the rest of the hot water in the copper, so she refilled it with cold water from a brass tap above it on the wall. Someone had thoughtfully fixed a piece of rubber garden hose to it so she was able to direct the water straight into the copper. The fire was drawing well and she added more coal. She was sweating before she had even started on scrubbing the pans.

Many of the smaller copper pans had been used for sauces and garnishes. They were tin-lined and easy to clean so she did those first, dried and polished them and lined them up in size order on the table. They glowed in the light from a window high on the wall over the sinks and she experienced her own glow of satisfaction from a job well done. She pressed on until all her drying cloths were wet and the table was filling up.

The greasy oven trays were worse and needed several goes at the scrubbing as well as another sinkful of hot water and soda for soaking. Her hessian apron was sopping and her arms were red up to the elbows. She pushed a stray lock of hair back under her cap and straightened her aching back.

'So this is where you've ended up.'

She whirled round.

'I've been wondering what happened to you.' Devlin Wilmot stood in front of her, dressed in riding jodhpurs and a tweed waistcoat over a woollen shirt. 'In fact,' he went on, 'I have been looking for you. I was in the stables when you arrived.'

He paused. She had nothing to say to him and his very presence reminded her of his hateful friend and the soreness between her legs.

'You were in a carriage with Cyril Belfor. What did he want with you?' His tone was firm and demanding.

She felt her colour rise and consoled herself with the fact that if her face was as red as her hands, a blush would not show. She wanted to say it was no business of his but realised that, as she was one of the servants now, she could not speak to him in the same way as before. She answered briefly, 'He brought me and my mother over from town.'

'Your mother is here with you?'

'Yes. Mr Belfor arranged it.'

He seemed taken aback.

'Cyril?'

'No, his father. We are living here now.'

He was puzzled. 'Both of you?'

Clearly he did not know about Mabel's recent behaviour towards his father and no one had seen fit to tell him since he returned from university. Well, it wasn't her place to enlighten him either.

'Goodman! Tea!'

Nell caught sight of Madge in the passage behind him. She stopped and stood quite still when she saw Devlin. 'I have to go,' Nell said to him.

He moved to one side. 'Yes, of course. Don't let me keep you.'

She rushed past him, anxious to ask Madge about Her Ladyship's old governess. 'What did Master Devlin want with you?' Madge whispered as they hurried to the servants' hall.

'I don't know,' Nell answered truthfully. 'I have to find my mother. She's supposed to be with the governess.'

'Does she know her, then?'

'She was meeting her at the vicar's. Will she

244

come down for tea?'

'T'old governess has it taken up to her, but not when she goes to the village.'

'Where is she? I've got to see my mother.'

The servants' hall was noisy with maids and footmen sitting chattering around the long rectangular table. They were helping themselves to cups of tea, bread and jam and squares of plain cake.

'This is Nell,' Madge called out as they went to sit down. A few glanced in her direction and went back to their conversations.

'My mother,' Nell reminded her.

'I don't know owt about your mother. I've never heard of the governess having a visitor back from the village.'

'She's staying with her.'

'What? Here? Who is she, then?'

Nell's anxiety mounted. 'She's my mother and I don't know where she is.'

'You'd better ask Mrs Quimby. She'll be here in a minute.'

The chattering stopped as chair legs scraped on the stone-flagged floor and everyone stood up. Mr Paget came in closely followed by the housekeeper. The large wall clock ticked loudly in the silence as he walked to the head of the table.

He did not look pleased. 'I've never heard such a racket at teatime and you don't have to tell me what you're gossiping about. Well, it is family business and not yours. As soon as this shooting party has left, we shall be having a visit from Her Ladyship's grandfather. He will be celebrating his birthday here.'

One of the maids murmured, 'I don't think Her Ladyship will be in any mood to celebrate.' It was the parlourmaid that Nell had met in the attics. She had put on her cap with lace streamers at the back and matching lace-edged apron. She looked very pretty; in fact, she was a very pretty girl with bright blue eyes and glossy black hair.

'You will keep your opinions to yourself and there will be no more talk of it,' Mr Paget thundered. He sat down with a thump.

Everyone else followed his lead. Nell kept her eyes on her tea plate. She was a long way down the table and no one was the least bit interested in her. But she was curious about the servants' hall gossip. 'What's going on?' she muttered to Madge.

'Not sure yet; it's something to do with the family. Nobody tells me anything but I'll find summat out.' Madge sounded confident.

'Can you find out about my mother as well?'

Madge turned to whisper to her neighbour. Valets and lady's maids came and went during tea and at one point a young gardener in corduroys and gaiters hovered on the threshold and called, 'Mrs Quimby, ma'am, they want more cake in the stables. They say there's over twenty of them today with the local gentry here an' all.'

Mrs Quimby, who was deep in a head-to-head discussion with Mr Paget, waved him away impatiently and replied, 'Go and ask Cook.'

The clock chimed and most of the remaining servants got up to leave. Not wishing to be noticed, Nell went with them and waited for Madge inside the scullery.

'Did you find out?' Nell asked anxiously when she returned.

Madge's eyes widened. 'There's going to be a wedding! Well, at least an engagement but it's all hush-hush until this shooting party has left,' she exclaimed. 'It can't be Miss Phoebe – she's well and truly on the shelf – so it must be Master Devlin. I wonder who his fiancée is. It won't be anybody from round these parts else we'd have heard by now.'

Nell was as surprised as Madge. Master Devlin's drunken behaviour was even more unforgivable if he had recently proposed marriage to some unfortunate girl. She supposed he must be in love with her; unless, of course, he was anything like his father who had married first for money and then for social position. She became irritated with herself for dwelling on it and said to Madge, 'I meant did you find out about my mother?'

'Oh yes, well, I think so. One of the housemaids takes up supper to the old governess and she's been instructed to prepare enough for two in future.'

'Where does she take it?'

'She'll show you. If you can get through your work in time you can go up with her.'

'Really? Oh, thank you. I've been so worried.'

'Well, you don't need to be. Miss Twigg's a nice old duck, even if she is old-fashioned in her ways.' Madge glanced at the table full of cleaned pans and cooking pots. 'You've made a good start in there. I think you and me are going to get along nicely.'

'I hope so.' Nell breathed a sigh of relief and went to check the water temperature in her copper.

She took one last look at the array of gleaming copper before she stacked them on to a wooden trolley for a kitchen maid to collect. As she did this she found a folded piece of paper under one of the small saucepans. To her surprise, it was a note to her from Devlin:

Dear Nell,

I must speak with you. Please be aware that I mean you no harm, but I have information that you should know. Meet me outside the stables archway after ten o'clock supper. I'll wait until 11.

It was signed 'Devlin Wilmot' so there could be no doubt it was from him. She screwed it up tightly into a ball in the palm of her hand. Well, she thought, it certainly wasn't wise to keep an assignation at that hour with a man who had shown himself to be capable of uncouth, unruly behaviour. However, when she thought about the way he had conducted himself since, he had certainly tried to make up for his drunken prank. He had even said so to her and she had rebuffed him. This made her realise that, in contrast with his friend Cyril, he was perhaps genuinely sorry.

She was tempted to throw the note in the fire. Instead, she pushed the ball of paper deep into her dress pocket. Devlin's information might concern Mother. George Wilmot had appeared kindly by offering them a home but Nell wasn't at all sure that he had her mother's best interests at heart and

Miss Phoebe certainly hadn't. If his son knew anything that might affect Mabel's welfare then Nell wanted to know about it too. She reasoned that several servants would be enjoying a smoke or a stroll in the fresh air at that time before retiring for the night, so her walk would not be questioned.

Grange servants began their day early and ate their main dinner in the middle of the day, usually before the family took luncheon. Then they had an afternoon tea to keep them going until a late supper of hot soup, cold pie and pickles, sometimes with bubble and squeak, and any cake left over from tea. Cook also made cocoa for them to drink, which was very popular.

A kitchen maid was responsible for preparing the servants' food and another was sent over to the stables for visiting parties. She cooked on the range in the coachman's kitchen and a carriage house had been converted into a servants' hall for outdoor workers. Madge explained all this to Nell when they had finished for the day, had rubbed salve into their wrinkled, reddened hands and were eating supper in the servants' hall.

'First thing in the morning,' Madge went on, 'you go over to the stable block to get the range going for their breakfast and do the washing-up from the night before.'

'What about lighting my copper for the breakfast things here?'

'Damp it down last thing tonight to stay in all night and bank it up in the morning before you go over there.'

'Right you are. Where can I find the maid to show me where Mother is?'

'Oh, I'd forgotten about her. You'd best look sharp. She'll be doing the tray in the still-room now.'

Nell rushed along to where the still-room maid brewed tea and coffee for the family and made Melba toast, Welsh rarebit and other simple specialities for the dining room. Sometimes Mr Paget or a senior footman used it for special requests from the gentlemen. The teapots here were silver, unlike the brown earthenware ones used for servants.

Nell introduced herself to this small, neat young woman who seemed put out by a change in her routine. She glanced disapprovingly at Nell and said, 'Keep quiet and don't get in my way. You can open the doors for me when I'm ready.'

Nell watched her at work. She was very quick and precise in her movements and the tray, though wooden and not silver, looked beautiful with a snow-white cloth and pretty china. Supper for Miss Twigg and her charge consisted of soup, toast and butter, thin slices of cold fowl with beetroot followed by plain cake and a large silver pot of steaming cocoa.

Mother will be very satisfied, Nell thought.

Miss Twigg, Nell discovered, lived in the old nursery at the Grange, housed on the floor beneath the attics. She had a sitting room that used to be the schoolroom, the nanny or governess's bedroom and a night nursery, which was now Mabel's pretty little bedroom with bedcovers that matched the curtains. The sitting room had a small range-style fireplace, where they could boil a kettle to make tea, and a tiny scullery off it. At the back of the scullery there was even a privy with a cistern to flush that was filled from a water tank in the attic above.

Nell waited on the threshold to be invited in. Mabel was sitting at the table with her back to the door, engrossed in a button-sorting task. The still-room maid deposited her tray, said 'Goodnight' and disappeared. Nell noticed Mabel's attention move from her buttons to the food on the tray.

Miss Twigg rocked back and forth in her rocking chair and stood up. She examined Nell closely, looking her up and down, but not in a disparaging way, and said, 'So you're the daughter. Yes, there is a resemblance. Come in.'

She was a tiny, wizened old woman with bright beady brown eyes and a squeaky, though well-to-do, sounding voice. Both her hands were heavily veined with the fingers twisted by arthritis. Nell stepped into the warm room and said, 'It's Nell, Mother. Did you have a nice afternoon in Keppel?'

Mabel turned around and said, 'There you are, dear. Have you come to take me home?'

'You live here now, Mother,' Nell replied. 'So do I and my bedroom is on the floor above you.'

'Can't you come down here to sleep?' Mabel seemed subdued.

Nell guessed she was tired. She answered, 'There isn't enough room for me as well. Do you like it here?'

'I liked it at the vicar's today. We played cards and had Dundee cake for tea.'

'Mrs Goodman was very helpful,' Miss Twigg

added. 'She held my cards for me and I told her which ones to play. Will you share our supper?'

'I had mine in the servants' hall earlier, thank you.' Mabel seemed contented and Nell hesitated before she went on, 'Miss Twigg, my mother is easily confused by new surroundings. You will come and find me if she gets upset, won't you?'

Miss Twigg looked reproachful. 'I see by your dress that you are employed in the sculleries. I do not venture below stairs.'

'But I need to know she is settled and happy in her new surroundings.'

'Miss Goodman, you may rest assured that your mother will be safe and well with me. I was Lady Clarissa's nanny and governess and I nursed her dear mama through her final years.'

'May I come and see her in my time off?'

'Of course, but be sure you are wearing a clean cap and apron, and be warned that Mrs Quimby's rooms are also on this floor.'

'Thank you.'

Miss Twigg nodded. 'Now, my dear, would you lay the table while you are here? My hands are not what they were. You will find all you need in the cupboard.'

Miss Twigg did not wait, or even expect a reply. She sat down with Mabel and helped her to clear away the buttons. She did this by making suggestions rather than giving her orders, which Mabel responded to very well. Nell stayed with them until they had finished their soup. When she left, she was much less worried about their situation at the Grange. Nell didn't mind how many pots she had to scrub if Mother was settled and happy.

She tried her utmost to push to the back of her mind the price she had paid this afternoon. It wasn't her mother's fault. It was hers for trusting in someone who had already shown himself to have dubious morals. She had been foolish to think that Cyril Belfor would take her direct to the Grange after leaving Mabel with the vicar's wife. She should have insisted on staying with her mother. She would do anything to undo the violence he had inflicted on her, but it was too late. What was done could never be undone and she had to live with it as best she could. But it was very difficult to forget such a cruel and selfish assault and she hated herself every time she relived it in her head.

The servants' hall clock was chiming as she passed the open door and it was well past eleven, far too late to go out for a walk. The room was empty and the passage and sculleries were in darkness. She lit an oil lamp, filled and ready for tomorrow's early risers, and took it with her to tend the fire under her copper.

The creaking of the fire grate's cast-iron door as she secured it for the night sounded eerie in the dim light and her movements cast strange shadows on the walls. She froze as she imagined footsteps in the passage and wondered if the Grange had a ghost. She shivered in spite of the warmth, hurriedly finished her task and picked up the lamp to make her way back upstairs.

There was someone in the passage. He came towards her as she approached the stone steps. She braced herself for a ticking-off from Mr

Paget for being late with her duties. Instead, Devlin Wilmot loomed out of the shadows and barred her progress.

'Nell, is that you? Did you find my note?'

'I did, sir, but I have been very busy.'

'No matter; you have finished now and I must talk to you.'

Nell was tired and whatever he had to say she did not want to be caught speaking to him. What if Mr Paget did a late round of the domestic offices? She said, 'I'll get into trouble if I'm seen.'

'You'll get into trouble well enough if you don't hear what I have to say.'

His serious and authoritative tone made her hesitate. It was the way he said 'trouble'. In the factory workers' terraces in town, 'in trouble' meant one thing only to an unmarried woman: a baby. 'What do you mean?' she asked.

'Is there anywhere we can sit? Perhaps somewhere out of this draughty passage?'

Her anxiety increased. 'We have the servants' hall,' she muttered.

'I'll take the lamp. If anyone comes in, I'll say I'm looking for Paget.'

He closed the door so no one would see the light and they sat at the end of the long dining table. 'I shan't keep you long,' he said, 'but I feel some responsibility for him, especially after the way we treated you on the track that day. I know what he's like.'

He was talking about Cyril, she realised, and the word 'trouble' assumed a real significance for her. Her mind was in turmoil. Dear Heaven, she might be having a baby. Once was all it took and it could happen the first time! She was aware of a blush rising in her face and she felt faint not knowing what she would do if she was.

The heat of embarrassment spread through her body. Had Cyril boasted to him about his conquest this afternoon? She began to tremble and stood up. 'I don't want to talk about it,' she said, 'so please leave me alone.'

'But you haven't heard me out yet!' He stood up as well and placed his hand on her arm to stop her going to the door.

She recoiled from him immediately and cried, 'Don't touch me!'

He removed his hand and seemed disturbed by her response. 'Calm down, Nell. I wish to speak to you, that is all.'

She folded her arms, hunched her shoulders and moved away from him. 'Well, I don't want to listen to you.'

'Maybe not but I am trying to help you.' He shrugged and added, 'Still, if this is how you react when a man comes near you, I don't think you need my advice after all.'

'I'll go then,' she replied. This time he did not stop her and she opened the door to the passage.

He called after her, 'Look, Nell, I can't let you go without saying this. I saw you arrive with Cyril Belfor. You were in his carriage, weren't you? I wanted to warn you about him.'

Her hand was still on the doorknob and she leaned on it for support. 'What about Cyril Belfor?' she said to the door.

'He has a weakness for a pretty face, especially if the girl wears a cap and apron.'

She kept her back to him. 'And why should that be of interest to me?'

'Don't pretend innocence, Nell. He must have offered you the ride in his carriage. I was an undergraduate with him so be careful. His favours do not come free.'

She grew hot again. Her heart was thumping and she didn't say anything for a moment. She took a couple of deep breaths to calm her anxiety then said, 'He was doing the favour for his father. Septimus Belfor arranged for me to come here.'

'So you said, but why?'

She let go of the doorknob and turned to face him. 'He's your father's lawyer, isn't he?'

'My father is involved? This doesn't make any sense at all.'

'Have they not told you about my mother? Surely Phoebe has told you about Mother's visits to the brewery. They want her out of the way and...'A sob threatened in her throat. She swallowed and coughed to cover her choking. 'Well, the alternative doesn't bear thinking about.'

She didn't want to appear weak and stared hard at him, hoping her welling tears did not show.

He shook his head and seemed genuinely concerned. 'I have not been a party to any of this.'

She believed him. Why would he know anything that had happened at the brewery or in town? He had not been at home for most of the last few years, and certainly had not rolled up his sleeves at the brewery as he used to when he was a boy.

Exhaustion swept over Nell. The day's events had taken a mental and physical toll on her and she was in danger of crumpling into a sobbing, sorry heap in front of him. Her intake of breath trembled. He noticed but she straightened her back and went on, 'If that is all, Master Devlin, I have to be down here again at six in the morning.' She hesitated for a second and then added, 'Goodnight, sir.'

She twisted round quickly and ran out of the door, stumbled up the stone steps and across the rear of the entrance hall until she fell into the lobby at the bottom of the back stairs. She didn't stop, not even to light one of the candles used by the servants, until she had reached the attics and her breath was coming in hoarse rasps. Then she paused, waiting until her breathing had calmed. The other girls would be asleep already and they would not thank her for waking them. She wanted them to be friends. She needed friends at the Grange.

Chapter 21

Scullery maids were the first indoor servants up in the morning. Outside, stable lads were already seeing to the horses but no one else was around. The kitchen was in a former coachman's residence in the middle of the block and resembled a homely farmhouse kitchen with a large cooking range. A long wooden table filled the centre, littered with mugs and tankards and bits of dried pie crusts from yesterday's supper. However, the fire had been properly tended the evening before and was easy to bring to life. A huge blackened kettle had been on the range hotplate all night and was already hot.

Nell cleared the table and took the pots through to the scullery at the back where there was an old-fashioned water pump at a shallow stone sink. She washed up then scrubbed the table, refilled the kettle and left it to heat up on the range. A kitchen maid, recognisable by her grey and white striped dress, came in carrying baskets laden with sausages, bacon, eggs and bread. The girl was bleary-eyed but grateful for Nell's efforts.

Back at her own scullery the washing-up seemed endless. It arrived regularly throughout the day. The Grange was full of guests for Lady Clarissa's shooting party and they brought valets and lady's maids with them, all expecting to be well fed, whether upstairs or downstairs. Trout, venison and grouse, of course, were served at just one dinner for the guests and two whole briskets of beef were boiled for the servants.

Servants scurried up and down the passage from early morning to late evening with only a brief lull after upstairs luncheon and before their afternoon tea. Those who were not needed were allowed a couple of hours' rest before the guns and followers returned, mud-spattered and hungry for toasted pikelets, scones warm from the oven and fruit cake with Wensleydale cheese. Afterwards, the guests took baths before they dressed for dinner and Nell's copper was drained by footmen carrying brass water cans upstairs to dressing rooms. In fact, all scullery and laundry coppers were emptied for bathing and Nell had to carry kettles full of hot water from Cook's kitchen range to her sink.

'Why don't they have gas coppers?' she asked Madge as they creamed their hands and went for tea. 'The well-off in town have gas geysers over the sinks for hot water. Mind you, I've heard they can be dangerous.'

'There's talk of gas being laid to the village. If that happens, we'll have it here, but not for this winter. They don't need it for light upstairs because they have electric light from a motor in one of the empty wine cellars.' Unusually, Madge lingered over her bread and jam and square of gingerbread and Nell asked why. 'The water won't be hot enough to go back yet. Why don't you get some fresh air for half an hour?'

'I'd rather pop upstairs and see Mother, if that's all right.'

'Go on, then, but don't let any of the guests see you.'

Nell ran up the back stairs and found the former nursery was empty. She stood on the landing outside, wondering where Mabel might be. The main staircase came up to the third floor and she heard raised voices from beneath her. Curious, she went to the top of the carpeted flight and peered down. Mrs Quimby was in earnest conversation with Miss Twigg.

'Take her back upstairs, Miss Twigg,' the house-keeper said. 'I have gentlemen guests bathing in these rooms.'

'She is looking for her daughter,' Miss Twigg replied. 'She thinks she is down here.'

Nell's heart sank. It was Mother, looking for

her as usual. She knew this would happen. She walked halfway down the stairs and called, 'I'm up here, Mother.'

Mrs Quimby gave her an angry look and came up to meet her. 'I knew it was you. Well, I don't know how you've wormed your way in here with her, but it won't do. It won't do at all. You will come and see me downstairs after supper to-night. Now take her back to where she belongs.'

Mabel had heard Nell's voice and called, 'Where have you been? I've looked all over for you.' She came into view at the bottom of the stairs.

Miss Twigg took Mabel's arm and said, 'Shall we have that cup of tea now, Mrs Goodman?'

Nell went further down the stairs, her eyes widening at the sumptuous carpeting and gilded decor on the second landing. 'And I've been looking for you, too.' She smiled.

Mabel shook Miss Twigg's hand free of her arm and linked it with Nell's. 'Which room is mine, dear? Will you show me?'

'You're upstairs, Mother; this way.'

Nell noticed that Miss Twigg struggled with the stairs. Her arthritis clearly went beyond her gnarled fingers. She was a very old lady and Nell went back to help her. 'Is Mother too much for you?' she asked quietly.

'No, Miss Goodman. She can be very helpful. She's very close to you, isn't she?'

'As if I haven't got enough to do with the Grange full for the shooting,' Mrs Quimby muttered as she overtook them. She swept past Mabel and along the landing to her bedroom.

As soon as they were back in the nursery,

Mabel brewed a pot of tea and sat in front of the fire with a toasting fork and dish of pikelets. It was something they had done regularly together on Sundays at home, Nell thought, as she laid the table and found a dish of fresh butter and a jug of milk. But she wondered if her mother would get used to Miss Twigg being there instead of her. She took the warm plate from her mother and said, 'Come and sit at the table now.'

Miss Twigg asked Nell to have tea with them. Nell knew she did not have time but agreed anyway. While they sat around the table she took the opportunity to explain to her mother how much Miss Twigg needed her help with her arthritis being so bad. Mabel half listened. She was more interested in the tea but she seemed impressed by Miss Twigg's genteel, old-fashioned ways. It must remind Mother of when Father was alive, Nell thought, and they lived in a big house with linen tablecloths and pretty china.

Miss Twigg was old and bent but she was intelligent and alert and had realised quickly that Mabel was 'difficult'. However, she seemed to be taking the situation in her stride. As Nell got up to go, she said, 'One of the stable boys will drive us to the village once a week in the governess cart for the whist drive at the vicar's. He takes me to church every Sunday, too, unless the weather prevents it. Why don't you both come with me?'

'Mother will, I'm sure, but I don't know about my time off yet, ma'am,' Nell replied.

'Lady Clarissa is very keen on church for the servants.'

It sounded like a warning to Nell and she

promised she would try to join them for morning service, although she had no idea how she would manage it. Madge might help, she thought, and the shooting party would have left by then. She left eventually to return to her scullery.

Madge was not in a good humour. 'Where've you been? I said half an hour!'

'I'll make it up, I promise. I'll come back after supper.'

'You'll have to! Take a look at that lot!'

The kitchen and still-room never stopped during shooting, from cooking the enormous breakfasts and game pies for the guns out in the fields to late-night suppers for the gentlemen in the billiard room. Luncheon was four courses and dinner seven or eight. Cakes were freshly baked for tea each day and shortbread biscuits for the bedrooms in case guests were hungry in the night. Valets and lady's maids frequented the still-room preparing bedroom trays of tea, coffee and chocolate for their masters and mistresses.

The servants, too, ate huge amounts and, at first, Nell wondered where they put it all. She soon learned that a long day of non-stop activity increased her own hunger. The scullery sinks were full of baking trays and saucepans and the table piled with crockery from the servants' hall. As soon as she cleared it, it filled again and her back was beginning to ache from lifting ewers of water and bending over sinks. It was much heavier work than bottle-washing at the brewery but she guessed she'd get used to it eventually.

The servants' supper came after the dining-room dinner and clearly one or two footmen had been sampling the dining-room wine. Mrs Quimby and Mr Paget, too, seemed in a more jovial mood. The housekeeper chose to ignore Nell, and Mr Paget was not interested in any of the female servants unless they caused trouble. Nell caught sight of Eddie and waved at him, but he was as busy as she. He ate and ran and she presumed he had a constant stream of muddy boots to clean and polish before morning.

Nell and Madge were downstairs maids and their grey dresses and plain serviceable caps meant they were more or less invisible to the up-stairs parlourmaids and footmen. Kitchen maids, who relied on them, acknowledged their exist-ence, but they ate with Cook's brigade in their own separate dining room. Madge said it was the custom in big houses. Nell asked her about church on Sundays.

'Oh, Her Ladyship is very keen. Everyone who can be spared is expected to troop down to the village for morning service. It's more of a get-together really,' Madge explained, 'but we do get a sermon from the vicar. They say Her Ladyship tells him what to say depending on what's been going on here. We all go, though, because it's time away from your duties on top of your half day.'

'Will that include me?'

'Oh aye, ducks. The shooting party will have left by Sunday and we'll be nearly back to normal. I say nearly because we've got the birthday party next week.' Madge's eyes widened suddenly. 'Be-sides, nobody'll miss next Sunday! T'vicar'll be reading the banns for the wedding so we'll know who he's marrying.' Madge smiled in a secretive way. 'Whoever she is I expect they'll have the ceremony here because he is the son and heir. Miss Phoebe had her nose put right out of joint by that.'

Nell thought about this and although she didn't like Miss Phoebe very much she said, 'Well, she is the eldest and she does run the brewery now. It doesn't seem fair that Master Devlin should have it all.'

'Aye. She's always been jealous of him because he's Lady Clarissa's favourite. I don't blame Miss Phoebe. She is her father's real daughter and he's adopted.'

'That's common knowledge, though, isn't it?'

'Her Ladyship wanted a son. She's old-fashioned, you see, about male heirs and all that. She couldn't have children of her own.' Madge clapped her hand to her mouth. 'I shouldn't have said that! It's not a secret but we're not supposed to talk about it.'

'I'm not a gossip,' Nell reassured her. Madge was the only person who saw fit to talk to her here, anyway, she thought. But the mention of children resurrected the worry about her own condition. She pushed back her chair. 'I'll have to get back now. Mrs Quimby wants to see me after supper so I'll be working until midnight at this rate.'

Madge followed her and whispered to her back, 'What does she want to see you about? You're the best scullery maid I've ever had here.'

Nell was honest with her. 'It's about my mother. I never know what she's going to do next so I think Mrs Quimby will want me to leave.'

'I'm not having that! You've only just started

264

and I didn't have to show you how to do anything. Don't you worry, lass. I'll make sure Cook knows 'cos the kitchen maids won't want you to go either.'

'Thank you.' Nell smiled, although she didn't think Madge's intervention would make any difference.

Mrs Quimby was stern-faced and marched Nell straight down to the butler's pantry where Mr Paget stored the silver. It was a large room and when he called out 'Enter!' Nell was surprised to see a huge thick iron safe door standing open. The safe was large enough to walk inside. She glimpsed shelves of shiny serving dishes and candelabra. Mr Paget emerged, leaned on the door to close it, then swung a large lever upwards and spun a dial on the outside.

'That's done for the night. Sit down, Mrs Quimby.'

The room contained a clerk's desk with ledgers on shelves behind it, a small table with two dining chairs, two further fireside chairs beside the grate and a bed. Good heavens, Nell thought, Mr Paget must sleep in here to guard the silver! He joined Mrs Quimby at the table and poured them each a small glass of brandy. Nell stood there quietly as they discussed her and sipped their drinks.

'I know she's a problem for you,' the butler said, 'and I don't want the little madam here any more than you do, but we're stuck with her for the foreseeable.'

'It's her mother that's causing the trouble.'

'I've heard all about it. Mr Wilmot's filled me in

and it's his wishes that they both stay.'

Mrs Quimby was indignant. 'Well, what does Her Ladyship say to that?'

'She knows nowt about it and it's best if it stays that way. She's up in arms about the engagement as it is.'

'*Pas devant*, Mr Paget,' Mrs Quimby said sourly.

Nell understood what she meant from learning French from the headmaster's classes at school. *Pas devant la bonne* was 'not in front of the maid'.

But Mr Paget glanced at her sharply. 'It'll be all round the village on Sunday anyway.'

'Yes and I'll lose my head parlourmaid.' Mrs Quimby sounded very cross.

'Now who's saying too much?' he warned.

'All right. Tell me what to do with this one.' She grimaced in Nell's direction.

'Keep her below stairs and out of sight. She'll behave because she doesn't want to see her mother in the workhouse and Miss Twigg has got the mother in hand.'

'Miss Twigg doesn't mind, then?'

'She's happy to have summat to do.'

Mrs Quimby gave an irritable sigh. 'If you say so.'

'I do. Another snifter?'

'I don't mind if I do,' Mrs Quimby replied. She glared at Nell and added, 'You can go now and don't think you'll ever move from the scullery, because you won't.'

'She'll be gone after the wedding, any road,' Mr Paget added. 'Everything will change after that.'

Nell breathed a sigh of relief. George Wilmot had kept his word and overruled Mr Paget. This

266

made her think that there was something in Mother's ramblings that worried him so much he didn't want it spread around. She wondered what it was and her imagination was fully occupied as she worked on until midnight, clearing the backlog of dishes for the next day. But suppositions were not truths and she gave up trying to fathom a reason.

Her thoughts turned to the head parlourmaid. Why would she leave? Unless, of course, she was the bride and that was why Her Ladyship disapproved? It was not beyond the realms of possibility nowadays and she was very pretty. She'd find out on Sunday, she thought, as she toiled up to the attics, aching and weary. Mother was content, which cheered Nell and enabled her to drift off to sleep despite her own worries.

As soon as the guests began to leave and Nell's washing-up eased a little, Madge took her out to the game larder. It was well away from the house, beyond the stables and next to the walled garden. The building itself was just a brick outhouse with a slate roof. Inside it was single storey and cold, with a few small high windows to let in daylight. A skinned deer hung by its hind legs over a tiled floor at one end. Its head had been removed and the neck stump was dark red with congealed blood. Nell felt her stomach lurch. A slate-covered bench went around the inside of the walls with iron hooks suspended from the ceiling above it. They mostly carried the recently shot grouse, with a few hare and rabbit.

'Cook wants a dozen brace plucked and gutted

for the banquet next week, but you can't start on them until she gives you the nod that they're ready.'

'Me?' Nell queried. She shivered and felt sick, not sure if it was the cold or the sight of all those lifeless carcasses. In town, she had usually purchased her meat ready butchered from a market stall, or ready cooked from his shop. If she bought a rabbit, the butcher skinned and gutted it for her.

'Aye, lass, plucking and gutting the wildfowl is our job in this household. I'll show you how. You've plucked a fowl before, haven't you?'

'Once a year at Christmas,' Nell replied, remembering sitting in the back yard with an old sheet spread on the ground to catch the feathers, and sore fingers afterwards. A dozen brace!

'I'll ask if you can do them on Sunday afternoon while it's quiet, then maybe I can give you a hand.'

'Thanks, Madge.'

'You'll have to help me black-lead the range if I do. I have to show you how to do that, any road.'

Nell smiled. 'I know how to clean up a kitchen range,' she reassured her.

'Aye, you're not the usual sort I get for the scullery. We can have a nice long chat when we walk to church on Sunday.'

Nell explained about going with her mother and Miss Twigg in the governess cart. Madge frowned at her in a benign way and repeated, 'Aye, not the usual sort at all.'

Chapter 22

On Sunday the number of guests at the Grange had reduced considerably, if the washing-up was anything to go by. In the servants' hall, there was an air of excited anticipation about the expected announcement in church, except for those who already knew. They were the most senior servants and they maintained a grim, tight-lipped silence when urged to tell.

Nell was excited about seeing Mother and riding in the trap to the village. She carefully arranged the trim on her best white blouse, brushed down her good skirt and jacket and polished her boots. Eddie, their driver, was holding the pony's head as she approached. He was spruced up, too, and looking forward to seeing his family in church. Nell realised that would include Joe and frowned. She liked Joe and would have been delighted to see him if she hadn't been so cruelly defiled by Cyril Belfor. He had made her feel dirty inside. She wondered if Joe would be able to tell just by looking at her what had happened in that deserted cottage in the woods. Her hand went automatically to her stomach. How long will it be before I know? she thought.

'You all right, miss?' Eddie asked.

'Yes. Why shouldn't I be? It's a lovely morning.' It was. The sun was shining and it promised to be hot by the afternoon. 'Here's Mother with Miss

Twigg now.'

Nell helped them both into the trap and climbed up beside them. Eddie closed the gate at the back and went back to gather up the pony's reins and they were soon on their way, overtaking a column of servants before they reached the village. Mother was in very good spirits and behaved well. It was only when she was left to her own devices that she brooded on the past and became agitated. She wore a summer frock with matching ribbon on her straw hat and Miss Twigg had changed from her everyday black to a grey muslin with ribbon insets.

Eddie left them at the lych-gate and they walked through the graveyard to find their pew before the other servants arrived. Everyone had to be settled before the Wilmots arrived. Eddie had said that Master Devlin was bringing them in his motor car.

It was a large church with three very fine stained-glass windows behind the altar. Miss Twigg had a pew not far from the front. Nell hoped it wasn't the same one as Mr Paget and Mrs Quimby. She suggested she move further back but Miss Twigg wouldn't hear of it. She must sit with her mother.

However, on the other side of the central aisle, Nell was extremely disconcerted to see Septimus Belfor with his frumpy wife and his son sitting at the front. What on earth were they doing here? Surely they worshipped at the parish church in town where Septimus was a trustee for the spire repair fund? Cyril looked over his shoulder, saw her and gave her one of his sly, crooked smiles. He was such a horrid, hateful man, the very sight of him made her freeze in her pew. She tried to relax, but what on earth would she do if she was having a baby? Both hands shifted to her stomach as she sat and stared straight ahead.

The pews in front of her filled up with the more senior servants from the Grange and then the family came in, led by Mr Wilmot, who stood aside to allow his son, daughter and wife to file in. He exchanged a nod with Septimus and then sat down beside Lady Clarissa.

She was a very grand lady, way above her husband in the social scale, but that did not appear to concern her unduly. She ran the Grange as it ought to be run and employed lots of local people on the estate. She was always gracious but known to say very little over and above what was required of the occasion. Nell noticed a significant gap between her and her husband in their pew and an even bigger one between her and Miss Phoebe. The vicar had followed them down the aisle and the service was soon under way.

Gosh, the singing was good! Nell and her mother loved the singing. The organ was at full volume and hymns filled the lofty building. Nell glanced round at one point to see a packed church with villagers standing at the back. She had only seen that before at the Christmas midnight mass. The announcements came at the end, when the offertory plate circulated. Often there were murmurings of conversation at this stage but today everyone held their breath. However, no one heard anything after the vicar had read the banns. They were too busy muttering to each other.

Miss Phoebe! Miss Phoebe was the one getting married. Not Master Devlin and certainly not

271

the head parlourmaid. Nell herself thought she hadn't heard it right: Miss Phoebe and Cyril Belfor. *Cyril Belfor!* No one could believe it, and the murmurings echoed around the congregation. Dear heaven, thought Nell, Cyril Belfor was going to marry Miss Phoebe and she might be expecting his child. A low buzzing filled her head and she thought she was going to faint. She closed her eyes and slipped to her knees on the hassock to recover. Her head fell forward onto her hands, resting on the back of the pew in front as though in prayer. It was a good cover until the organ bellowed into life again and the Wilmot family followed their vicar out of the church.

'Are you feeling quite well, Miss Goodman?' Miss Twigg enquired.

Nell pulled herself together. 'Yes, thank you. It's become very warm in here, don't you think?'

'Not really, my dear,' Miss Twigg replied. 'I hope you are not sickening for something.'

The Belfors had gone with others who were in their party. What were they doing here anyway? They should have been in their own church to hear the banns read there, Nell thought irritably. Outside, the sun shone brilliantly and they were in time to see Devlin's motor vehicle followed by two horse-drawn carriages drive off towards the Grange. Miss Twigg liked to read the newest gravestones for inscriptions and Mabel joined her as they wandered around the church yard in the warmth.

Crowds of servants and villagers spilled out into the open air, heads together in gossip about the news. Nell overheard a few comments and agreed silently. She knew both Miss Phoebe and Cyril Belfor better than she wanted to, and it really was a most unlikely match. But her feelings about Cyril Belfor were still very raw and she did not wish to be drawn into any of the conversations. Instead, she went off in search of Miss Twigg's pony and trap and had to walk down a long tree-lined lane past several other carriages to find it. She welcomed the cooling shade and put her hand to her forehead. Perhaps she did have a fever?

'Nell! I was hoping I might see you. Eddie told me you were at the Grange.'

'Joe! How are you?' His friendly, welcoming face cheered her up.

'Pleased to see you.'

He emphasised the 'you', which made her feel even better. She asked after his parents and he in turn enquired about Mabel.

'I'm glad you're both settled. Do you get a half day?'

'Once a fortnight on a Wednesday. Apparently, the other maids walk to the omnibus terminus and go into town.'

'I know,' he said. 'If you go with them, I can bring you back to the village in the cart when I fetch Mother.'

'Oh, would you? That's very kind. I can stay quite late at the market then.'

'Well, in that case, will you have tea with me at the Copper Kettle?'

'Oh Joe, I'd love that. I really would.' It was just what she needed to take her mind off her worries and she wanted to hug him.

273

'I'll come in early and meet you. You just say when.'

They talked easily for several minutes until they heard the church clock chime.

'Time to go,' Joe commented. 'Eddie'll be looking for his trap. I said I'd bring it round to the lych-gate for him. It gives him more time to see his friends in the village.'

Joe is such a nice man, Nell thought as he helped her climb up to sit beside him. He walked the pony and trap down the lane to the church then handed the reins to a waiting Eddie. Nell said goodbye to Joe and went to find her mother and Miss Twigg. They were at the far end of the church yard and she had to call to attract their attention. She had to hurry; she would have to start on the grouse after dinner.

Mabel had not set eyes on Lady Clarissa before the service and she made one or two less than flattering comments as they rode back to the Grange. It was not only the content of her remarks that embarrassed Nell, but the way she said them, which was nothing short of rude. Lady Clarissa was not a handsome woman, and, although she was beautifully dressed, she had no bosoms to speak of and would not have needed any padding when bustles were fashionable.

'Mother,' Nell chided, 'please be quiet. Lady Clarissa is Mr Wilmot's wife.'

'Well, at least she's not a trollop like the first one.' Mabel turned to Miss Twigg. 'He said he'd marry *me*, you know, after she died.'

Miss Twigg's face showed surprise but she did not respond. Nell wondered if she had orders to report to Mr Wilmot anything Mabel said.

'Weren't you married to Father at the time?' Nell queried.

'George killed him and stole all his money,' Mabel stated. 'He felt guilty, you see.'

Nell distracted her by pointing out the beautiful wrought-iron gates as they came into view. They passed the spot where Devlin and Cyril had attacked her. She had thought that Devlin was as bad as Cyril then. Now she knew different. She stared unseeing into the distance.

'Are you sure you are quite well, Miss Goodman?' Miss Twigg prompted.

'A little tired, that's all. I am adjusting to my new duties.'

Servants' Sunday dinner of boiled shoulder of mutton and onion sauce followed by spotted dick and Bird's patent custard was eaten as soon as they returned from church. Afterwards, Madge handed Nell her sacking apron and took her straight round to the game larder.

'Tackle them a brace at a time. Save all the feathers in these pillow shams and put the guts in that bucket by the old horse trough. The pump's a bit rusty but it still works.' Madge set her up with groundsheet and chair on the shady side of the building.

It was so quiet that Nell could have been sitting in the middle of the moors. A few bumble-bees buzzed around. She had to work quickly to get the gutted birds back in the larder before the blowflies got to them. Fortunately the flies seemed more attracted to the bucket of guts, which turned her stomach every time she leaned over it.

However, she soon got into a rhythm of stretching the skin and tugging the feathers in the opposite direction. The trick was not to tear the skin as it would ruin the appearance of the finished bird for the table. Inspired by this morning's hymns, she began to sing a country folk song that she'd learned at school to keep herself company.

She faltered when she heard the snort of a horse and looked up to find Master Devlin leading his hunter round to the trough. He was hot and sweaty, his hair tousled and his boots dusty, as though he had been riding hard. His sober church dress had gone; he had taken off his waistcoat and opened his shirt at the neck. This was a different Devlin, altogether more primitive, she thought. Nell frowned, as he was more akin to the drunken Devlin she had first met on the track. She glanced around nervously for Cyril but Devlin seemed to be alone.

'Don't stop,' he called. 'I remember that song from my schooldays.'

He did not sound dangerous. 'Good afternoon, sir,' she replied, but did not resume her singing.

'I had forgotten about this old pump,' he commented as he worked the handle a few times. It screeched and whined before water gushed into the trough. He continued pumping until there was enough for his horse to drink. She watched him for several minutes flexing his arm and back. He examined his horse's flanks and fetlocks, stroking, patting and murmuring. Suddenly he looked directly at her and, embarrassed, she quickly resumed her plucking. As soon as he left she could go over to the bucket to gut this grouse and start on the other.

He won't be long, she thought, it must be time for luncheon and he has to dress.

After another few minutes he took the horse's bridle and walked him over to where she was sitting. 'What are you doing here, Nell?' he asked.

She thought that was obvious but answered, 'Cook wants a doz–'

'Not plucking grouse,' he interrupted. 'Why are you working in the sculleries at the Grange? You used to be in the office at the brewery before I went away. Madge told me you came from the bottle-washing plant.'

'Times have changed, sir?'

'Don't call me "sir".'

'Very well, Master Devlin.'

'Not that either; not when we're alone. What's wrong with "Devlin"?'

'Nothing at all.'

'Good. Well, why don't you tell me what's been going on in my absence?'

'You need to speak with your father – or Miss Phoebe.'

He tethered his horse to an iron ring in the wall and took a few steps closer. 'I want to hear your version. Why is my father doing everything Septimus Belfor asks of him?'

What could she say? If you knew the rumours my mother was spreading about your father, you'd see that it was sound advice? 'Both gentlemen have been very helpful to me and my mother.'

'You wouldn't have needed to come here if you

had still been in the office.'

'Yes I would. I have to keep a close eye on Mother and I couldn't do that at the brewery.'

'You could have had an alms house in town,' he stated.

A dream, Nell thought. They were an alternative to the workhouse for those who had the right connections, or the means to pay. 'I couldn't afford that for her.'

'The brewery donates regularly and it has a welfare fund. Mother insisted on it. It's what her family do: they look after their servants.'

Miss Phoebe and her father must have known that all along and never even offered! Nell pursed her lips but answered civilly, 'Mother is contented with Miss Twigg. She knows how to keep her occupied.'

'Miss Twigg had a good effect on me when I was growing up, but she arrived too late to influence Phoebe. I'd have thought you could do better than the scullery.'

'I have no complaints,' she answered. It wasn't strictly true and she looked down at the freshly plucked bird on her lap.

'Tell me what you know, Nell. It's not so much what Septimus Belfor is doing, but *why*. Why is he suddenly so involved with my family's affairs?'

And mine, Nell added silently but she said, 'You ask me that when his son is going to marry your sister?'

Devlin guffawed. 'That makes even less sense than you and your mother taking up residence here! Cyril's taste is not for my sister. His appetite is for chambermaids, innkeepers' daughters, Lot-

278

tie in the tearooms–' He stopped and stared at her.

Alarm had spread across Nell's features. Dear heaven, did he know about Cyril and her?

However, to her relief, he misinterpreted her concern. 'Mother forbids such behaviour here, of course,' he added.

Nell's heart began to thump. She was just another girl in a defenceless situation that Cyril had taken advantage of, except that he planned to continue his appalling behaviour with *her* after his wedding. And this man in front of her was his friend! She wished he'd go and leave her to pull out the entrails of the grouse. It made her retch but it was infinitely preferable to continuing this conversation. She stood up, holding the plucked bird by its legs and said, 'I have to get on with this.'

'Talk to me, Nell. Tell me what's going on here.'

'I don't know,' she answered, irritated by his persistence. 'Ask Cyril Belfor. He's your friend, isn't he?'

'He's no friend of mine. We were undergraduates together and from the same town, that's all. We're cut from very different cloth.'

'Well, Madge will be back in five minutes and I have another bird to pluck.'

He seemed to accept this and took the legs of the plucked grouse from her. 'I'll gut this one. You start on the other.' He carried it over to the bucket, came back for the last one, and gutted that as well. Then he hung the last brace in the larder while she stuffed the remaining feathers in the pillow shams.

He pumped more water and they stood side by side in silence to rinse their hands in the trough.

'Won't you be late for luncheon?' Nell remarked.

'I made my excuses. I needed a hard ride over the moor,' he answered shortly.

When Madge arrived he untied his horse and picked up the bucket of giblets. 'I'll take this round to the kennels. They're on my way.'

Madge waited until he was out of earshot. 'You want to watch your step, young lady. He's gentry and he's sniffing around you. They love and leave you, they do. Ask the head parlourmaid.'

'But that wasn't Master Devlin!' Nell exclaimed.

'No, it wasn't. Who told you?'

'I ... I don't remember,' she muttered.

'Well, she's having a bairn, so let that be a lesson to all of you young 'uns. She hasn't said as much but us women know about these things and Lady Clarissa is hopping mad to be losing her. She's not telling Mr Paget about the bairn either, 'cos he's giving her a testimonial on condition she doesn't talk about the goings-on with you-know-who.'

No, that would never do, Nell thought petulantly. The daughter of the house is to marry a gentleman of dubious character who put the head parlourmaid in the family way! Nell closed her eyes in horror. And the scullery maid, she added silently. Surely she should have started by now? She racked her brain for dates and counted the days on her fingers behind her back.

'I'm surprised Miss Phoebe still wants to marry him. I wouldn't,' Nell said.

'Miss Phoebe doesn't know. Listen to me, lass.

If you're staying here you have to understand that the Grange runs on two railway lines that never meet. Lady Clarissa and Cook on the one track, with Mr Wilmot, Miss Phoebe and Mr Paget on the other.'

'What about Mrs Quimby?'

'Sits on the fence between them, she does. She'll have a seizure one day, mark my words.'

'And the rest of the servants?'

Madge laughed. 'We just get on with our work. Nowt surprises us any more.'

'Not even this engagement?'

'Maybe. We all thought Miss Phoebe was well and truly left on the shelf so snaring a handsome young fellow a few years younger than her sounds all right to me. She's not too old for bairns yet, but he'll have to get a move on with her.'

Bairns again! Nell wished that Madge would stop mentioning them. 'Shall I go back to the game larder after tea?' she suggested.

'No, I'll do the rest of the grouse. I want you to clean the kitchen range for me. They can manage with just the still-room for tonight.'

Wire-brushing and black-leading a warm range was hot work and the lofty kitchen seemed airless to Nell. She felt limp and sticky well before she had finished and by the end wanted nothing more than to put her head under a cold water pump. She scrubbed her blackened nails, took off her sacking apron and went in search of Madge who was plucking the last of the grouse.

'Phew, it's warm this afternoon,' she said, and flopped down on the grass by the shady wall.

'You look done for,' Madge commented.

'It was hot in there.'

'You can slow down a bit, you know. It's quiet on a Sunday afternoon with no guests.'

'May I go and see Mother?'

'Best not, ducks. Miss Twigg'll be having a nap after this morning's excitement. Go for a little walk instead.'

Nell's heart lifted. It was a beautiful afternoon. 'Can I?'

'Stick to round the back of the walled garden. You'll find the kitchen garden and yon side are the gardeners' bothies. I'd keep clear of them if I were you 'cos they're a lively bunch. Don't go inside the high walls either in case the family are out for a stroll. Take one of them baskets from the larder and if anyone sees you, you'll look like you're delivering summat.'

'Thanks, Madge.' Nell scrambled to her feet.

'Our tea's at half past five on Sundays.'

'I won't be late.' She set off with a spring in her step.

Chapter 23

It was so peaceful wandering through the vegetable plots picking the pea or bean pods and sampling the contents. Stick beans were in flower and bumble bees hummed around them. A boy, who couldn't have been more than twelve, was filling watering cans from a rainwater butt and carrying them to a bed of young winter greens.

Nell's eyes followed the drainpipe upwards and realised that beneath the ivy covering this wall was part of a building. A small wrought-iron gate beside it offered a tempting view of the walled garden. It was huge and on the far side a line of glasshouses leaned against the high brick wall.

Espalier fruit trees spread across the warm bricks and regimented beds of soft-fruit bushes and canes linked by raked gravel paths filled the centre. She heard the squeak and clang of another iron gate, out of sight and to one side of her, then the crunch of gravel underfoot.

'What is this building?' she asked the boy.

'Dunno,' he replied. 'Never bin in there mesenn.' He stopped watering and bent to pull a few young carrots that he dunked and washed in the watering can. He offered her one. She accepted it with a smile and crunched on it. As he chewed he pointed to the gate and grinned. 'Is that your fancy man?'

Nell followed his gaze. One of the footmen had come round the side of the building to smoke a cigarette and was waving to her through the intricate ironwork. She had noticed him in the servants' hall because he was the one who had been kind to her on that day Mr Paget had seen her off the premises. She doubted that he was aware of her existence.

'You're the new scullery maid, aren't you?' he asked now.

She nodded, not sure whether he was friend or foe in this divided house. 'I didn't think servants were allowed inside the walled garden.'

'We're bringing out the tea. Lady Clarissa has

283

tea in her garden room every Sunday if the weather allows. Do you want to see?'

'May I?'

He put out his cigarette on the wall and pocketed the stub, then opened the gate for her. The garden room was a small single-storey red-brick building with stone slabs laid in front of it and a pair of very wide glazed doors that opened onto the paving. The glazing was made up of many small panes of glass and all the woodwork was painted white to match the whitewashed brick walls. Most of the walls were hidden by folding screens decorated with scenes from the Orient. The floor was made up of simple red quarry tiles. The footman held open the door for her and she stepped inside. Another footman, wearing white gloves, was polishing tea knives and spoons and laying them carefully by delicate gold-edged porcelain on a white linen tablecloth.

The table was laid for six. Dishes of butter curls, strawberry jam and thick cream were dotted around a large Victoria sponge cake in the centre. A side table held silver spirit burners that Nell had seen in the still-room. They were used for keeping tea kettles hot or making scrambled eggs in the dining room for late suppers. It was very pretty and Nell gazed, enchanted, for a few moments, aware that her mouth was watering. She swallowed.

A boy in livery arrived with a large salver, covered by a silver dome. He was about the same age as Eddie and Madge had pointed him out to Nell as the hall boy. 'Just cucumber sandwiches and scones today,' he said. 'Mr Paget said Lady

Clarissa didn't order any pikelets.'

'I'm not surprised. They've only just finished luncheon,' Nell's companion responded, pulling on his white gloves. He took the salver from the boy and placed it on a side table. 'Go and fetch the hot water then,' he prompted, and the hall boy left swiftly. The other footman began to arrange the tiny crustless triangles daintily on the porcelain sandwich plates. It was a peaceful setting that was suddenly shattered by a piercing whistle and both footmen looked up wide-eyed.

'That must be old Paget already. He's early. It's not five o'clock yet.'

'I'd better go,' Nell said.

'No time. He'll be at the gate and see you. Quick, over here.' He pulled one of the Oriental screens forward and pushed her behind it, kicking her basket out of sight after her, just as Mr Paget's bulky figure loomed in the doorway.

'Get your skates on, lads,' Mr Paget boomed. 'They're on their way.'

'But the tea's not here yet, sir.'

'They'll walk round the garden first.'

Nell held her breath. She peered through the gap where the screen was hinged and hoped no one could see her. Both footmen stood to attention at the back of the room and Mr Paget waited outside on the stone slabs. She heard him say, 'They're looking at the peaches and apricots but the kettles are here, so light the burners.'

'Shall I slip out before they come in?' Nell whispered through the crack.

'Shhh, Paget might hear you. You'll have to stay there until they've gone back in the house.'

Nell blew out her cheeks. The family could easily sit for an hour over tea. Madge would think she'd run away. She heard two people arrive quite quickly and peered through the crack to see George and Lady Clarissa sitting at the table.

Lady Clarissa was clearly not in a good humour. 'Wilmot, how could you be so foolish?' she demanded. 'I should have thought that you of all people would understand the importance of a good marriage. Phoebe cannot marry this ... this *tradesman*.'

'The law is a profession, dearest.'

'It amounts to the same thing. He plies his trade in the market square. He might as well be a boot-maker or a shopkeeper.' There was a pause before she raised her voice and called, *'Paget!'*

'Yes, my lady.'

'Take these footmen outside with you and close the door.'

'But the tea, my lady—'

'Do as I say.'

'Very well, my lady.'

Nell held her breath and slid noiselessly to the floor. Through the crack she could see Lady Clarissa's white kid shoes and silk stockings. She was tapping the point of her parasol on the stone floor. Mr Wilmot's polished black boots were visible at the other side.

'May I remind you that when we married we made an agreement?' she went on.

'I've kept my side of the bargain,' George Wilmot countered. 'Have you forgotten the "All my worldly goods" part?'

'Don't try to be clever with me, Wilmot. It

doesn't suit you. You know what I mean. Unless you want my family and all their connections to disown us, we shall live our life my way, according to my rules.' Nell heard her inhale before continuing, 'And that includes making sure the daughter of the Grange does her duty and marries either a title or wealth. This match is neither. It cannot go ahead.'

'But Phoebe wants it, my dear. She told me so.'

'Nonsense, she is an unattractive spinster flattered by the attentions of a handsome young blade. He had no interest in her before the summer.'

'He was waiting until he had finished his education. His father has promised him a partnership when he marries.'

Lady Clarissa made a disapproving clicking noise with her tongue. 'He is not suitable and the marriage will not endure. I do hope you have not offered him a dowry.'

'Well, none of the gentry you picked out for her were interested in her without one.'

'Then she would do better to remain a spinster as I did and live graciously off her father and brother. There will be widowers enough for her in the future.'

'That will be too late for her to have a child. Cyril is her last chance and Phoebe is my blood.'

'Do not remind me that her mother was an innkeeper!' Lady Clarissa tapped her parasol more insistently and stood up. The ribboned edge of her silk gown quivered. 'This marriage cannot take place! We have a son and I shall not allow the daughter of a ... a ... *a trollop* to inherit any part of the Grange. That is the right of our son and his son.'

'Phoebe and Cyril can have the brewery. She does a fair job of managing it for me.'

'Are you out of your mind? Without the brewery there is no Grange. Wilmot! Do not let me down here. You must forget this dalliance of Phoebe's and look to Devlin's marriage. His Majesty did not see fit to grant you a title despite my connections. But our son shall have one. The Lord Lieutenant of the Riding has already commented on his abilities.'

'He was always your favourite, wasn't he?' Nell thought that Mr Wilmot sounded anxious and a little breathless. She slid her back up the wall to get a better view through the crack. He was red in the face and appeared much angrier than he sounded. He went on, 'But I don't see how Phoebe's marriage will affect Devlin.'

'Of course you don't because you have learned nothing about being a gentleman apart from how to dress and eat.' Lady Clarissa's face was as white as the table linen and she was trembling with rage. 'Who of consequence will consider Devlin with a *tradesman* as his brother?' Her Ladyship moved out of Nell's view and called, 'Paget! We have mice in here. Deal with them!'

Nell froze. She had been as quiet as possible but it was cramped behind the screens and now she was in danger of being discovered. The door opened with a squeak and she recognised the footman's voice.

'I'll see to it, my lady. I think it's a bird that flew in earlier.'

'Very well. Paget! Paget! Ah, there you are. I need some air.'

Nell listened as Mr Wilmot pushed back his chair and stood up. She had a good view of him and saw him take a silver hip flask from his pocket and drink. The footman put his head around the edge of the screen and pressed a finger to his lips. He said out loud, 'It is a wren, sir. I see it.' He pushed in beside her, grinned and gave her a light kiss on her lips. She recoiled immediately, moving the screen. Her body went rigid and the footman looked cross. He put his fingers to his lips again, then said, 'I've got it, sir.' He backed out of the tiny space with his empty hands cupped together and pushed the screen to its original position with his elbow. 'I'll just put it outside, sir,' he added and left.

Mr Wilmot called after him, 'If you see Septimus Belfor, tell him I need a word before Her Ladyship returns.'

Nell despaired of ever getting out of her prison. She leaned against the wall and closed her eyes, only to open them sharply when the door opened and footsteps echoed on the stone.

'What do you want, George?'

'She won't have it, Septimus,' Mr Wilmot said. 'I told you what she was like. All this gentrification comes at a price, you know.'

'It's the brewery that pays for it, old fellow.'

'Be reasonable. She can take all this away with a few words in the right ears. No more brewery deals with shipping lines and hotels; no more shooting parties and hunt balls for either of us.'

'Do I have to remind you that you hold the

purse strings, George?'

'It's not that simple. She can ruin me if she wants.'

'So can I, old fellow, and don't you forget it.'

'You're a crook, Septimus Belfor, and your son is the same.'

'No, George. You are the crook, and I have the paperwork to prove it. Now, my good friend, you know my terms. My Cyril marries your Phoebe and you give them a half share in the brewery as a wedding gift. Then you leave the other half to them in your will.'

'But that's Devlin's half!'

'And who is he? He's just some foundling that your barren wife felt sorry for.'

'She won't stand for it, Septimus. She wants things done her way.'

'Then you'll just have to persuade her otherwise, won't you?'

'Or what?'

'Or I start listening to Mrs Goodman's rants. Her daughter's not stupid. She'll soon work it out. That's why you need to keep a close watch on them both.'

Nell strained her ears for every detail of the conversation, her face a mixture of shock and disbelief. Mother's fanciful ideas might not be so fanciful after all! And these two men knew the truth of it. Perhaps Cyril did too, and he had found his own way of trying to keep her under his control. Her heart began to thump as the spectre of a baby – Cyril Belfor's baby – loomed in front of her.

But within a few seconds she was distracted as

290

the garden room filled with people. The party crowded in and Nell peered between other tiny gaps to see who was there. Cyril, Miss Phoebe and Master Devlin came in, followed by Mr Paget and his two footmen.

Mr Paget said, 'The sun was too hot for Her Ladyship, sir, and she has gone back to the house.'

There were murmurings of sympathy from Lady Clarissa's family and guests, and a few comments on George Wilmot's overheated appearance as they sat around the table.

'If you will excuse me, sir,' Mr Paget continued, 'I shall return to Her Ladyship indoors.' He left his two footmen to serve tea.

The conversation was dominated by the younger folk and was quite jovial to begin with. But it was difficult for Nell to make out who was saying what as one of the footmen blocked her view; except, of course, when Miss Phoebe spoke as her voice was distinctive.

'Have you made the arrangements with the vicar in town yet, Father?' she asked.

'Are you sure this is what you want, dear? Your mother says that a daughter of the Grange must marry in the local church.'

'Don't start that all over again!' Miss Phoebe sounded agitated.

'It's a village occasion, Phoebe dear,' George pointed out.

Phoebe remained stubborn. 'The parish church in town is bigger and grander.'

'But your mother–'

'Cyril said you had persuaded her!'

'Calm down, Phoebe.' This was a different male

voice, Devlin's, who added, 'Father, perhaps the footmen should leave us.'

'Good idea, lad. We need to thrash out our differences here and now.'

Nell grimaced as she realised she would be left alone, hiding behind the screen. As soon as they had left, Miss Phoebe turned on her brother. 'You should leave too. My marriage has nothing to do with you.'

Devlin remained calm. 'Everything this family does concerns me. It's my family as well as yours.'

'No it is not! I am Father's flesh and blood and you … you are just an interloper–'

'Phoebe, that's enough!' her father interrupted. 'I've told you before to curb that loose tongue of yours.'

'Well, it's true. He's only here because Mama wanted a boy. She'll have another son at the Grange as soon as I am married to Cyril, so Devlin can go off and do whatever he wants with all his fancy learning.'

'Is that so?' Devlin had his back to her but Nell recognised his voice. He added, 'Have you thought to ask me what I want to do? Or do you think you can order my life as you seem to have done Cyril's?'

'Cyril will help me to run the brewery,' Phoebe snapped. She turned to her fiancé and added, 'Won't you?'

Nell had a good view of Cyril's face and she saw that familiar, crooked triumphant smile. 'I shall be your partner in every way, dearest.'

Nell saw Devlin's hands clench into fists by his side.

292

He said quietly, 'When did you agree to this, Father?'

George appeared flustered and stumbled over his words. 'We, that is me, I mean I ... I thought you might like to travel before you settled down, you know, carry on your education and...' His words trailed away as though he wasn't totally convinced of the notion himself.

Septimus Belfor, who had been silent until then, took up his argument. 'You have the world at your feet, Devlin. You need to find yourself an heiress to wed. It shouldn't be difficult with your looks and your father will give you an allowance. I'm reliably informed that America has rich pickings, m'boy.'

Chapter 24

'I am not your boy, sir. My home is here and my future is at Wilmot's Brewery.'

'Dev, old friend,' Cyril responded, 'there isn't room for both of us in the brewery.'

Devlin sat back in his chair and stared at him. 'You're right.'

For a moment Cyril's confident smirk wavered.

Devlin continued, 'You don't fool me, Cyril. You have no more affection for my sister than you had for your studies.' He shifted in his chair to address his sister and stated, 'Phoebe, you are making a mistake. Cyril does not love you.'

'Yes he does! He told me so!' Her father placed

a calming hand on her arm, but she continued in her high-pitched screech. 'You're jealous of me, Devlin, because I am Father's favourite and he's giving me the brewery. You do love me, don't you, Cyril?'

'Of course I do, dearest heart. Why else would I wish to marry you?'

Nell sank back against the wall, astounded by his capacity to lie. She had experienced Cyril Belfor's deceitfulness at first hand and knew how sneaky he could be. She felt sorry for Devlin who seemed to have everyone against him, including his own father. But not his mother, she thought. She was the only one on his side. Apart from me, Nell realised. She had had her differences with Devlin Wilmot but had found him, in the end, to be straightforward and honest.

Foundling or not, Cyril Belfor and his father were squeezing him out of his inheritance and they had no right to do that. What had George Wilmot done in the past to allow them to behave in such a way? And how was he going to pacify Lady Clarissa? Clearly, she was not in agreement and there was no doubt that her influential connections were essential to the brewery.

'I think I'll go and see how mother is,' Devlin said. Nell heard chairs scraping on the stone floor and the door opening. She closed her eyes and prayed silently that they were all leaving and she could escape from her hot and stifling confinement.

The final snippet of conversation she overheard was between Cyril and his father. They must have been alone by then because Septimus said, 'We'll rename the brewery as Belfors after a year or so. But be sure of this, son, there's no going back once you are married. You will have to stay with her and give her some Belfor heirs.'

'I'll follow your example, Father.'

'Just make sure your wife and mother-in-law don't find out.'

'My mother doesn't know about your mistress, does she?' Their voices faded as they left.

A minute later the kind footman pulled the screen back. 'It's safe to come out now. They've gone back to the house and Mr Paget's indoors with Her Ladyship.' He picked up the plate of cucumber sandwiches and offered them to her. 'They haven't eaten much.'

'They argued for most of the time,' Nell answered and put a tiny triangle into her mouth. It was the softest white bread without any crust, the freshest of butter and the slenderest of cooling sliced cucumber. It was delicious and she ate another.

'All that money they've got,' the footman said, 'and they can't stop rowing, not even for a wedding.'

'Well, do you think it's a good match?' she asked, reaching for another sandwich.

'Not my place to say,' he said. 'Not yours either. Want some cake?'

Nell shook her head. 'Madge'll wonder what's happened to me.'

'Yeah, she finished the last of the grouse ages ago. Run along then.' He gave her bottom a pat and then a squeeze. Nell froze and her mouth went dry. He didn't appear to notice as he continued clearing and stacking delicate china. 'I'll see you later, after servants' hall supper,' he added.

He had been kind to her but she did not want any of his attentions, least of all the sort he had in mind. She said, 'I ... I don't think that's a very good idea.'

'Is that so?' he queried without taking his eyes off his task. His tone wasn't friendly.

Clearly, as a lowly scullery maid, she ought to have been flattered by his interest in her. Now he had taken offence and she didn't want to make enemies. She stammered, 'Th-thank you for showing me the garden room, Mr ... er, I don't know your name.'

'It's the head footman to you.'

The other footman jerked his head in a gesture for her to leave, which she did and hurried back to the sculleries.

Madge asked her where she'd been and she said she'd got lost. Madge didn't believe her and tutted, 'I told you to stay away from the gardeners' bothies.'

Nell didn't respond. Her attention was taken by a wooden packing crate on her scullery table with the words GLASS and FRAGILE stencilled all over it. 'What's this?'

'Master Devlin's sent it down with a special request for you to clean it up, because you've done bottle-washing at the brewery.'

Nell reached inside, scattering straw on her scrubbed table top, and retrieved a conical glass container. 'This isn't a bottle. What's it for?'

'I don't know, but the gardeners use funny-shaped glass things for ripening bunches of grapes in their hot houses. Maybe it's summat like that.'

Nell rummaged around finding glass tubes in wooden stands, funnels and globe-shaped containers with long necks. Madge picked up one of them. 'They use summat like this for their shooting practice, only they fill 'em with feathers.'

'Feathers!'

'Aye, they catapult them in the air like a real bird and when they hit it, the feathers go all over.'

'Funny-shaped birds,' Nell commented. 'I can't do them in my stone sink. I'll have to use your wooden ones.'

'You'd best leave them till last thing at night then?'

'But I like to see Mother before I go to bed!'

'Hark at you! Who do you think you are?'

'Madge, please, they are for Master Devlin.'

Madge sighed irritably. 'Well, the family are out for luncheon tomorrow, so I suppose I can take my half day then if Mrs Quimby agrees. You can use my scullery while I'm gone.'

'Thanks, Madge. I'll need some more bottle brushes.'

'They're sending them over from the brewery.'

Nell had to wash the weird shapes carefully because they felt more like wineglasses than beer bottles and she couldn't even imagine what they were for. She was engrossed in her task at the sink when Master Devlin came into the sculleries to find her. She heard his footsteps and turned her head, straightening up as soon as she recognised him. Some of the glassware was already

297

finished and waiting on Madge's dresser against the wall.

He picked up a wooden rack of tubes and examined them against the light from the high window. Nell stood to attention with water dripping off her reddened hands. He must not have gone out with the family because he wore boots and leather gaiters over corduroy trousers with a woollen waistcoat and plain shirt. He could have been one of the gamekeepers, except that he was not so ruddy-faced. He had a very handsome face, she thought, and lovely thick hair. He turned his head quickly and caught her staring at him. Embarrassed, she looked at her feet and put her hands behind her back.

He picked up a drying cloth and handed it to her. 'Stop for a minute and dry your hands. I want to ask you something.'

It was very quiet below stairs as Mr Paget and Mrs Quimby had gone out in a trap with the head gardener and his wife. Most of the other servants were upstairs in their rooms or seeing friends in the stables. However, one or two were in the servants' hall playing cards.

'Is everything in order, sir?' she asked, drying her hands.

He nodded. 'Pack it back in the crate when it's dry. I'll send round fresh barley straw.' He continued to examine the pieces.

'Very well, sir.' After a short silence, she said, 'May I ask you a question too, sir?'

'You may.'

'What is it for?'

'My glassware? It's for my laboratory at the

brewery. Father seems to have forgotten that the reason I agreed to university was to learn about science. The head brewer and I are going to make sure that every one of our barrels holds the best ale in the county.'

Nell put her head to one side. Drinkers were the first to complain if their ale was in any way below their expectations. And it did happen occasionally, even with Wilmot's ales.

'Wilmot's barley wine already wins prizes,' Nell commented. 'Mother used to say it was my great-grandmother's recipe.'

'Is that so?' He was very relaxed and he smiled at her. He was even more handsome when he smiled and she felt a flutter of appreciation in her stomach. He leaned against the edge of the dresser. 'A lot has happened while I have been away. Don't you agree?'

'I wouldn't know, sir.'

'Oh, but you would, Nell. Tell me, what is it like working at the brewery under Phoebe's rule?'

'It's different from in your father's day. He used to walk round and talk to us. He'd ask us what we were doing and why we did it.'

'I can't imagine Phoebe doing that.'

'No, she never comes out of her office. Her charge-hands tell her what's going on.'

'Do you miss working there?'

'I miss my friends, but I've not had any time for them lately, anyway, with Mother needing my attention.'

'Would you go back?'

She shook her head. 'I can't. Not now.' Especially if Cyril Belfor is running it with Miss

Phoebe, she thought.

His face became very serious. He focused his dark eyes on hers and said, 'Well, I wish I knew what has really been going on in my absence.'

She felt accused, as though somehow he thought it was to do with her. She was flustered and she blushed but remained silent.

He went on, 'I think you know more than you're saying, Nell Goodman.'

Heavens, that was true, but only because she had eavesdropped on private conversations in the garden room! She wondered if she ought to tell him about Mother's accusations and her suspicions. She wanted to because ... because ... because, she realised that, out of all the Wilmot family at the Grange, he was the only one she trusted.

'You'll have to tell somebody someday, Nell. There is more to this engagement than meets the eye. I know what Cyril Belfor is really like.'

So do I, Nell thought. She was embarrassed by her rising colour, and simply said, 'Will that be all, sir?'

'For the present,' he replied. 'I shall be distracted by my great-grandfather's birthday for a while. But I'm determined to get to the bottom of this fiasco.'

She felt feverish. She was overdue. She had checked and double-checked her dates and she was late. She was unable to close her eyes without a vision of herself in a workhouse dress, her baby farmed out to some childless couple who would only care for it in return for an unpaid servant when he or she grew up. She couldn't do that to her baby. She'd have to run away, go to one of the big cities where they had homes for fallen women run by Church people who at least might find her a position where she could keep her baby with her while she worked.

But what would happen to Mother? Who would look out for Mother if she left? She couldn't leave. She would have to stay and face everyone who knew her and they would ridicule her and shun her because she had lost her virtue and given birth out of wedlock and she'd be forever labelled as a harlot or a trollop. Not for her the respectability of a husband and home with their children growing up around them. Only the shame and degradation meted out to women such as her. She despaired of what to do and she could not share her desperation with anyone.

But all was not doom and gloom for Nell. Her spirits lifted when she thought of her mother and the way she had settled with Miss Twigg. Mabel was content helping her with physical tasks and accompanying her in a trap on outings to the village. Nell thought that her life had rewound a few years to the time before she moved to bottle-washing, when Mother was able to occupy herself at home with her housekeeping or shopping in the market. When Nell was up to her elbows in dirty greasy water, she reminded herself that it was a small price to pay for Mother's well-being.

Nonetheless, discord between the Wilmots was worrying, in as much as Mother did have knowledge, albeit confused, of George's past behaviour. Nell told herself that family upheavals at

301

the Grange were not her concern. Her involvement was no more than the head parlourmaid's misfortune. She had decided to leave. Nell didn't have that choice and she knew she would have to confide in someone sooner or later about her predicament, before anyone guessed the truth. But on the day before Lady Clarissa's birthday celebration for her grandfather, the servants' hall erupted into turmoil.

Word had filtered down as far as Madge and Nell that the family quarrelled at every mealtime. Miss Phoebe and her father snapped at the footmen and parlourmaids for no apparent reason and Lady Clarissa spent most of her time speaking with Cook in the morning room or sitting alone in her boudoir.

The servants were busy but not overstretched. Septimus Belfor and his wife were in residence, with Cyril of course. Her Ladyship's grandfather had arrived in a modern closed-in motor car with his chauffeur, who was housed in the stable block, and with his attendant. His attendant, who had been a medical orderly for injured officers after the Boer War, slept in the dressing room adjacent to the elderly gentleman's bedroom in order to provide assistance during the night. He considered himself above the servants in status and gave orders to Mr Paget as though he was a gentleman himself. Consequently Mr Paget was not in a good humour and his irritation quickly spread.

More of Her Ladyship's aristocratic relations were expected on the day of the birthday party, when all servants were expected to work from dawn until dusk until the last guest had left.

Madge and Nell arrived at the servants' hall early for breakfast. The head parlourmaid and one of the under-parlourmaids came in together. The parlourmaid was crying and her superior took her to a chair by the fire.

The head footman was in Mr Paget's place at the table relishing a large plate of bacon, sausage and fried bread. He said through a mouthful of food, 'You can't sit there. That's Mrs Quimby's chair.'

'Stay where you are,' the head parlourmaid ordered the weeping girl. 'It's time we had this out in the open. Fetch Mr Paget.'

'I'm not doing that! He's left me in charge this morning while he has his breakfast with Mrs Quimby in her room.'

'Well, I want to talk to him now!'

'I wouldn't do that. He's in a foul temper. He was up in the middle of the night fetching brandy from the cellar for the old geezer upstairs.'

'Well, can you use his telephone? I want the police here.'

'Police? What's happened? Who's been murdered in his bed?'

'He's got to be stopped. Look at her!' The head parlourmaid was pointing to the maid who sat shuddering in the chair, trying to suppress her sobs.

She really was very distressed, Nell thought. Something dreadful must have happened.

The head footman put down his knife and fork. 'It's not that gentleman's gentleman the old geezer brought with him, is it? Mr Paget said he was trouble.'

'No it's not. It's Miss Phoebe's so-called fiancé.

He can't keep his hands to himself.'

The servants' hall went silent. Most of the maids knew what she was talking about but none of the footmen were aware of the head parlourmaid's condition and who had caused it. Nell's mouth dropped open and her knife and fork clattered down to her plate. No one turned in her direction. All eyes were on the parlourmaids.

The head footman looked angry. 'You shouldn't go around saying things like that here. She probably flaunted herself at him while he was still in his nightshirt.'

'I did not!' the maid cried. She stood up, shaking all over, and went on, 'He forced himself on me and I'm not staying while he's here.'

The head parlourmaid added, 'That makes two of us. We're going upstairs to pack this minute and you can tell Mr Paget from me that we are leaving and neither of us is coming back.' She took the girl's arm gently. 'Come on, love. I'll take you to my auntie's in the village. She can put both of us up.'

Nell's stomach churned and she felt sick as she watched them walk out. She pushed away her half-eaten breakfast and said, 'Madge, I need some fresh air. I'll be in the courtyard.' Madge nodded in a distracted way. She was already exchanging whispered gossip with a laundry maid.

The cool morning air helped to calm Nell and she wandered around in the early sunshine. She wanted to go with the parlourmaids; to get away from all the lies and deceit that seemed to be infecting this house. The head parlourmaid had mentioned the police. She could go with them to the police station. Surely they would believe three of them.

Madge didn't come for her and she lingered long enough to see the two maids leave with bags and carrying a travelling box between them. She hurried over.

'He shouldn't get away with it,' Nell said. 'Will you go to the police?'

'No point,' the older maid replied. 'Not round here, anyway. His father knows the magistrates and the circuit judge. But don't you worry, word'll get round about him and one day he'll get a beating from some girl's father or brother.' She half smiled at Nell. 'You're pretty. Stay below stairs, love, and keep well away from him.'

Nell went indoors, expecting a telling-off for being late. Madge wasn't in her scullery and Nell set to work filling her sink with hot water from the copper. She worked on through her routine and when Madge didn't appear Nell began to worry that she'd been taken ill. She asked the kitchen maid who came in for the clean pans.

'I've not seen her,' the maid replied, 'but there was a to-do this morning with the parlourmaids that's set the cat among the pigeons, right enough. Do you know what it was about? Cook won't tell us.'

'Don't ask me.' Nell shrugged. 'I haven't been here long.'

Disappointed, the girl left with her trolley. Nell refilled and refuelled her copper then went next door to tackle the dining-room silver and china in Madge's scullery. The head footman came in when she was up to her elbows in hot suds.

'Who told you to start in here?' he demanded.

'Nobody, but they need doing. Do you know what's happened to Madge?'

He ignored her question and said, 'I'm in charge so you should've asked me first. You can carry on, but don't get any ideas. I'll be counting the knives and forks later.'

The atmosphere in the servants' hall was subdued at dinner time. Neither Mr Paget nor Mrs Quimby appeared and Madge slid in beside Nell as the stew arrived from the kitchen. A few other, older female servants sat down at the same time.

'I've done your washing-up,' Nell whispered.

'Good lass. I'll miss you.'

Alarmed, Nell's mind raced with possible explanations for Madge's remark. 'What do you mean?' she asked.

'Stop gossiping down the end there,' the head footman called.

'I'll tell you later,' Madge replied.

Dinner was the quietest Nell had known since she arrived and everyone went back to their work as soon as they had finished eating. Madge followed Nell into her scullery. She was shaking her head in a sad way.

'Have I got to leave?' Nell asked anxiously.

''Fraid so,' Madge said. 'It was you or me, ducks.'

Chapter 25

'But why did they ask you to leave? I don't understand.'

Madge gave a big sigh and leaned against the table. 'Mr Paget and Mrs Quimby have been arguing all morning. With two parlourmaids gone and Lady Clarissa's party arriving today, Mrs Quimby can't manage upstairs. She's been seeing all the older downstairs servants about moving above stairs, just for the time being, like.'

'But that's good, isn't it?'

'If any of us had wanted to be housemaids we would be, wouldn't we? Cook's not letting any of her brigade go and none of the laundry women are interested, so that left me. Well, I'm not spending all day on me 'ands and knees at my age. I told her straight.'

Nell's heart seemed to sink to her feet. 'You didn't suggest me, did you?'

'No, I didn't. I don't want you to go but Mrs Quimby said you'd have to. And I'll tell you summat for nowt, she didn't like it any more than me; neither did Mr Paget, but Cook was there an' all and she told them you'd be all right for above stairs.'

'Do I have to do it?' Nell protested.

'I said it was you or me, ducks. Two of the regular housemaids will do the parlourmaids' jobs and you'll do theirs.' Madge brightened. 'Mrs

Quimby's getting a local lass to help me in here.'

'It's all settled, then?'

'Aye. Get yourself off to the sewing room for your uniform.'

Nell exchanged a plain grey dress for one in a green and white stripe. Her caps and aprons were starched cotton instead of calico but without lace embellishments. She had a pair of sleeve protectors and a hessian apron for fireplaces and scrubbing. The former head housemaid was collecting the green dress of a parlourmaid, and clearly very pleased with her new status. She gave Nell a list of her duties and Nell asked who she would be working with.

'There were only the two of us so you're on your own. We'll help out upstairs if we've the time and Mr Paget'll give you the hall boy to carry coals when he can.' She glanced at the elderly seamstress before going on, 'I'd send him in to do early-morning fireplaces in the gentlemen's bedrooms, if I were you.'

'But they won't want fires.'

'You'll have to clean up any soot that's come down.'

'I don't suppose you will do them?'

The new parlourmaid picked up her stack of lace aprons and caps. 'Wearing these? Certainly not!' She twirled in front of a cheval glass, admiring her new dress. 'Besides, I'll not cross the threshold of you-know-who until he's safely dressed and gone to breakfast.'

As if that would stop Cyril Belfor, Nell thought.

The parlourmaid went on: 'Get through early because Cook's assistant has made fancy stuff for

our late supper so we can have a party as well.'
She skipped out cheerfully.

Nell looked at her list. Early-morning duties included hall, front door and steps, dining and drawing rooms. After her breakfast, she was to do the fireplaces and carpets in the bedrooms and dressing rooms under the direction of the head parlourmaid, then the landings and staircase. After the servants' midday dinner it was the breakfast and morning rooms, and the library while the family were at luncheon, then the dining room again when luncheon was over.

The list went on. There was more than enough work for two housemaids, Nell considered. Eddie showed her where to find the housemaids' sinks and cupboards but neither had time to stand and talk. They agreed to see each other at servants' supper and she set off with her housemaid's box stuffed full of cleaning paraphernalia.

Lady Clarissa used her morning room to write letters and speak to her housekeeper and Cook, but breakfast was usually over by eleven so Nell started in the dining room: sideboard, dining table, carved chairs, removing food debris and buffing up the shine. She retrieved a journal from one of the window ledges and placed it on the sideboard, then forgot about it as she tackled the carpet on her hands and knees with a stiff brush and dustpan. She used a feather duster on the woodwork of doors, windows, skirting boards and picture frames within reach. Then she checked the two enormous fireplaces with marble sur-rounds, one at each end of the room, which were hidden behind ornate brass fire-screens.

There was a sprinkling of soot down in one hearth that she had to clean up very carefully so as not to spread the sticky stuff, and she was on her hands and knees finishing this task when the door opened. She expected it to be the parlour-maid come to inspect her work.

'Have you seen my journal?' Nell recognised Devlin's deep tones immediately and scrambled to her feet. He was searching along the seats of the chairs.

'On the sideboard, sir,' she called. Her voice echoed across the empty room.

'Oh, it's you, Nell.' He picked up his journal and walked over to her. 'I see you are a house-maid now. Mother was muttering about some servants' upheavals at luncheon. She was quite cross, actually. What's been going on? Not fighting amongst yourselves, I hope?'

She wished she could tell him because she was sure he wouldn't make light of it if he knew the truth. He would probably believe it, too, but the last thing she wanted was for him to suspect anything about her involvement with Cyril Belfor. She bit on her lower lip and kept quiet. Servants didn't have opinions or feelings, according to Mr Paget; put up and shut up was his maxim.

Nell wanted so much for Devlin to think well of her. She didn't care what any of the other Wilmots thought, but ... but she respected Devlin. He seemed honest and sincere.

'You're frowning, Nell. What happened?'

'You must ask Mr Paget, sir. We are all very busy preparing for tonight's birthday dinner, sir.'

He smiled and nodded. 'Good servants never

gossip. Well, Great-grandfather will be grateful. We shall all be, and you will have your own party below stairs later. Mother insists on it when you've all worked so hard.' He waved the journal in the air. 'Thank you for finding this.'

Nell experienced an urgent desire tell him everything she had overheard and her fingers itched to place them on his arm so that he would not leave. She didn't, of course, and he departed as quickly as he had arrived. The cavernous room felt even more empty than before. She got on with her work and wished desperately that she had a friend at Wilmot Grange, someone to confide in about her situation. But would she have the courage to tell her about Cyril, even if she had?

The head footman came in to inspect the dining room and asked her to polish the table again while he stood by and watched. It didn't need any more buffing and she guessed he was just being difficult because she had turned down his advances. Fortunately for her, his junior footman came in with a tray of silver to prepare for the banquet and he dismissed her abruptly. Nell went in search of the head parlourmaid for permission to go and see Mother during the quiet afternoon period.

Below stairs was abuzz with activity as guests were arriving with valets, lady's maids and multiple pieces of luggage. Everyone was rushed off their feet and no one had time to speak with her. Madge told her to report to the sculleries after servants' tea and sent her off to help in the still-room meanwhile. The still-room maid needed help with trays of tea and scones for newly arrived travellers who were resting in their rooms.

'You haven't forgotten Miss Twigg, have you?' Nell enquired as she polished teaspoons.

'I have only one pair of hands,' the still-room maid replied.

'Shall I prepare it for you?'

'Yes do, although I don't know who will take it upstairs this afternoon.'

'I'll do that, too.'

'Very well, but change your apron. Mrs Quimby is up there with the new parlourmaids.'

Nell chose the delicacies that her mother preferred and hoped Miss Twigg liked them too. Then she dashed to her cupboard for a clean cap and apron before carrying the loaded tray, with enough cakes for three, upstairs. Miss Twigg and her mother were resting. Nell made up the fire and put the kettle to boil. It was already hot and before long both ladies emerged from their bedrooms.

Nell hugged her mother and asked Miss Twigg if they were coming down to the servants' party later that evening.

Miss Twigg responded, 'Her Ladyship has invited me to the banquet. I am well acquainted with her grandfather and several of her guests. Mrs Goodman will help me with my hooks and buttons.'

'In that case, may I fetch Mother down to the servants' hall later?' Nell assumed a positive reply and continued, 'Would you like to come to a party, Mother?'

Mabel was already excited by the preparations and answered, 'Oh, yes please. I like a party. Will you be there, Nell?'

'I'll come and fetch you. After tea, we shall decide what you will wear.'

Mabel frowned. 'I haven't got a gown grand enough for here.'

'Yes you have, Mother. We'll choose something from your cupboard together.'

Nell spent the remainder of her time before servants' tea pressing ribbons and steaming feathers with her mother. She laid out her best mauve gown with overskirt and flimsy jacket on her bed. It was long and old fashioned but the colour suited Mabel and she always looked pretty in it.

'Wait here for me,' Nell said as she kissed her goodbye, 'and I'll come and get you before supper.'

After servants' tea, Nell put on her hessian apron and sleeve protectors to help Madge in the scullery. Mrs Quimby had given her a young girl who looked about twelve to do Nell's former job and the child had to stand on a stool to reach the bottom of the sink. Nell took over and directed the girl to keep the fires going and the water topped up in both coppers.

'What's your name?' Nell asked after introducing herself.

'Edith, miss.'

'Where are you from?' Nell asked.

Edith lowered her head and mumbled something into her chest.

'Beg pardon, I didn't hear.'

Edith mumbled again.

Nell turned to look at her. 'Can you speak up, please?'

'Union workhouse,' she muttered.

Nell tried not to react but something must have shown on her face because Edith's lower lip trembled and she looked scared. 'Don't tell anybody, will you? Mrs Madge said she wouldn't.'

'Of course I won't if you don't want me to. How old are you?'

'Nearly fourteen. If I get a place here I can leave.'

'Have you no family at all to take you in?'

Edith shook her head. 'I was born in there. My ma were taken in, you see, when she were 'aving me. And then she died.'

'Oh, I'm very sorry about that. Do you remember her?'

'She died when I were born.' The implication of this made Edith blush and look away.

Poor child, Nell thought. She has only known the life of an orphan in the workhouse. Nell felt a twinge in the pit of her stomach. If she was with child she would be dismissed and she and Mother could end up in the workhouse. She might die in childbirth and this could be her child in fourteen years' time. No family, no means of support, nothing but the workhouse.

Nell stopped scrubbing a heavy iron oven tin. It had been used for roasting bones to make the stock for Cook's demi-glace. Lady Clarissa's guests were having nine courses at dinner tonight. She wondered what they were eating in the workhouse. It wasn't as bad as in the old days when they just had gruel and soup, but plain and frugal were the parish watchwords.

'Mrs Madge is nice, though,' the girl said.

'Yes, she is,' Nell agreed.

She resumed her pan-scrubbing. Edith must have had a father, who might still be alive. Perhaps he did not know of her existence. Her mother probably told no one she was with child to avoid the ensuing shame and degradation. Nell understood that because she herself had no intention of telling Cyril Belfor if she was carrying his baby. Yet she ought to, she thought, because he had a responsibility for the infant. And she knew she wasn't the only woman to bear a child of his.

Nell recalled a newspaper report of a court case in town where the father of a wronged girl had sued the man who had seduced his daughter for the means to bring up the child. The man had refused to marry the girl and it had caused a huge scandal and endless tittle-tattle in the market. The girl and her mother were shunned but her father had no hesitation in bringing the case to court, determined to make the man pay.

Another twinge in her back caused Nell to stop scrubbing again. She stared at the painted brick wall in front of her. Cyril Belfor should be made to pay.

The evening of never-ending greasy pots and pans dragged on. She didn't know what time it was when someone, a junior footman, yelled, 'Goodman! Where are you?' from the passage. She took her arms out of the soapy water and answered, 'In here.'

He appeared at the door. 'You're wanted upstairs with your stuff.' He pulled a face. 'Not like that. Get yourself cleaned up.'

Nell dried her hands and pulled off her sleeve protectors and hessian apron. 'Who wants to see me?'

'Mr Paget. Wait for him outside the dining room.'

Nell picked up her cleaning box from the cupboard in the passage, ran up the stone steps and through the green baize door. She felt hot and feverish as she hovered in the marble-floored hall wearing her clean cap and apron. She wondered if she was coming down with something and prayed that she was for the alternative made her insides tremble with worry. A silver-topped decanter and glasses stood on a hall table for stiff and weary travellers. She was tempted to help herself to a tot of brandy to warm her stomach and calm her nerves. Then a junior footman emerged through the green baize door carrying Cook's roasted grouse decorated with the tail feathers. He caught sight of her and called, 'Idiot! Don't let Mr Paget see you there! Use the back stairs entrance.'

She remembered the ornate screen in the dining room that hid the servants' entrance and followed him through the small door to the dimly lit lobby. When he came back from depositing his tray on the dining-room sideboard she asked, 'What does he want me for?'

'Clean up that spillage just the other side of the screen. You'll see it and they won't notice you 'cos they're having a right old ding-dong in there tonight. Her Ladyship's not 'appy, and the master's ready to explode.' He hurried away for a second tray of grouse.

Nell crept in to wait behind the screen. The

dinner-table conversation was not friendly in its tone and when the second tray of grouse arrived she stepped out to see who was present. The glittering scene startled her and she stopped to catch her breath. It was a family party, relatively small for the size of the dining room. The guests were seated at the table she had lovingly polished, although several of the sections had been removed to make it smaller. It was laid with shiny silver and crystal and the fine green and white Rockingham china that Madge took great care of. The centre was punctuated by three ornate silver candelabra interspersed with dishes of unusual fruits from the glasshouses. The gentlemen wore white ties and evening tail-coats and the ladies … oh, the ladies were sparkling in jewels and feathers and glistening dresses. Even frumpy Mrs Belfor wore a jewelled ornament in her hair.

Lady Clarissa and George Wilmot were at opposite ends of the table, both of them looking angry. Her Ladyship's grandfather was flanked by his attendant and Miss Twigg, who leaned forward and moved a wine glass out of the elderly gentleman's reach. Nell thought they were the only guests who appeared unruffled by the raised voices, apart from Devlin.

Nell's eyes lingered on him as he looked so different in evening dress. He was handsome, of course, but confident too and … and *noble*, yes, noble like a duke or earl, or what Nell imagined they would look like. Miss Phoebe and Cyril seemed very agitated and his mother and father were attempting to calm them both. Mr Paget

317

and his head footman were studiously occupied with serving the grouse.

George Wilmot was red in the face and shouting, 'Am I master in this house or not?'

Lady Clarissa responded in her controlled and cultured voice, 'Don't be ridiculous, Wilmot. You are making a fool of yourself. I am simply stating that if you insist on permitting this unfortunate match then they will not reside at the Grange.'

Miss Phoebe's shrill tones split the air. 'Where do you expect us to live, Mama?'

Lady Clarissa seemed to enjoy her reply and said, 'If you had taken my advice on your choice for a partner you would not have to ask that question.' She raised her delicately arched eyebrows at Cyril. 'Well, what is your answer, young man?'

George did not give Cyril a chance to speak. 'Why should they have to go anywhere?' he said. 'Phoebe is my daughter and the Grange is big enough for all of us!'

'A wife must be mistress in her husband's home. No house is big enough for two mistresses.'

'But I can help you run the Grange, if you will let me.'

Lady Clarissa ignored this comment and said to Phoebe, 'If you insist on this marriage going ahead you must live outside the county.'

'Leave the county? Now wait a minute—' Cyril began.

'I have not finished. George will buy a hotel in Liverpool – one that serves the Atlantic shipping lines – and you may install yourselves there and run it to keep you occupied.'

This time Septimus Belfor responded. 'I cannot allow that, my lady, I need my son here. He will be a partner in my business.'

Lady Clarissa stared hard at George. 'Wilmot knows my views on that.'

'You're a snob, Clarissa,' he said.

'Is that not why you married me, Wilmot, so that I should bring influence and status to your wealth? I expect at least as much from Phoebe. She is her father's child, is she not?'

George reddened even further and looked flustered.

'Which is more than you can say for Devlin!' Phoebe shrilled. 'Why has he come back? He is the one who should be leaving!'

Devlin had remained silent until then, along with the elderly guest of honour who, it appeared, was rather enjoying the argument. 'If you are going to drag me into this, Phoebe, take care,' Devlin said. 'I agree with Mother that this marriage is wrong for you, but for different reasons.'

'You were always Mother's favourite.'

'I should be happy for you if I believed that Cyril loved you.'

'Hey, old boy, I thought you were my friend. Of course I love her,' Cyril responded.

'Of course he does,' George echoed.

Phoebe looked smug and the silent guests were looking at their plates with unusual interest. Mr Paget had finished serving the grouse. Lady Clarissa picked up her knife and fork and others did the same. George called for more wine and for a few minutes the embarrassing conversation ceased.

A footman dumped a stack of dirty dishes in Nell's arms to take down to the scullery where she spent a few moments being quizzed by Madge about the party. She was rescued by a kitchen maid asking her where all the footmen were as the next course was ready. She went upstairs in search of them and could hear raised voices in the dining room from the back lobby. She opened the door to the shrill tones of Miss Phoebe. 'Well, if she's here, Paget, go and fetch her!'

Paget poked his head around the screen, his face like thunder. 'I knew you'd be trouble,' he snarled. 'Get in here and do something about that mother of yours!'

Chapter 26

'My mother?' Nell pushed by him into the dining room.

Mabel, in her old-fashioned full-skirted gown, was standing by George with a frown on her face. A footman hovered behind her, clearly not sure what to do, and Devlin had risen to his feet, napkin in hand.

'Mother?' Nell said.

'Nell, my love, where shall I sit? George won't tell me.'

'Take her out of here,' George grunted. The footman grasped Mabel's arm.

Mabel squealed, 'You're hurting me!'

'Leave her alone!' Nell dashed forward and

gently took Mabel's other arm. 'She doesn't mean any harm!'

'Oh, but she does, lass,' George argued. He half rose, leaning on the table with his hands as though he needed the support. He was breathing heavily. The white linen table napkin tucked into his collar contrasted sharply with the purplish red of his face. 'You have to keep her quiet! None of what she says is true. I didn't kill her husband. Everyone knows Goodman died of heart failure like his father and mother before him.'

'It was your fault!' Mabel said. 'You said you'd look after me.'

'Well, I am doing, aren't I?' George sounded weary.

Devlin had moved off his seat and indicated for the footman to stand back. He took the footman's place beside Mabel, for which Nell was very grateful.

Miss Phoebe was very annoyed. She cried, 'But why does she have to live *here*, Father? Why can't you send her to the asylum?' Cyril had a firm hand on Phoebe's arm, preventing her from standing up.

'She's not *mad*,' George argued.

'Well, she's certainly not sane,' Cyril said. He turned to his father, seated further along the table. 'Don't you agree, Father? You've dealt with her sort before.'

Her *sort?* Nell was so angry with him that she could have hit him and if she had had anything to hand she might have thrown it at him.

Septimus Belfor was as impassive as Lady Clarissa, but Nell guessed that his stony expression was one of suppressed anger; his wife actually looked frightened. She had two bright spots of colour in her cheeks and was twisting her hands in her lap.

'Mother, come with me,' Nell said. 'This is not our party.'

'Oh, but it must be. Miss Twigg is here, and George.'

The room went quiet. Everyone's attention was on them apart from Miss Twigg's whose main concern appeared to be keeping Lady Clarissa's grandfather sober. The elderly gentleman appeared to be enjoying himself and he stretched painfully to reach his wine. Miss Twigg moved the glass further away.

Devlin broke the silence. He gave a small bow and said, 'Good evening, Mrs Goodman.' Then he held out his arm and added, 'Shall we find your party?'

Mabel looked up at his face and recognised him. 'Oh, it's you,' she said and took his arm.

Nell flashed him a brief, grateful smile and followed them out of the dining room.

'Bring brandy, Paget,' Devlin said to the butler as he held open the door, 'and a tray of tea to the morning room.' It was the nearest room, directly across the hall.

'Please don't leave your guests, sir,' Nell protested. 'I can take Mother downstairs.'

'It's not much of a celebration now. The gossip about it will be all round the county by next week.'

'I'm so sorry, sir.'

'It's Devlin.'

She gave in and repeated, 'Devlin.' Then went on, 'Mother has been very settled with Miss Twigg. But seeing your father sparked off her memories. She was the same when she went to see the house we used to live in.'

'Tell me about that.'

Devlin took the brandy tots from Mr Paget and sent him for the tea. Nell made sure Mabel was comfortable in an upholstered chair then wandered into the bay window and began to describe the incident at the house where the sergeant was called.

'Your mother has said some shocking things,' Devlin commented. 'Do you think there is any truth in them?'

'I believe so, but it's hard to know how much. My father and yours were partners in the original brewery years ago and Father did die suddenly when I was a baby.' She paused as her mother came over to join them. 'I don't want Mother to hear this.'

'Isn't this a charming room?' Nell said to her and suggested she look at the wall hangings and bookcase.

While Mabel was distracted, Nell took a deep breath and said to Devlin, 'Septimus Belfor knows more about it than he says. I think he was involved in drawing up the original brewery partnership.'

'Well, he and Father have always been as thick as thieves.'

She didn't know whether he was making light of it or not. But the conversation she had listened to in the garden room indicated something crooked between them.

Devlin went on, 'He's my father and I love him but his genial manner covers a darker nature.'

Nell had recently found that out for herself and wondered if she had been taken in by him over the years. She sympathised with Devlin. He had been away being educated for too long and was out of touch with his sister's scheming.

Mabel came over again and said, 'Will you take me back to the party now?'

'Our party is downstairs, Mother,' Nell explained gently.

Devlin smiled at Mabel and said, 'You don't want to go back to the dining room, Mrs Goodman. They spend all their time arguing.'

'It's much more fun in the servants' hall,' Nell added. 'They have a piano.'

'Do they? And singing?'

'And singing.'

Mabel started to sing to herself and then hummed the tune when she forgot the words. A footman brought in a tea tray laid with a silver teapot, cream jug and sugar bowl, delicate silver-edged china and a cake stand of tiny biscuits and sweetmeats especially baked for the guests. He did not hide his surprise to see Nell in the morning room with her mother and Master Devlin. She knew it would be the talk of the servants' hall tonight.

Mabel volunteered to pour the tea and Devlin said, 'Shall we sit down?' He went over to a small couch opposite Mabel's chair and gestured to Nell to join him. She did, a little anxious about Mabel handling the expensive china. One hand

324

was on the couch by her knee, ready to lean forward and help.

Devlin placed his large warm fingers over hers and she looked down at them, startled. He gripped her fingers gently. She glanced at him and he was smiling. 'I'm glad we're friends again, Nell.'

Me too, she thought. What should she say? She was a servant here and, even though she trusted him, they were from very different backgrounds. Could they be friends as adults? She said, 'Thank you. So am I.'

He seemed very pleased and stroked the back of her hand gently with his fingers. 'When this family business is settled,' he said, 'we shall be able to spend time together and get to know each other better, much better.'

'I should like that very much,' she said. It was the truth but she wondered if it was wise to say so. He leaned towards her and she was sure he was going to kiss her cheek. What was she thinking of? What would he think of her if he knew she was carrying another man's child? She recoiled instinctively and murmured, 'Don't.'

He seemed surprised and glanced at Mabel who was busy deciding which of the tiny cakes to eat first. 'I'm sorry,' he said softly. 'We need to be alone.'

Nell felt devastated. He was giving her clear signs that he cared, without knowing that she could never return his affection. She had to reject him and her heart wept.

She leaned forward to take the cake stand from Mabel who was about to choose another cake. She offered them to Devlin and said, 'I expect we shall have to leave in the morning.'

The moment was over. He declined a cake and asked, 'But where will you go?'

'I thought I might find a live-in position in the village.'

'Let me help you. Septimus Belfor is administering a small estate that includes the old charcoal burner's cottage in Keppel Woods. Cyril is acting as agent to oversee the renovation of a dwelling. I rode by there recently and it's habitable—'

'Oh, I couldn't go there!' she interrupted hastily.

Devlin frowned at her. 'Why not? It would at least give you and your mother a home for the time being. I'll talk to him.'

'No, please don't. Truly, I don't want anything to do with the Belfors.'

Devlin's frown turned into a demanding question. 'What do you know about them, Nell?'

Cornered, Nell found herself flustered and blushing. 'You ... you, yourself, have warned me about him ... his ... his ... Master Cyril's inclinations. He will have to visit the cottage ... to inspect ... people will gossip...' She ran out of reasons and wished she could tell him the truth. She wanted to but could not. She found it impossible to speak of it to anyone. But neither did she wish to lie to him, so she stayed quiet.

He was thoughtful and the silence lengthened until Devlin said, 'He has promised to leave his wild days behind him now he is to be married to my sister.'

'Well, that won't stop him,' she mumbled.

'What did you say?'

Nell glanced at her mother who was examining

326

the needlepoint on a cushion. She respected Devlin too much to keep evading the truth. He ought to know at least some of the stories about his future brother-in-law. She said, 'Two parlour-maids left today because of him; and because Mr Paget says the prettiest maids should expect young gentlemen to be playful with them and they must put up with it.'

She bit back the words *and one of them is carrying his child* out of loyalty to the former maid and a sudden, trembling rush of her own fear. Devlin wasn't naive; he had simply been away for too long and had no knowledge of what had been going on in the brewery or the town. Nell felt that she had nothing to lose as tomorrow would bring dismissal without a doubt. She went on, 'Mrs Quimby will be angry with me for telling you because even Mr Paget does not know the full extent of ... of Cyril's behaviour.' She shrugged. 'I don't suppose it matters now that I am leaving.'

'Of course it matters!' He was clearly shocked – and angered – by this revelation. 'What have I come home to? I cannot persuade Phoebe not to marry Cyril so he must certainly mean it when he promises to change his ways or he will answer to me! Phoebe and I may have our differences but she is still my sister.'

His raised voice caused Mabel to look up from her cushion and she dropped it to the floor. Devlin's eyes flashed angrily and Nell considered that it would not be a pleasant experience for any man to cross swords with him. But she was too exhausted to continue this exchange and sighed,

'Yes, of course, I understand your unease. But all I am concerned about at present is my mother's welfare.'

He calmed down and said, 'I apologise. I should not have drawn you into my worries. Shall I take you downstairs now? I have to return to our guests at some time.'

He was polite but, to Nell, it felt like a dismissal. He had retreated totally from the intimate moment they had shared earlier. She had read too much into it. He was the young master and she was a housemaid. What was she thinking of? He had no personal responsibility for her. He had simply saved his mother from embarrassment by removing the source of disruption. 'Come with me, Mother,' she said. 'We're leaving now.'

However, her words were drowned out by the door bursting open and an agitated Mr Paget calling, 'Master Devlin, come quick, your father has been taken ill!'

Devlin spread his arms in a helpless gesture and rushed out after Mr Paget. He left the morning-room door open. Nell glanced at her mother. She was choosing another of Cook's delicacies to try. 'Wait here for me,' she said to her and went after Devlin, closing the morning-room door behind her.

Across the hall the door to the dining room stood open. Chairs were pushed back as some guests were standing and agitated; others remained impassive and seated. Mr Paget looked shocked and his footmen hovered around him, unsure of what to do. George Wilmot was on the floor, half hidden by the table, with his overturned chair by his side. The attendant with Her Ladyship's grandfather was kneeling down beside him and Devlin stood over them, obviously alarmed and breathing heavily.

'Paget,' Devlin called, 'telephone for my father's physician.'

Mr Paget seemed frozen to the spot. His face was ashen.

Devlin raised his voice. 'Now, my good fellow!'

The head footman jumped to attention and said, 'I'll do it, sir.' He tugged at Mr Paget's sleeve and half dragged him out of the room, pushing him onto a hall chair. When the footman noticed Nell he said, 'Give him a brandy,' and jerked his thumb in the direction of a side table.

Nell obeyed, pouring a similar measure to the one he had just brought her. Through the open door, the consternation of Her Ladyship's guests was obvious. Two of the ladies had succumbed to weeping and were comforting each other; their gentlemen companions stood with heads together, muttering. Everyone's attention was focused on the motionless form on the floor.

A couple of years ago, Nell would have been as distressed as the wailing ladies at Mr Wilmot's sudden illness. She had thought of him as a kindly uncle rather than her employer. But since then he had distanced himself from her and her mother and it appeared that he had good reason. George Wilmot had something to hide about his past involvement with Nell's family – something that Septimus Belfor knew and something that George Wilmot did not want to be revealed to his aristocratic and influential relations.

The notion seemed as fanciful as her mother's ramblings. Yet after overhearing the garden-room conversation even those now seemed to be rooted in the truth. A hidden thought surfaced. Nell had considered it in the past and pushed it away as nonsense. But now she wondered if, just possibly, she could be... She hadn't considered it seriously in a long while, although when she was younger she had believed it was quite likely. Why would a wealthy and well-connected gentleman such as George Wilmot take such an interest in her and her mother if there were not a long-buried, and perhaps shameful, reason? A bastard child, she thought: me.

Mother had never hinted that she was guilty of such a scandal and was, indeed, scornful of women who showed any inclination to be of dubious morals. She had taught Nell from an early age the value of her virtue and had been truly distressed when Queen Victoria had passed away. Mabel had greatly admired the monarch's principled example of loyal devotion to her family. Surely Mother had never been an unfaithful wife to Father? But, as Nell knew to her cost, it was possible for a woman's wishes to be ignored and overcome in such matters.

However, she could not believe that genial George Wilmot had ever forced himself on her mother. Yet if he was guilty of dishonest dealings with her father, he was not the kindly gentleman she believed him to be. Was it possible that he was her real father? Possible, certainly, and it made sense of Mother's more outlandish accusations. The queasy feeling in Nell's stomach returned.

Was this her real father, struggling for life on the dining-room floor?

Devlin half disappeared from her view as he sank to his knees. Nell forgot about her housemaid's position and the pomp of the gathered guests. The glitter and gloss of the dining room faded as she walked around the table to see for herself. Her mouth dropped open. George Wilmot's face was grey and his lips were blue. The attendant had his head on one side, against Mr Wilmot's chest, listening for a heartbeat. Devlin's face was distorted in anguish. For a brief second he glanced up at her with disbelief in his eyes. At that moment all her sympathies were for him and not for his ailing father. If this was her father on the floor, he had treated her and her mother very ill of late.

She heard the footman return and say, 'The physician is on his way, my lady.'

Nell noticed that only Lady Clarissa and her grandfather appeared unmoved by the drama. The aristocracy were noted for their ability to hide their emotions, Nell thought; unless Her Ladyship, like she, was unsure where George Wilmot's loyalties lay. Miss Twigg's attention was taken up by the elderly gentleman, who was the worse for drink, as she attempted to dissuade him from taking another glass of wine.

The attendant stood up. 'It is too late for a physician,' he said. 'Mr Wilmot is dead.'

Nell choked back an involuntary sob of shock. A gasp rippled around the room as Devlin removed his coat and covered his father's face.

He stood up and looked at the footman. 'Take

the ladies into the drawing room.' He moved quickly to his mother's side but she brushed aside his offer of a helping hand. Nell frowned at this reaction. Lady Clarissa did not appear to be distressed. If she felt any sadness, she did not show it at all.

Her Ladyship rose stiffly to her feet and addressed her remaining guests. 'You will excuse me; gentlemen, you will be shown to the smoking room.' She turned to her elderly guest of honour. 'Grandfather, will you take brandy in your room?' She did not wait for a reply but went on, 'Your man must stay with Wilmot until his physician arrives. Miss Twigg will assist you.' She smiled indulgently at her former governess but as soon as her grandfather had left the room, Nell noticed that her pleasant expression turned to one of undisguised anger. As the frightened guests filed out into the hall, Paget recovered enough to announce that coffee would be served in the drawing room.

Cyril Belfor and his parents remained in the dining room, although Mrs Belfor had wanted to leave with the other ladies but her husband had prevented it. Nell stood in the shadow of the screen, unnoticed by Lady Clarissa. Servants were normally invisible to the gentry anyway.

Her Ladyship turned her venom on Miss Phoebe. 'I blame you for this,' she stated. 'If you had done your duty as his daughter this would not have happened.'

Nell stared at the lifeless form on the floor, his contorted face obscured by Devlin's evening coat. If this man was her father then Miss Phoebe was her half-sister. She stared at the woman whose actions had torn apart her life.

Miss Phoebe's nostrils flared and she cried, 'It is not I who is to blame! It's her!' She pointed an accusing finger at Nell. 'This is your fault! You and your crazed mother have caused this! If you had not wormed your way into our lives with your slanderous lies, my father would still be alive!'

Alarmed, Nell backed away until Septimus Belfor stepped forward to assume control. His expression was unreadable as he directed his silent wife to take Miss Phoebe to her room and give her brandy. Then he barked at his son, 'Do something about that skivvy. She knows too much already. You must take charge, son. You will be master here soon enough.'

Chapter 27

'Very well, Father,' Cyril replied. He did not appear in any way upset or shocked at George's death. If anything, Nell thought, he was working very hard to hide his pleasure. He said to Miss Phoebe, 'Go with Mama, dearest, and take the brandy. I'll send the doctor to you when he arrives.'

Miss Phoebe seemed undecided at first but eventually went upstairs with Mrs Belfor. Septimus Belfor left to pacify the guests in the drawing room, leaving Cyril alone with Nell and the body of a man who may actually have been her father.

She was anxious to return to her mother before she came looking for her and walked towards the open door.

Cyril barred her progress. 'You don't leave until I say so,' he said and closed the door firmly.

'Let me pass,' she protested. 'Your father does not wish me to stay and neither do I.'

'Well, I do, at least until I can arrange the cottage for you.'

'But I told you–'

'You don't tell me anything. You heard my father. I shall be master here within the month and without old George to protect you and your crazy ma, you'll do as I say.'

'No, I shall not. Do you hear me? I'm not doing it!'

'Yes you are. You don't want to see your mother in the workhouse and that is your only alternative because Phoebe will throw you out.'

'Lady Clarissa won't let her.'

'You don't understand, do you?' He spread his arms. 'None of this belongs to Lady Clarissa! She can live here as the dowager if she wishes but she won't want to. The Grange belongs to Phoebe now and as soon as we are married I shall be master. Her Ladyship can't tell me or Phoebe how to run the place like she did old George. She'll go soon enough when I turn her out of her rooms.'

Nell was almost speechless. 'How dare you? You're a monster and your father is the same.' Angrily she elbowed him aside. 'Get out of my way,' she snapped, and pushed open the door. She heard him laugh. 'It's the workhouse or the cottage, Nell,' he called after her.

The hall was empty apart from a junior footman carrying coffee towards the morning room. Nell dashed forward and said, 'The guests are in the drawing room.'

'This is for the morning room,' he answered and balanced the heavy tray on one arm to reach for the door handle.

Nell opened it for him to see Devlin and her mother seated side by side on the small sofa. 'Oh! I didn't know you were in here, sir,' she said.

He stood up as she entered and said, 'You will need coffee. I haven't told her yet. I thought it would be best coming from you.'

Nell sat down next to her mother and Devlin took an adjacent chair. Nell took her mother's hand and said, 'The party has had to be cancelled, Mother. Someone has died.'

'Oh dear, I am so sorry. Was it anyone we knew?'

'It was George, Mother. George Wilmot.'

'George? No, he can't be dead. He just asked me to come and live here.'

'I'm sorry, Mother, he is. It was very sudden.'

'No, not George.' She looked directly into Nell's eyes. 'He was looking after us both, wasn't he? He said he would and he did in the end, didn't he? He said he'd look after us when your father died. It was his fault, you see. He killed him and stole his money. That's why he has to look after us. He can't die and leave us now.'

Nell glanced appealingly at Devlin, who was listening with interest. 'Don't worry, Mother. We'll be all right.'

'Will we? Has he left you half the brewery? And

the barley wine. It's yours by right. That Phoebe thinks it's hers but it's not. Your great-grandma's barley wine was the envy of the Riding.'

Mother was rambling again, and now she was in full flow. 'George shouldn't have let her have it.' Mabel's face suddenly dropped into sadness. 'He can't stop her now, can he?'

Devlin handed her a tiny coffee cup. His face was ravaged by grief but he managed a small smile and said kindly, 'No, he can't, Mrs Goodman. But I can.'

Surprised, Nell raised her eyebrows and detected an almost imperceptible nod in response from Devlin as he handed her coffee as well. He lowered his voice. 'I shall root out the truth. My adoption was legal. Why is my sister so against me?'

'Perhaps because her fiancé is determined to have the brewery and the Grange for himself?' Nell suggested.

'And his attentions to my sister have clouded her judgement,' Devlin murmured. 'He has not shown an interest in her until recently.'

Nell thought for a minute and chose her words carefully. 'I believe Septimus Belfor has been planning this for a while now.'

'What do you know, Nell?' he prompted.

Nell wanted to tell him everything she knew but it was not for her mother's ears. She glanced at Mabel. She had not drunk her coffee and her eyelids were drooping. 'Mother is tired,' she said, 'may we talk of it another time?'

'Of course.' He stood up and offered a helping hand to Mabel.

Nell murmured, 'I'll put her to bed. Good-night, sir – Devlin.'

Nell worried herself to a restless sleep that night, and for much of the night she lay awake listening to the soft rhythmic snores of the other maids in her attic, waiting for the dawn. Where would she and Mother go now?

But when the sky began to lighten there was a joyous respite for her. She felt the stickiness and had a show on the back of her nightdress. Thank heaven! She was not with child! As she searched for her rags in the dimness, her future did not look quite so bleak. She would not be kept on at the Grange but she could look for another position with confidence. She must go as far away as she could from any place where Cyril Belfor had influence.

The household was subdued as the servants came to terms with the master's sudden demise and it went into mourning. The sewing room in contrast was busy making black armbands for Mr Paget and Mrs Quimby to issue to all servants, including the outdoor ones. During the day, carriages came and went as preparations for the funeral began. However, routines continued as normal, although Lady Clarissa did not emerge from her rooms until her dressmaker had visited.

Mrs Quimby came to find Nell while the family were at breakfast. The head parlourmaid had instructed her not to enter any of the rooms so she was on her hands and knees brushing down the carpet on the stairs. As she worked she re-considered her options. Mabel already had acquaintances in Keppel. She looked forward to the church gatherings organised by the vicar's wife. And the Wainwrights were nice people who had been very helpful. It made sense to try to stay in the area. She really did not want to resort to living in town and working at a factory, leaving mother alone all day. She was so deep in thought, she didn't hear Mrs Quimby's footsteps on the carpet.

'I knew you'd be trouble,' the housekeeper began. Nell continued with the step she was working on until Mrs Quimby added, 'Stand up when I'm talking to you.'

Nell put down her dustpan and brush and obeyed, smoothing down her apron.

'Mr Paget will see you now in his parlour,' the housekeeper said.

Nell guessed this was her dismissal. She wondered how much notice she would have. 'Shall I finish the stairs first?' she suggested.

'You do understand the meaning of "now", don't you?'

It was clear that Mrs Quimby was firmly on Mr Paget's side. Nell went downstairs to the butler's parlour and knocked on the door. The sneer on his face prepared Nell for his scorn. 'I knew you wouldn't last long. Pack your bags. You and your mother are going before dinner.' Then he smiled as though he took pleasure in saying it.

'Must we leave immediately, sir? We have nowhere to go.'

'The workhouse would take you both in.'

'You are sending us to the workhouse?'

'If it was left to me,' Paget pointed out, 'I'd have your ma in the asylum but that costs money so

338

Miss Phoebe has decided on the workhouse.'

'No! You can't send us there. I am able-bodied and I can work.'

Paget sat back in his mahogany chair and uttered a coarse laugh. 'Aye, that's been noted right enough. You must have a friend upstairs,' he grunted. 'Your sort always does.'

Devlin? Nell wondered. Had he put in a good word for her?

'You certainly don't deserve it, especially after your ma's exhibition in the dining room,' Paget continued grudgingly. 'Miss Phoebe wanted the workhouse cart here before breakfast, but Master Cyril has a kinder heart.'

Nell's stomach lurched and she swallowed nervously. 'What has Master Cyril to do with me?' she asked.

'He will soon be Master of Wilmot Grange, that's what. He knows of a cottage you can use.'

Nell's heart missed a beat and she babbled, 'I can't afford to pay rent, sir, not without a position.'

His sneer returned. 'Well, it's not charity! You'll be grafting for a roof over your head. The place has had the masons and carpenters in and needs a proper clean-up.'

Nell closed her eyes in despair. Cyril was determined to have his way and his betrothal to Miss Phoebe meant nothing to him! She felt panic rising in her throat. 'But if it's only a cottage, Mr Paget, there won't be enough room for Mother–'

'Hold your tongue and think yourself lucky that we have Master Cyril in charge now. He'll keep you on if you do a good job for him.'

Her legs were in danger of buckling beneath

her. 'I ... I can't go there, sir, it's ... it's too far from the village for Mother.'

'You don't even know where it is yet! And who do you think you are to pick and choose?'

'Where exactly is it, Mr Paget?'

'It's in Keppel Woods if you must know, and it's either there or the workhouse for you, Goodman. So which is it to be?'

Nell chewed on her lip silently. She didn't mind going to the workhouse. She would get out again as soon as she obtained a position with somewhere to live. But if Mother went into the workhouse, they'd never let her out again. Too many influential folk wanted her there.

Her heart began to thump as she realised she was trapped into accepting what Cyril Belfor had so 'kindly' offered. In desperation she argued, 'Please don't make me go there, sir. There are no neighbours and I shan't feel safe alone with Mother in the middle of the woods. We might be set upon by vagrants!'

'Aye, you might,' Mr Paget replied with a humourless smile. He seemed to enjoy being cruel to her and went on, 'So you'll just have to keep the door locked, won't you?'

Well and truly, she thought; night and day, whoever calls. The locks were substantial, she recalled. Nell had to accept this cottage in the short term to put a roof over their heads but she determined to move on quickly. Mrs Wainwright might be able to help. It was a long walk to Keppel, especially for Mother, but it was a thriving village.

'Am I due any wages, sir?' she asked. She didn't

expect much.

'Wages? Your wages are forfeited for the damage you've done. Now get out of my sight. There's a cart waiting for you in the yard.'

Nell ran up to the old nursery for Mabel and found that Miss Twigg had already packed her belongings and sent the box downstairs. She seemed quite sorry to hand over Mabel, who was dressed in her outdoor coat and hat. But her only comment was, 'I'm sure this is for the best.'

Nell reassured her mother that all would be well and they climbed to the attic to collect her own things. 'We have been given a cottage to use,' she explained. 'It needs cleaning and it's only temporary until I find another position.'

'Is it my fault we have to go?' Mabel asked.

Nell gave her a hug. 'No, Mother. It's because George has died.'

'Did he leave you half of the brewery?' Mabel asked brightly. 'You ought to have half by rights. If he has, shall we have to live in town again?'

'We'll see,' Nell replied.

Eddie was waiting with an old dog cart to take her and Mother away. Nell was pleased to see him but he said little as he took her bags and helped them aboard. Outdoor staff, at work in the stables or gardens, stopped to watch when they trundled by. The small cart was heavily laden and drawn by an ancient pony, so progress was slow.

'I wish they wouldn't stare,' Nell muttered.

'You can't blame them. They'll be wondering if they are next.'

'What do you mean?'

'When the master dies there's always change.

You are the first to go.'

'Oh, I'm sure Lady Clarissa won't get rid of any servants.'

'It won't be her choice, will it? She's just the widow now.'

'But surely the Grange is her home?'

'Miss Phoebe will want her out. It's no secret that they hate each other.'

'I'm sure Master Devlin will not let that happen.'

'They say he's not entitled because he's not family.'

'Who says?' she cried irritably. 'Of course he is family!'

Eddie looked at her with raised eyebrows. 'It's all round the servants' hall. What's it to you, anyway?'

'Nothing.' She shrugged. 'It doesn't seem fair, that's all.'

'Aye, you're right, it doesn't. He's a decent sort is Master Devlin, but Miss Phoebe has always been jealous of him.'

'I'm sure George loved them equally and he'll have left a will.'

'Well, we won't know until after the funeral,' Eddie chatted away. 'Do you know the old charcoal burner's cottage? I use to play there as a nipper. The spinster who lived there had a maid called Biddy and she used to give us jam tarts on her baking day. It's been empty and shut up for years. Biddy moved on after the old lady died. Will you be the housekeeper now?'

'We shan't be there for long. How is your mother keeping?'

Eddie talked of his family at length, including Joe and how he was thinking of expanding his father's workshop into a small factory and taking on more men. They turned off the main track into the woods. It was still summer now, Nell thought, with warm sun, leaves on the trees and lush grass underfoot. But it would be cold and dark and sinister in winter. She shivered at that thought.

Eddie noticed and commented, 'Someone just walked over your grave.'

It was an old wives' tale but it did not help to alleviate her anxiety. She repeated out loud to reassure herself, 'We shan't be there for long.'

'Master Cyril said you'd be living there. He said to tell you to charge your supplies to the Grange.'

'When did he speak to you?'

'This morning. He came to find me in my boot room and gave me the front door key. He told me to chop you some wood and get the range going for you. And you're to give me a list to take to the village, you know, food and soap from Miller's. They'll deliver out here for you. That was thoughtful of Master Cyril, wasn't it? He'll be the new master after the wedding. I think it'll be all right at the Grange with him as the new master.'

They were approaching the clearing, the cottage came in sight and Nell's memories came flooding back. She suppressed the nauseous loathing that was constricting her throat.

'Eddie, would you...?' It came out as a strangled croak and she coughed. 'Eddie,' she repeated, 'I don't suppose you could stay for a day or two? I'm nervous of being on our own at night.'

'Aye, it can be a bit spooky out here. It never

worried Biddy, though. Any road, I can't help you there. I have to be back for dinner and I've put in for hall boy so I don't want to be late.'

'Is the present hall boy leaving?'

'He's going to be a footman. I'll tell you what, though. While I'm in the village, I'll ask our Joe to drop by when he can and see how you're getting on.'

'Oh, would you? Would he do that? I'd be so grateful.'

'Whoa, girl!' Eddie pulled up the horse gently and gazed at the cottage. 'Well, look at that all spruced up. Who wouldn't want to live there?'

Me, thought Nell. She wished she could appreciate how pretty it was with the new thatch on the roof, half-timbered walls freshly painted in white and a shiny brass doorknocker on the solid front door. Mabel was enchanted and Nell might have been too if it did not harbour such awful memories for her; memories that Nell could not even share with her mother, or indeed anyone.

'You and your ma'll be fine and dandy here,' Eddie went on, 'once you've got used to it.'

'We're not staying long,' Nell repeated. She planned to be up early in the morning to walk into Keppel and search for a new position. 'How far is it to the village?' she asked.

Eddie hunched his shoulders. 'A couple of miles or so, I reckon. I remember the track being really muddy when it rains. I'll get your luggage inside and then chop some wood. You'll find a water pump in the scullery.'

Eddie handed her the heavy iron key from his pocket then tethered the horse. Nell stood on the front step for a full two minutes before she plucked up enough courage to unlock the door. Mabel was wandering around the outside and peering through the windows while Eddie stacked their belongings on the path. Eventually, Nell blew out her cheeks and turned the key.

'I'll get the fire going for you if you like,' Eddie volunteered. 'I expect the lamps need their wicks trimming as well.'

'Thank you, Eddie. I haven't got any refreshment to offer you.'

He turned to her and grinned. 'I asked one of the kitchen maids to pack a basket to keep you going.'

Mabel felt like crying. 'Oh, Eddie, you really are kind.'

'Our Joe asked me to watch out for you up at the big house. I think he's sweet on you.'

The thought had crossed her mind but she had not allowed herself to dwell on it with the worry of a baby hanging over her. Joe Wainwright wouldn't be sweet on her if he knew the truth. She felt soiled by Cyril Belfor and unable to think of ever having a sweetheart of her own. Besides, she didn't think of Joe in that way, she realised. Her longings were in another direction. She pulled herself together and stopped dreaming of the impossible.

Chapter 28

When she stepped over the cottage threshold Nell could not bring herself to open the door to the front parlour. It was difficult enough to go into the back kitchen. But she did, and on through to the scullery, where she had pumped water at the stone sink.

The squeak and whine of the pump brought back a sharp memory of pain and soreness, of humiliation and disgust. How could she live here? How could she even spend one night in a place that held so much degradation and self-loathing for her?

Nell gritted her teeth and pumped water, throwing away the first rusty bowlful until it came through sparkling clear and icy cold. She filled a blackened kettle, then the boiler in the kitchen range. The boiler had a brass tap fitted for drawing off the water when it was hot.

Mabel stood at the kitchen table unpacking the basket but stopped halfway through as she discovered more of the teatime treats she had enjoyed the day before. She sat down and started eating them. Nell took them from her and suggested they explore upstairs.

The only staircase was narrow and winding. There were three rooms on the first floor. 'I shall have this one,' Mabel declared, standing in the middle of the largest bedroom. It had a fine window that overlooked the front garden.

'I'm the housekeeper, Mother; we'll sleep upstairs,' Nell explained and climbed the final flight of stairs to the attic. It was a huge room stretching right across the house with front and rear-facing tiny windows that peered out from under the thatch. One end was stacked with furniture and chests under dust sheets. Mabel sat down on a box and said, 'I want to go back to the Grange.'

'We can't, Mother. But we shan't be here for long, I promise you. Come and look out of this window.'

The back garden was overgrown but there were fruit trees and bushes, also brick outhouses including one big enough for a stable. Nell took Mabel's hand and they went downstairs to explore. The outhouse doors were locked. The first whiff of smoke curled away from the chimney and Eddie came outside.

'I'm away off to the village now.'

'Won't you stay for a bite to eat?'

'No time. Have you got a list for Miller's?'

'Give me a minute. Mother, come inside and look for the keys to the outhouses.' Nell went indoors to find her writing box. Eddie paced impatiently as she sat on the stairs and scribbled a list then pushed the piece of paper into his hand. 'It's not much. I shan't be here…'

'…for long,' he finished for her. 'So you keep saying. Ta-ra.'

A moment later, the dog cart rattled away.

'Nell! Come and look!' Mabel called from the kitchen. She had found china in a cupboard and was arranging it on the dresser. 'Isn't this pretty?'

It was, and very delicate too, so Nell knew they oughtn't to be using it. 'Put them back, Mother, and let me wash down the shelves first,' she said.

Mabel stopped, disappointed.

'We'll go upstairs and make up a bed while the water's heating,' Nell suggested. 'Did you find any keys?'

'What keys?' Mabel replied.

'I'll look for them later.'

She found a bed big enough for them both in the attic and bedding in a trunk. It was a fine sunny day and she carried blankets and covers downstairs to air outdoors. They had cold mutton, bread and lettuce hearts with tea to drink from the picnic basket. Nell found a bunch of keys in a dresser drawer and tied them to her belt on a piece of string from the scullery. She felt like a medieval chatelaine.

As she suspected, one of the outhouses was a privy. Next to that was a garden store containing rope for a washing line, which she fixed up using some old wooden steps. Across the yard, the stable had one loose box for a horse and enough room for a governess cart. But it was empty apart from some old bales of straw. The windows were small and high and the air inside was chilly considering it was late summer.

Mabel discovered the front parlour and spent the afternoon removing dust sheets and arranging the pieces of furniture. Then she sat on the chaise longue and called out to Nell, 'Can we have tea and cake now?'

'Not today, Mother,' Nell replied from the kitchen. 'I'm making mutton broth for our tea.'

She could not bring herself even to step inside that room and went outdoors to bring in the blankets. The keys rattled as she moved and she found the sound comforting. As soon as they had eaten the broth she locked the front door and sat at the kitchen table with Mabel, sorting and cleaning the various knives and other cook's tools that they had located. They were both tired and yawned in succession although it was still early and not even twilight.

'Go and use the privy, Mother,' Nell said, 'and then I can lock the back door.'

'Did you find a po in the attic?'

'I did. You won't have to come down in the night.'

Nell went to the front door to bolt it. Through the small window at the side she saw a carriage approach down the track and froze for a moment as she recognised it. It was the same one that had brought her to this cottage for the first time and with the same driver. A cold hand clutched at her heart. Quiet as a mouse, she crept back to the kitchen and out through the back door to catch mother just as she was going into the privy.

'Later,' she whispered, and when Mabel turned her head in surprise Nell placed a finger to her lips. She took her hand and led her across the yard and into the stable where she locked and bolted the door as silently as she was able. 'We're hiding, so don't make a sound,' she said softly.

'Is it the rent man?' Mabel said.

Nell ought to have been amused because they had never been obliged to pay rent so she wondered where Mabel had seen such behaviour. But as she was too anxious even to smile, she whispered, 'It's a nasty man,' and put her finger to her lips again.

They stayed with their backs against the wall under the windows so as not to be seen and Nell strained her ears. He could get inside the cottage through the unlocked back door, so he would know she had moved in. It would not occur to him that she could really have been unwilling. Her palms began to sweat and she visualised the large cook's knife she had been cleaning earlier. Dear heaven, she might kill him if he came near her again! Eventually she heard him opening and closing the outhouse doors and her heart almost stopped when he rattled the stable door.

'Nell Goodman,' he called, 'are you in there?'

Mabel's eyes widened and Nell shook her head silently. She had no idea how long they stayed there except that the light through the windows faded totally. Eventually, Mabel went over to sit on the straw and dozed off. Nell was quite chilled when she decided to risk going back to the cottage. She unlocked the door carefully and the creak of a rusty hinge disturbed Mabel.

It was quiet in the yard outside and Nell crept around the side of the cottage from where she could see the track. The carriage and its driver had gone. She hurried back to Mabel who was wandering around in a disorientated manner, unsure of where she was. Nell led her to the privy, took her to the scullery to wash and then upstairs to bed. She was too tense to sleep herself and went downstairs again to damp down the range fire, wondering when Cyril Belfor would be back.

She was lucky to have seen him arrive, but she couldn't lock herself and Mother in the stable every night. Her sense of urgency to get away from this place kept her awake. Although she did sleep some of the time it was not for long and she watched the dawn break, wide-eyed and anxious.

Mother woke early too and they rose together to resurrect the fire and make tea, which they drank with the last of the milk. The sun was warm on their backs when they set off to walk into Keppel. Mabel was excited and Nell promised a visit to Miller's tearoom before they returned.

Nell called at Wainwright's first and was delighted to find Mrs Wainwright in the shop.

'You don't look too well to me,' the older woman said after their initial exchange of good wishes. 'But our Eddie has told us what's gone on. You'll be all right looking after that old cottage in the woods.'

'It's just a temporary position,' Nell informed her. Mabel was occupied looking at the boots and shoes on display.

Nell moved closer to the counter and lowered her voice. 'I'm looking for something more permanent nearer the village. I was wondering if you knew of anyone needing a housekeeper.'

'Oh, I think you'd be better off where you are. Once you've cleaned it up you'll have little else to do outside the shooting season. Eddie seemed to think it's been done up very nice.'

'It's too isolated for Mother, and ... and I am nervous at night.'

'Aye, Eddie mentioned that an' all. The old lady

in there before only had a maid with her and they were safe enough. We don't get vagrants in Keppel Woods as a rule. Any road, our Joe said he would look in on you if you want. He'll pop over at twilight and make sure there's nobody lurking about and you're safely locked in.'

'I should like that but it's too much to ask.'

'It's no trouble for him. He enjoys a walk in the fresh air after a day in the workshop and he can chop a few logs for you as well.'

'Well, if he doesn't mind, I should be very grateful.'

Nell thought Mrs Wainwright was very pleased with this arrangement and she shrugged away any further hints from Nell about housekeeping posts in Keppel. Nonetheless, Nell looked forward to having Joe around at a time when Cyril Belfor might appear and she was in a lighter mood when she left Wainwright's shop. She went on to the game dealer for a rabbit, which he said he would send over later that day. She had seen his delivery boy in the main street on a large black bicycle with a basket at the front. Obviously the ladies and housekeepers of Keppel did not carry home their provisions as Nell had done regularly from the market. When she offered to pay for the rabbit, he looked offended and said he would render his account at the end of the month, according to his usual practice.

Mabel liked rabbit stew and used an old recipe with apple and prunes so they went along to Miller's for the prunes. A fresh-faced young man in white shirt, black waistcoat and long white apron served her. After he had asked for a delivery address he said he'd put them with her order for that afternoon, and did she need anything else? Mabel had wandered over to the tearoom and was peering through the glass panel and trying to open the door.

'Is it open?' she asked.

'I'll call Miss Charlotte,' he replied and went off to find her.

Mabel had become quite restless by the time she appeared so Nell ordered shortbread with chocolate to placate her. But once agitated, Mabel was slow to calm and kept asking when the vicar's wife was coming.

'Not today, Mother. I'll take you to her on Wednesday. Miss Twigg will be there.' Nell hoped that Miss Twigg would not shun Mother after her behaviour at the Grange.

'But when will she get here?' Mabel insisted, rather too loudly.

Charlotte scowled across at her and, after a few more customers arrived, came over and asked her to be quiet.

'Finish your chocolate, Mother,' Nell said gently. 'We must get on.'

'Are we going to the vicarage now?' Mabel asked as they left Miller's.

The main street was busy, not only with shoppers but with traps and bicycles toing and froing in the morning air. The occasional carriage rumbled by and Nell was mortified to see Cyril Belfor approaching. He was driving Miss Phoebe in the same carriage he had used last night. They were both dressed in black and progressing relatively slowly through the village. Several villagers stopped to stare but Nell took hold of Mabel's hand and backed against a wall until they had passed.

Mabel resisted this and, as the carriage drew level with her, pointed and cried, 'That's her! She's very grand now.' She put out her hand to a passing lady and said, 'You know her mother was a trollop, don't you?'

'Mother!' Nell closed her eyes and sighed. Miss Phoebe had heard her and she was – oh dear Lord, she was furious and why shouldn't she be? Nell saw her exchange a few heated words with Cyril, who responded in the same angry way. She heard him say, 'Very well, I'll do it!' He threw a malevolent look in their direction and Nell's heart sank even further.

She snatched at Mabel's arm and drew her away from the village lady who was, quite rightly, bothered about being accosted by this strange woman. 'Mother, please be quiet,' Nell pleaded. 'You really must not say things like that.'

'But it's true,' Mabel said.

'And it's very rude to say so,' Nell answered firmly, 'especially when others can hear you.'

'Well, I don't know why George married her.'

'George has passed away, Mother,' Nell reminded her. Mabel blinked at her. 'Oh dear, what are we going to do, Nell? He said he'd look after us.'

'We're going to be all right, Mother. But we ought not to talk about it in the street, ought we?'

Nell thought she sounded like one of her school teachers and felt guilty as Mabel looked sheepish and stayed silent. Nell wondered if that was the approach Miss Twigg had taken with her. The carriage had moved on. Further down the street it turned into the vicarage driveway. A few yards away, the accosted lady was talking to another lady and casting glances in their direction. The whole episode could not have lasted more than a couple of minutes but it had drained Nell of all her energy. She blew out her cheeks and suggested they go back to the cottage.

The weather was fine; they picked sour apples for the rabbit stew and pears to ripen off in the outhouse. A cart arrived with their provisions from Miller's. They were carried indoors by a cheerful lad. The rabbit came with him too as, apparently, the butcher's boy did not like riding the woodland track on his bicycle.

After a broth-with-bread dinner, Mabel took out a chair and dozed under an apple tree. Nell gave the kitchen and scullery a thorough clean, jointed the rabbit and put it to stew for tea. But she jumped every time she heard the crack of a twig underfoot or a bird flap out of its roost. She fretted, too, that she had done nothing about finding another position. Tomorrow, she decided. Tomorrow, she would find lots of things to occupy Mother in the cottage and go into town alone.

During the afternoon, she tied a square of calico over her hair, carried an armful of housemaid's equipment up to the attic, and set about making it as comfortable and pretty as she could. There were two windows in the gables at each end of the attic, and she opened them wide. As she brushed and dusted and scrubbed, she prayed she would not be sleeping here for many more nights. A position and a room to rent were all that she needed.

The rabbit stew was delicious and afterwards Nell returned to the attic to finish before the light faded. The sun had set and it was already growing dark among the trees when Mabel called up the stairs to say somebody was coming. Nell left her brushes and cloths in the attic and was clattering down the stairs with a roll of rug she had found, intending to drape it over the washing line and give it a good beating in the fresh air. Mabel was standing at the open front door.

'Go into the kitchen, Mother.' With her heart in her mouth she dropped her burden in the hallway and began to close the door. It wasn't a carriage or a cart, but someone on foot and to her immense relief she recognised Joe Wainwright swinging along the track.

'Joe!' She stood back and waited for him to walk up the path.

'Eddie told me what happened at the Grange.' He stood in the hallway and looked around. 'You've fallen on your feet here, though. It'll only be used for the shooting.'

Nell managed a smile and said, 'Would you like some tea?'

'Just what the doctor ordered,' he replied.

'I hope you don't mind the kitchen,' she said and bent to pick up the roll of carpet.

'Here, let me,' he volunteered.

She did and he took it outside for her, heaved it over the washing line and gave it the beating of its life as she and Mabel made the tea. He sluiced the dust off his hands and face in the scullery before joining them at the kitchen table. The twilight was closing in and Nell lit a lamp.

'Will you be all right walking home in the dark?' she asked.

'I know these woods like the back of my hand and I'll not leave until I hear you bolt the door behind me.'

'Thanks, Joe. I won't be staying here long.'

'But you must! We can really get to know each other now. You know, properly.' He smiled, first at Nell and then at Mabel, who seemed to like him.

However, his statement caused a lull in the conversation as Nell didn't know how to respond. She liked Joe very much and he was a good friend but she didn't feel any passion towards him, at least not the kind that Eddie had hinted at earlier. She wasn't 'sweet on him'. She tried to think of something non-committal to say and couldn't.

He continued to smile at Mabel and eventually added, 'Well, if your mother approves of me. Mrs Goodman, I'd like very much to walk out with your daughter.'

'That's nice. You've got a sweetheart, Nell.'

'What do you say, Nell?' Joe urged. 'We can see each other every Sunday at church and I can take you into town on your half day when I collect my mother from the market. Mother likes you, Nell.' He stared at her for a few seconds and added, 'So do I.'

'Will you take us in your carriage?' Mabel asked.

'It's only a cart, Mother,' Nell answered in her usual gentle fashion. She realised immediately that she had said the wrong thing: in order to explain to Mother she had been rude to Joe.

Joe was embarrassed and he went on in a rush, 'I'm going to have my own workshop soon. Father is buying a lease on the coach house next to the old forge and I'll employ journeymen so it'll be a factory – only a small one to begin with but ... well, it has rooms above to live in, big enough for a family.' He stopped to draw breath. The implication embarrassed Nell. She ought to have been flattered but she was sensitive about the slightest hint of babies and became quite flustered. She picked up the teapot but no one's cup was ready for a refill. 'I'm sorry, Joe, I didn't expect–'

'No stop,' he interrupted. 'It's my fault. I'm rushing you. Don't say anything now. I'll come every day to see you safely locked in for the night. Give me an answer when you're ready.'

Mabel smiled at him and said to Nell, 'Can we go and live in Keppel, Nell?'

Chapter 29

A few days later Nell heard a cart rattling along the track and rushed into the hall to see who it was. It was late afternoon and broad daylight, but even so ... if it was Cyril... With her heart thumping in her throat, she peered out of the small window by the front door. It wasn't Cyril; it wasn't even Joe Wainwright. It was a closed-in wagon drawn by a heavy horse and ... and the sergeant was sitting upfront with the driver. It veered round to pull up and she saw the writing on the side, ominously painted in black. *Union Workhouse:* the words hit her like a sledgehammer between the eyes.

She was trembling but she straightened her back. The sergeant had been helpful to her in the past. He was fair-minded and a good soul. She smoothed down her apron and pushed stray hair under her calico square.

The sergeant climbed down and walked to the back of the wagon where he opened the door and helped down a middle-aged woman. She wore the plain black dress and pleated cap of the workhouse matron. Nell had seen a picture of her in the local newspaper and occasionally passed by her in town. She opened the door before they knocked.

'Good afternoon, sir.' Nell looked pointedly at the matron but the sergeant did not introduce her. Nell nodded politely at her but she did not smile. 'Is something wrong, Sergeant?' she asked.

'Nothing more than usual,' he replied. His face was very serious, which made Nell wary. He went on, 'We've come for Mabel.'

'What do you want with her?' Nell put her hand on the side of the door to bar their entrance.

'Now come on, lass. You don't want to be making this harder than it has to be. If you tell her it's for her own good she'll come quietly.'

'She's not going with you.' Nell began to close the door.

The sergeant put his boot in the doorway. 'I did warn you, Nell, when she went round to that house in town. You've done your best for her and nobody's blaming you, but folk are complaining ... powerful folk...'

'No!' Nell banged the door against his foot. 'You're not taking her to the workhouse! I won't let you! I can look after her. I've got a position here and she helps me. She can stay here with me so she's got somewhere to live and you've no reason to take her.'

The sergeant put his arm against the door to hold it open. He sucked in air through his teeth. 'You see, Nell lass, that's not what I've been told. She can't stop here because the owner won't have it.'

'You mean Phoebe Wilmot won't have it!'

'Mr Belfor, if you must know. He is responsible for this place.' The sergeant put his other foot in the doorway. 'Where is she, lass?'

'You're not taking her!' Nell repeated. Her mind was racing as fast as her heart was beating.

The sergeant pushed by her, looked up the stairs and called, 'Mabel!'

Nell followed the sergeant's gaze and said, 'She's resting.'

The matron had followed the sergeant inside and now spoke for the first time. 'Can we get a move on?' she muttered. 'I've got another widow to fetch from Keeper's Drift this afternoon.'

The sergeant's tone hardened. 'Go and get her, Nell.'

Nell folded her arms and stood her ground.

'I'll get her myself then.' He turned to the matron. 'You'd best come with me.'

Nell waited until they were halfway up the stairs then hurried through to the back kitchen

360

and out into the overgrown garden where Mabel was wandering about. She had heard her name called and looked frightened. 'Who is it, Nell? Is it the nasty man?'

'Quickly, Mother, we're going to hide in the stable again.' Nell ran down the garden to take her arm, one hand already searching under her apron for the stable key.

Mabel stared past Nell. 'It's not her, is it? I know her!' Nell twisted to see the matron striding out of the back door.

'She's out here, Sergeant,' the matron called and added, 'Come along with me, Mrs Goodman.'

'Nell?' Mabel squeaked. She was frightened and clutched at Nell's arm as the matron approached them. Nell realised there wasn't time to reach the stable and placed herself between her mother and the matron. 'Stay away from her!' she cried.

'Now step aside, Miss Goodman. She's coming with me.'

'No, she is not!'

Suddenly, Mabel's grip on Nell's arm relaxed and she said, 'Oh, we'll be all right, love, the sergeant is here now.'

He did not look pleased as he came out of the back door. 'Now then, Nell Goodman, I always thought you were a sensible lass. Mr Belfor went to the magistrate and the Parish Council about Mabel and it's not as though folk don't know about her. We can't have her out and about being a nuisance now, can we?'

'But she won't be, I promise!'

The matron made a tutting sound. 'Don't be ridiculous! You're lucky it's me and not the asylum wardress that's come for her.' She took a step forward.

'Don't come any nearer!' Nell cried.

'Nell,' the sergeant warned, 'you don't want to get into a tussle here, do you? Your mother might get hurt.'

Nell's heart seemed to rise into her throat and she was close to tears. 'I thought you were our friend.'

'I have my job to do. Now you explain to your ma where she's going and bring her quietly round to the cart and nobody will get hurt.'

She had tried so hard to avoid this but it was exactly what Septimus Belfor had wanted all along. This was the advice he had given to George, God rest his soul, and George had had enough of a conscience to take them in at the Grange instead. But George was gone now and Phoebe had always wanted Mabel put away. And of course it suited Cyril's depraved plans for using her to survive his loveless marriage to Phoebe Wilmot.

'I ... I can't do it. I can't,' Nell replied. 'I can't let you take her to that place. We've never been apart, ever.' Her eyes were brimming as she appealed to the sergeant. 'Why can't she live here with me?'

'Because she has been evicted, that's why. I have papers saying so, lass. You can't have her here with you. And if you don't watch your step with your betters, lass, you'll be out on your ear as well.'

'And in the workhouse with your mother,' the

matron added. She was becoming increasingly impatient. 'Now can we get a move on?'

'Nell?' The sergeant raised his eyebrows.

It fell to her, Nell realised, to explain to her mother what was happening. But she couldn't. And she could not stand there and watch her being carted away in the workhouse wagon. She turned to face her.

Mabel's eyes, too, were shiny with tears. She didn't need to be told; she knew who the workhouse matron was. 'I don't want to go back there,' Mabel said in a small voice.

'I can't stop them taking you, Mother,' Nell explained, 'but I can come with you.' She turned to the matron. 'I can admit myself to the workhouse if I am homeless, can't I?'

The matron blinked at her then glanced warily at the sergeant. 'You said the daughter had a position here.'

'Mr Belfor told me—'

Nell interrupted him. 'They want a proper housekeeper who can cook as well and I was only a scullery maid at the Grange so I'll soon be dismissed again. I might as well come into the workhouse now.'

The matron looked angry and the sergeant was perplexed. 'Don't be daft, Nell, Mr Belfor knows you.'

'Well, I'm not staying here on my own at night! It's spooky in the middle of the woods and there are vagrants about. I might be murdered in my bed.'

'You've got a position here, Nell,' the sergeant said firmly.

'No, I haven't. I'm not staying without Mother.' She faced the matron and said, 'I am homeless and without a job so I am applying for admission to the workhouse.'

The matron let out an exasperated sigh. 'Sergeant?' she queried, expecting him to deal with the situation.

Nell did not give him a chance. She went on, 'If you won't take me in today, I'll sleep on the church steps in town. The vicar will find me and bring me along to you himself.'

The sergeant frowned. 'She won't be with you for long,' he said to the matron. 'There's plenty in town that'll take her on as a housemaid.'

'The workhouse doesn't have money to waste on the able-bodied who don't need us.'

'Well, I'm sure she can earn her keep while she's with you.'

The matron made a tutting sound with her teeth again. 'This is most irregular, Sergeant. The guardians will never approve.'

'Isn't Mr Belfor a guardian?' the sergeant asked.

'Mr Septimus Belfor? Indeed he is.'

'I'll have a word with him, Matron. He knows about these two.' The sergeant turned to Nell. 'Will that satisfy you, Nell Goodman?'

'Give me a minute to collect a few things,' she answered.

'We haven't got room for possessions,' Matron snapped, 'and we provide all you want.'

'I'll have to damp down the fire and lock up. Perhaps you would return the key to Mr Belfor and explain to him about my ... er ... my shortcomings for the position here.'

364

'Can we just get on?' the matron responded tetchily. 'How far is it to Keeper's Drift?'

Mabel was clutching even harder at Nell's arm. 'But it's nice here. I want to stay.'

Nell pressed her lips together and blinked away her tears. 'We shan't be in the workhouse for long,' she explained. 'I'll soon find somewhere else for both of us, I promise.' Nell wished she was as confident as she sounded.

'I don't want to go there. It's horrible.'

'It won't be so bad nowadays,' Nell reassured her. 'And I'm with you this time.' It won't be easy, though, she thought, and her fears deepened as they rattled along inside the dingy wagon with the testy, impatient matron. She held Mabel's hand tightly and stared out of the tiny window. Everyone on Keppel high street stared as they went by.

It was worse than she'd expected because they were separated as soon as they arrived. Nell was ordered to take a hip bath and wash all over with carbolic soap, including her hair, and she assumed that Mabel was asked to do the same. A wardress gave her some calico underwear, thick stockings and strong stiff boots to wear. The frock was made of some coarse heavy material that was too hot for summer. Her own possessions were wrapped up in a brown paper parcel and taken away 'for safe keeping'. She asked to see her mother and was told that 'family time was on Sunday and she'd be too busy earning her keep until then'.

Mother must be terrified, Nell thought, and fretted about her constantly for the remainder of the day.

Her way out was obvious: marry Joe, for he had all but asked her and he was very keen to involve her – and Mother – in his future. But she did not love him and he would not be quite so earnest if he knew the truth about her, and she could not trust Cyril Belfor to keep quiet.

She saw Mother in the cavernous dining room at tea but was stopped by a wardress from going over to speak. They waved to each other. The food was plain but adequate: soup, bread and cheese and an enamelled mug of strong tea. Nell was given sewing to do by an oil lamp in the evening and wondered how Mabel was coping. She planned to creep out of bed in the middle of the night and find her dormitory.

'Is Goodman in here?'

Nell put aside her needlework and stood up.

'Master's office; follow me. You have a visitor.'

The Master's office had carpet on the floor and two desks. The Master sat at the largest, looking through a file of papers. A typewriter stood in isolation on the other. He had comfortable chairs by the fireplace and a gentleman was sitting in one with his back to the door. Nell saw his black arm-band before he rose to his feet and turned.

'Devlin?'

He came towards her, examining her features closely. 'This must be dreadful for you. How are you?'

'I am well but I'm worried about Mother. How did you know we were here?'

'The workhouse cart doesn't drive through Keppel without everybody knowing who was in

366

it. I didn't believe it at first.' He turned to the Master and asked, 'Perhaps you can explain?'

The Master behaved in a deferential way towards Devlin. He read the details of their admission from a sheet of paper in his hand, which gave Devlin his answer.

'So Miss Goodman is free to leave?' Devlin confirmed.

The Master nodded.

'I won't go without Mother,' Nell said hastily.

'Of course not,' Devlin said kindly, then addressed the Master again. 'I shall take responsibility for Mrs Goodman. I have a nurse to care for her.' Nell raised her eyebrows. Devlin went on, 'Miss Twigg at the Grange will look after her. Now, sir, if you will arrange for Mrs Goodman to join us we can leave immediately. My motor carriage is outside.'

'But your sister...?' Nell began.

'I'll explain later,' Devlin answered. 'We'll stop at the Crown first.'

Nell was hugely relieved. She didn't mind if she slept in a stable as long as Mother was safe.

The Master seemed flustered and said, 'I must have your signature on these papers, sir, and they cannot leave in workhouse clothes.'

Devlin took a leather wallet from inside his jacket and put two banknotes on his desk. 'I shall arrange for the return of your property, at which time you may consider this security payment as a donation. Now get on with it, my good fellow. Where do I sign?'

The formalities were completed before Mabel arrived. Nell hugged her tightly. 'We're leaving,' she whispered and they filed out down the stone steps and out of the main entrance to Devlin's waiting vehicle. Brown paper parcels tied with string containing their own clothes were already on the seats.

Devlin drove the short distance to the Crown Hotel in town where he asked for a private sitting room and tea with shortbread biscuits. The room had gaslights on the walls and only then did Nell notice Devlin's grazed knuckles.

'What happened to you?' she asked.

'I wanted some answers from Cyril.' He smiled and offered Mabel the biscuits. 'If you have no objection, Nell, I'll take you and your mother back to the cottage tonight. It's my father's funeral tomorrow and I shall be—What is it, Nell? What's wrong?'

Nell went hot and cold all over. Her nerves were already in shreds and she began to tremble. 'I can't. I can't go back there.'

'Why not? It's very pretty and the woods are patrolled by my gamekeepers.'

Nell shook her head emphatically. 'I won't live there. I'd ... I'd rather go back to the workhouse.'

Devlin frowned. 'You were like this before when I mentioned the cottage. I thought it was ideal for you—' He stopped.

Nell continued shaking her head. 'It's not ... it's ... it's...' She glanced at Mabel.

Devlin took her arm – with more firmness than he ought, she thought – and said, 'Mrs Goodman, we're just going to sit over there while you enjoy your tea.' He settled her in another chair and demanded, 'What *is* the matter, Nell? You're shaking. What are you frightened of?'

Nell breathed deeply to control herself.

'Tell me,' Devlin insisted.

'It's ... it's ... Cyril, he ... he...' She couldn't say it.

Devlin rubbed his grazed knuckles. 'I've got the measure of him,' he whispered, 'and his crooked father. They had persuaded my father to change his will in Cyril and Phoebe's favour. But Father had not signed it and they were foolish enough to forge his signature.'

This news didn't surprise Nell at all and she wondered if Septimus had done something similar with her own father's will. But it wasn't that that worried her about Cyril now.

'He'll come to the cottage. I can't go back there,' she said quietly.

'Just tell me if he gives you any trouble. I have evidence of his malpractice. I've got him over a barrel, so to speak.' He sounded triumphant.

Oh, how much she loved Devlin, she realised now. She gazed at him with tears in her eyes. She wanted him to wrap his arms around her and hold her. But it was all too late. The damage was done. She felt like weeping.

'You're really distressed about this, aren't you?' He frowned. 'What has happened, Nell? You must tell me.' He paused, looked down then directly into her eyes. 'I know all about the head parlourmaid,' he murmured.

Tears squeezed out of her eyes. The words were easy to form in her head, less easy to say out loud. 'At the cottage...' She inhaled with a shudder. 'He ... he raped me,' she whispered. After she

369

had said it, she repeated it, more to herself than to Devlin. Then her tears flowed. She didn't know for how long. At some time Devlin gathered her gently into his arms and she sobbed silently into his shoulder.

Mabel came over with the biscuits. 'Please don't cry, Nell love, you're making me cry as well.'

Nell pulled herself together and sat up. Mabel took Devlin's linen handkerchief and wiped her eyes. Then she held it over her nose and said, 'Blow,' just as she used to when Nell was a child. Nell smiled at the memory and Mabel said, 'That's better, dear. I'll fetch you a cup of tea.'

Devlin's face was set in a granite expression that Nell found alarming. He was rubbing his grazed knuckles with his fingers. Eventually he said, 'I'm taking you both to the brewery for tonight. You can stay with my head brewer and his wife. They have plenty of room – their house used to be an inn.'

'At this hour?' Nell cautioned. 'It's very late to call on folk.'

'I'll send a message ahead. They won't mind, I get on well with my head brewer and his wife.'

'I am very grateful to you, Devlin,' Nell added, 'but this is too much to ask of a ... a ... friend.'

'We are more than friends, Nell, you must know that.'

No, she didn't. They had been friends as children, growing up, before he went away. Yet he had distanced himself from her, and now they were adults her feelings for him had strengthened. She loved him with all her heart, but what was she to him?

370

He went on, 'Father's funeral is tomorrow so the brewery is closed. You are both welcome to attend, of course. My head brewer will bring you in his carriage.'

'Thank you, we should like to pay our last respects,' Nell said. It seemed an inadequate response for all he was doing and she added, 'I don't know how to thank you.'

'Your happiness is all I ask. I want your happiness.' He gazed into her eyes and went on, 'Then I shall be happy too.'

For a second Nell was sure he was going to lean over and kiss her but the moment passed and he said, 'Why don't you change out of those clothes? I'll wait for you in the hotel lounge.'

It was much later, in the middle of the night, that Nell realised why Devlin was so kind to her. She woke suddenly, convinced he too believed her to be George Wilmot's daughter. Did he think of her as a sister? Was that what he meant by 'more than friends'?

Chapter 30

Mabel's memories of the old Navigator Inn were resurrected by her night's stay and she wandered around inside the building, exploring every corner. Nell had difficulty in getting her to leave on time for the funeral the following day. When they arrived at Keppel church, in their borrowed black mourning dress, it was full, although places had been reserved for them near the front.

Nell was surprised that neither Septimus Belfor nor his son Cyril attended. Phoebe sat in the front pew with her brother, Lady Clarissa and Her Ladyship's grandfather. Afterwards it took a long time for all the carriages to take their passengers out to the Grange for the wake. Nell spent half an hour listening to Madge chatter about preparations for the wake, then Joe Wainwright approached. He was a Grange carriage driver for the day.

He knew about the workhouse. 'It must have been a mistake?' he said. 'Are you pleased to be in the cottage again?'

'I'm not in the cottage, Joe. I'm not going back there, not ever.'

He frowned. 'Where will you live?'

'I don't know, but I'm at the old Navigator with Mother for now.'

'But I can help you, Nell,' he said. 'Have you thought any more about–'

'I'm sorry, Joe. My answer is no. You and your family have been very kind to me and I hope we can still be friends but I ... I, well, I don't love you.'

His mouth twisted. 'I know,' he said. 'I've always known your heart was elsewhere.'

'You have?'

He seemed resigned to her answer and, thankfully for Nell, he was called away to fetch the carriage he was driving. Nell glanced around anxiously for Mother and relaxed when she saw her with Miss Twigg. The former head parlourmaid was looking on from a front door across the road and Nell walked over to see how she was. She looked extremely well and appeared cheerful.

'Have you heard what's happened to him?' she said, not expecting an answer.

Nell didn't know who she meant at first.

'Cyril Belfor,' she went on. 'Somebody went to his house late last night and beat him up good and proper. I told you they would. Not before time, if you ask me. He daren't show his face now. It's all around the town.' She seemed very pleased about this and, Nell admitted to herself, so did she.

'Do you know who did it?' Nell asked.

'Who cares? He had it coming. Apparently the sergeant was called, though, and there was a right to-do. His ma and pa cleared off this morning. The butcher said they've gone abroad and left Master Cyril to fend for hisself.' The girl was clearly enjoying relating this news but went on, 'Is that Miss Twigg over there trying to attract your attention?'

It was and Nell hurried over to speak with her. She wished to take Mabel back to the Grange in her trap and wondered if Nell would care to ride with them.

The doors of the dining, drawing and morning rooms stood open as mourners filled the ground floor of the Grange. Even the library housed a cluster of gentlemen discussing business in hushed tones. Footmen circulated with silver trays of sherry and those tiny tasty mouthfuls that Cook excelled at producing. The atmosphere was subdued underneath a constant hum of lowered voices. Nell stayed in the company of the head brewer and his wife. They seemed to think that she and Mabel would be sleeping at the Grange that night.

Devlin was fully occupied supporting his mother and sister, swathed and veiled in black, although he did acknowledge Nell from a distance. She noticed he didn't remove his gloves and when he took off his black top hat indoors his eyes were reddened and his face slightly discoloured. She guessed most would put it down to grieving but Nell knew differently.

Lady Clarissa went to her boudoir to rest after an hour of receiving condolences. Nell saw Devlin lead Phoebe into the library and close the door. Shortly afterwards the business gentlemen emerged to be claimed by their impatient wives. Miss Twigg had already taken Mabel upstairs to her rooms.

Mourners began to leave as Paget announced their carriages. Nell's hosts assured her that she needn't return with them as she was staying at the Grange and that Devlin would speak with her as soon as he was able. Nell wondered if she should go down to the servants' hall to wait but they said no, wait for him in the morning room. And so Nell sat on the small sofa where she had imagined not so very long ago that Devlin was going to kiss her and wondered what he wished to speak to her about.

She saw him come out of the library with Phoebe and glimpsed her ravaged, tearful face before she pulled down her veil. She was holding onto his arm as he crossed to the morning-room door and said, 'I'm taking Phoebe to Cyril. Will you wait here for me? Paget will bring you tea.' His face was definitely bruised but he managed a smile and added, 'I have much to tell you.'

She gave up speculating and was distracted by Paget – the man himself – bringing her tea. The change in his demeanour astounded Nell. He addressed her as Miss Goodman and as he was leaving the room said, 'I hope you will forgive me, miss, but the Grange will not change in the way I had anticipated. It seems that Master Cyril was not the gentleman we thought he was.'

He left before Nell had a chance to respond.

Devlin was a long time but eventually she heard his motor carriage outside the morning-room window, so she put aside a novel she had found in the bookcase and went into the hall. He had returned alone. Paget took his motoring coat and gauntlets, exposing Devlin's sore knuckles.

'Thank you for being so patient, Nell,' he said. 'We'll talk in here.' And he led her back into the morning room.

Nell sat back down on the sofa but Devlin remained standing and gazed out of the window at the sinking sun.

'I heard about Cyril,' Nell said. 'Is Phoebe very distressed?'

'She is, especially on top of losing Father. She loved him.'

'Of course she did.'

He whirled round suddenly and added, 'Dammit, Nell, she loves Cyril, too! I cannot persuade her to give him up.'

'Does she know what he's done?'

'She blames his years in Cambridge for leading him astray, and his father for the fraud.'

Fraud? Nell supposed that was forging George's will.

'She is right about his father,' Devlin continued. 'He's the crook and Cyril is weak. He did as his father told him. Maybe Phoebe can make something of him, running a shipping hotel in Liverpool.'

'Are they leaving, then?'

He nodded and came to sit beside her. 'Now she knows more, my sister sees the sense in that.' He picked up her hand and added, 'So much of this involves you, I don't know where to start. The sergeant knew a lot more than he admitted. But he told me enough to challenge Cyril.'

Nell frowned at his face. The skin around both his eyes was darkening and an angry bruise was coming out on his cheekbone. 'It was you who gave him the beatings, wasn't it?'

'It was. The first time was to get the truth out of him – and the keys to his father's office.' He looked apologetic for a moment and said, 'Have I shocked you?'

'Well, yes,' she admitted.

'But what can you expect from a foundling?' he said with a shrug.

'Your mother would not approve,' Nell commented.

'Perhaps not, but she has told me my parentage. She has kept it a secret all these years and nobody suspected. She wouldn't say, of course, while Father was alive. My mother has a deep-rooted sense of duty.'

Nell had a sudden horror that he might be George's son born out of wedlock and possibly her half-brother. 'You're not George's, are you?'

'I thought I was and, interestingly, I once thought you might be too, especially when Father brought you to work in the office at the brewery. My feelings towards you were not brotherly. It was why I stayed away so long, even during vacations.'

'But you're *not* George's, are you?' Nell reiterated.

'Definitely not.'

'And me?'

'Definitely not. The sergeant watched your mother and father courting. Your parents' marriage was a love match. You are Harold Goodman's daughter.'

'So what exactly did your mother tell you?'

'I'm a bastard child, all right, but from a second cousin of hers and an unnamed aristocrat.' He shrugged. 'I'll never know who, as my real mother died.'

'I'm sorry.'

'Me too.' He paused. 'It still left the question of why my father looked after you and your mother when your father died. Septimus Belfor would have left you both to your fate in the workhouse.'

'I've wondered about that myself. Mother's ramblings didn't help.'

'I found the answers in the Belfor safe. Septimus kept every single document. He took quite a small percentage from the brewery at first but became greedy as he grew older. He was determined to have the Grange and the brewery for his son.'

His grip on her hand had tightened and she raised her arm. 'Ow,' she said pointedly with wide eyes.

'I'm sorry, Nell. You mean so much to me I'm frightened I'll lose you. Father tried to do his best for you but Septimus wouldn't let him and he had evidence of the fraud.'

'What is this fraud, Devlin?'

'Your father invested in Navigator Ales with his barley wine, his loyal labour and a good deal of hard cash. He should have had a half share in the brewery when he was twenty-one. Septimus and my father swindled him out of it with some company sleight of hand that bankrupted the Navigator and set it up again as Wilmot's Brewery.'

Nell was speechless. Mother had always told her she was the boss's daughter and she hadn't believed her!

Devlin continued, 'It was the shock of losing everything he'd worked for that killed your father. Your mother too had a breakdown and never properly recovered.'

She listened intently. Half of the brewery ought to have belonged to Mother!

'My father had made a will leaving equal shares of his estate to you, Phoebe and myself, as long as Mother could continue to live at the Grange. He had a signed copy of it in his papers here. Septimus had written another will in Phoebe and Cyril's favour but Father hadn't signed it when he died. So Septimus simply forged his signature.' He winced as he shifted his position.

Cyril must have fought back hard because

Devlin was in some pain, Nell thought. She said, 'Shall I ask that medical attendant to take a look at your bruises?'

He shook his head. 'I've had worse. I used to box at Cambridge.' He went on, 'As soon as Father's legal will is proved, you will own a third of the brewery.'

Nell found this hard to believe and shook her head unconsciously.

'It's true,' he insisted. He inhaled sharply as he moved and said, 'Would you pour me a brandy from the hall?'

When Nell returned with the glass she said, 'You need your physician to take a look at you.'

'I've sent him to tend Cyril. His need is greater. Phoebe will stay and look after him.'

'Is he very bad?'

'Yes, but he'll recover without any lasting damage.'

Nell experienced a sense of satisfaction. She would have done the same to Cyril if she had been able and she understood why, sometimes, men – and women – resorted to fighting. But to give Cyril a second beating seemed excessive. She said, 'Why did you go back a second time?'

'After you told me what he did to you? Well, he's lucky to be alive.'

Nell pressed her lips together and looked down. Cyril deserved it and she hoped it would bring him to his senses. 'What's going to happen now, Devlin?'

'That depends on you, Nell.' He slid to the floor on one knee and pulled a small worn leather box from his pocket. 'I love you, Nell. I want you to be my wife. Will you? Will you marry me?'

Her mouth dropped open. She watched wordlessly as he opened the box, took out a sapphire ring and lifted her left hand. He held the ring for a few seconds, poised to slip onto her finger.

'You have to give me an answer first,' he prompted.

She laughed nervously. Of course she'd marry him! 'Ye-e-es,' she squeaked.

'It was my great-grandmother's betrothal ring so I may need to alter it for you, but I want you to wear it now.'

The ring was too big, just a little, but Nell did not mind in the least. She threw her arms round his neck and kissed him. If she hurt him, he didn't say. He was too busy kissing her too.

Acknowledgements

I enjoy writing all my novels and this one has been no exception, so I am grateful for the support I receive in the process. In particular I should like to thank my agent Judith Murdoch and my editorial team, Manpreet Grewal and Marina de Pass, at Sphere for their hard work towards the final publication of this book.

The publishers hope that this book has given you enjoyable reading. Large Print Books are especially designed to be as easy to see and hold as possible. If you wish a complete list of our books please ask at your local library or write directly to:

Magna Large Print Books
Magna House, Long Preston,
Skipton, North Yorkshire.
BD23 4ND

This Large Print Book for the partially sighted, who cannot read normal print, is published under the auspices of

THE ULVERSCROFT FOUNDATION